Ferdinand Dennis was born
and moved to Britain 1964.
broadcaster and university lecturer. He is the author of three novels, '*The Sleepless Summer*', '*The Last Blues Dance*' and '*Duppy Conqueror*'. His non-fiction works include '*Behind the Frontlines*' (winner of the Martin Luther King Memorial Prize), and '*Back to Africa*'. '*The Black and White Museum*', a collection of his short stories, will be published by Small Axes in 2021. Ferdinand Dennis lives in London.

'The skill the author brings to his portrayal of character is matched by the vivid realism with which he depicts place'

The Times

'*Duppy Conqueror* presents a giant's eye view of the exiled African psyche. An ambitious and compelling novel, it takes vast strides through the mystic paradise of Jamaica in the Thirties, the racially fraught underworlds of postwar Liverpool and London, and the defunct utopianism of African repatriation plans in the Sixties ... Although the book has epic ambitions, it does not feel an epic read. Dennis drives it along through a narrative bubbling with eccentric characters and poetic descriptions.'

Independent

By the same author

Fiction

THE SLEEPLESS SUMMER

THE LAST BLUES DANCE

Non-fiction

BEHIND THE FRONTLINES:
JOURNEY INTO AFRO-BRITAIN

BACK TO AFRICA

Duppy Conqueror

FERDINAND DENNIS

SMALL AXES

HopeRoad Publishing
PO Box 55544
Exhibition Road
London SW7 2DB

www.hoperoadpublishing.com

This edition first published by HopeRoad in 2020

A CIP catalogue record for this book is available from the British Library

ISBN: 978-1-913109-03-5

eISBN: 978-1-913109-10-3

Printed and bound by Clays Ltd, Bungay, Suffolk, UK

10 9 8 7 6 5 4 3 2 1

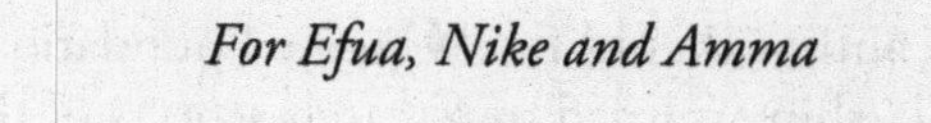

For Efua, Nike and Amma

The author thanks the Wingate Foundation
for the scholarship awarded to research aspects of this book.

PART I

I

On the morning his exile from Paradise began, as he walked the dusty road to Port Columbus, Marshall Sarjeant remembered the day he lost belief in Blyden's story of the creation of Jamaica. It was during the second week of Teacher Lee's disappearance and on that day he and four schoolfriends decided to play truant rather than subject themselves to the sleep-inducing monotony of the substitute teacher.

They met on Buchanan Ridge under the wild tamarind tree, its vermilion blossoms scattered in the silver-grey grass, and proceeded to the Blue Hole, where they romped under the waterfall, compared pecker sizes, dived from luminous white rocks into the placid water and shouted for the water spirit Mamadjo to come and join them in their delinquent revelry.

Fats Wally had brought a bag of mangoes and when the boys had devoured them, Scoop Fearon and Marshall caught two rainbow fish and, after many false starts, grilled them over a fire.

Enlivened by the succulent flesh, Fats Wally decided that Mamadjo had not appeared to them because their earlier summons had lacked conviction. So he positioned himself on a large egg-shaped rock and, with legs apart, cupped his hands to his mouth and began bellowing: 'Mamadjo, Mamadjo, Mamadjo-o-o-o-o!' Fats was very dark and had a mighty stomach, and as the sunlight bathed his black heaving figure he seemed like a pulsating, glowing apparition. His shouting climbed to a feverish pitch which infected the others, and they joined in, part-singing, part-shouting.

When the futility of their discordant chorus dawned on them they fell about laughing at Fats Wally, who continued booming like a ship horn until his voice went hoarse and he threw himself into the water, creating a splash as great as his disappointment at Mamadjo's refusal to answer his call. Then they cooled off under the limpid water, which cascaded down the rock face as if escaping from a tear in the seams of heaven.

Later that day the boys headed for Black Rock Beach. They walked through the Morgan banana plantation and were chased off by one of the workers for stealing. They had better luck in an orange grove owned by Mr Grimes, and left there sated. They stopped again at Clearwater where Billy Hearne suggested to Fats Wally that here he might have more chance of seeing a water spirit. This was a spot where, according to local legend, water nymphs who looked like Arawak Indians, the original inhabitants of the land, bathed on full-moon nights and combed their luxuriant dark hair as they sang liquescent songs that could drive mortal listeners crazy. But Fats Wally claimed tiredness, and besides, night was some way off.

The person who drew the errant schoolboys to Black Rock Beach was Blyden, the oldest fisherman in Paradise. His best days at sea were long gone, and late in the afternoon, when the sun hovered over the promontory known as Cuffee's Point, as the fishermen gathered on Black Rock Beach to repair their nets, children would descend onto the sand and call upon Blyden to tell them stories. Skinny and gnarled and dark like a piece of driftwood washed ashore, buried in the sand for years, then unearthed and baked in the sun, Blyden had the ruminative air of one who had known many defeats and they had left him with profound respect for life's enduring mysteries.

It turned out to be an unusual afternoon on Black Rock Beach. Prester, a young fisherman, had the previous day caught a two-hundred-pound shark and, still drunk on his conquest, which effectively ended his apprenticeship, he dominated the gathering with the arrogance of victorious youth.

When Blyden tried to recall his own victorious battle with an elusive marlin, Prester interrupted and ridiculed him with cruel, mocking laughter, and likened Blyden's fishing days to the setting sun, except that he, Blyden, would never rise again. But on the insistence of the children, with Marshall amongst the most vociferous, Blyden once again told his story of creation and in that act regained his authority.

'In the beginning, when the ocean covered most of the earth and there were only a few barren rocks, most living creatures dwelt many fathoms below the surface. An unhappy Fish became curious about life above the surface of the ocean and began swimming there daily. Then one day he saw a fabulous feathered creature sunning itself on a rock. He asked the creature its name and it replied in a musical voice, "I'm Bird," spread its vast dazzlingly multicoloured wings and flew towards the sun.

'Fish watched in wonder as Bird soared up and across the immense sky. He had never seen anything so wonderful and from thereon was determined to see Bird again. Fish returned to the rock every day to see Bird and after some time decided that he loved Bird more than any creature in the sea. When he declared his love, Bird fluttered her wings and said: "But I am a creature of the air and you a creature of the sea, we cannot love each other." "Then I will become a creature of the air, too," Fish retorted. Bird laughed at the impossibility of Fish's ambition, but the magical sound of her laughter only inspired Fish to greater heights of love.

'The two creatures continued meeting for a long time, and, one day, tormented by his love for Bird, Fish went to the goddess of the sea and begged to be released from its waters. He pleaded with the goddess for feathers to replace his scales, for wings instead of fins, and a beak instead of gills, so that he might be united will Bird, his loved one. The benevolent goddess agreed to grant Fish his wish on one condition: all the offspring of his union with Bird would belong to the sea. Fish consulted with Bird and both agreed to the goddess's condition. So Fish acquired feathers and wings and set up home with Bird on the rock where they had first met.

'Soon Bird laid three eggs. But the prospect of having to part with their children upset Fish and Bird, and they began to plot escape from their bargain with the goddess. Bird knew of a mountain that rose from the sea and reached the clouds. If they could get to it, they would escape the sea goddess. But the goddess overheard their treacherous plan, and sent the sea crashing over the rocks. Bird managed to rescue one egg and Fish another. But the angry sea rose up and snatched at them as they tried to climb beyond its reach to the safety of the mountain. In the struggle, both were forced to drop their eggs. The spot where Fish's egg fell became the island, Bird's egg became the people of the island, the third egg became the flying fish which swam plentifully off the coast of Paradise.'

Blyden told his story with the usual dramatic flapping of arms, squeaky and musical voices, but this time it left Marshall strangely unmoved. Up until that moment he had seen the island through Blyden's eyes and saw magic everywhere, in the majestic mountains, the meandering rivers and the turquoise sea, and loved it with the adamantine strength of his pure, innocent heart. He took pleasure in knowing the names of plants, cultivated a vegetable garden of okra and callaloo, collected seashells, and could spend dreamy hours watching opalescent clouds drift across the mountains like vast swathes of white muslin cloth unfurling in the breeze. And when, for whatever reason, he felt melancholy, a few hours in the company of the old fisherman, listening to his fantastic tales, was an effective cure. But now he walked away from Blyden's company wrestling with an immense feeling of disappointment, a visceral emptiness, like hunger in its gnawing intensity. The fisherman's tale seemed hollow, maddeningly untrue. Strolling home with the other boys Marshall pondered the tale, puzzled over why it seemed to lack the enchantment of the past.

They had not long passed the vandalised statue of Queen

Victoria, with its missing arm, when Marshall turned to Scoop and said: 'You believe Blyden's story, Scoop?'

Scoop, a slim boy with a long ectomorphic face, had been whistling and in response to Marshall's question he stopped and seemed to think for a long time, then, with an affectedly deepened voice, said: 'Course not. But that Blyden, he's a master storyteller. I've to give him that.'

Scoop's swift and confident response made Marshall feel foolish because he realised that up until then he and Scoop had been listening for different things in Blyden's tale. He, Marshall, for truth, and Scoop for pleasure.

'Have you never believed it?' Marshall asked.

'Course not,' Scoop said firmly. 'Nobody knows how Jamaica make. Except God. And my father says that God run 'way and leave it 'cause so much evil happened here.'

'That's not so,' said Marshall.

'It is, too,' said Billy Hearne. He was a short, stocky, brown-skinned boy with naturally red lips. 'You should ask your aunt about Sarjeant's curse. That's the real truth about Paradise. My mother says all Sarjeants are cursed. Even those who seem normal.' Billy Hearne laughed and the others followed suit.

'That's a lie, Billy Hearne, and you know that. That's a bare-faced lie.' On another occasion, he might have dismissed his friend's provocation but Marshall was feeling irritable and inexplicably cheated by the anticlimactic effect of Blyden's performance. Suddenly enraged, he pushed Billy Hearne and as Billy fell threw himself on top of his friend. The other boys surrounded them as they rolled in the dust.

Both boys were bleeding by the time Pharaoh Sarjeant, who had been passing by, intervened. A tall, lean man with a booming voice, he seized the boys by their shirt collars and without partiality – he was related to Marshall – lectured them severely, then ordered them home with the fierce authority that all grown-ups in the town exercised over young miscreants. Marshall did not try to appeal to his relative, as his aunt, with whom he lived, had often warned him to avoid Pharaoh Sarjeant.

'Greet your Aunt Binta for me,' Pharaoh said to Marshall, and signalled with his head that Marshall should go home immediately.

'Yes, sah,' Marshall replied respectfully, though he felt that Pharaoh Sarjeant's intervention had cheated him of certain victory.

Marshall hurried away, feeling more ashamed than defeated because a relative had caught him in a fight. He swore to himself never to talk to that donkey-faced fool Billy Hearne again. Scoop, who was his best friend, ran after him and tried to explain that Billy had only been repeating the gossip of malicious market women. But Marshall would not listen. Immured in his injured pride, and now ashamed that he had lost self-control, he ignored his friend and trudged home alone through the swiftly falling dusk.

Marshall's day reached an ignominious nadir when his aunt, Binta Sarjeant, punished him for the first time in almost a year. She had not only heard about his absence from school – cause enough to upset her – but his bloodied and torn shirt betrayed that he had violated one of her cardinal rules: to stay out of fights. Livid and pitiless, refusing to hear his excuse, she reproached him in the high-pitched whinnying voice that overcame her on such occasions. She ordered him to chant the rosary for thirty minutes beneath the portrait of the Madonna and Child, and the wooden crucifix, which hung in a corner of the small living-room. When he had finished she sent him to bed without dinner.

Marshall resignedly accepted his punishment and retired to his closet of a room, clinging to the hope that sunrise would bring food and sympathy from his beloved Aunt Binta. As he lay in bed the rumbling and hissing of his rebelliously empty stomach did not agitate him as much as the inexpressible sense of loss and the mysterious sadness that weighed down his spirit. It was as though on this day something inside him had gone, borne away on a nocturnal breeze laden with the mournful, eerily maternal sound of the manatees in faraway Legge Cove.

Far into the night, kept awake by his unquiet mind, he decided he could live without a heroic Blyden, and would henceforth regard the old man as a fisherman past his prime and now destined to end his days with telling simple tales to simple children for their simple amusement. And he was no longer one of those children.

But no sooner had he reconciled himself to Blyden's mortality than the darkness began to echo Billy Hearne's insult to his family name. He, Marshall, was well aware that the Sarjeants, one of the oldest families in Paradise, included members with physical defects which set them apart from ordinary folk in Paradise. Uncle Willie, an albino with a shrivelled left arm, was famous for his rum-drinking prowess, as well as the extraordinary strength of his right arm. The market day he had mounted an angry bull after it had gored three people, and steered the bucking, stomping beast into the town square, where he'd wrestled it to the ground, had entered the folklore of Paradise.

Hyacinth, a dwarf, possessed an almost celestial soprano voice which could send an audience away weeping or leave them feeling as joyful as the air after a heavy rainfall.

Then there was the enigmatic Pharaoh Sarjeant, who had stopped the fight. He lived alone on Manning Ridge. As far as Marshall knew Pharaoh did not have a physical disability but many people considered him crazy, and held him responsible for vandalising the statue of Queen Victoria which stood in the town square. No matter how often the statue was repaired, the outstretched arm bearing the sceptre was always broken off and Marshall vaguely remembered that Pharaoh Sarjeant had been imprisoned for that crime.

There were also the five women at Banyan, who cared for Nana Sarjeant, his bed-ridden great-great-great-great-grandmother. Pearl had a club foot, Louise a hare lip, Norma was dumb, and Velda was a hunchback. Only Eleanor was normal. Even Binta Sarjeant, his guardian, Eleanor's grandniece, belonged to the ranks of physical misfits. Half of Aunt Binta's face was covered in lumpy purplish skin, which ran from her forehead to her neck, as if a permanent fungal growth had invaded her face. And there were other, more distant, relatives, some of whom did not bear the name Sarjeant, scattered in the hills and valleys around Paradise. Surveying those families in his mind's eye, Marshall could not think of one without a cripple or a blind, deaf or dumb member.

Drifting into sleep, he saw his own freckled face and body with its head of brownish hair which had a tendency to redden in reaction to strong sunlight and earned him the sobriquet Red Sarjeant from friends. If there was such a thing as Sarjeant's curse, though fortunate in escaping its more extreme effects, he too was a victim and therefore had a right to know the truth.

The following morning, a Saturday, Marshall worked with sedulous care to melt the glacial visage that Aunt Binta adopted whenever he incurred her displeasure. Up early, he watered the vegetable garden, which he was inclined to neglect, gathered the fallen limes, swept the yard, the veranda and the house, and washed his bloodied shirt with the fervour of a criminal removing evidence. He wore a dolorous countenance that owed more to gnawing hunger than genuine contrition.

When Binta called him in for a late breakfast, believing she had forgiven him, he went to join her at the table. He did not waste time posing the question with which he had fallen asleep and which had grown in importance with his demonstrative labouring.

Binta Sarjeant dismissed it with a firm retort: 'You know better than to listen to rumours.' But noticing how she touched the lumpy purple skin on her neck, averted her gaze, then determinedly concentrated on her food, Marshall concluded that Aunt Binta was both still cross and concealing something. Patience and persistence, virtues Aunt Binta often extolled, he was certain, would be rewarded.

Binta Sarjeant, slim and straight-backed, had the languid air of a woman weakened by protracted mourning. In fact, she enjoyed a reputation as the finest and quickest dressmaker outside Port Columbus, the nearest city to Paradise. She had dressed the bride in almost every wedding held in Paradise over the past decade, and even attracted customers from Nancy, a town nearly thirty miles away. Her popularity as a dressmaker was, in part, due not only to the speed, but also the artistry with which she transformed cheap cloths into fabulous gowns that uplifted even the poorest weddings. But many a young bride also believed that a wedding dress stitched by the childless spinster with the ugly facial rash was invested with some power that guaranteed the wearer's fertility and the fidelity of the husband. Most importantly, it helped to cure the wanderlust that afflicted the men of the island and caused them to abandon wives, lovers and children in search of imaginary wealth in other Caribbean islands and the American continent.

Although the deceptively languorous dressmaker herself made no such preternatural claims for her modest gowns, her diffidence heightened a reputation which ensured that she and her nephew never went hungry. She possessed a fiercely independent spirit, which defied her congenital facial disfiguration, and made her something of an outsider in her family. She had not only chosen to live close to Paradise, far from the family home, Banyan, which was five miles away up in the hills behind the town, she worshipped in an alien church. She was a Catholic and held her faith in defiance of several religiously intolerant members of the Sarjeant family who claimed to be Baptists. She had estranged those same family members when she enrolled Marshall in the newly established Catholic Missionary School, St Christopher's, rather than the common Baptist Free School. She did not conceal from her nephew her disdain for the noisy services of the Baptists. Sometimes when she was very angry with Marshall, she reminded him that she had fought to save his soul, and if he wanted to send her to her grave a proud, happy woman, he would control his violent temper by serving the Church.

Marshall had had to work hard in the past to regain his aunt's confidence and trust. And now that the issue of Sarjeant's curse was troubling him, he resolved to work harder than ever to demonstrate the depth of his remorse for getting into yet another fight. So over the next twenty-four hours his behaviour bordered on the saintly.

After Mass that Sunday, he approached Aunt Binta, who was relaxing on the veranda, sat at her feet, and, assuming his sweetest, most endearing little boy's voice, said: 'Auntie, is it really true that all Sarjeants are cursed?'

She sighed with a weary expectation and said: 'Guess you going to start hearing 'bout Sarjeant's curse from all sorts of loose-mouth people, so you better hear the truth.'

Binta Sarjeant prefaced her account of Sarjeant's curse by denying its existence altogether. She conceded that the frequent deformities among the Sarjeants were a sign that something was amiss, but attributed them to incest and diseases transmitted over many generations. But she admitted that no family member shared her opinion. Every Sarjeant known to her believed the story that had been handed down the generations.

2

Around 1810 Robert Buchanan, a Scot eager to escape the oppressive beauty of Paradise, sold Banyan Plantation and its three hundred African slaves to Neal Sarjeant. Solemn and reticent, with the ascetic's spare frame and an erect carriage, Neal Sarjeant was a former soldier turned artist. He had travelled the world many times and fought in many mercenary wars, and in early middle age, with his warrior spirit tired and disillusioned, the wealth accumulated from those exploits gave him the freedom to indulge, without regard for the opinions of art critics and collectors, the passionate delusion that he could paint.

The muse of that delusion was his much younger wife, Sybil. She had persuaded Sarjeant to settle in Jamaica and inspired him to purchase Banyan Plantation. Sybil was a swarthy woman of indeterminate national origins, with piercing green eyes and luxuriant long brown hair framing a face that was pretty rather than beautiful. Her thin lips were permanently set in a curious half-smile which gave her a supercilious air and left many people with the unsettling impression that she knew some secret about them. She was, undoubtedly, the animating force in the marriage.

The Sarjeants moved into Banyan House with a great volume of superb French and English furniture transported from Port Columbus in a convoy of twelve wagons. Sybil Sarjeant's personal possessions included a grand piano, a giant harp and so many clothes that they alone filled three wagons.

From the outset Neal Sarjeant dedicated the daylight hours to his art, and was seldom seen on the grounds of the plantation without easel, brushes and oils. One of the bedrooms in

Banyan House was converted into a studio where he worked when the weather was too inclement to paint the landscapes and scenes of slaves labouring. Sybil, meanwhile, spent her days instructing a group of selected female slaves in the finer points of domestic etiquette.

Then, three months after they took up residence at Banyan House, an extraordinary third member joined the Sarjeant household. He rode into Banyan Plantation on a grey mare, and his name was Alegba.

The presence of Alegba, a mute, bald-headed, powerfully built African, exercised the tongues and imagination of everyone in Paradise, Europeans and Africans alike. Soon after Alegba's arrival Neal Sarjeant called an assembly of slaves, and the European employees retained from the previous owner. There he expressed distaste for the institution of slavery, outlined the new, liberal rules by which the plantation would be run, and astonished everyone when he introduced Alegba as his second in command, the head overseer, empowered to dismiss workers and punish slaves as he saw fit.

Outraged, the bookkeeper, Tom Mayall, resigned on the spot but changed his mind overnight, after his quadroon wife pointed out that his misplaced racial pride would render her and their eight children homeless. Mayall was further humilated when Neal Sarjeant, looking up briefly and impatiently from the canvas he was working on, directed him to Alegba as the person who had the authority to re-employ him, which duly happened.

Owned by the Sarjeants and run by the mute African, Banyan Plantation was a much improved place for the African slaves. The Sabbath became a day of rest for everybody, except the lazy and insubordinate, and Alegba decided who fell into those categories. He was a ubiquitous figure among the slaves. Astride his mare, he supervised the field hands, communicating with them by means of grunts and hand signals, and never failed to make himself understood. He hunted down and punished runaway slaves, but undertook these tasks with a swift, joyless efficiency, reserving the severest punishment – lashings with the cat-o'-nine-tails – for persistent runaways and the most violently rebellious slaves.

Four weekends each year the Africans were allowed to celebrate in their own way, with drumming and dancing, praisesongs to half-remembered gods and lamentation for their enslavement. Alegba sometimes attended these celebrations, but he remained apart, and more than once confounded his fellow Africans by weeping openly at their songs of captivity. None the less, he continued to hunt and bring back the runaways and administer the floggings himself.

His lack of empathy with the slaves led many to believe that he was a mischievous African god who had entered into partnership with the Sarjeants for his own indecipherable ends. They could find no other explanation for his uncanny ability to make himself understood without speech. Only the fantastic could explain his daily presence at dinner with the Sarjeants and the fact that he slept under the same roof as the master and mistress.

The planters in Paradise were equally puzzled by the relationship between the Sarjeants and the strange African. Seeking to ingratiate himself with a potential future employer, Tom Mayall was, in the first instance, their main source of news on the peculiar arrangements at Banyan House. He reported after-dinner soirées at which Sybil Sarjeant played the harp, with both Neal Sarjeant and Alegba seated in Chippendale armchairs, smoking pipes and sipping fine Portuguese sherry.

That Alegba accompanied the Sarjeants on some of their early forays into planter society confirmed Mayall's reports. Alegba, silent and alert, was never far from their sides. His intelligent eyes registered that he understood every conversation, and his mannered clapping of the musical ensembles imported from Port Columbus to entertain those gatherings left many guests too shocked to be offended. None the less, the Sarjeants' socialising ended in their second Christmas in Paradise. With Neal indisposed for unknown reasons, Sybil outraged decent society when she not only strolled into the annual seasonal ball escorted by Alegba dressed in the fine raiment of an English gentleman, but also proceeded to waltz with him. Several offended guests departed early. The Sarjeants would receive no further invitations from their planter neighbours.

Some days later, Emily Spender, an English planter's wife, accosted Sybil Sarjeant in the town square, and accused her of degrading that Christian occasion by being in the company of a pagan savage.

Sybil replied: 'Don't worry, madam, you won't have another opportunity to take offence at my choice of escorts and your husband will soon be free to spend more time in Port Columbus with the Spanish whore he keeps there.'

The next day Emily Spender, struck down by what was diagnosed as malaria, took to her bed, where she died within weeks. That incident, combined with the undeniable success of Banyan Plantation – its sugar, cocoa, oranges and spices commanded the highest prices in Port Columbus and its African slaves seemed, if not happy, at least contented – focused the envious and mystified attention of the planters on Sybil Sarjeant. The salacious speculations are not worth repeating, being entirely baseless and the product of rumsoaked imaginations, but the belief that Sybil Sarjeant and Alegba, viewed as shaman or witchdoctor, had entered into a diabolical pact gained a sizeable number of adherents. Neal Sarjeant was regarded as a willing accomplice, blinded by love for Sybil, and needy of the profits that accrued from their evil machinations so he could continue to indulge his vain artistic ambition.

For many years the Sarjeants seemed indifferent to the hostility their unusual arrangement attracted. But in their sixth year strains began to appear in the household. They first became evident in Sybil Sarjeant when she suffered a miscarriage four months into her pregnancy. The same misfortune struck her repeatedly over the next three years. The only occasion one of her pregnancies lasted the full term, the baby emerged stillborn. As these fruitless pregnancies multiplied, she grew thinner and frailer. The evening musical performances stopped and she was inclined to lose her temper at the slightest mishap. She daily admonished the house slaves for their laziness, stupidity, incompetence and dishonesty. One day she personally supervised the whipping of a pregnant scullery maid who had been caught stealing food. Only Neal Sarjeant's timely intervention brought a halt to that vicious, excessive punishment. Informed some weeks later that the girl had lost the baby, a cruel smile of satisfaction crossed Sybil's lips.

Gradually, Sybil withdrew, remaining in her bedchamber for days at a time. The rare occasions when she ventured out, she never stepped beyond the balcony.

As Sybil weakened, Alegba seemed less capable of maintaining control over the affairs of the plantation. His unblemished record of catching runaways was lost when four men escaped into the mountains. He often appeared to be confused, unsure of himself, gave contradictory orders, became forgetful, and lacked the energy of his earlier years. One Easter he completely forgot himself and joined in the all-night celebration of the Africans, frenziedly danced and issued the plaintive guttural cries of a caged beast. Then, as if suddenly emerging from some spell, he fled the company of his fellow Africans and returned to Banyan House. He too became a shadowy, seldom seen figure, as if sick with sympathy for Sybil.

Neal Sarjeant, meanwhile, wandered through these difficult times as though oblivious to the slow disintegration of the Caribbean idyll of his weary soldier's heart. But as Sybil's behaviour became more erratic and Alegba weakened, the daily strain began to show on him too. He was now seen more often out of his studio, and without the paraphernalia of his painterly obsession, as if defeated by the weakness of his talent and vision.

It was shortly after he had made a bonfire of the canvases representing five years' work that he succumbed to a malaise familiar to the long-corrupted planters whose advice and fraternity he had shunned. He sought comfort in the arms of a female slave, Nana, who was the daughter of Athena Morgan, the cook. As Sybil slept, he made his way to Nana's cabin with a frequency that could have only one result. Nana became pregnant and bore her master a son, who was named Thomas. Before Sybil Sarjeant discovered that the mulatto child she sometimes saw in the plantation grounds was not the offspring of some feckless soldier from Port Columbus but her husband's, Nana was pregnant again.

Sybil's swift descent into madness destroyed the vestiges of normality in Banyan House. She persecuted the house slaves, striking them for the slightest misdemeanours, or imagined offences. Athena Morgan was accused of attempting to poison the Sarjeants and, as punishment, banished to the fields, the fate suffered by all her successors.

Then early one windless November morning Sybil was seen leaving the house with Alegba, who seemed half asleep. They rode away on a horse-drawn cart, but where they went nobody knew. Sybil returned alone the following dusk, her clothes dishevelled and bloodstained, her face bruised and covered in scratches but wearing a triumphant expression, as if she had been victorious in battle.

That same night Banyan House was destroyed by fire. It started with smoke billowing from the roof as Sybil Sarjeant, dressed in a Parisian white cotton nightgown, stood on the upper-floor balcony, gripping the railing, her eyes closed. Her luxuriant hair, now streaked with grey, streamed behind her on a wind of growing ferocity and inexplicable origin, for the day had been stultifyingly still. It was as though Sybil were summoning the wind to fan the flames of her wrath.

The heavy doors and window shutters, installed by the previous owner of Banyan House to withstand assaults from rebellious slaves, resisted the efforts of rescuers. When they finally gained entry they found a drugged, almost asphyxiated Neal Sarjeant at the bottom of the stairs. The flames and smoke made access to the upper floor impossible, and the rescuers settled for saving the semiconscious master of the house.

At the height of the fire, a figure drowning in flames burst through the blaze. Some witnesses swore they saw, at first, Alegba and not Sybil. But it was definitely Sybil, her clothes and hair on fire, who staggered towards the prostrate Neal Sarjeant with outstretched arms, grasping the air. She collapsed yards from the blazing building. Dying of burns she none the less summoned up the energy to utter the curse for which she would be remembered: 'I curse you, Sarjeant, for bringing me to this hellish paradise. I curse you and your nigger children and their children's children. I curse you for ever.'

Neal Sarjeant would never recover from the death of his wife and the destruction of Banyan House. He freed his slaves, abandoned the plantation to them and squandered the wealth he had accumulated over many years in the gambling salons and brothels of Port Columbus. Broken in pocket and heart, he drifted back to Paradise and was taken in by Nana Sarjeant, who had given birth to twin boys and adopted the surname Sarjeant. He soon abandoned her cabin and went to live in a derelict stone watchtower on the edge of Paradise. Although he shunned his mulatto children, now three boys, and their mother for a reclusive life, he was not deserted. Nana Sarjeant visited him once a week and arranged for a dutch pot of food to be left at the fortified door of the watchtower.

For many years Neal Sarjeant marked the anniversaries of his marriage and his wife's death by taking potshots from the roof of the watchtower at unwary travellers on the Port Columbus road. Local inhabitants came to recognise a pattern to his murderous madness and knew on which days of the year to avoid that route. But two years after emancipation, the Governor of the island, Sir Harold Frances, was touring his domain with an entourage of foreign dignitaries. As they neared the watchtower a sudden blast of buckshot caused pandemonium among the travellers, and they were forced to flee their carriages and fine mares and seek shelter behind rocks and trees. The enraged Governor ordered his soldiers to storm the watchtower and arrest the culprit. As the soldiers crashed through the door, Neal Sarjeant turned his rifle on himself and blew his brains out. His last reported words were: 'Damn Paradise. Damn Paradise!'

3

The story of Sarjeant's curse did not immediately preoccupy Marshall beyond his recognising an ancestral thread of continuity between himself and the planter-artist whose ill-fated Jamaican years had ended in disillusionment, madness and death. For he heard it at a time when vague artistic ambitions had begun to stir inside him. From an early age he had demonstrated a talent for drawing, filling notepads and scraps of paper with detailed pencil sketches of Paradise scenes and faces. Drawn from memory, and accurately highlighting the person's best features, the pictures of family members and friends had earned him encouraging praise from subjects surprised by his skill and flattered by his portrayals. The greatest encouragement, though, had come from less biased quarters.

Teacher Lee had spotted his raw talent, taken him aside and urged him to develop it. She had spoken to him of great art as consolation and exaltation inspired by religion and mythology. She had mooted the possibility of a scholarship to a Kingston college and presented him with an attractive vision of a future beyond school. By singling him out as a boy of promise, she had, moreover, won the violent affection of his young heart and become the subject of a schoolboy crush that made her and the idea of art as a vocation inseparable. Her prolonged absence caused him far more anxiety than the legend of Sarjeant's curse. So, three weeks after she first went missing, with rumours now circulating that she had run away to Brazil with a strange Haitian, a distracted Marshall found it impossible to resist playing truant again.

On this occasion his sole companion was Scoop Fearon.

The other boys, led by an unforgiving Billy Hearne, had declined to join them. For most of that day Marshall was a boy free of worries, lost in the laughter of mischief. The pair bagged three ground doves with their slingshots, caught a fat goatfish, stole a hand of green bananas from one farm and some cocoa yams from another. They roasted the scrawny birds and fish, boiled the bananas and yams in a kerosene pan and had a feast. Then they frolicked in the Blue Hole for hours. Late in the afternoon, as the boys lay on rocks shaded by giant fern leaves, Scoop brought up the subject of Teacher Lee's sudden disappearance.

'Wonder if Teacher Lee reach Brazil yet.'

'With that funny-looking Haitian?'

'So them say.'

'I don't believe Teacher Lee would go away just like that,' Marshall said emphatically.

'You don't know them Haitians,' Scoop said. Because his father had worked on the Panama Canal, Scoop regarded himself as a great authority on Caribbean matters.

'But I think I know Teacher Lee. A little anyway. She wouldn't run off with no funny-looking Haitian.'

'You just vex 'cause the Haitian thief your sweetheart.' The two boys laughed.

The events preceding Teacher Lee's disappearance were by now common knowledge. The Haitian, Hippolyte Jacmel, had booked into the town's only boarding-house and begun to make enquiries about a young woman, whom he claimed had jilted him. Dressed in a black three-piece suit and black homburg, he spoke in heavily accented English, and provoked uncomfortable laughter wherever he went because of his formal manners and the odour of death emanating from his undertaker's clothes. He had described her as having eyes as black as ackee seeds and a hint of China in their shape, the high cheekbones of a Red Indian, the statuesque height and languid walk of a princess from the African savannah, the rich golden complexion of one who is a confluence of all the peoples in the world, and she was likely to dress with extreme modesty to disguise a beauty that was a gift of history.

Only one woman in Paradise fitted that exalted description – Teacher Lee. She always wore a white or cream-coloured long headscarf with matching fussy high-neck blouse, which also covered her entire arms, and ankle-length loose skirt or dress that rested on sturdy closed shoes. As she taught at a Catholic school some people mistakenly assumed that she belonged to an order of nuns who had forsaken the more familiar habit and headdress for secular clothes of even greater and more forbidding chastity. She was not, in fact, a nun.

In one rum shack, Hippolyte Jacmel was told about the tragedy which had befallen Penton Frances, whom Teacher Lee had employed to carry out repairs on her cottage. The bachelor carpenter had become feverishly infatuated with her, and one night hid himself in the Victorian wardrobe in her bedroom to catch a glimpse of the body concealed beneath her fastidiously chaste clothes. Whatever he had seen had struck him dumb and, following two days of excessive drinking, he rode over Cuffee's Point on his bicycle. The bicycle, a mangled wreck wedged on the rocks, was the only remaining evidence of Penton Frances's brief madness.

Hippolyte Jacmel had spent a day at Cuffee's Point deep in thought. Then he had started to appear at the school gate, bearing bouquets of flowers, which he attempted to press on Teacher Lee while addressing her in French. She had ignored him with the same blank expression she presented to all men in Paradise, regardless of their status and the ardour of their appeals. The flowers would wilt in his hands but the following day he would return, clasping a fresh bouquet to his chest. He had stopped following her home only after she reported him to Constable Royston. But Constable Royston – sharing the view, common among most Paradise men, that a woman of such peerless beauty couldn't possibly be satisfied with a routine of prayers, work and domestic solitude – had not been as vigilant as the situation required. He had merely warned Hippolyte Jacmel that he, the constable, was alert to the unwanted attention the visitor was showering on the good Teacher Lee. On the same morning Teacher Lee had failed to show up at school, Hippolyte Jacmel's landlady, Mrs Elaine Macfarlane, complained to Constable Royston that the Haitian had absconded the previous night without paying his bill.

'Besides,' Scoop said when they'd stopped laughing, 'I wouldn't blame her. Who'd wan' to spend all their life in Paradise, it's the end of the world?'

'I do,' said Marshall. 'If I go to Kingston, I'm coming right back here. Not catching me wandering round the world.'

'Not me,' said Scoop. He stood up and stretched his thin body so taut that his ribs pressed again his dark skin. 'I'm gonna see the world.'

'And how you gon do that?' said Marshall.

Scoop laughed drily and said, 'Marshall, you know me. I'm gonna lie me way round the world or my name ain't Scoop Fearon.'

They laughed again. Scoop had a reputation as a teller of monstrous lies, and took sheer pleasure from inventing and making people believe them. His real name was Milton Fearon but on his insistence everyone addressed him by the name he had claimed for himself. When their laughter abated Scoop, more serious now, said: 'Fact, I might be leaving school soon. My pa says the best education's not in no school but in life itself.'

'You joking, Scoop?' Marshall said, suddenly raising himself on to his elbows.

'Nope,' Scoop said, and dived into the water and started shouting: 'Gonna see the world, gonna see the world.'

Disappointment crept over Marshall like lengthening shadows in the afternoon sun. Scoop was his best friend and without him school, already robbed of Teacher Lee, looked set to become unbearably tedious. Marshall's mood had plunged so low that when Scoop, insensitive to the crushing effect his casual disclosure had had on his friend, observed that they should set off home if they were to get back to Paradise before dusk, Marshall could not find the willpower to move. Petulantly, he told Scoop to go ahead; he would catch him up. Scoop departed, whistling.

Marshall remained beside the Blue Hole ruminating on how much he would miss Scoop, the whereabouts of Teacher Lee, and whether Aunt Binta had learnt of his absence from school. Then he closed his eyes.

Marshall had not intended to doze off, and when he woke the weak light and cool air inspired him with a sense of urgency. Setting off at a brisk pace, he decided to take the short cut through Cooper Vale and alongside Mr Collins's pimento farm. He estimated he'd reach the cotton tree on Manchioneal Hill before dusk and from there he could stroll into town. But he had forgotten that the path he had chosen, being seldom used, was covered in high guinea grass, which slowed his progress.

Nevertheless Marshall reached Cooper Vale in good time: there was still plenty of light. Cooper Vale's grove of cedar, eucalyptus and mahogany trees festooned with vines – associated in local lore with sightings of a rolling calf, a laughing cowboy on his three-legged horse and other apparitions – was the sort of place most sensible people avoided at night.

Midway along the grove, the fencing of the pimento farm visible ahead, he was arrested by the sound of someone calling his name from within the grove. It sounded like Scoop Fearon. Marshall immediately thought that Scoop had taken the same route and was waiting here to frighten him, send him fleeing so he could tease him later. Refusing to be scared, he entered the grove and followed the sound. A few yards into the semi-dark cluster of trees he stepped on something soft and yielding. He looked down and saw the leg, then the body, and he was startled and leapt backwards and panicked and then froze still in one fluid continuous moment of absolute fear.

A woman lay prostrate on the ground. Her face was turned away and one knee was drawn up to her waist while the other leg was straight, giving her the appearance of someone blissfully sleeping. She was almost naked but for the scant remnants of shredded white cloth, strips of which, strewn around her, seemed like petals violently torn from some giant flower. Her entire body and limbs were covered in symbols, ideograms, mathematical formulae, verses, musical notes, Roman numerals, Chinese characters and pictures of animals and snakes and a multitude of other, unrecognisable, images, which all seemed to be animated, whirling and merging into each other as if they were alive, though she was deathly still. And large red ants, flowing into and away from her head, blazed a shimmering crimson path across the ground like a river of flames, like a stream of blood. Marshall remained transfixed, in the grip of an icy fear, until she stirred and with a sudden jerky movement, raised and turned her head, revealing a skeletal face as white as the sea-washed, sun-bleached remains of a fish on the beach. Then he turned and ran. How he ran!

Many days later he would remember running through the dusk, the scent of pimento bushes, the slight change in temperature above the vale, the sprawling branches of the cotton tree, the faint trace of the sea, raw and salty, the white clouds lazily drifting across a pale moon, the fading lights in the distance. But he would never remember exactly when the light went out, when he started running through pure darkness, viscid like the air before an August rainfall. He was certain memory guided him for a few minutes before he crashed into the first garden fence and someone, Mr Henry, seized him roughly and said: 'Bwoy, you been drinking white rum or what?' And he answered: 'Ah can't see. Ah can't see.'

Marshall initially accepted his sudden blindness with calm and optimism. This owed much to Binta Sarjeant's forgiving and sympathetic nursing, bolstered by the professional opinion of Dr Paul Da Costa, a member of the Church. The young physician swiftly diagnosed that the boy was merely suffering from shock and reassuringly predicted that he would soon see the sun again.

Marshall, meanwhile, enjoyed the admiring attention of constant visitors, especially his schoolfriends, who regarded him as a hero for having discovered Teacher Lee's body. A party of men led by Constable Royston had found the lifeless body of Hippolyte Jacmel dangling from a tree in the grove. The macabre murder and suicide had even been reported in the *Daily Gleaner,* giving Paradise brief infamy.

But as Marshall's blindness continued he became irritable, Binta Sarjeant's growing anxiety became palpable, and with each visit Dr Da Costa sounded far less confident. Finally the doctor admitted to being perplexed and promised to consult his medical reference books and write to his former professor in Edinburgh to seek advice. He was no clearer on the next visit, made one night a month into Marshall's condition. But he did not hurry away, as he had done in the past, as if embarrassed by his overly optimistic prognosis. He sat on the veranda with Binta Sarjeant, within earshot of Marshall, and related an account of the real Teacher Lee that would send the worried aunt first to the priest, then in desperate search of ancient remedies.

According to the reports filtering back from Port-au-Prince – the destination of the bodies – Teacher Lee was born Antoinette Louise Cane to Françoise Cane, the creole-mulatto mistress of a successful, but low-born, New Orleans merchant. Aspiring to enter society, he kept both his mistress and their child a secret, though without her advice he would have remained a mere store-front clerk. Angered by her lover's repeatedly broken promises, Françoise Cane poisoned him and fled to Haiti, where she invested the remainder of her fast vanishing youth in Christophe Melange, a charismatic politician who preferred the salons of beautiful women to the intrigue needed to secure real political power.

Françoise had dabbled in African sorcery in New Orleans,

and in the Haitian capital, Port-au-Prince, she immersed herself in this arcane art. She became high priestess of the city's most powerful Voodoo sect. She conspired with all sorts of evil characters, and gods who only answered to the most precious sacrifice – innocent life. When a child went missing in Port-au-Prince, it used to be said: 'Madame Cane has made another gift to the spirits.' Françoise's ruthlessness did help Christophe Melange's political career. He was appointed Vice President in Jean Devereux-Baptiste's government and seemed destined to one day occupy the highest office in the land. Françoise Cane saw herself as his First Lady.

So when Françoise Cane learnt that President Devereux-Baptiste had no intention of allowing his rather indolent Vice President to succeed him – had, in fact, already identified his successor in an energetic military man – she lost all reason. A spate of child abductions in Port-au-Prince followed. The President, who had until then enjoyed a healthy life, fell critically ill. For months the old man clung to life with the tenacity that had seen him dispose of innumerable political rivals over the twenty years of his misrule. More children died, but the President still lived. Insanely desperate, Françoise Cane decided to make a personal and ultimate sacrifice: Antoinette.

Young Antoinette had by now grown into a teenager of spellbinding beauty and charm, qualities enhanced by the mannerisms she learnt from the English governess hired both to educate the girl and prevent her from getting under the feet of her megalomaniac mother. The governess, who loved the child dearly, was dismissed from her position and driven out of Haiti. Some days later Antoinette was drugged and surrendered to the priests, to be prepared for the rarely performed ritual sacrifice to the god Damballah. Washed in rosewater and goatsmilk, her entire body – from her neck to her ankles, including arms – was tattooed with myriad symbols and incantations intended to convince Damballah that the sacrificial victim bore all the knowledge and love the high priestess possessed.

But on the night of the ceremonial sacrifice, as Françoise Cane looked upon the innocent face of her daughter, her maternal instinct must have rebelled against her political ambition. She cancelled the ceremony. Chaos ensued. She had transgressed by teasing Damballah with false promises and now both she and Antoinette would have to be punished to appease the angry deity. Melange and his coterie – the priests whose sacred beliefs she had offended – all came looking for Françoise Cane and her daughter.

Somehow mother and daughter managed to escape to Hispaniola, pursued by the cultists. There followed a peripatetic decade which saw them live in Puerto Rico, Dominica, Trinidad, Venezuela, Nicaragua and Cuba. In the Cuban city of Santiago de Cuba Françoise Cane, physically and mentally exhausted by the endless flight, expired, leaving her daughter, now a woman, to fend for herself.

Meanwhile, in Port-au-Prince, Antoinette Louise Cane had become a legendary figure among voodoo devotees. They believed whoever possessed her would acquire instant encyclopaedic knowledge of the most powerful voodoo rituals, which would bring inestimable wealth and unlimited power. Hippolyte Jacmel, the son of the tattooist who had inscribed the secrets on Antoinette's body, was the most obsessive hunter. But when he caught a glimpse of the now serenely beautiful young woman in Port of Spain, love, not the desire for power and wealth, inspired his continuing pursuit. None the less the fugitives eluded him, the trail went cold time and again, and Jacmel wasted several aimless years wandering around Europe in search of Antoinette.

When Hippolyte Jacmel found Antoinette Louise Cane in Paradise, Jamaica – found death and love – he changed the trajectory of Marshall's life. Marshall would no longer draw the faces and places of Paradise, his schooling ended abruptly, and the fragments of the religious faith he had started to acquire, though firmly lodged somewhere in his soul, would remain just fragments. They would have to co-exist with other spiritual, and more urgent secular, concerns.

4

Binta Sarjeant did not take lightly the decision to transfer Marshall to Banyan, the family home. Dr Da Costa had spent many nights poring over his medical tomes, and Father Kennedy, the priest at St Christopher's Church, had intoned volumes of prayers on the boy's behalf. All to no avail. Restless with boredom, determined to move about, Marshall had practically destroyed every breakable object in the house. He was a danger to himself. Exasperation and desperation forced Binta to swallow her pride and seek help from quarters she had earlier rejected. Rejected in the belief that Banyan and her relatives there were trapped in another age, imprisoned by the superstitious beliefs of an old woman who refused to die.

Marshall had often visited Banyan with Aunt Binta, and knew it only as a place where he was fussed over by elderly female relatives. He cared little for Aunt Binta's disagreements with the family. He just wanted his sight back.

Although Banyan was only five miles inland from Paradise, it was a world unto itself. The house accommodated six people and easily found space for one more. A sprawling bungalow, it had acquired a ramshackle appearance from the many rooms added over the years, and its uneven flooring initially proved treacherous for Marshall. But its roof kept out the rain, and specially selected trees and shrubs kept it cool and free of mosquitoes. Water came from a well behind the house, kerosene lamps provided light and wood, cooking fuel. Daily visitors brought provisions, or came to purchase the herbs and concoctions that the women packaged and bottled in the kitchen and which Aunt Binta hoped would cure her nephew. None of those remedies worked, but at Banyan he found the equanimity to accept the perpetual night that had descended on him since he saw Teacher Lee's naked body.

Banyan gave him an open space to roam and work off a frustration that, as long as it persisted, prevented him from adjusting to his blindness. Marshall now discovered that thought he was sightless, there were still pleasures to be derived from these uniformly dark days. First with the women's help, then with a stick or the ingenious device of strings tied to the veranda posts, he daily walked to and from the house to shady spots where he would sit and whittle soft wood into the shapes of animals and birds preserved in memory and evoked with patience. None the less it was a relatively sedentary life and he put on weight at an alarming rate. Binta Sarjeant, who visited weekly, was kept busy sewing new pants and shirts for him. The mountainous meals of yams and dumplings that the Banyan women served up – food for walking great distances over a hilly land or working long hours in the merciless heat – broadened and lengthened him monthly. The daily surplus energy kept him awake at night and it was during those hours that his favourite sights in Paradise were replaced by favourite sounds. Then the snoring of the women, the breeze, the crickets and cicadas, the frogs and the owls sounded like wind instruments, and the rhythm of the rain on the roof and on the ground and on the leaves, and the ripe breadfruits crashing through leaves and bouncing off branches and exploding on the ground sounded like percussion instruments. And if he concentrated really hard, he could hear the intermittent throbbing of the land, as if the island itself were one immense bass drum and the night an epic musical symphony.

One day Eleanor Sarjeant, who headed the household, asked Marshall to help shell a bag of gungo peas. Other tasks requiring only touch followed. This way, Eleanor, a busy, bustling woman, drew Marshall out of his solitude and into the garrulous company of the women in the kitchen, at the back of the house. When the goats had been milked, the chickens fed and the yard swept to remove the invisible footprints of the many ghosts that had passed during the night, they settled into a working day punctuated by meeting the needs of Nana Sarjeant.

That incredibly old woman was the heart of Banyan. Twice daily, morning and afternoon, she would be brought to the veranda and seated in a bamboo rocking-chair. There she would hum lowly, almost inaudibly, like the sound of a distant brook. She still possessed some vestiges of sight, hearing and speech, but as she tired easily nothing was demanded of her except that she continue to breathe. Marshall often sat at her feet in silence, her ancient presence as reassuring and comforting as the landmark a traveller looks for when nearing home. Before being wheeled away she might stroke his head and face, her wrinkled palms like dried banana leaves on his skin.

Back in the kitchen, as he shelled the peas they had placed before him, or ground whatever bark, soft stone or plant they had placed in a mortar, Marshall came to understand the unique power of the women, whose individual laughter and voices mixed with various scents and odours to create a sense of occupying an inviolable and timeless space. They were memory as flesh, historians and museum keepers as well as apothecaries and midwives. They argued over minor details of past events, which were recounted almost daily, as if they feared forgetting. Though they seldom left the grounds of Banyan they knew everyone's business in Paradise. But mostly they talked about the Sarjeant family; that was their consuming passion. Marshall could sense the anxiety in their voices when they discussed the pregnancy of a relative, their fear that the baby would be born with the wretched affliction they called Sarjeant's curse. He heard the story behind the curse so often, heard it told with such conviction of its absolute veracity, that he came to believe their account, which differed in many important respects from Binta Sarjeant's version.

The women of Banyan did not portray Nana Sarjeant as the victim of a dissolute plantation owner and failed artist, the passive recipient of Neal Sarjeant's amorous attention, an empty vessel into which he poured his frustration. The master of Banyan House did descend into melancholy then despair as he struggled to paint without his muse, Sybil, whose failed pregnancies had turned her into a semireclusive termagant who emerged from her solitude only to terrorise the female slaves. They feared her, then they hated her, then they declared war on Sybil. When Athena Morgan, the cook and Nana's mother, began lacing his meals and drinks with herbs that weakened his will and made him notice the lamplight in Nana's cabin and then gravitate towards it like ants to sugar, all the women had agreed on this strategy, including Nana. Nana's own motives were mixed. She felt compassion for Neal Sarjeant. She surrendered her body to him and became pregnant not merely to wound Sybil but to give him life and immortality, the very things that Sybil could not give him. In anticipation of Sybil's anger, the women of Banyan simultaneously worked to eliminate Alegba. They could not fathom his relationship with Sybil, but they were certain he would be the instrument of her wrath against them. His ability to withstand a quantity of poison that would have killed a bull elephant left them wondering whether he was a god. Without Alegba they hoped Sybil would be too weak to retaliate and resign herself to what was a common arrangement on other plantations.

If Nana and her accomplices underestimated Sybil's power — they did not foresee the slaying of Alegba, whose body was never found, the destruction of Banyan House, its intended use as a funeral pyre for Sybil and her husband, the strength of Neal Sarjeant's love for his wife – then Sybil had also underestimated her opponents. Over a century later, Nana, stubbornly alive in the belief that her presence would limit the power of the curse placed on the Sarjeants by Sybil, was still battling her.

Nana held Sybil responsible for the fact that her first-born, Thomas, whose birth ignited Sybil's fury, later turned against his mother and ran away to sea in his early teens, joined a merchant ship in Port Columbus and was never heard from again. She recognised Sybil's handiwork in Robert, the wild, hard-drinking twin, who had fathered six children – two of whom were born crippled – by the time he was twenty-five, and led a peasant strike and protest march on the government office in Port Columbus. Despite appeals for clemency from Church leaders and Nana Sarjeant, Robert Sarjeant and three others were hanged for fomenting unrest among the peasants. When she defied the Governor's orders and drove a horsecart to Port Columbus, single-handedly fought off the vultures to cut down her son from the gibbet, and brought him back to Banyan, where she buried him, she was not, as many people thought, challenging the Crown. She did it to save his soul from Sybil.

She recognised the family nemesis, too, in Robert's twin brother, John. Born with a withered right leg, withdrawn and prone to melancholia, but hard-working, John Sarjeant shot himself in 1854 because he could no longer continue dragging around the withered dead leg, though he had a loving, loyal wife and four healthy children, only one of whom showed a sign of the curse in a disfigured face.

When the children of her children started reproducing and there was in every family a child who bore signs of the curse, Nana swore to stay alive and protect the line she had created with Neal Sarjeant. They, the women of Banyan, her great-great-grandchildren, were her aides. But much as these women loved and revered Nana they were aware that she could not live for ever. They believed her death would have disastrous consequences, that then Sarjeant's curse would become more widespread, visibly affecting not just one or two members of each family, but everyone born with Sarjeant's blood. Sybil's victory would be complete.

Sometimes Marshall heard things that were not meant for

his ears. The kitchen walls did not meet the roof and on one side was a rough bench where everyone sat when needing a break from the work. He was sitting there one afternoon, silently listening to the sounds of a day approaching its end. Unaware of his presence, Norma and Louise began to talk about Ruth Sarjeant, Marshall's mother. He knew she had died giving birth to him and believed what he had been told about his father disappearing to Kingston. He found out now that his mother had also been a victim of Sarjeant's curse, and much more.

Ruth was the only child of Joshua and Annie Sarjeant. Joshua, the great-grandson of Robert Sarjeant, was one of many Sarjeants who left the island in search of work and vanished into the insatiable belly of the Americas. He left behind Annie and Ruth, who, as she grew older, was the sort of child on whom everyone looked with pity while thanking fate for giving them normal offspring. She was a simpleton, and with age, her behaviour became disturbingly strange. She spoke to the cows and goats in the fields, wallowed in the mud with the pigs and slept in the chicken coop. She went through a phase where she dined on aromatic but bitter-tasting hibiscus flowers, consuming them in secret feasts betrayed by the stains on her hands and lips.

Those idiosyncrasies were forgotten when she developed a more disturbing habit: she began to wander. She was twelve years old when Harold Miller, a neighbour, found her walking towards Port Columbus with the gritty determination of someone persevering through exhaustion. In her slow, heavy-tongued speech she told him she was accompanying a woman in a flowing yellow dress and carrying a multicoloured parasol. He brought her back to Annie Sarjeant's house, and gave his worrying account. Over the next year Ruth went missing at least once a month. On a few occasions, despairing of ever finding her, fearing she had come to some harm, Annie raised the alarm in the town and search parties of men scoured the fields, vales, riverbanks and shoreline for the missing child.

Annie tried all sorts of remedies before resorting to brute force. For a whole year Ruth was kept on a leash tied to the veranda post, a tree or her bed. When this extreme measure was suspended, Ruth resumed her wandering, but it now acquired a predictable pattern. If night came and she was not home, she could be found on the beach, under a fisherman's boat. She spent whole days on the sea wall, staring out into the vast emptiness of the ocean as if it were a book. One day a fisherman asked her what so fascinated her about the sea, and she said she was listening to the songs of the drowned. He spread the word. From then on many people regarded Ruth Sarjeant as a girl who spoke to spirits. Before retiring at night, they searched under their houses and inspected their chicken coops in case she chose their property on which to hold her diabolical conversations and so bring misfortune to their already difficult lives.

They became even more wary of her when it was discovered that there were, indeed, ghosts in the sea off the Paradise coast. A year after Ruth claimed to hear the drowned, several rival groups of American divers descended on the town like an invading horde. They were searching for the wreck of the *Catalonia,* a Spanish ship laden with gold and jewellery for the King of Spain, which sank in a storm in 1625. The Americans attracted an army of migrants from other parts of the island and this influx helped to transform Paradise, until now overshadowed by its proximity to Port Columbus, into a proper town. Shops sprang up, the police station was enlarged, and there was even talk of extending the railway line from Port Columbus to Paradise as construction on several holiday villas started. The divers were around for almost six months. They did not find the sunken galleon but they did discover a wreck with the floating skeletal remains of four hundred African slaves.

Marshall was conceived some months after the divers left, while men in search of work still straggled into town, stopping overnight or for a few days, then moving on. Ruth had been kept away from the sea front during the gold-rush months, a restriction that should have lasted much longer because Paradise had ceased to be a small town where everyone knew her and looked out for her. But hindsight was no consolation to her mother, who discovered, quite by accident, that Ruth's swelling stomach was evidence not of fat acquired from her latest eating craze, a passion for raw sweet-potato leaves, but of pregnancy.

Blinded, separated from friends and displaced to Banyan, where the dust of the family past was daily disturbed and examined, Marshall listened to the women's account of his origins and then stumbled away in loud, tearful distress. Norma and Louise, who had unwittingly illuminated that unlit corner of his life, could not comfort him. For some days he returned to sitting under trees and whittling the shapes of animals and birds, this time with a violently careless impatience which left his hands bleeding from knifecuts

It was Eleanor Sarjeant who came to him one night, as he sobbed quietly in bed, came and held him as if he were a baby and said: 'Whether a person born under rock stone or born in mansion, whether 'im mother is queen or a pauper, is less important than the life 'im live. So be strong, me child, be brave, be a duppy conqueror.'

5

Marshall's losses continued to multiply when Binta Sarjeant, who had constantly reminded him that he could return to living with her if he was unhappy at Banyan, implicitly withdrew that option and announced that she would be moving to Kingston. Awakened to the disturbing signs of advancing years in the appearance of a few grey hairs, she had been seized by a sudden desire to experience living in the capital for a few years. She was determined not to allow her disfigurement to prevent her from knowing, however briefly, life beyond the tranquil insularity of Paradise. Monthly letters and occasional parcels of new clothes replaced her weekly visits to Marshall. Eleanor Sarjeant read him the letters, which helped to palliate his inevitable feeling of being abandoned, and he came to take heart from, and pride in, the exemplary courage of his doughty aunt.

Around the same time Binta Sarjeant left Paradise, Scoop Fearon departed for Port Columbus, where an uncle had secured him a job on the docks. Scoop, who had left school some months after Marshall went blind, was the only former schoolmate who regularly visited Marshall at Banyan. Marshall missed Scoop's visits, missed the exaggerations and lies which Scoop insisted on telling, as if testing his own skilfulness in mendacity and Marshall's credulity. He missed those amusing accounts of supposed adventures told in such great detail and with such absolute conviction that they would have convinced the sighted, let alone the blind. If Scoop were to be believed, he had helped Constable Royston apprehend two thieves who tried to steal a barrel of salted pork from the Chinese grocery store; acted as go-between in an illicit affair between Mavis Banks, the wife of Joseph Banks, and Carlton Harris, and then saved Carlton Harris's life by warning him that Joseph Banks had discovered the affair, and was heading for him with a freshly sharpened machete; beaten Will Morris, an infamous drinker, in a rum-drinking contest; and followed Father Kennedy one rainy night to a goat field where an indescribable act took place. All these events had occurred between two visits divided by a week.

So a year later, as he sat under the guinep tree, Marshall was happy to hear the approaching sound of Scoop's inimitable whistling above the familiar chirping of the birds.

Scoop was back in Paradise temporarily. While working as a banana loader in Port Columbus, he had been offered a job on a boat and was taking a deserved break before embarking on his first voyage. His hands were larger and rougher, his voice deeper, and he spoke a language sprinkled with pungent profanities acquired from his fellow dock workers. For the duration of his visit Scoop excited Marshall's imagination with vivid descriptions of the wonders of Port Columbus – its movie house that transported audiences to remote corners of the world, its silent automobiles gliding along on cushions of air, and its glamorous female American tourists, who wore shoes with heels as high as stilts and heat-resistant ice necklaces to keep themselves cool. That account, along with Scoop's worldly air and self-confidence, made Marshall aware of how stagnant his own life had become in the dark, timeless ambience of Banyan.

Nevertheless, it was a wonder of Paradise that had Scoop in the grip of febrile agitation when he next called on Marshall some days later. He had helped his father deliver a cabinet to the house of Mrs Duncannon-Henriques, who owned one of the largest banana plantations in Paradise, and there he saw a girl so beautiful he momentarily forgot his own name. He was hopelessly, sweetly, ecstatically in love. Infected by his friend's excitement, Marshall asked him to describe her.

'Her name is Soledad and there isn't another girl in Paradise like her, in the whole of Jamaica, the whole of the Caribbean. You know that time a day when the sun setting over Cuffee's Point and the sky streaked all shades of red and the sea calm and look like it's covered in a million hibiscus? That's what she look like, but twice as beautiful.'

'I still can't see her,' Marshall said.

'All right, you know when you take a piece of lignum vitae and polish it, shine it, and the two shades of the wood, light and dark, dancing in and out of each other. That is Soledad. She is the most perfect specimen of womankind a man will ever set his eyes on.'

'How do you know you love her?' Marshall said.

''Cause since I saw her I haven't eaten a thing. Can't eat. Can't even drink water, not even coconut water. I'm starving from love. Feel my ribs.' Scoop took Marshall's hand and pressed it against his ribcage and Marshall felt the bony protrusions, which convinced him, though he had never known a fleshy Scoop.

Scoop calmed down and gave a more prosaic description of a tall, willowy girl with smooth dark skin. Although he doubted that she had noticed him yet, he was determined that she should do so.

Marshall felt duty-bound to share with Scoop the rather discouraging information he had on Mrs Duncannon-Henriques and her stepdaughter, Soledad, learnt from the women of Banyan. He did not need to remind Scoop that Mrs Duncannon-Henriques refused to chop down the poison mango tree which overhung her wall, and whose fruit had given many unwary children and passing strangers violent stomach cramps, because, the lady had always argued, it taught respect for other people's property. Scoop knew that already. Marshall recalled the story, told him in the kitchen, how a decade before, Mrs Duncannon-Henriques had caught her husband and the maid in a compromising position and he had died soon afterwards, and how you could hear his pain-racked shouts as far away as Cuffee's Point, and the maid gave birth to a baby so hideous that the midwife had fainted and on recovering decided that it was better off dead. The women of Banyan held the opinion that Mrs Duncannon-Henriques regarded her stepdaughter, Soledad, as a lifelong companion adopted and nurtured to give her solace in the infirmity of old age and keep vigil in the final hours of a life marked by jealousy and selfishness.

Scoop listened but he would not be discouraged. He possessed a temperament that made the pursuit of youthful dreams, however wild and fantastic, the forge of failure or success from which the man would be born. Marshall's caution merely transmuted the fearsome Mrs Duncannon-Henriques into the dragon Scoop would have to slay, the river of fire he would have to cross if he were to win Soledad.

On his subsequent visit Scoop reported that he had stood at the gate of the house on Bonny View Hill and seen Soledad again, on the veranda, a vision of beauty and all he desired. He had waved at her, but she ignored him. Although hurt, he was undaunted. He would persevere through the pain. He would be patient.

Scoop's suffering was suspended when he was prematurely called away to Port Columbus to start work as a cabin boycum-deckhand on a steamer that transported migrant workers and sundry cargo around the Caribbean. His first voyage lasted four months. The Scoop who returned had grown even more confident for having realised one of his youthful dreams, to travel the world. He had been to Kingston, Santiago de Cuba, Havana and Miami, Florida. His next voyage, a fortnight away, would take him to New Orleans. These forays into the Caribbean had now sparked a great ambition: to see New York, where, according to Scoop, the Empire State Building was as tall as the Blue Mountain.

'What about Soledad?' Marshall asked.

'Not a day went by when I didn't think about her, saw her face in the clouds, reflected in the sea, in the night sky.' He had brought her a present from Port Columbus, a silk scarf bought from an American sailor, and even as they spoke he was hoping that the maid he had entrusted it to was delivering it to Soledad. Far from having lost his feelings for Soledad, he found his love reaffirmed and strengthened by his first voyage. 'After a week at sea you don't see much to get excited about,' said Scoop. 'You dream about home or the next port.' When he had dreamt of home, he dreamt always too of Soledad. But the voyage had made him wiser. He now recognised that he needed to make his fortune before he could lure her away from Mrs Duncannon-Henriques. Between now and then he would concentrate on winning her heart with gifts, tokens of his love. This was his grand scheme and he would pursue it wholeheartedly. 'You can't eat okra soup with one finger,' Scoop concluded.

It was a somewhat less buoyant Scoop whom Marshall next saw. The lovestruck sailor had spotted the maid to whom he had entrusted the headscarf for Soledad, wearing the item in town. Soledad had refused to accept the gift, told the maid to keep it or return it to its owner. Stung by that rejection, Scoop had come to Marshall both to complain and seek the warm breeze of friendship to stir his ship of love miserably stuck in the doldrums. Marshall did not fail him. He made an inspired suggestion: Scoop should write her a letter.

Scoop seized on the idea and said: 'You have to help me, Marshall. You were always better at spelling and grammar than me.'

Marshall agreed, with no small measure of trepidation. It was late in the day so Scoop stayed the night at Banyan. Under the light of a kerosene lamp, casting and recasting sentences, abandoning words that were too long because they were not sure how to spell them and there wasn't a dictionary in the house, they laboured through the night in search of words to express Scoop's devotion. At some point Eleanor Sarjeant evicted them on to the veranda because their noisy disagreements disturbed the house. It was Marshall who kept Scoop awake, insisting that they finish the letter, as if it were more important to him than his somnolent, forlorn friend. Largely dictated by Marshall and written in Scoop's painstakingly tidy and tiny script, the love letter to Soledad was finally finished after more than twenty-four hours. It read:

Dear Miss Soledad,

For what seems like an eternity I have been trying to see you. I have stood at your gate for hours through rain and sunshine, on moonlit nights and dewy mornings hoping to see you on your veranda. Failing each time, I have returned home and dreamt about you. I have seen your face in Kingston, your eyes in Santiago de Cuba, your lips in Havana. And in Florida I saw your smile.

Words cannot describe how I felt when you rejected the headscarf I sent as a token gesture of my affections for you. If you knew the hurt that rejection caused, if you could have seen my pain, you would have taken pity on me and regretted your action. I am sure no lady as refined and beautiful as you would wish to see even a dog in the pain I went through. The scarf was sent by one whose feelings for you are strong and true. Though you have spurned me, these feelings remain as strong and pure as you are beautiful.

I am a sailor and my work takes me away from Paradise for months at a time on long, lonely voyages where a man can go crazy with nothing to do. It would strengthen my heart if you would become my sweetheart. The person who I can buy gifts for when I am in foreign ports, the person whose love will help me endure the long, lonely days at sea, survive the perilous sea, the person whose smile will be here in Paradise waiting to greet me on my return, like the sunrise after a dark night.

I will soon be travelling again. It would strengthen me if you would reply to this letter. If you do not yet feel able to reply, but would like to send this lovesick sailor off on his next voyage with a stronger heart, please show me this sign that there is hope. Allow me to see you, though from afar, on the veranda. Just one glimpse of you will be like a flash of sunlight in a clouded sky, a tonic that I will bottle and take away with me and sip from when I feel lonesome and homesick. My longing to see you is unlike any ordinary pain. It is consuming my whole body. Please put me out of my misery. I will be standing at your gate on Thursday noon, hoping, with my humble and undeserving heart, that you will grant me this small wish but one that would fill my eyes with tears of joy.

Yours blind with love,

Sgn: Scoop Fearon.

The letter was entrusted to the same maid for delivery. Scoop went to Soledad's gate on Thursday at noon but he saw no one. A week later there had still not been a reply and Scoop's shore leave came to a fruitless end. He departed for Port Columbus, determined to buy her the most delightful gift he could afford in New Orleans.

Some days after Scoop's departure Marshall was sitting under the guinep tree, playing a bamboo flute, when he felt a series of stabbing pains shoot through his head. He dropped the flute and clasped his head and shouted in agony. Suddenly, shafts of brilliant light, light so bright he had to close his eyes, struck him repeatedly and sent him rolling in the dust in loud pain. Eleanor Sarjeant came to his rescue and brought him back to the house. Velma gave him the bitterest bush tea he had ever tasted and as the pain subsided he fell into a deep sleep.

When he woke he realised it was a new morning and then realised that he knew it was morning not by the sounds of the women who had started their day but because he could see the window surrounded by a cream lace curtain, pale light, the green trees outside and the room in which he had slept.

He leapt out of bed and dashed from his room shouting, 'I can see, I can see,' plunged into the cool, moist, morning air and hurtled into the backyard, scattering the chickens.

The women stopped their morning chores and stared in amazement as he dashed about, feasting his eyes on this new morning of his life. He could see the cocks crowing in the trees, a ripe lime buried in the leaves of the lime tree, the light blue sky, the rambling house, the dew-laden flowers. He could see his own hands and face, bulbous with fat, his rotund body. He could see again. The women gathered around and hugged him, and Velma and Pearl cried and talked of miracles and said how they had prayed every night for the return of his sight.

Later Marshall watched Nana Sarjeant being wheeled on to the veranda. He had no memory of ever having seen her before, though she had been as looming and permanent a fixture in the background of his life as the Blue Mountain. He was struck by the shrunken, frail figure who was helped into the bamboo rocking-chair. Fantastically old, with tight wrinkled skin that resembled parched earth, she seemed to have discarded all superfluous flesh, becoming skin and bones, kept alive by the power of an indomitable will. She sat grimly still, and her eyes, though cloudy, reacted to every sound and seemed to see far more than anyone else.

She signalled with a slight trembling gesture of her hand for Marshall to approach. He did so, and she stroked his hair. Then in a weak, barely audible whisper, clearly requiring great effort, she said: 'Now you must learn to see properly.'

Now you must learn to see properly. They were the only words Marshall ever heard her utter.

6

The full meaning of Nana Sarjeant's words escaped Marshall's understanding until the day, less than a month after he had regained his sight, Eleanor Sarjeant called him to the veranda where she was speaking to Pharaoh Sarjeant. In the three years Marshall had lived in Banyan, Pharaoh had been an occasional visitor, whom the women of Banyan treated with unalloyed respect. Their high regard for Pharaoh contrasted with Aunt Binta's view of him as a dangerous person to be avoided, and surprised Marshall, especially because they had also revealed that Pharaoh had been to prison for offending the King of England. His visits, which always included a few minutes alone with Nana Sarjeant, were usually short, but he and Eleanor had been engrossed in talk for hours before they summoned Marshall.

Marshall stood at the foot of the steps leading to the veranda where Eleanor and Pharaoh sat like a royal couple receiving a supplicant. Seeing them together, he recognised the family resemblance. Although darker than Eleanor, Pharaoh shared her height and coffee-brown eyes. They were cousins, but to look at they could have been brother and sister.

Pharaoh congratulated Marshall on his recovery, then said laconically: 'And now what?'

Marshall looked at him blankly before grasping that he was being asked about his future. He answered truthfully, 'I am not sure.' It was a matter he had been thinking about as he reacquainted himself with his favourite sights in Paradise. The novelty of regaining his vision had been accompanied by an awareness of the time he had lost in the limbo of blindness. How things had changed! His schoolmates had galloped into the outside world. Worst of all he seemed incapable of sketching even the simplest-looking objects. The impulse to draw might well have had an ancestral source, but the ambition to become an artist – with all the hard work, sacrifice and self-belief that entailed – had expired with Teacher Lee. Only his love of Paradise and the desire to spend his life here remained undiminished.

'Here's something to think,' Pharaoh said: 'I will complete your education. Teach you all that I know.' Pharaoh rose from his chair and gazed at Marshall with imperious severity, which made the boy conscious of the fat acquired over recent years. Pharaoh was tall, lean and had the straight-backed stature more common in the Sarjeant women. Eleanor Sarjeant looked at Marshall with beseeching eyes as if seeking his immediate and grateful acquiescence.

Marshall sensed that not only was he being honoured with this offer, but refusal would cause offence. Placing himself under Pharaoh's tutorship would be both an act of loyalty to the family and repayment for the care he had received from the women of Banyan. There was, too, something both likeable and curious about Pharaoh Sarjeant. Growing up with Aunt Binta, who had quarrelled with the entire family, Marshall had not known many men. Now Pharaoh Sarjeant seemed like someone worth knowing.

'Think about my offer,' Pharaoh said and left.

Watching Pharaoh walk away with long, powerful strides, Marshall knew he would accept the offer, despite the niggling reservations, which had as much to do with Aunt Binta's prejudices as his knowledge of Pharaoh's criminal past.

Left alone with Eleanor, he was shocked by her mindreading ability when she said: 'I hear Binta telling you to say no. But he's a good man, Marshall. When you're a little older you'll learn that some crimes are necessary.' She left him sitting on the veranda steps, pondering his future and Pharaoh Sarjeant.

Marshall did not yet know what Pharaoh did abroad, but

he knew about the actions that had led to his incarceration. Pharaoh Sarjeant had spent almost thirty years outside Jamaica. On returning to the island he lived in Kingston and there assumed the mantle of his great-great grandfather, Robert Sarjeant, who had been hanged for fomenting peasant protest, but he preached a different message. He spoke in apocalyptic tones of an international race war between Blacks and Whites and warned dark-skinned Jamaicans that they faced annihilation unless they stopped collaborating in their own oppression. He swooped on rum bars, playing-fields and beaches, and harangued and exhorted young men and women to join his crusade. The sight of the tall, stately man striding through the scorching afternoons, without a bead of perspiration to betray his exertion, sent children scattering, and even the noisiest dogs ceased barking.

Every Saturday morning he stood on a soapbox in Victoria Square and delivered lengthy speeches on the need for the darker people of Jamaica to uplift themselves. He excoriated their slovenly dress, their lack of manners, their poor standard of hygiene, and the weak minds which allowed them, a century after emancipation, to remain the victims of mental slavery.

But Pharaoh's speeches fell on the ears of folk principally concerned with the price of staple goods like yam and kerosene. If they thought about race at all, they were proud of being subjects of the British Empire, the mightiest empire in the world. One Kingstonian, a veteran of the First World War, dressed in a lovingly preserved uniform, took to following Pharaoh around, singing throughout his speeches: 'Rule Britannia, Britons never, never shall be slaves.'

The greater their mockery, the closer Pharaoh brushed against the little-used sedition laws, which forbade him insulting the King of England. He was given several warnings, but these threats only emboldened him. His speeches became more seditious. Inevitably he was arrested, tried, found guilty and sentenced to six months' imprisonment. On release, he returned to the quiet of Paradise and appeared to refrain from the racial demagoguery that had landed him in prison. But when the statue of Queen Victoria in the Paradise town square was damaged overnight, the authorities came looking for Pharaoh Sarjeant. His protestation of innocence did not convince them and he was taken to Port Columbus Penitentiary to await trial. The charges against him were dropped because the statue, which had been quickly repaired, was again vandalised while the main suspect languished in prison. None the less many people in Paradise still believed Pharaoh was responsible for constantly smashing off the right arm of the Queen Victoria statue.

Marshall's early visits to Pharaoh's home were undertaken with a vague desire to please Eleanor Sarjeant and the other women of Banyan. If the exercise proved to be too demanding, he was ready to abandon it and seek employment on one of the banana plantations where several of his less bright but equally unadventurous schoolmates worked.

Pharaoh lived thirty minutes' walk from Banyan, on a secluded bank of the Rio Grande River, in a forty-by-twenty cabin. It was simply furnished with a steel bed, a curtained clothes closet, three cane chairs, and a large table below a packed bookshelf. The entrance area to the cabin was a small covered portico, which also served as a kitchen, and at the far end a wide window gave a tranquil view over a slow, tenebrous stretch of the river, and farmland and green hills in the distance. He took pride in this modest, simple way of life. In the privacy of his home the former political demagogue turned pedagogue was not as severe as the mask he wore on his solitary walks around Paradise. He seldom smiled but when he did his eyes sparkled and his face betrayed a hint of mischievousness that belied his mature years and involuntarily evoked in Marshall's mind an image of Anancy, though he was certain that Pharaoh, who grew most of what he ate and bought the rest from nearby farms without haggling over prices, would see little to admire in the cunning, lazy character of that fabled creature.

Marshall was so charmed by Pharaoh, who combined the autodidact's love of knowledge with the instructor's pleasure in sharing, that he began to look forward to the quiet hours of reading in the cabin by the river. Unexpectedly, he was subjecting himself to a rigorous regime of study which stirred dormant knowledge and extended what he already knew in several new directions. The long walk to and from the cabin, coupled with physical exercises Pharaoh insisted were an essential complement to serious study, stripped him of two stones in weight over as many months. As he shed fat he began to carry himself like Pharaoh, straight and erect, but he had to practise the direct gaze.

Surprisingly, despite his learning and years abroad, Pharaoh shared with the women of Banyan a deeply ingrained streak of superstition. It compelled him to sweep the yard around his cabin as a morning ritual, he never left clothes hanging outside overnight, and when he expected to be out at night he always carried a little salt in case he met some wandering vengeful spirit.

One day, as he struggled with a trigonometry problem, Marshall sought distraction and asked Pharaoh if he believed in Sarjeant's curse.

Pharaoh's response was swift and firm: 'I knew the world of spirits before I knew the material world. A truly wise person believes in the existence of both worlds and strives to understand the connections between them. And the wisest person I have known in my life is Nana Sarjeant.'

He revealed that he had spent much of his childhood in Banyan and so knew Nana Sarjeant before the meditative silence of incredible old age limited her speech to rare strained utterances. Before urging Marshall back to work, he promised to tell him about an adventure he had had in his youth, but when Marshall finished the lesson and asked about that adventure, Pharaoh distracted him by allocating him another task, an evasive manoeuvre that would be repeated many times, instilling in Marshall a curiosity that would not be satisfied for a few years.

Pharaoh was less mysterious about other episodes from his past. Some evenings he strolled back to Banyan with Marshall and as they walked he recalled the women he had loved, friendships formed and destroyed, hard times in foreign countries. Told with the dusk falling around them and continuing into the hours when fireflies cut luminous trails through the warm night, the sharing of these intimacies drew Marshall closer to Pharaoh, filled him with admiration for this relative who had lived so fully. It was on one such occasion that Pharaoh recounted the events that culminated in a prison sentence in the United States and deportation back to the island, ending his years abroad.

Pharaoh Sarjeant had worked on enough merchant ships, seen enough of Europe, and fought and won enough fights for respect from white shipmates when an implacable longing for terra firma inspired him to jump ship in Limón, Costa Rica, and head for the Panama Canal. Appalled by the pay and working conditions there, he became involved in trying to unionise the workers and acquired a taste for rabble-rousing, which earned him such hostile attention from the bosses that common sense rather than cowardice advised him to flee the Panama heat under the doubly protective cloak of a stormy night. None the less, the experience imbued him with a powerful desire, if vague and unfocused, to help make the twentieth century a better place for all humanity. From Panama he travelled to Miami, Florida, then New York City, and was sucked into a Harlem crackling and exploding with laughter and music that made him feel at home. For a time he drifted from one odd job to the next and through days of dissipation. Then he encountered Cornelius Delancey, a soapbox orator who delivered racial upliftment speeches on Harlem street corners and ran the International African Advancement Organisation.

Impressed more by Delancey's brilliant oratorical skills than his back-to-Africa message, Pharaoh became a follower. The potential of Delancey's message sunk in when he remembered a rainy afternoon in Banyan and Nana Sarjeant sighing deeply as she watched the rain fall, sighing as if the rain had washed away the topsoil of some painful ancient memory. He'd asked her what was wrong and she'd said: 'Jus' dreaming of Africa, son. Jus' dreaming.' Delancey had found the key to the soul of black folk. Not long freed from the chains of enslavement those people now yearned to express their African selves, and returning to their ancestral continent was one way of doing so. Pharaoh had found his cause. He worked with tireless energy for the organisation, became one of Delancey's lieutenants, and was instrumental in bringing about a sudden surge in membership.

The organisation sold shares in a steamship company and bought a steamer which plied the Caribbean-New York route and was captained by a man whose impeccable maritime credentials should have raised doubts about their authenticity.

The steamship company formed part of a more ambitious project, a massive repatriation scheme aiming to send a million African-Americans back to Africa. As money poured in from all over the United States of America and the Caribbean, the organisation began negotiating a land deal with the Liberian government, which would give its members five hundred thousand acres of farmland. Rather prematurely, Delancey announced a departure date for the first shipload of repatriates.

Pharaoh Sarjeant was the youngest member of a five-man delegation dispatched to finalise the Liberian land deal. They sailed to Monrovia, the capital, and when his feet touched the African soil Pharaoh fell on his knees, kissed the soil and thought of Nana Sarjeant, who had first spoken to him of this ancient continent.

The euphoria of arrival was short-lived. With hindsight,

Pharaoh recognised the auguries of failure, such as the angry woman who broke from the crowd lining the main highway through Monrovia and spat at him. A mad woman, he was told. Later he learnt that she had been the first wife of an intractably belligerent tribal chief killed by the army of the Black colonisers.

More obvious was the undiplomatic behaviour of the Liberian President. He kept the delegation waiting for a fortnight. They were kept busy – feted and shown palatial houses built in the style of the Southern plantation mansions, owned by the Americo-Liberians. Then they were taken on an extensive tour of the interior, along roads so rich with iron ore that their surfaces shone, where they met tribal chiefs who promised them fertile mineral-rich land.

Finally the President granted them an audience and negotiations began. At the end of the first day, the President entertained the visitors with a fabulous banquet. Skimpily clad native girls danced and tribal warriors enacted mock battles against the backdrop of the Atlantic Ocean, the insistent rhythms of which were echoed by a band of drummers.

Preparing to retire for the night, the President, a gigantic brown-skinned man whose father had emigrated to Liberia from South Carolina, steered the delegation leader and Pharaoh out to the balcony of his grand official residence, placed his arms around their shoulders and said: 'You realise we can't let you guys in. You guys would spoil the party.'

Refusing to believe ears clotted by the raucous drumming or trust senses dulled by wine, the delegation members arrived the following day at the President's office to resume negotiations. They were informed that the President had fallen ill and his doctors had ordered an indefinite period of rest. In case they didn't get the message, they were ordered to leave Liberia on the next New York-bound ship.

The crestfallen Pharaoh arrived back in New York on the same day that a minor story in the *New York Times* revealed that the Liberians had just sold one hundred thousand acres of land to an American rubber company for a dollar an acre.

By now it was evident that corruption and incompetence were vying with personal rivalry and jealousy to cripple the organisation. The most seaworthy of the steamships had run aground off the Honduran coast and the captain with the spotless sailing record had abandoned it to the rats. Delancey was having an affair with his secretary and his wife was suing him for divorce while publicly denouncing the organisation as a sham, run by crooks, swindlers and philanderers.

When the date for the first shipload of repatriates arrived, ten thousand people, hopeful travellers and well-wishers, gathered on the docks. Renowned for his fearlessness, Pharaoh was chosen to deliver the disappointing news: there would be no Africa-bound ship that day.

Thereafter the organisation's total collapse was swift and inexorable. Delancey and his lieutenants were charged with mail fraud. Of the ten defendants, eight fled, leaving only Delancey and Pharaoh to face the charges. They were found guilty and served eighteen months in jail. Released from prison, Pharaoh was deported to Jamaica, where he tried and failed to create a new organisation driven by ideas acquired from Delancey.

Pharaoh reflected on that episode with a measure of ambivalence. He now saw himself as vain and conceited. The ego to which Delancey appealed would perhaps have been more effectively expressed and satisfied on the dramatic rather than the historic stage. Nevertheless, he left Marshall in no doubt that neither prison nor age had weakened his belief in an idea of Africa inspired but improperly realised by Delancey. He was proud that he had once been a sort of soldier in what he saw as a difficult, centuries-old war which began with the enslavement and transportation of their African ancestors to the New World. He said: 'It's the worst kind of war any soldier has to fight. The enemy is both within and without. It's a war with the self, to bring peace to a divided soul.'

That night Marshall retired to bed wondering what Pharaoh had meant by the phrase 'a divided soul' and what connection that had with the divided soul he vaguely recalled hearing in Father Kennedy's sermons. He wondered whether he, too, should seek to make an impact, to, as Pharaoh had put it, 'help make the twentieth century a better place for all humanity'. He drifted into sleep imagining himself addressing a rally in some faraway city, though the skyscrapers of his imagination remained stubbornly green, like the Paradise hills.

When he woke in the morning, as he strolled to the cabin through the cool morning air watching the sunrise over the mist-enshrouded mountain, and heard the music of the birds, he decided that he did not possess whatever quality – a taste for adventure? wanderlust? – made of a man a soldier, like Pharaoh, or a sailor, like Scoop Fearon.

7

Scoop Fearon had made little progress in his efforts to scale the fortress of Soledad's heart. The letter composed with Marshall's help had not been graced with a reply and she had rejected all the gifts he brought back for her from his voyages around the Caribbean. He blamed Mrs Duncannon-Henriques for isolating the young lady, denying her the chance to participate in the life of the town: but he remained determined to lure her away from the house on Bonny View Hill. He continued to bring back gifts for Soledad, and for Marshall tales of encounters which he claimed formed part of a grand scheme for his future with Soledad.

In preparation for the day they were united in matrimony, he had taken a string of girlfriends around the Caribbean, gathering experience that would make for a happy marriage, one free of all temptation to stray into supposedly greener pastures, or succumb to the guiles of women. If he were to be believed, wherever his boat had docked, from Havana to Port-au-Prince, from Santo Domingo to Aguadilla and down the archipelago of the Windward Islands, he had left a love-struck girl pining for his return, clutching her inflamed heart on some pier or promontory, though she knew that his heart belonged to Soledad back in Paradise.

In between these amorous escapades, Scoop had won and lost small fortunes in cockfights and poker games, and almost killed a man in a fight for calling him a cheat. Since that incident he always walked with his trusty flick knife, constantly alert to the danger posed by a defeated opponent intent on revenge.

Gone were the days when Marshall could easily disentangle

the truth from Scoop's wild embellishments. If Marshall, picking up on some minor inconsistency, dared to challenge Scoop, his friend produced evidence. There was the photograph of the girl in Castries, St Lucia. He bared his chest to show the ugly perpendicular scar he had earned defending his honour in a Guadeloupean bar. Days after Scoop's departure Marshall would remember a glaring contradiction which undermined the adventurer's narrative, smile to himself and look forward to his friend's next visit.

The adventure that seemed to bring about a breakthrough in Scoop's campaign for Soledad was beyond question: he was shipwrecked. It happened in the year of Hurricane Isabella. Inured to hurricanes, Paradise folk used them to divide long periods of time and Hurricane Isabella was an unforgettable visitor. It started as a strong wind blowing from the direction of Mexico, bending the coconut and palm trees as if they were mere cornstalks, turned into a persistent downpour which lasted for three days, then, within twenty-four hours, escalated into a storm of malevolent ferocity. The coastal road between Paradise and Port Columbus was impassable, entire houses were blown away and the churches became refuges for hundreds.

The hurricane lasted for a week, waxing and waning, and afterwards it seemed as if the world had been turned upside down, the natural order of things reversed. Houses floated in the sea and boats were found up to a mile inland, nestling in trees and smashed against rocks. Farmers reaped crops of fish, and fishermen hauled in nets laden with corn cobs, sugarcane stalks, coconuts and yams. Two fishermen rescued a cow and a pig from Humbert Cay, a barren, inhospitable isle two miles off the Paradise coast. How the farm animals reached there alive was the subject of speculation for months afterwards.

While Paradise was still recovering from the hurricane, news came from Port Columbus that Scoop's boat, the *Pegasus,* had been reported missing. This was swiftly followed by reports that the boat's masthead had been found floating between

Port Columbus and Santiago de Cuba. For days Marshall went down to the beach and kept vigil, praying that somewhere in that desolate sea, now calm after days of fury, his friend was still alive, clinging to some flotsam – or better still marooned on an island.

With the news that they had found the captain's sharkravaged corpse, Marshall gave up hope of ever seeing Scoop again. In homage to Scoop's memory he spent an entire night alone on Black Rock Beach. At dawn he built a memorial of rocks to his departed friend.

Over a week later Scoop was brought to Paradise on the back of a donkey cart, his body covered in blisters, his clothes hanging off his emaciated body. He had spent three days in the water, deterring sharks by eating garlic which he had stuffed in his pockets on the advice of the boat's aged cook, a Venezuelan who had survived three shipwrecks. A Brazilian-owned ship had taken him to Havana, where he stayed until he recovered strength, and he was then put on an American cruise liner to Port Columbus.

Marshall was one of the first of many visitors to call on the sole survivor of the *Pegasus.* The experience seemed to have changed Scoop, robbed him of the lightness with which he'd lived life, as if being shipwrecked had awakened him to its fragile, impermanent nature.

He attributed his survival to a miracle. He told Marshall that after a day in the water, being tossed here and there by giant waves, he was on the brink of abandoning hope, releasing his grip on the door that had kept him afloat, when a bright circular light appeared and in its centre stood Soledad. She leant forward and urged him to persevere through the night. She kept him awake over two interminably dark nights by singing:

When death nears and you're all alone
Remember me, I am the light of home.
When your strength and hope fades

Remember me, I am the light of home.
Remember me, remember me.

Scoop's conviction that Soledad had, by some act of magic born of a powerful love for him, rescued him from the raging sea grew in strength with his recovery. He scoffed at Marshall's suggestion that his delirious mind, rather than an epiphanic manifestation of love, might have been responsible for the singing apparition. There was now no question of leaving Paradise to make his fortune and return for Soledad; he was determined to take her with him, to rescue her from the cruel isolation imposed by the selfish stepmother. He implored Marshall to assist him in this mission.

Serendipitously, Marshall discovered that he was better placed than before to help Scoop. He learnt from Eleanor Sarjeant that a distant cousin, Pearline Barham, had recently started working as a maid in the Duncannon-Henriques household and Soledad had quickly grown fond of her and shared confidences with her. Marshall enlisted his cousin's help. Pearline, a short, pretty, buck-tooth teenager with honest eyes, was now entrusted to deliver a series of letters written daily by Scoop with Marshall's help.

After seven letters Scoop finally received a reply in the form of a brief note that simply read: 'You are invited to Sunday lunch with the Duncannon-Henriqueses next week. Please bring a friend.'

Scoop and Marshall were excited and bewildered by this strangely terse and cold response to the passion-filled letters. Had Soledad shown the letters to her stepmother? And, if not, how had she persuaded that famously snobbish woman to entertain a commoner like Scoop? Marshall, of course, would have to accompany him.

To be invited to anybody's house for Sunday lunch in Paradise was regarded as a great honour: to be invited to Mrs Duncannon-Henriques's house was a rare and great honour. Only her farm manager and other persons indispensable to the running of her business had enjoyed the privilege of eating in the stately dining-room with its twelve-feet-long mahogany table and matching red-velvet-upholstered chairs, of being served crab de creole from silverware dishes, of drinking guava juice from Waterford crystal, and eating escoveitch fish on fine Wedgwood china plates. And only a few of those fortunate visitors had known their soup spoons from their dessert spoons, their fish knives from ordinary knives. Marshall and Scoop did not count among the latter group.

Dressed in their finest clothes, Scoop looked like the pimp that he would later become in a suit that he had bought off an impecunious American sailor. Marshall looked like the country hick that he was, albeit a rather dignified one, in a brown mohair suit that Aunt Binta had sent from Kingston. It was far too small and painfully uncomfortable.

The meal got off to an awkward start. Scoop sat opposite Mrs Duncannon-Henriques, a stern-looking, large woman with a stiff bearing and an expression that seemed to suggest a preparedness to endure rather than enjoy the occasion. Marshall was seated opposite Soledad. Seeing her for the first time, he understood how Scoop could lose his senses over her. Slim and dark, she had skin that was smooth, unblemished and brought to mind a cloudless night sky when all the stars in the firmament are visible, filling you with mystery and wonder.

Scoop sat through the meal in awed silence, lost for words. It was Mrs Duncannon-Henriques who broke the ice by asking Marshall about the health of Nana Sarjeant, whose longevity she admired. Marshall's expansive answer seemed to relax her and she spoke at length about her own battles against the many small discomforts of ageing. The conversation lightened up somewhat when Soledad, speaking with a fluting, clear voice, playfully chided Mrs Duncannon-Henriques, whom she called 'Mother', for worrying unnecessarily about her health.

Throughout the meal Scoop kept his eyes lowered, but he

found his voice when they retired to the drawing-room, the windows of which afforded a panoramic view of the sea. He recalled in great detail his shipwreck, rescue and journey back to Port Columbus. When Mrs Duncannon-Henriques asked where he had found the reserve of strength which had saved him, Marshall tried to signal to his friend not to mention the singing apparition of Soledad. But he failed, and Scoop in what would be the single greatest moment of truth in his life, answered honestly. Soledad gasped when he sang the refrain from the song, and Mrs Duncannon-Henriques's expression underwent a dramatic transformation from laboured patience to visible horror.

A long moment of dense silence, during which Scoop gazed fixedly at Soledad, was broken by Mrs Duncannon-Henriques, who said calmly: 'I am pleased that an image of Soledad inspired you with strength, Mr Fearon. But don't you think you have ambitions above your station?'

'My ambitions are honourable and motivated by love, Ma'am,' Scoop said, with a defiance all the greater for the sincerity in his voice.

Those words marked the end of their Sunday lunch with Mrs Duncannon-Henriques and Soledad. The hostess glared at the young sailor, accused him of insolence; then rang the bell for a servant to show the guests out. Her final words to Scoop were: 'You will never again see Soledad or set foot in this house.'

A lesser man than Scoop would probably have left town the next day, but he was made of sterner stuff. With Marshall's help he wrote another letter, and was rewarded with a note from Soledad asking him to meet her at the rear of her garden at an hour when her stepmother would be taking her siesta. Again he was instructed to bring a friend, and again Marshall accompanied him.

Marshall allowed Scoop and Soledad privacy, but he could not help overhearing Soledad, tremulous, almost breathless, tell Scoop how for two nights in the hurricane, she had dreamt of a drowning sailor and woke up with an unfamiliar song in her memory, the very same one he had recalled before her stepmother. Nor could Marshall help overhearing Scoop's declarations of his unvanquishable love for her, his impassioned entreaties for her to run away with him because theirs was a divine love, a gift from God, their destiny.

Soledad's responses were cool, detached. She apologised for her stepmother's snobbery, which she made clear was not an attitude she shared, but offered Scoop nothing more than friendship based on the strange coincidence. There was now a great bond between them, one that would last all their lives, but it would never, she warned him, transcend Platonic boundaries. Having said that, she ended their meeting with a promise to let him know when it would be safe to meet again.

Scoop was not interested in the consolation prize offered by Soledad. He believed so strongly in their shared destiny that he insisted on seeing hope where none existed. She had already chosen to defy her Draconian stepmother. He would not give up.

When his subsequent letters went unanswered, he slumped into bouts of despair from which he emerged more determined than ever. Every minute of his waking day was taken up with thoughts of Soledad, and she strolled across the landscape of his dreams, too, filling his nights with the fever of unrequited love. Daily he walked past the spot where they had met secretly, hoping she would be there, and though he was always disappointed, the memory of that rendezvous fuelled his perseverance.

Concerned about his friend's behaviour and perplexed by Soledad, Marshall quizzed his cousin Pearline Barham and gained an insight into the Duncannon-Henriques household which would have benefited Scoop had he been prepared to listen.

The relationship between Soledad and her stepmother was not simple. While it was true that Mrs Duncannon-Henriques had adopted Soledad as an infant from the Port Columbus orphanage and reared her with disciplinarian rigour, Soledad's obedience was not just due to gratitude. Gifted with uncanny powers of intuition, from the moment Soledad saw the stern-faced Elsavet Duncannon-Henriques, she recognised a woman craving for a chance to give and receive affection: she recognised her saviour.

She had chosen her stepmother as much as her stepmother had chosen her. She had picked a fight with a docile doe-eyed boy and allowed herself to be beaten, cried a river and won the visitor's sympathetic attention. Though Elsavet had gone to the orphanage in search of an older child and preferably a boy, the tearful little girl who clung to her side proved an irresistible choice. Soledad the child, out of an intuitive awareness that Elsavet Duncannon-Henriques could only love those over whom she could exercise absolute power, had shown her stepmother absolute obedience. And over the years, especially after the death of her husband, there had developed between them a bond of affection as deep as that between a daughter and natural mother.

With maturity, the gratitude and affection she felt for Elsavet had been supplemented by profound admiration for her courage in preserving her independence from predatory suitors who had come a-wooing before the earth had settled on her husband's grave. They came offering condolences and comfort while trying to ascertain how much she was worth, and spread calumnies when she had seen through their dishonesty and rejected their insincere advances.

If the servants in the Duncannon-Henriques household had never seen Soledad disagree with her stepmother, this was not due to a lack of nerves on her part. She held her guardian in too high esteem to disagree with her openly. Besides, she knew innumerable subtle ploys for getting her own way. Elsavet suffered from excruciatingly painful attacks of migraine, which only Soledad's hands seemed capable of massaging away. During these therapeutic sessions, she was susceptible to most suggestions. There was no risk of Soledad abusing this power. She exercised it only in relation to small domestic matters, such as what to have for dinner, where to hang pictures. In the fundaments of their lives, its peaceful orderliness, its gentle pace, they were in absolute agreement.

Scoop's letters had affected Soledad. But she placed too high a value on the magnificent view of the sea from the veranda, the extensive garden teeming with flowers, the soothing sight of the mountains from the rear of the house, to succumb to the impetuous desires of youth, which, to be sure, she experienced, but quashed with a mixture of pragmatism, common sense and formidable willpower. She was content with her solitary sedentary pursuits: composing poetry; teaching herself Spanish, and learning to play the piano; stitching tapestries, reading to herself and to Elsavet.

Compassion for Scoop had moved her to deploy every weapon in her considerable armoury to persuade Elsavet to host a Sunday lunch for him. Elsavet initially balked at the proposal and relented only after Soledad had pointed out that entertaining Scoop, a local hero, the survivor of a shipwreck, might help to appease the banana workers who had emerged from the hurricane infected with trade union ideals and who were threatening to strike for higher wages. It would show that the owner of the largest banana plantation in Paradise had sympathy for the suffering of common folk.

Now, on Soledad's advice, Mrs Duncannon-Henriques had started making donations to the Free Baptist School. In Pearline Barham's opinion: 'That young lady knows exactly what she wants and it isn't Scoop. Don't think it's any man.'

Marshall did his best to take Scoop's mind off Soledad and bolster his spirits. He tried to revive their earlier boyhood activities – swimming and fishing in the Blue Hole, bird-hunting; reminded him of the Castries beauty who had promised to remain celibate until he returned, even if that took a decade. He tried to reawaken in Scoop the ambition to travel the world, see New York. But Scoop showed such little interest in these distractions of the past that Marshall began to wonder whether this unhealthy obsession with Soledad was being fuelled by a fear of the sea.

8

A hot, dry spell settled over Paradise. No rain fell for weeks and the stagnant airless nights caused universal lethargy. Hummingbirds flapped their wings at a slower pace while trying to feed on hedges of drooping hibiscus flowers below which lay the twitching, exhausted bodies of other hummingbirds. Dehydrated dogs hugged shaded spots and emitted dry, raspy barks that sounded like pleas for water, and even the lizards ignored them. The sea stroked the shore with a sluggish reluctance and its surface, with its hard, glassy sheen, seemed to throw the heat back onto the land. Market traders watched helplessly as their callaloo, ackee and okras wilted and dried up. Only the ghosts, the duppies, the memories of the island, were untouched by the heat as they roamed the night searching for careless homes to penetrate and share the burdens of their terrible solitude.

The intemperate heat claimed some unlikely victims. Pharaoh, that indefatigable old soldier, a man for whom a siesta was an extravagant act of laziness, was now forced to rest through the afternoon hours when the humidity became a suffocating blanket, as oppressive and enervating as an incubus. Years ago, he had slept rough while waiting for a ship in Marseille, and contracted an unknown ailment which was mostly dormant but erupted sporadically, causing aching joints and lassitude and a metallic taste in his mouth. A herbal concoction specially prepared by the women of Banyan gave him some relief until it passed. Stretched out on his iron bed, shirtless, his chest covered in grey wiry hair, he would drift in and out of sleep, fighting to remain awake. He was not always successful. Sometimes he lapsed into somnolent soliloquies, in which an unnamed woman by whom he had fathered a child in a city called Liverpool recurred, as though the heat were agitating memories of Pharaoh's past transgressions. On another day, as he stirred restlessly, covered in sweat, he repeatedly muttered something about the warriors needing to end the war and all wars, as if he were addressing a crowd on a Harlem street corner.

Marshall had offered not to trouble him until he felt better but Pharaoh insisted they carry on with the lessons. He was not allowed to pause until he had finished his allocated tasks for the day, then he would be free to do as he wished. But one day, though he tried hard to concentrate through Pharaoh's semiconscious ranting, the repetition of Nana Sarjeant's name, its volume and intensity caused him such anxiety that he shook Pharaoh awake. Startled, he sat up and glanced out of the window at the almost dry river-bed and parched land, as if getting his bearing, then asked Marshall to bring him a cup of water.

When Marshall brought it, Pharaoh looked at him for a long time and that curiously arch smile Marshall had noticed in the past creased his lips.

He enquired after Scoop, and after Marshall answered said: 'You know, I like you, Marshall. I like your loyalty. A guy like Scoop isn't going to have many friends in life. But he'll always be able to rely on you.'

'Isn't that what friends are for?' Marshall said.

'Yes. That's why you got to choose them carefully or you'll end up carrying them through life, always carrying. The best kind of friend walks beside you, not behind or in front, and when he's in need you have to press your help on him 'cause he won't want to load you down with his troubles.'

'Scoop's no burden to me,' Marshall said. 'We go way back. I'm not doing anything for him that he wouldn't do for me.'

'Time is longer than rope. We'll see. As I said, you're a loyal person and that's a fine quality in a man.'

Despite the open window and door, the air in the cabin was close and stale. Marshall stole a glance at Pharaoh, who was drinking the water, and sensed a man friendless by choice, and unknowable.

'You were talking in your sleep,' Marshall said.

'About?'

'Something about Nana Sarjeant. It wasn't clear.'

Pharaoh glanced away, became pensive for a while then said: 'Yes. Nana Sarjeant. The wisest person I know.' There was an ironic note in his voice. Then he said wearily and ruefully, 'Why the blasted hell she had to get entangled with Neal Sarjeant and that witch of a wife, I don't know.' He launched into an embittered monologue about Nana Sarjeant and the accursed line she had helped create, then said more calmly: 'You know, I was like you once. Young, with no particular ambition except to enjoy this glorious land. This damned Paradise. But I didn't realise what it meant to be a Sarjeant. There's no ordinary life for you if you're a Sarjeant. You can't marry and settle down and look forward to rearing healthy children because you'll never know when one is going to show signs of the curse, how bad that sign will be, and every time you see that crippled or disfigured child, your child, you'll feel guilty for perpetuating an evil. You'll never know happiness as a Sarjeant ...'

Pharaoh fell silent and slumped back on the bed, his breathing laboured and loud. He said wearily: 'Sometimes a man gets tired, and he just wants to lay his burden down. Lay it down for ever.' Then he fell into a deep sleep of such silence that Marshall had to check that he was still breathing.

Marshall finished his exercise for the day, and wandered around the cabin. He had never given any thought to the implications of the curse for his future. Pharaoh's illness had exposed a secret bitterness and in so doing it had made Marshall aware that being a Sarjeant was no privilege. He envied Scoop now, his apparent ability to love so fearlessly, so deeply. He, Marshall, would never be able to allow himself such powerful feelings for a woman. Could never dream Scoop's dream of marital bliss. Yet the curse had not stopped the women of Banyan from procreating; they were defying it by taking chances, gambling that enough of their offspring would be normal. Why shouldn't he follow their example, rather than Pharaoh's, which seemed like an admission of defeat?

Later he re-entered the cabin and found Pharaoh sitting up on the bed. Sleep seemed to have refreshed him and he showed no embarrassment for his earlier uncharacteristic outburst of despair. Instead, he reminded Marshall of a promise he had made early in their relationship. It concerned an adventure he had had before leaving Paradise and the island. Then he asked Marshall to look under the bed and pull out a wooden box. The box Marshall saw there was roughly made and without a lock.

Pharoah swung his legs over the bedside and opened the box. He took from it an old spear, which he said was his only souvenir from the Liberian trip. While Marshall examined the spear, Pharaoh took out a much smaller box, filled with bits of paper. He held one piece and called it to Marshall's attention. The paper was old, and looked like a map.

'This,' said Pharaoh, 'is a part of Sarjeant's curse, and it's time you learnt about it because this is also your legacy.'

Although the disappearance of Alegba remained a mystery to most people familiar with Sarjeant's curse, a few people knew what had happened on that morning over a century ago when Sybil Sarjeant was seen riding away from Banyan House with him. The swift descent into poverty experienced by Neal Sarjeant made no sense, for he was evidently a wealthy man, and even after freeing his slaves it was expected that he would still have ample funds, but didn't.

What had happened was this: Sybil Sarjeant had filled a chest with gold coins, the bulk of the Sarjeant fortune, and took it with Alegba towards the base of the Blue Mountain. At the precise point she had marked on a map, she ordered

Alegba to dig a hole the depth, width and length of a grave and place the box in it. When Alegba finished, as he rested in sleep before refilling the hole, Sybil Sarjeant slashed his throat with one swift movement, then rolled his body into the hole, on to the box of gold. His spirit would remain there to guard the fortune.

Neal Sarjeant somehow got hold of the map she had drawn of the site. No one knew whether he made an effort to retrieve the gold. After the burning of Banyan House, before he plunged into his final and terminal phase of insanity, he gave the map to Nana Sarjeant. It was his other legacy to his children and it had been in the family ever since.

Robert Sarjeant, the elder of Nana's twins, had been the first to try to retrieve the gold. He failed but from his attempt came the knowledge of the spirit guarding the gold, and it is likely that Robert was driven to acts of excess, from his womanising to his politics, by what he saw.

When Pharaoh reached the age of twenty-one, having proved himself to be fearless, Nana Sarjeant revealed the existence of the map and chose him to retrieve the gold, to become the duppy conqueror. Pharaoh did not shirk this honour. He was young and brave and felt the world was his to conquer.

With map in hand, and pickaxe and shovel, he went in search of the gold. He dug for what seemed like an eternity. Finally, the pickaxe struck a box through the hard, dry earth. But at that precise moment, Pharaoh became aware that the sky was receding as the hole deepened of its own volition. From the box came a chilling, malevolent laugh that filled Pharaoh with the novel feeling of fear. He deliberated for a moment whether to remain in the hole and face whatever thing had curdled his blood, or escape. He chose escape, and scrambled out of the hole with the help of the pickaxe.

Standing on the edge, looking down into a hole that was now twice as deep, he saw a bald-headed figure standing akimbo, looking upwards at him with blazing red eyes and a chest glistening, and he was laughing. Seeing that terrible spectre, he knew he was facing something that he had neither the strength nor the wit to defeat and had the sense to admit that to himself. His only act of composure was to refill the hole, achieved with the same amount of earth he had removed, and with each shovelful the laughter decreased until it stopped altogether. Then, though exhausted, he made as speedy an exit away from the site as was possible.

He did not return to Banyan House immediately. For weeks he wandered around the hills, living off berries, until the shivering that racked his body subsided and he felt he could face Nana Sarjeant with his failure. It was after that that he went to sea.

'So there you have it, young Marshall,' Pharaoh said when he finished recounting the tale of his encounter with Alegba's spirit. 'You once asked me if I believed in Sarjeant's curse. As I travelled and taught myself to understand science, and became aware that men are either actors in history or the acted upon, whenever I was seduced by the power of the knowledge that now governs the world, I reminded myself of that experience.'

'And did you ever go back?'

'Yes. When I first returned to the island. The same thing happened. Only this time I stared long and hard at that terrible figure and it stared back at me and I knew that I was staring at my death. How do you kill a memory, how do you conquer a ghost?'

'I don't know.'

'Neither do I. Many nights I've lain awake thinking about it. But so far nothing. Yet we have to keep on trying. That's our legacy. Maybe you could try, maybe you would succeed where I failed.'

'Me!'

'Yes. I heard about the incident that blinded you. I know how you survived those blind years. You showed courage. Maybe you'll be the duppy conqueror. But not yet, not yet. You're still young, too young.'

Marshall was flattered that Pharaoh saw him as a suitable candidate for a task that he had failed at. And as his mind had in recent months turned to the practicalities of living in an adult world, he estimated the value of the fortune that would accrue to a victor. It would transform the Sarjeants from a family of small farmers to landowners wealthier than even Mrs Duncannon-Henriques. Banyan House could be demolished and rebuilt in grand style. He could live like a gentleman, and, though he could not love for fear of perpetuating the evil of Sarjeant's curse, he could find other pleasures. He did not think of failure; he thought only of victory.

For days he carried the secret of the map around in his head, quietly excited. The only person he told was Scoop Fearon but, still distracted by Soledad, Scoop appeared to show little interest. Marshall was left alone with the puzzle Pharaoh had posed: How do you kill a memory, how do you conquer a ghost?

9

The return of gentler weather, hot mornings and rainy afternoons, coincided with a rare visit from Binta Sarjeant, bearing joyous news of her betrothal to a carpenter in Kingston. The simple gold ring on her finger and the photograph of her fiancé – a stocky, dark man with an open face – were brandished about like hard-won trophies, and sent the women of Banyan dancing and shouting like excited schoolgirls.

But neither imminent marriage nor city life had changed Binta. Family affairs still brought out her quarrelsome nature. She openly voiced her disapproval of the relationship between Marshall and Pharaoh, whom she stopped short of calling an ex-convict, and charged her cousins and aunts with neglecting Marshall's religious education. Privately, she accused Marshall of abandoning the Catholic faith, implying that she had lost him to the women of Banyan, then dragged him to Sunday Mass at St Christopher's, and extracted from him a promise to resume attending church.

'I should've had you confirmed when you were younger, that way they wouldn't be able to steal your soul,' she said.

Marshall found himself quite tongue-tied with this difficult but loving aunt whose solicitude, preserved and nourished by time and distance, was more appropriate for a young teenager than a young man. Her departure for Kingston, delayed by two days as she tried to correct other failings elsewhere in the family, came as a great relief to everyone. Although he resolved not to allow himself to be browbeaten by her again, the following Sunday he went to Mass at St Christopher's to quieten a conscience as devastated as a cornfield after a hurricane. But sharing the news of her engagement with Scoop, he could only recall her with uncritical fondness.

It was shortly after Binta's departure that Marshall began to notice some new faces in Paradise: a party of Europeans. He first saw them in the town square, near the Queen Victoria statue, and again some days later beside the sea wall. The Whites who lived in Paradise were well known to everyone, but these were obviously foreigners, conspicuous by their smart linen clothes and inquisitive air.

It was Marshall's cousin Pearline Barham – still acting as an intermediary between Scoop and Soledad – who furnished the strangers with identities and purpose. They had dined with Mrs Duncannon-Henriques and Pearline had overheard enough to satisfy Marshall's mild curiosity.

They were English tourists and were staying in one of the seaside villas constructed in the aftermath of the false gold rush and now owned by Mrs Duncannon-Henriques. The party consisted of Mrs Frances Castle, her twin teenage children, Constance and Alexander, and a man in his late twenties whose relationship to the others seemed indeterminate because he bore no resemblance to the twins and was too young to be Mrs Castle's husband. It only later became apparent that this fourth member, Jacques, was Mrs Castle's lover, a Frenchman. Mrs Castle was a widow; her late husband, an industrialist, had died of a heart attack and left enough money to keep three generations of Castles in wealth without their having to work. Although Mrs Duncannon-Henriques had seemed slightly deferential towards Mrs Castle, Pearline had overheard her remark to Soledad: 'Mrs Castle seems like a parvenue who had obviously married into new money. But she's had the good sense to give her children the best English education.'

Pearline drew the visitors to Marshall's attention again some days later when she brought him an invitation to a tea party being staged by Constance and Alexander. No adults would be present. It seemed that they were keen to make the acquaintance of people their own age and Soledad had included his name on a guest list they had asked her to recommend. He surmised that Soledad had included his name and not Scoop's to avoid arousing her stepmother's suspicions should she see the list. It was her way of inviting Scoop. Marshall asked Scoop to accompany him and Scoop leapt at the opportunity to see Soledad again.

As the event approached, it was much talked about because people were surprised that Mrs Castle should give her teenage children licence to hold a social at which there would be no adults. Such freedom would never be granted in Paradise, where a mummified sense of Victorian morality imprisoned most young adults and often sent enraged fathers on missions to haul their errant twenty-odd-year-old sons away from bad company. The murmurs of misgivings subsided when it became known that Mrs Duncannon-Henriques, the paragon of parental protectiveness, had consented to Soledad's presence, marking the first occasion that Soledad would be seen outside the Duncannon-Henriques home without her stepmother or an approved escort.

There was in fact little to worry about. The Castle twins had thrown similar parties in other places. They received their guests like a married couple holding open house in a new neighbourhood, and circulated among them with the ease of people practised in meeting strangers, disarming them with charming smiles and an openness that quickly created a relaxed, convivial atmosphere. There was no alcohol, and the fare had been prepared by Mrs Duncannon-Henriques's servants.

Fascinated by the self-assured twins, and dazzled by the villa with its huge French windows which opened on to a lawn, Marshall felt out of his depth and acutely aware of how isolated he was from people his own age. None the less he was determined to find his feet. Leaving Scoop with Soledad, he drifted between several groups before settling with a group dominated by Denzil Stewart, a local who had recently graduated from his Kingston school.

They were soon joined by Alexander who, now separated from his sister, appeared to be less at ease. His discomfort showed in the fidgety shifting of his hand from his trouser pocket to his thick flaxen hair, and the unintended arrogance of the shy person. Nervousness probably accounted for the odd intensity with which he began to speak about the imminence of war in Europe. But once he had his audience he spoke with great authority about the actions of a 'nasty chap' in Germany who was determined to liberate the Germans from the humiliation of the Versailles Treaty and was building up a formidable armaments industry and army.

Denzil Stewart was the only person present capable of engaging Alexander in this discussion, while the others, Marshall included, remained mute spectators. But Denzil's concerns were parochial. He was more worried about West Indian independence than an imminent world war, and rounded on Alexander as if he were a plenipotentiary of the British government. He gave a little speech about the inevitability of independence, which, though lacking Alexander's fluency, was full of passion.

Alexander listened with patrician indulgence, then effortlessly dismissed Denzil's argument by rejecting the notion that the West Indian colonies were viable national entities.

'Besides, however strong the case for independence is, until the danger of war has been averted it cannot be an issue.'

Articulate, confident and knowledgeable, Alexander steered the conversation back to the ominous events unfolding in Europe. Denzil did not allow the young Englishman's superior airs to intimidate him and kept returning to the issue of West Indian independence. Both seemed to enjoy the contest of opinions, the disagreement, and when both revealed that they had political ambitions – Alexander to become a Conservative MP, and Denzil to serve in the Jamaican legislature and first government – the foundations of a mutual admiration society were erected.

Marshall tried to appreciate this window into world affairs, but the view was obscured by years of complacent insularity.

Constance's sudden presence interrupted them. She said: 'Don't get Alexander going on about politics or you won't be able to stop him. He sees every conversation as an opportunity to practise for the day he's elected to the House of Commons.'

She placed an arm on her brother's shoulder, as if to protect him, threw back her thick, lustrous brown hair, and smiled. Her broad face, sprinkled with minute freckles, seemed darker than her brother's, though both were tanned. Still holding her brother, she recounted his unsuccessful attempts to learn the charleston and the jitterbug in Philadelphia, teasing him about his stiff, awkward movements, which had caused his American instructor to give up in frustration.

Alexander flushed and laughed with his sister, and candidly admitted that he would have needed a whole year of daily lessons to approach even a simulacrum of decent dancing American style. 'Our American cousins have more space to be loose-limbed,' he said.

'Maybe it's because they're politically freer,' Denzil said, refusing to be diverted from politics.

Alexander seized on Denzil's remark and their political debate resumed with a tension that almost pushed it beyond disagreement and into conflict, and made them the centre of attention. But as they calmed down, their arguments became more obscure – littered with allusions to Aristotle and Plato, de Tocqueville and Rousseau – and Marshall's attention strayed.

He next found himself briefly alone with Constance. When she pointed out that they were both freckle-faced, he laughed with gusto, which quelled a nervous tremor induced by the realisation that she was very attractive, beautiful in her own alien way.

She revealed that the Castles would be staying in Paradise for another month as their mother, who was spending the afternoon with Mrs Duncannon-Henriques, was tired and had quite fallen in love with this quaint little town. They were on a tour of the Americas, which had so far included Canada, Washington, New York, Philadelphia, Florida and several British West Indian islands.

'My mother seems to have a fascination with places called Paradise,' Constance said. 'This is the sixth we have visited. Every West Indian island seems to have a Paradise. But this is the only one we have actually stayed in, and, it should be said, the closest I've come to seeing one that deserves the name. Alexander thinks so too. It's splendid. Simply splendid.'

Constance's enthusiasm for Paradise – the simplicity of life, the calm sea, the lush flora – was boundless. She wished she could stay longer but was resigned to returning to London and, like her brother, obeying her calling. Though she had more natural confidence than Alexander, she did not share his certainty about a career. Divided between the theatre and medicine, she was prepared to forgo either as she did not want to start a family too late in life.

'Equally, I don't want motherhood to be all I do,' she said. 'And what career have you chosen, Marshall?'

Marshall was momentarily nonplussed but recovered quickly to answer: 'Maybe a farmer.'

The sudden entry of Scoop and Soledad from the garden created an opening to avoid a more elaborate answer, which he did not possess. He steered Constance towards them, and they formed a foursome, which Scoop dominated with moderately tall tales from the sea. The party ended soon afterwards.

The Castles' tea party left Marshall feeling strangely elated. The twins represented a world beyond his imagination. They had been travelling for almost six months, staying in hotels and rented houses without concern for the expense involved. On returning to England, Alexander would be going to university, while Constance would give more thought to her future. Their choices seemed staggeringly infinite, their world inconceivably vast, their future unassailably secure.

Listening to the women of Banyan preparing to close the day, speaking in their dense patois as the familiar night sounds rose up from the darkness, Marshall felt as though he had been absent longer than five hours and further than the edge of Paradise, the location of the villa. The feeling of having journeyed afar gave him a heightened sense of security in this intimately known and cherished surrounding.

Two nights later, unable to sleep, Marshall went to sit on the veranda steps. The stars glittered and a quarter-moon hung like one parenthesis. The longer he looked up at the glittering sky, the more the stars seemed to acquire the shape of an immense question mark. Since the Castles' party he had been wrestling with a vague unsettledness, an inner disharmony that eluded identification.

Suddenly he heard a rustling noise and saw Scoop furtively stepping out of the night. He spoke low and fast in a taut, almost tearful voice, and kept glancing over his shoulders.

'I'm leaving Paradise, Marshall. I've got to get away. You coming with me? We can get jobs in Port Columbus, make it to America from there. You coming with me?'

Marshall slowed him down, and asked what had brought on this sudden rush to leave Paradise. What about Soledad?

Scoop explained that Soledad was the cause of his flight. Emboldened by the pleasant time he had spent with her at the Castles' tea party, Scoop had made one last bid to persuade Mrs Duncannon-Henriques of his seriousness. He had called at Bonny View during Mrs Duncannon-Henriques's precious siesta hour, and demanded an audience with her. Pearline, who had answered the door, pleaded with him to call back another time because to disturb Mrs Duncannon-Henriques at that unfavourable hour would only add to his troubles, and more than likely implicate her in the disturbance. But Scoop had insisted.

Mrs Duncannon-Henriques had eventually come downstairs, wearing an expression of violent displeasure. She'd listened without interruption to Scoop's appeal to be allowed to call on Soledad openly. When he had finished, Mrs Duncannon-Henriques, impassive and stiff, called Pearline, and instructed her to bring the walnut case from her bedroom. Pearline had returned with the case, given it to her employer who asked her to leave the room.

When they were alone again Mrs Duncannon-Henriques had opened the box and taken out an ivory-handled Colt .45, pointed it at Scoop and said: 'If I catch you creeping around my property, anywhere within the walls of Bonny View again, I will not hesitate to use this against you. This is the only warning I will give you; there won't be any further warnings. Now get out.'

Scoop's knees had buckled involuntarily, and he obeyed and left Bonny View under a cloud of defeat and humiliation. But it had not ended there.

The following day, as he was making his way up Bonny View Hill in the hope of seeing Soledad, three vultures had appeared from nowhere and swooped down on him. He had had to run for cover in a poinsettia bush and there he found a stout piece of stick to defend himself against the John Crows. He had managed to make it home, but on every daylight excursion the birds had appeared, hovering in wait for an opportunity to attack him. Now he could only safely move about at night and no longer doubted that Mrs Duncannon-Henriques deserved her evil reputation. The vultures were her emissaries, her attempt to drive him out of Paradise, and she had succeeded. But he was only leaving Paradise temporarily; he would return when he was wealthy enough to claim Soledad.

Sympathetic though he was to Scoop's latest mishap, Marshall declined Scoop's invitation. He tried to explain why he could not leave Paradise – the lessons with Pharaoh, the task for which Pharaoh would soon start preparing him, Nana Sarjeant, the women of Banyan. Besides, the skyscrapers of New York held no appeal for him: he was happy in Paradise.

Refusing to be defeated by Marshall's intransigence, Scoop continued pressing his case until frustration gave way to anger. He began to curse Marshall, showered him with the sort of vile imprecations that fractious market women hurled at each other on profitless days. He called him a coward, a worthless country bumpkin who would not amount to anything in this backwater place. Then he was gone. Shocked and wounded, Marshall stood and listened to the retreating sound of his oldest and dearest friend, and long after he could no longer hear him, the night resonated with Scoop's furious, bitter disappointment.

The full extent of Scoop's fury only began to dawn on Marshall the next morning when he arrived at the cabin to find Pharaoh nursing a head wound. The previous night someone had broken in, knocked Pharaoh unconscious and stolen the map of the site of the Sarjeant treasure. Yet Pharaoh was remarkably blasé about the incident. He had suffered worse concussions in bar fights, and woken up with worse heads in his time. Nor did he seem to be overly concerned about the theft, for he knew the exact location of the gold, which he was certain would still be there when Marshall was ready to mount his challenge on Alegba's spirit, a task only a Sarjeant could undertake.

This cool, optimistic reaction assuaged some of Marshall's anxieties. But other, graver, unspoken worries began to preoccupy him. He was confident he knew the identity of Pharaoh's attacker and the thief: Scoop Fearon. He was the only person with whom Marshall had shared Pharaoh's secret. Was the theft Scoop's revenge for what he regarded as Marshall's betrayal of their friendship? If so, Scoop had in turn betrayed their friendship.

Over the next few weeks, when Marshall's mind turned to his treacherous friend, he often found himself wishing that Scoop had drowned or never returned to Paradise. The rotting corpse of their friendship exuded a sickening, foul stench, and made him realise that he had not known the real Scoop. And if he had not known Scoop, who could he ever know or trust?

10

Scoop's treacherous act and the secret guilt of his own complicity in the affair were still agitating Marshall on the day he went to town to buy exercise books, and spotted the Castle twins with Denzil Stewart. They stood near the Queen Victoria statue and Denzil, sweeping a hand in wide arcs like a property owner showing off his estate, seemed to be holding forth. Preoccupied and irascible, Marshall was in no mood to be friendly but he could not avoid them, so decided to be civil at the same moment that Constance Castle waved to him.

As he approached she greeted him with a broad, warm smile and formally addressed him as 'Mr Sarjeant'. Although this formality was perfectly normal amongst islanders who placed a high premium on respect, it elicited from Denzil Stewart a half-suppressed laugh, an offensive snigger. Marshall instantly decided that Denzil, the scion of a wealthy Paradise family and a former pupil of the island's most prestigious school, had allowed his familiarity with the visitors to compromise his manners. He shot Denzil a glance of naked hostility which should have left its target without any doubt that he did not take kindly to being laughed at.

But Denzil ignored Marshall's warning, smirked and said: 'Mr Sarjeant, you must tell me who your tailor is. You're always so well dressed.' He was referring to Marshall's trousers, which were clearly too short and tight. Amused by his own irony, Denzil guffawed like a well-fed donkey.

'Yes, I must say, the sartorial standard of some Paradisians leaves much to be desired,' Alexander said. Denzil Stewart erupted into laughter.

Many years had passed since Marshall last lost control of the bad temper which had earned him repeated censure from Aunt Binta, but he now had to struggle to keep it in check. He glared at them and said: 'If you fly with a John Crow, you'll eat dead meat.'

Denzil immediately understood this proverbial insult to his character, fell quiet, and looked somewhat chastened.

Marshall stiffened with dignity, retained enough composure to excuse himself with Constance, and as he walked away he heard her say: 'That was very rude, Alexander, you should apologise.'

Alexander caught up with him and said: 'Marshall, I am sorry. That was terribly rude of me. I forgot my manners.'

Marshall accepted Alexander's apology, they shook hands, and Denzil and Constance came to join them. In a gesture of contrition, Denzil mentioned that Marshall came from one of the oldest families in Paradise and suggested to Marshall that maybe he could show the Castles the countryside around Paradise, as he, Denzil, would be away for a few days. This much friendlier and more civil exchange touched Marshall and made him feel that he had perhaps overreacted to Denzil's harmless ribbing. When both Alexander and Constance leapt on Denzil's suggestion with enthusiasm, Marshall further thawed and felt that refusal would be mean-spirited and inhospitable. They were, after all, decent sorts.

Thus began a friendship – given further encouragement by Pharaoh, who released Marshall from the study regime in the claustrophobic cabin. Over the two days, he discovered that beneath their metropolitan sophistication and precocious self-assurance the Castle twins retained the capacity for enjoying the simple pleasures of countryside walks. But they showed their appreciation in different ways. While Constance communed with this alien landscape in respectful silence, Alexander quizzed Marshall on the names of plants, birds, butterflies and insects, and took obvious pride in being able to recall their Greek or Latin names, recording them in little notebooks which he kept in various pockets. Initially Marshall had no objection to these questions – indeed he was quietly amused to hear the common plumrose referred to as *Colassa argenta*, and the castor-oil plant as *Ricinus communis* – but by the afternoon of the second day, he began to find Alexander's habit of translating every answer he gave an annoying intrusion. By applying foreign names to familiar plants and creatures, classifying and categorising them, Alexander seemed to be possessing them, then subjecting them to the cold intellectual scrutiny of the scientist. When Marshall started feigning ignorance, the questions abated. But Alexander would not be silenced.

On one occasion, standing on Diablo Ridge in the stance of an explorer, his chest inflated with theatrical pomposity, he declared: 'Paradise has forced me to question whether the alienation of man from nature, and therefore himself, is too high a price for progress. The greatest challenge facing the twentieth century is to maintain the delicate balance between preserving nature and exploiting it for the good of all mankind. When I become the British Foreign Secretary, I will ensure that no heavy industries ever reach this corner of the empire, this primeval and exuberant garden, this Eden. It will for ever remain green, abounding in flowers, and its people will be free to continue living their simple, pastoral lifestyle.'

Marshall shared some of Alexander's sentiments but wished he had sounded less patronising.

While he searched for the words to articulate his ambivalence, Constance said: 'Perhaps the people of Paradise would like a say in their own future.'

Marshall laughingly agreed, and Alexander scowled and fell into a ruminative silence, as if contemplating some intractable problem. But his restless intellect did not allow him to remain withdrawn for long and he was soon seeking Marshall's opinion on nature and progress.

That gentle reproof from Constance, and Alexander's meek

response, was one of many instances which gave Marshall an insight into the unusually close relationship between the twins. He sometimes felt as though they were two parts of the same person, with one acting as a balance to the excesses of the other. And Alexander was not always in the wrong. Constance was inclined to linger at spots which captivated her and retreat into reverential silence, as if confronting an awesome mystery. On such occasions Alexander would make a gentle, almost imperceptible gesture that brought her out of her reverie. Witnessing the closeness between the twins not only made Marshall feel excluded from their company, it made him conscious of a personal loneliness, an incompleteness.

If the Castles exposed that loneliness, they also, for a time, helped Marshall to overcome it on long languorous days that started with a morning walk followed by a lazy afternoon on Paradise Cove, a sandy indentation on the coast, where a wind-sculpted sea-grape tree provided a natural shade. With Denzil Stewart's return they formed a quartet.

Denzil and Alexander were keen swimmers, and held noisy racing contests to the mouth of the cove. Marshall, who was not a natural competitor, quickly tired of the swimming races. While the others swam, he was often alone with Constance, whose quiet company he preferred to their loud competitiveness. Constance read to him from paperback novels, or told him about life in England. In return he amused her with stories about some of the harmless ghosts that haunted Paradise, but took care to avoid mentioning the Sarjeants' own cast of spectres. Walking back to Banyan each evening, Marshall sometimes skipped and even whistled, as if his newly found companions had relieved him of some burden and restored something lost during his years of blindness.

These halcyon days reached a climax when one morning Marshall turned up at the Castles' villa and was greeted by Mrs Castle. Petite and blonde-haired, she bore a strong resemblance to Alexander. Marshall had never spoken to her, as she seemed to spend much of her time in bed with her French lover, who was an even scarcer sight. She addressed him as Denzil, invited him into the house and left him alone in the living-room to wait for Alexander and Constance.

While he waited, he heard what sounded like an argument between Constance and her mother. It was an intimation of discord that destroyed Marshall's view of the Castles' transient household as a peaceful, harmonious one under a shelter of wealth.

Eventually Alexander appeared and explained that he had caught a chill the previous evening and would be staying indoors. He looked rather weak in his silk dressing-gown, his flaxen hair tousled, his voice a feeble whisper.

Constance then marched into the room, ignored Alexander, and said: 'Marshall, would you like to go for a walk with me? I've got to get out of this house.'

Marshall glanced at Alexander, who turned away, then agreed. Alexander calmly wished them a good time, but only Marshall heard as Constance was already out of the door.

Some yards from the house, Constance revealed that arguments with her mother were common because she believed that her mother showed more affection to Alexander. 'She pampers him rotten,' she said angrily. She did not say what had brought on this pique, but railed for a while about the injustice of having always to take second place to Alexander. Then, as if she had unburdened her troubles, she fell quiet. When she next spoke, she was again the reasonable, pleasant companion, the gentle conversationalist with whom Marshall had spent many hours on the beach, and who had over the days become the focus of a silent, growing affection.

Marshall and Constance planned to walk around the outskirts of Paradise, but they did not get far. As they approached the four-hundred-year-old cotton tree, the sky darkened suddenly and released a deafening clap of thunder, followed by lightning, then huge drops of rain began to splatter on the ground. The nearest shelter was the cotton tree and on Marshall's suggestion they dashed there and stood in the diamond-shaped mouth of the hollow where the mixture of damp wood, decaying leaves and dead insects generated a feculent yet sweet odour. It was more than a passing shower. The globulous drops spattering the ochre-coloured dirt track on either side of the cotton tree beat out an escalating rhythmic tempo that climaxed in a steady sheet of rain that pounded saplings into the ground and strained the strongest branches. Earth cavities filled with tiny animated lakes and cart tracks with streams that rushed nowhere fast. The rain abated briefly and then resumed with renewed ferocity as if it had been merely catching its breath for a new level of assault, which now fell with a terrible aural and visual beauty. Hypnotised into silence by this majestic act of nature, enveloped by the pungent immortal trunk of the cotton tree, watched by the spirits of many past generations, with Constance beside him, Marshall viewed the rain fall over the Paradise of his lonely heart.

When the spell wore off, Constance said: 'Alexander likes you. He thinks you have great dignity, and seem trustworthy and honest.'

'He's found a category for me?' Marshall said.

She laughed lightly. 'You have to forgive Alexander's little idiosyncrasy. He's a compulsive classifier.'

'There's nothing to forgive. That's how he is. I like him, too. You two seem very close.'

'We used to be closer. When we were much younger I could tell what Alexander was feeling or thinking, even when he was in another part of the house. But as we grow older, we seem to be growing apart. He's becoming someone I know less and less.'

'It sounds as though that saddens you, that growing apartness.'

'Alexander and I will always be close, but the closeness of our childhood is lost, and, yes, that saddens me. It's like losing a part of one's self. And you, do you have brothers and sisters?'

'No. I am the only one. When I am with you and Alexander I feel as if I've always been alone.'

'But you have not been lonely?'

'Maybe that's what I meant. I am beginning to know loneliness.'

'Because of us?'

'I don't know,' he said, and thought of Scoop and his betrayal.

The rain fell on the leaves in a discordant patter until it ceased altogether. The light over the mountains brightened and the parting clouds exposed aquamarine blue patches of sky. The air was charged, as if it had been cleansed of all impurities, leaving only the odour of fresh earth and wet leaves.

They stepped out of the cotton tree and continued their journey. But the hour they had spent watching the rain from the hollow of the tree had wrought some subtle, nebulous change between them. They walked closer together, and Marshall did not, as he often did, name the plants they passed. For in the beginning the plants had no name.

The scheduled morning walk stretched, by tacit agreement, into an afternoon at Paradise Cove. They sat under the sea-grape tree and watched the long sunset cast a golden path across the sea.

Constance said: 'I've had a perfect day, tranquil yet full of marvels. I wish every day could be like this, but our time here will soon end and we'll return to England, to the grime and fog of London and the threat of war.'

'Will you write to me?' Marshall said. 'Write long letters telling me about London?'

Constance did not reply, but looked at Marshall and tears started rolling down her cheeks. She said: 'Marshall, will you hold me, please?'

He complied with awkward hesitancy, placing an arm

around her shoulders, and as her body pressed against his, it seemed to belong there and he held her until the sun sank into the sea, leaving a crimson sky, and when he released her he felt as though something inside him had either been destroyed or awakened or both. Finally they kissed, gently, then passionately.

Suddenly Constance pulled away and said: 'We've got to go. It's getting dark.'

The abrupt termination and her words snapped Marshall out of a trance. 'Yes. It's getting dark,' he repeated in a daze of stupefaction.

He held her hand until they reached the coastal road, where Constance shook her hand free of his grip. He began to sense a barely perceptible change in her mood, a faint trace of regret for what had happened in the cove. The feeling continued to grow as they walked through the dusk in silence broken only by her wondering aloud how Alexander had spent his day. At the gate of the villa, Constance smiled stiffly, bade him a perfunctory farewell and hurried inside without looking back.

Marshall waited until she had closed the door, then made his way towards Banyan, lost in a swirl of elation and confusion. For she had definitely withdrawn, become more distant, after the kiss. Perhaps she felt she had made a mistake; perhaps she had been playing with him. Now he would have to wait until the day after next to know whether it had all been an error because Soledad had invited the Castles to spend a day on Bonny View Hill. He would behave towards her as if nothing had happened.

But Marshall did not get a chance to find out the meaning of Constance's kiss. On the same day that the Castles visited Bonny View, Britain declared war on Germany, and this news, received over the wireless, threw the Castle household into turmoil as plans for their immediate departure were put into action. Caught up in their preparations to leave the island, the Castle twins became once again the metropolitan sophisticates, the worldly-wise travellers with ships and planes to catch.

Marshall spent a half-hour at the villa hoping that he could talk to Constance alone, but she seemed distant and detached, as if she had already left the island. He wished both Constance and Alexander *bon voyage,* then left the villa, feeling low and dispirited.

Over the next few weeks Marshall wrestled with a strange and painful emotion that was inseparable from his memory of Constance Castle, who had given him his first kiss. The morning they watched the rain fall from the snug, scented hollow of the cotton tree, their walk through the damp forest afterwards, the kiss on the beach – all replayed in his mind with tormenting clarity. Some nights, as he lay awake in bed, he imagined he heard her voice on the breeze, a soft, liquescent music which filled him with such sadness, such longing, such an overpowering feeling of lost love, that he sobbed gently into his pillow.

Constance was not the only cause of his sorrow. He grieved also for Scoop, his dearest friend, his soul companion. In this lachrymose state he forgave Scoop the theft of the map and wished only for his return, so that he could share with him the tragedy of his heart.

II

News of the war fever which had infected the globe reached Paradise intermittently through the *Daily Gleaner*, the island's only newspaper, and touched everyone's life. Children abandoned mundane games like marbles and cricket for war games, played with wooden guns, in which the German Führer and the devil were shot at with the imaginary bullets of their innocent hatred. Young men fled half-ploughed, rock-strewn fields to enlist in the army because the glory of war seemed more easily attained than crops from stubborn soil. A group of First World War veterans formed themselves into the Paradise militia and, bearing rusty archaic rifles and waving the Union Jack, paraded daily through Victoria Squre, and spread rumours of an imminent German or Japanese invasion due to the island's supposed strategic importance to the British Empire. In one risible incident four night fishermen arrested by a squad of bow-legged septuagenarian veterans played along with the martial game until they realised that the geriatric island guards intended to execute them for spying, at which point one of them pleaded with his grandfather, who was one of his captors, to recognise him.

Marshall did not succumb to this war fever. With time, the effects of Constance's ambiguous kiss and the feeling of loneliness that the interlude with the Castles had exposed weakened, and he settled back into the routine of studying and physical exercises under Pharaoh's guidance. Love and friendship, he resolved, would have to wait until after he had claimed the gold, the legacy that would give him a secure and comfortable future. In vivid daydreams he dreamt of wealth enough to purchase a banana plantation and rehouse the women of Banyan in a grand modern building that would be the envy of all Paradise. Sometimes, worried that his mentor might have forgotten the exact location of the gold, he sought and received reassurance from Pharaoh that he would know exactly where to dig when the right time came.

'It's your destiny, and my task is to ensure that you are prepared to meet that destiny with a better chance of victory than me,' Pharaoh always said.

Pharaoh never mentioned the possibility of failure, nor did he reveal his secret plan for defeating Alegba. But Marshall trusted Pharaoh, and believed that that knowledge would eventually be passed on to him closer to the day he was due to meet his special destiny.

Then late one afternoon, a year into the war, several abengs – cowhorns – sang out, full of urgency and alarm, across the hills of Paradise. As Marshall stood outside with Pharaoh, wondering what had caused this uproar, a small boy came running towards the cabin, shouting: 'Nana Sarjeant's dead, Nana Sarjeant's dead!' With this news, Marshall's studies came to an end for the day, and he threw himself into helping with the funeral, believing her death would hasten his confrontation with the duppy. How wrong he was.

Death had claimed Nana Sarjeant before. The most memorable occasion had happened ten years past her centenary, when she slept for ninety days. Cornelia Sarjeant, now deceased, had called in Dr Da Costa Snr, who inspected the body and pronounced the matriarch dead. Cornelia had then ordered a coffin and arranged a funeral. On the night before the funeral Nana Sarjeant stirred in her coffin, then sat up slowly, looked at all the mourners gathered round, and asked in a chillingly feeble voice for a cup of the bush tea that was widely believed to be responsible for her astonishing longevity. Some years later the same coffin was enlarged for Cornelia Sarjeant's burial.

There was less doubt this time. On the morning Nana Sarjeant died Eleanor Sarjeant saw her spirit wandering about the yard looking confused and lost because, as everyone knows, the newly dead share the disorientation of the newly born. Shortly afterwards a visitor reported that the four-hundred-year-old cotton tree on the edge of Paradise had erupted in flames that gave off neither heat nor smoke and could not be extinguished. Further irrefutable proof was provided by the fact that no one had heard the abengs but Marshall and Pharaoh, and the small boy who had brought them the news of Nana Sarjeant's death was neither known to the women of Banyan nor ever seen again. Nevertheless, they did not announce her death until Dr Da Costa Jnr had examined the corpse of the shrunken old woman and hesitantly certified her dead. The doctor then went to St Christopher's Church, prayed fervently for an hour, and went home and drank himself to sleep with a bottle of overproof white rum in case he had repeated his father's infamous error. The following morning he called at Banyan, confessed his uncertainty to the family, and carried out another examination, which reaffirmed what they already knew was true.

The very precise burial instructions Nana Sarjeant had left charged Eleanor and Pharaoh Sarjeant with responsibility for her safe crossing of the great river between the living and the dead. Their heads were shaved and the shorn hair burnt to prevent them from accompanying the deceased on the long, lonely crossing. Eleanor, and only Eleanor, had to sleep in the bedroom with Nana Sarjeant's corpse to discourage the confused spirit from taking up residence in the house. Further defence against the danger of Nana Sarjeant's spirit haunting the house was then provided by four strangers who would remain at Banyan until the last rite. Three very old women and a man – all strangers to Marshall, though they were known to Pharaoh and the women of Banyan, who showed them great deference – were brought to the house on separate donkey carts, and they slept on mats in the parlour, to where the corpse was now moved. These silent, wrinkled observers, whose presence seemed to hint at the passing not so much of a person as of an entire epoch, were the closest the deceased had to contemporaries. When in doubt about the finer points of the funeral rite, Eleanor and Pharaoh turned to them for advice.

News of Nana Sarjeant's death spread throughout the island and brought to Banyan a steady stream of near and distant relatives who would eventually number almost two hundred, with many deformed and disfigured members, who all showed the indomitable will of the Sarjeants to make the best of their disadvantages.

Binta Harrison (née Sarjeant), heavily pregnant and already the mother of a fifteen-month-old daughter untouched by Sarjeant's curse, was among the first to arrive, with her devoted carpenter husband in tow. A restless, energetic man, he immediately set about erecting sleeping shelters outside the house for other mourners, who could not otherwise be accommodated.

Binta's swift response to the news caused some surprise. She had not been fond of Nana Sarjeant, seeing her incredible longevity as an unnatural achievement. But marriage and motherhood had softened Binta. 'When you live in a city, you grow to value your roots outside it,' she told Marshall.

The Sarjeants were not alone in acknowledging the passing of the woman whose life had come to seem like a monument to the possibilities inherent in the human will. A Sunday atmosphere prevailed over Paradise, and visitors from miles around, including people who seldom left the tiny farms off which they subsisted, filed to see the corpse which lay in state, preserved on ice, in the parlour. Then they stood about outside and ate and drank while swapping stories of the ailments her herbal potions had cured, the wise counsel she had given, the exemplary fortitude she had shown in the face of adversity. There was no sadness to this farewell. It was a celebration. It was a sharing of strength for the irreversible crossing.

The funeral service, held in the Baptist Church, was the

one part of the exequy that had not been requested by Nana Sarjeant, who had never entered a church. But as her death belonged to the entire family, many of whom were Baptists, Eleanor and Pharaoh made no objections, and the council of elders gave their approval. Nine days after her death, Nana Sarjeant's coffin was transported on the back of a truck – loaned to the family by Mrs Duncannon-Henriques – to the Port Columbus Crematorium. A mile-long procession of people dressed in white followed the vehicle, singing and drumming and blowing abengs and shaking tambourines.

Pharaoh ceremoniously brought the ashes back from Port Columbus and, following her last will and testament, scattered half into the sea from Cuffee's Point, and the other half into the wind. On that day, the cold, odourless flames on the cotton tree died down and the leaves covering it were now young and bright green, as if the death of the oldest person in Paradise had given it a new lease of life.

That same evening, when Pharaoh returned from Cuffee's Point, he ordered that the heads of all male Sarjeants under the age of twenty-five be shaved and oiled with coconut in preparation for a final ritual that no one seemed to be expecting. Most people had already departed, and the more devout Christians who remained refused to participate or allow their children to take part and drifted away. But Pharaoh persuaded a substantial number to stay and their numbers were augmented by outsiders.

Head shaved and oiled, Marshall and twenty other young men, following Pharaoh's instruction, went to stand in the centre of a large circle of people seated on the ground before the veranda, on which sat the four elders and the women of Banyan, whose faces wore an impassive expression. A troupe of drummers began to play as six women, dressed in white robes and turbans, weaved their way among the young men, giving each a drink from a clay cup. Sweet and thick, with the odour of fermentation, the drink warmed Marshall's throat and stomach and made him feel oddly euphoric and yet calm. The women were then joined by six men, barefoot and naked to the waist, faces covered in chalk, and they started dancing around the huddled young men, while the circle hummed and swayed.

Marshall began to feel light-headed as the drumming seemed to increase in volume and tempo, and the white-robed women and chalk-faced men pulled and shouted at the young men and urged them to dance. He started stomping his feet and soon he could not stop, as if the drumming had possessed him, robbed him of all volition and dictated that he continue moving. With sweat pouring down his face and body, his vision became blurred, his perceptions dreamlike, and while part of him was imprisoned in this peculiar ritual another part hovered above it all with detached serenity.

Pharaoh, who had been sitting on the veranda, now strode through the circle and sat cross-legged with his head bowed while the dancers stomped their feet in time to the drumming. He appeared to drift into a trance, and when he stood up the drumming and dancing stopped and the silence that reigned bore no sign of the usual night sounds. Cupping his palms, arms outstretched, as if bearing something, Pharaoh walked among the young men, looking each in the eye, then stopped at Marshall. As he stood before Marshall, the drumming resumed. Marshall involuntarily stretched out cupped palms and Pharaoh placed something in them, something invisible but palpably real, for he could feel its weight, its ovoid shape and its faint throbbing. Then Pharaoh removed from his own neck a gold locket, placed it around Marshall's neck, and instructed him to put the object in the locket. Marshall obeyed and though whatever he held in his hand seemed too large, he felt its weight transferred to the locket and he clicked it shut.

Suddenly the other young men rushed towards Marshall and the drumming quickened, abengs and conches joining in to create deafening music. A multitude of hands started to undress him, stripped him of all his clothes. As Marshall stood there naked, Pharaoh turned a full circle slowly, the gathering fell silent and the drumming softened to quiet, rhythmic pulsation.

Then Pharaoh spoke loudly, to the crowd, to Marshall: 'In accordance with Nana Sarjeant's wish, her ka has been entrusted to Marshall Sarjeant who has been chosen to return it to Africa, where it will be buried in the soil, and bring an end to the curse which has hung over the Sarjeant family for over a century.'

The crowd released a tumultuous roar, the drumming started again, the young men danced around Marshall, stomping their feet and chanting his name ...

Marshall woke up in Pharaoh's cabin with such hazy memories of the ceremony that he thought he had dreamt it all. He felt the gold chain around his neck and its peculiar weightiness, and when he opened the locket he saw nothing but could sense the presence of the object, and remembered how it had come into his possession, the great honour and terrible burden it represented.

He looked around the cabin and saw Pharaoh gazing at him with imperturbable stillness and a stern expression on his face. Then Pharaoh gave him an explanation.

Fearing that her death would unleash the full effects of Sarjeant's curse, Nana Sarjeant had requested that her ka be taken back to Africa where it was to be buried in the soil. When this task was fulfilled the battle she had fought against Sybil Sarjeant's curse would come to an end. Failure to fulfil it, she had believed, would result in the extinction of the Sarjeants and triumph for Sybil.

Arrangements had been made to get Marshall as far as Europe. When the war was over, he was to find some way of getting to Africa. He would be on his own, dependent on his own resources, and until he had fulfilled his mission he was not to return to the island. On his return, he could challenge the spirit of Alegba for the Sarjeant gold.

'The war is an inconvenience,' Pharaoh said, 'but it will not last for ever. Another two years at the most. I'd advise you to sit it out in Europe.'

Pharaoh left Marshall fingering the locket containing the ka of Nana Sarjeant while contemplating the onerous task that had been placed on his shoulders. The honour he felt for being chosen jostled with a powerful feeling of being burdened with an unwanted task. It seemed to him that they could not have chosen a more unsuitable candidate. With a taste for adventure limited to the boundaries of Paradise, within which he wished to spend his life, he felt as though fate had played a cruel trick on him. 'Why me?' he asked himself repeatedly. And as he searched for an answer, he wondered whether Pharaoh and the women of Banyan had all along known he would be chosen for this mission before being given a chance to claim the gold.

Marshall did not get an opportunity to put this suspicion to Pharaoh until the next day. When Pharaoh appeared, he carried a cardboard grip of clothes for Marshall, and gave him an address in Port Columbus where he was expected.

Taking the items, Marshall said: 'Did you know I would be chosen to do this?'

'Yes,' Pharaoh said. 'But not when.' He paused, then, preempting Marshall's next question, said: 'I certainly thought we would have reclaimed the gold before Nana Sarjeant died. But nobody can predict these things. Do I sense reluctance, unwillingness?'

'No,' Marshall lied.

'Good. It will take no more than two or three years. Less, if you're lucky and the war ends. That's a small price to pay for finally ridding the family of that wretched curse. And think about what's waiting for you when you get back: a fortune that would take you three lifetimes to accumulate.'

Pharaoh allayed Marshall's suspicions but he did nothing to rouse his enthusiasm. He was given a day to say farewell to family members. He spent hours with Binta, who had given birth to a boy and was staying in Banyan until she was well enough to travel back to Kingston. She knew of the mission but, as if the ministrations of the women of Banyan had converted her to believing in the curse, she said nothing to discourage Marshall. Before he parted from her, she gave him a silver crucifix and they prayed together while the baby slept and her daughter looked on.

But Binta's kisses and hugs and those from the women of Banyan merely intensified Marshall's reluctance to leave Paradise. He returned to the empty cabin and the day of his departure came and went. When Pharaoh came to his cabin and found Marshall asleep, he stirred him awake and lectured him on the need to face up to the responsibilities of being a Sarjeant. Then he left with a look of disgust on his face which did far more than his words to rouse Marshall from the lethargy induced by resentment and, he had admitted to himself, fear.

The final impetus came later that day when Marsall wandered down to Banyan and received tragic news from Eleanor. Before they could name him, Binta's baby boy had died in the night, and one of the women had dreamt that same night that Sybil Sarjeant's ghost had wandered through the house. Marshall wanted to see Binta, but Eleanor would not allow him access to the grieving mother.

She said sternly, 'You know your aunt: she will recover and she will try again. If you want to help, you must leave Paradise with the first light and don't look back until you've reached your destination.'

The next morning, with his grip in hand, and the moon still visible, Marshall, now fully resigned to the necessity of his journey, left Pharaoh's cabin. He did not know when he would again see his beloved island. On that morning of exile, as he trod the dusty road to Port Columbus, Marshall Sarjeant remembered when he first heard the story of how Jamaica was created.

PART II

I

Marshall Sarjeant arrived in Britain in November 1943 as a member of the West Indies Volunteer Force, a body of men drawn from the British West Indian colonies and dispersed throughout the embattled British Isles to help in the war effort.

From the chains around his neck, concealed beneath layers of clothes issued by the colonial office, hung his ancestor's spirit and the symbol of his uncertain faith. Quiet and reserved, he lived in a boarding-house occupied exclusively by other West Indian volunteers, and worked in the Clayforth ammunition works.

Like the rest of the country, Liverpool was in a perpetual state of grim alert. Air raids had reduced huge swathes of the city to rubble, and stray bombs had blasted holes in streets of terraced houses where rooms of rose-patterned wallpaper were exposed to the snow and the rain. The occasional wedding, christening or peal of abandoned laughter could momentarily defy the reality of the ongoing war, but once the illusion had passed, dispelled by news of bomb raids or numbers killed in battle, the war seemed all the more terrible, a mad, unfathomable event.

Many of Marshall's co-workers were women with husbands in the army, and during the course of a week in early December he witnessed three newly widowed women being comforted by their colleagues as the effort to maintain appearances crumbled and they surrendered to the sorrow of their loss and the warmth of consoling arms.

This atmosphere of destruction and death in a cold climate fuelled a powerful nostalgia. In private moments, Marshall held the locket containing Nana Sarjeant's ka and the silver crucifix Binta had given him, and sought refuge in the cavernous memories of the island with a town called Paradise where daylight was not a few brief hours of dusky light, where snow and cold were unknown except on the mountain peaks, where the trees were not leafless and seemingly dead but full of exuberant foliage. But as the winter settled in, the solace of nostalgia seemed insufficient, and he took to wandering into the Catholic church near the boarding-house where he would silently pray for the war to end so that he could continue his journey to Africa.

Marshall was not the only member of the West Indies Volunteer Force for whom the war was an inconvenient obstacle to great ambitions. Two brothers from Trinidad, Augie and Bernie Parker, who both worked in a factory which made surgical equipment, shared an adjoining room in the boarding house, and on his rest days Marshall sometimes sought diversion in their company. Skinny and tall, Augie was a calypsonian with an irreverent, mocking sense of humour and a talent for mimicry which spared no one and no subject. Bernie was younger. As tall as his brother but fuller in figure, he had the handsome face and slow smile of a man who seemed destined to die from excessive love. He was also a musician, though he preferred sentimental ballads and was so full of music that he sang in his sleep.

The brothers regarded themselves as pioneers of calypso music. After the war they planned to head for London, to find work in nightclubs. In contrast to Marshall they had reached their destination but shared with him an impatience for the war to end.

Augie and Bernie helped Marshall survive his first English winter by providing a sanctuary of friendship where laughter and reminiscences of tropical islands generated a warmth that insulated him against the stressful war atmosphere, the cold of the land and the frostiness of the natives. They helped to immunise him against the daily slights he received from the

English workers at the ammunition factory and the austerity that kept the temperature of the boarding-house a little above freezing point. Augie Parker did a side-splitting impersonation of the boarding-house manager, John O'Casey, who was reported to have said to the owner, Mrs Philomena Cork, that he would be glad when the war ended so they could get the 'darkies' out of their home. Mrs Cork was a plump, jocose woman with red cheeks and a fondness for gin, which staled her breath from early morning and put her in maudlin mood as she listened to the war news on the wireless in the evenings. John, whose mountainous stomach had not been deflated by four years of rationing, was supposedly her cousin, but it was obvious to even the least observant they enjoyed more than a relationship of mere consanguinity. What they got up to behind closed doors was the subject of numerous ribald skits by Augie.

The Trinidadian brothers were inveterate revellers. They did not allow the war or the English weather to dampen their natural ebullience. Augie's birthday fell on the last Saturday of February and he observed it by inviting everyone who was not working to a party. Augie somehow managed to secure both a guitar and a bottle of rum. From midday a party atmosphere prevailed as other men gravitated to the Parkers' room, where they were entertained with melancholy love songs sung by Bernie, or humorous calypsos sung by Augie. With the beds leant up against a wall there was ample space to dance. The chambermaid, Edna, happened to be around and she was invited in, and after a few sips of rum lost all inhibition and gave the men a display of Irish dancing that filled everyone with delight.

Suddenly, John O'Casey burst into the room, shouting with an anger that turned his face beetroot red. There were many boarders in the building who were sleeping in preparation for their nightshift and the party noise was a disturbance. He ordered Edna to leave the room, then rebuked the men with a severity which intimated that it was the chambermaid's presence, rather than the excessive noise, that had caused offence.

After O'Casey left Gladstone McPherson, a Jamaican, expressed violent indignation and swore that if O'Casey did not behave himself, he, Gladstone, would cut him with the flick knife that he had had to show more than one disrespectful native. He demanded that Augie and Bernie resume their playing and singing and slowly the party built up again. This time when O'Casey came bursting into the room, Gladstone was prepared for him. Somebody turned out the light and from the sudden darkness came a loud cry of pain. When the light came back on, O'Casey was bent double, holding his stomach with an expression of shock and incredulity on his face.

It turned out that his wound was only superficial, despite the copious bleeding. But the incident brought to the surface a mutual antipathy that had been poisoning the air for weeks. Altercations between John O'Casey and the men became a daily occurrence.

Eventually someone from the colonial office came up from London and attempted to act as mediator between the now disgruntled landlady and the recalcitrant colonial volunteers. His solution, reluctantly pursued because finding alternative accommodation would not be easy, was the ignominious eviction of the troublemakers. Gladstone McPherson had long disappeared, but John O'Casey took the opportunity to rid the house of men with whom he had had even mild disputes. Among those to move were Augie and Bernie Parker, although the only violence they had inflicted came from Augie's sharp tongue.

Marshall, the youngest of the volunteers, was regarded as a decent young man led astray, and so escaped eviction on the condition that he observe the rules of the house. There was now little chance of him breaking those rules. With the departure of the Trinidadian brothers a funereal silence settled over the boarding-house and Marshall's longing for

Paradise and an end to the war became as palpable as a missing limb.

But Marshall had not seen the last of the Parkers. Some weeks later, with the weather improving, the trees greening, and buds appearing on shrubs which had seemed dead, he received a visit from Bernie Parker. Bernie told him that he and his brother were now resident musicians in a nightclub called World's End and invited Marshall to drop by. Marshall took up this offer on his next weekend break and, on a spring Saturday afternoon, made his way to the Toxteth area in Liverpool. From the moment he entered the neighbourhood, he was enveloped in a warm aura of welcome and familiarity. There were dark faces on the street and the passers-by greeted him and called him brother or 'bro'.

Bernie and Augie Parker lived on the top floor of a Georgian house on a wide avenue. Over drinks and a card game Marshall learnt that Toxteth was an old meeting place of Africans and Europeans, the only part of the city where men from his part of the world could feel at ease. In the early part of the evening, Augie took Marshall on a tour of the area. Wherever Marshall went he met men from the islands and the African continent. They received him with such warmth, such bonhomie, that he wondered how he had managed to survive so long without this quality of human contact.

That same night saw the first performance of the Trinidadian brothers in the World's End Club, which was a basement in the house where they lived. Bernie was the singer and Augie the lead guitarist, an old Nigerian sailor played saxophone and a little Somalian called Ali played the drums. As the night wore on the club filled up with men and women. Most of the women were white, and the men dark or of mixed race. With the windows blackened out, the club had such a permanent feel of night-time that when Marshall emerged from the basement he was shocked to discover that if he didn't hurry he would miss the start of his shift at the munitions factory, for it was late Sunday afternoon. He hurried away amazed that time could pass so quickly in a country where he had so far counted every minute of the day.

On his next visit Marshall was introduced to the proprietor of the World's End Club. Stocky and dark, with a broad bright smile, and an insouciant air, Holy Joe was married to Anne, the Englishwoman who worked as the barmaid. He seemed concerned that Marshall was living so far from Toxteth and promised to find him a room in this isle of hospitality.

The next week Marshall moved into a room below the Trinidadian brothers. He was further from work, but he felt much more comfortable here. It was almost like being at home and when his longing for Paradise assaulted him he sought sanctuary and comfort in World's End.

Marshall struck up an immediate rapport with Holy Joe. His new landlord was a master raconteur and an eternal optimist who had lived in Liverpool since the First World War and claimed to have escaped or survived numerous misfortunes because he was protected by the spirits of his ancestors. The latest had happened early during this war. He had signed up on a merchant ship as first cook but a week before the ship was due to sail he was visited by benevolent ancestral spirits. Their disembodied voices warned him that if he sailed, it would be his last voyage, but that they would intervene on his behalf. Three days later, Joe was in the galley as the ship listed violently and a large tin of cooking oil fell and crushed his toes. Incapacitated, he could not sail. The ship was torpedoed outside Birkenhead and only ten men survived. If there was anyone who would understand Marshall's mission to deliver Nana Sarjeant's ka to Africa, it was this genial Sierra Leonean. There were times when Marshall was sorely tempted to share the burden of his secret with him.

It was here, in the World's End shebeen, that the quiet, reserved youngman who had left Paradise and then Jamaica with a single purpose in mind began to discover the pleasures of the night. Cheap whisky loosened his tongue and his body, imbued him with verbal and physical eloquence, shook him free of the iron armours of responsibility and purposefulness, and enabled him to float through nights of increasing dissipation. Here he was introduced to the thrill of gambling, throwing dice or playing cards, and discovered that he possessed a lucky streak that deepened and widened and rewarded him as he learnt to trust his instincts.

Among the World's End's rough habitués, he learnt that women found him irresistibly attractive and during one dissolute week he slept with five different women over as many nights. On the Sunday of that week, woken by guilt, he rose early and attended Mass for the first time in months, and from there returned to the scented room of the woman who had given him such sweet satisfaction that she had aroused memories of swimming in the Blue Hole of his boyhood days. As he lay in her bed, his lust momentarily sated and his pride swollen by her effusive compliments to his vigorous manhood, he worried that he was allowing himself to be distracted by carnality. Yet it seemed to him, on that morning of guilt and pleasure, that he was in a state of stasis until the war ended. With peace he would book his passage on the first ship sailing to an African port. He fondled the locket and crucifix around his neck, then reached for the soft, pale body of his companion whose appetite was as insatiable as his own.

But there was a more serious side to Holy Joe's establishment. Some nights the men talked and argued about the inescapable fact of the war, and what it meant to them. These discussions were not new to Marshall, but while he had previously been a spectator, he now drew on Pharaoh's teachings and his own growing confidence, and became a vociferous and articulate contributor to heated discussions that sometimes went on into the mornings.

There was unanimous agreement that Nazi Germany was an evil that had to be defeated. But there was less agreement about Europe. Had the Europeans who were the target of the German aggression not themselves conquered and subjugated other peoples around the globe under the guise of spreading civilisation and Christianity? Was Hitler's persecution of the Jews not merely an old practice, rooted in an equally old belief that one part of humanity was somehow less human? Were they, the habitués of the World's End Club, not all the victims of a white man's world? The men in the World's End chewed over these questions with the same rough passion that they invested in dancing, gambling and womanising.

Every now and again, Marshall was invaded by a powerful sense of witnessing the end of one age and the beginning of another, one built out of the ruins of an inevitable war. None the less, he did not allow such grave matters to preoccupy him while there was so much fun to be had. Besides, he did see himself as a part of that rebuilding, however strong his views were. A wilful myopia kept his sights focused on returning to Paradise, to the love of his kinfolk freed of the ancient curse, to the battle that awaited him there, and the tranquillity that would follow victory.

That August Marshall was given a two-week holiday. Bernie and Augie had taken to making occasional forays to London, returning with stories of a city ripe for musical conquest, and teeming with Africans and Black American GIs. So when they invited Marshall along, he seized the chance to take a look.

They left Liverpool on an overcast Wednesday morning, intending to return on Sunday night, all three in a merry mood.

Marshall did not, in fact, see much of London on this visit. The Trinidadian brothers had contacts in the East End of London, and they slept by day and spent their nights in the Casablanca Club, which was run by a wily-looking Somalian called Jimmy. It was frequented by drifters similar to those found in the World's End Club, and overrun by good-time girls of various nationalities and easy virtue. Both Augie and Bernie were familiar with these women, and on the Saturday night their entry into the club attracted the attention of three women whose liberal consumption of alcohol sent inviting signals to the visitors.

Marshall wasted no time in making the acquaintance of Liza, who reciprocated his advances by clinging to him with the tenacity of one who had staked a claim. With a broad cockney accent, a licentious smile, and a voluptuous figure, she was by far the most attractive of the women, and massaged Marshall's vanity.

When Bernie disappeared with Liza's friend Sue – followed soon afterwards by Augie with the other, Lyn – Liza's suggestion that they go to her room seemed as natural as the drink Marshall held in his hand. She did not live far away and they walked through a cool morning, passing bomb sites that reminded him that he was in a war. Liza walked close beside him, and asked him about his island. Her questions troubled him and he deflected her attempt to know him by flattering her. He was so intent on distracting her, that he paid no attention to where they were going.

Marshall woke up in the afternoon with Liza's fleshy naked body beside him in a small room that smelt of lard and lavender, and admitted only a faint trace of daylight down the sides of heavy, dark curtains. He fondled the locket and crucifix and wondered about Bernie and Augie, but the knowledge of where to meet up with them quelled a disquiet which he attributed to being in a strange city. When he woke up again, Liza had prepared some slices of stale bacon and bread, and these restored his strength, and inspired him with a concupiscence that brought Liza back to bed until late evening. At nightfall Marshall left Liza's room with instructions on how to get to the Casablanca where he expected to meet Bernie and Augie. She promised to come later but he knew from the tone of her voice that she, like him, had exhausted a happy adventure of the flesh, all the happier for it being between strangers, and neither possessed the imagination or the desire to take it further. As he strolled he promised himself to find a church on Sunday.

Half an hour later, Marshall was still wandering the streets with the growing realisation that he was lost. It was a warm night and he carried his jacket slung over his left shoulder, and his shirt was open to his chest. He stopped to get his bearings when suddenly the air-raid sirens went off and piercing wails rent the air, followed by the distant sound of explosions. He knew he ought to seek shelter, and started running but with no idea where to run to. He decided to return to Liza's room, but its location now seemed uncertain.

A couple raced past him and he followed them until they entered a terrace, the door of which slammed with resounding firmness. Confusion came over him and he urged himself to remain calm. Then just as he spotted a landmark that he had set in his sights for such an eventuality, the shrill, piercing sound came closer and he heard an almighty explosion. The chains holding Nana Sarjeant's ka and the crucifix flew off his neck at the same time as several sharp, stabbing pains pierced his arms and legs, and he fell into a pit of total darkness.

2

Marshall surfaced briefly from a deep sleep and felt the constriction of bandages on his legs, torso and arms. Then he touched his neck and the realisation that the locket containing Nana Sarjeant's ka was not there filled him with an anguish that caused him to scream, although he could not hear his own voice.

In the darkness that followed the recurring nightmare began. It always started with a rainfall on an island and children scampering for cover. Separated from his friends, he sheltered in a cave and from there watched the falling rain change colour, becoming as red and as viscous as blood. When it stopped he became an adult and emerged from the cave to find the island transformed and his friends nowhere in sight. Bullet-shaped, metallic fruits hung from stunted trees with leaves as sharp as razorblades. The sticky red earth made a crunching noise as he stepped on calcified bones. He wandered about until he came to the sea, and there on a beach swarming with minute gold-coloured crabs, he saw a nun kneeling before a giant luminous cross which hovered above the ocean. He called out to her and she stood and started running. He pursued her along the shore, then through forests and across mountains. When, at last, he caught up with her and she turned to him he saw with horror that her face was white and fleshless and skeletal. As he stood there in a daze she fled again. He chased the skeletal nun to a green wooden house where a dark, withered old woman sat on a veranda in a rocking-chair, rocking with all the calm of time itself. The skeletal nun turned and laughed at him, walked up the steps to the old woman and squatted at her feet. The old woman stroked her bony cheeks and, yearning to be stroked so gently, he approached, but the old woman burst into laughter and from her toothless mouth gushed a vast, violent body of water which swept him away back to the beach where he saw the skeletal nun kneeling before the luminous cross. Then the chase would start again.

When Marshall next regained a semblance of consciousness, blurred figures stood over him and he heard an exchange which confirmed his worst fear.

The first voice said: 'This one's in a bad way. He keeps asking for something that sounds like ka and a locket. But we didn't find any jewellery on him.'

The second voice replied: 'We'll keep him until he's mended physically, then transfer him to Wickham Psychiatric Clinic.'

He knew then without doubt that he had lost the locket containing Nana Sarjeant's ka, and that knowledge combined with the pain in his chest and legs to drive him back to the island and the red rainfall which signalled the start of the dream of the skeletal nun.

When his physical pain began to decrease, he was conscious for longer periods, and often lay in the darkened ward listening to a medley of sounds that included the sort of maniacal laughter which some people, faced with the inevitability of disaster or death, release in defiance and terror and resignation. He knew when the man in the neighbouring bed had died in the night and had been replaced by another dying figure only because the new pain-racked whisper had a different quality, carried a higher pitch. He had never seen his previous neighbour and he would not see the new one either. Or the one after that. He came to recognise the nurses by their individual odours, the pitch of their voices, the outline of their bodies, the quality of their touches. One nurse made him think of flowers and damp earth and hers was the gentlest touch, yet firm and reassuring of life. Much of the time, though, he was insensate, barely aware of his surroundings, unsure which was reality, the hospital ward or the dream which invaded his mind night after long night.

One day a nurse removed the bandages on his arms and legs, washed him down, then wheeled him through the ward, past rows of beds around which women and children huddled in quiet meditation, as if seeking communion with God to beg for healing, to plead for lives teetering on the precipice of death. This slow unending passage through the hospital brought back other memories of the war, the ravaged buildings, the women weeping in the factory, and he resolved that should he ever recover and find himself amongst men who spoke casually of war, of doing battle, of killing other men, he would raise his voice in opposition. But he feared that they, the nurses and the doctors, had abandoned any hope of him recovering, that he was dead and witnessing the disposal of his body. He lost consciousness and woke up in another bed, in what seemed like an entirely different building.

Marshall's sleep was still haunted by the dream of the skeletal nun, but during his waking hours, a growing awareness of time made him realise that he had begun a tentative, hesitant journey back to normality. He began to recognise in the nurses and doctors regional accents, facial expressions, personalities, and understood that in this new hospital the patients' physical injuries were secondary to their mental wounds.

The hospital staff often held conversations over those patients who seemed dead to the world, and one day Marshall heard a doctor remark to a nurse: 'The survival instincts of the human race are really rather amazing. As long as men are capable of retreating into what we call insanity our species will continue. For madness is our most desperate defence mechanism. It rearranges our perception of reality.' Marshall would later learn that the doctor was called William Jones. A tall, shuffling, untidy man, he was a First World War survivor whose empathy with his patients was based on more than one involuntary safari into the wilderness of his own mind.

Dr Jones's remark resonated in Marshall's mind for the

remainder of the day. Had he fled into madness, a semi-vegetative state, an interior of the imagination, to an island of a perpetual nightmare? If so, how could he escape it? Did he want to escape it? Some nights later, when the bloodstained island with its macabre figures invaded his mind and he was chasing the skeletal nun on the beach, he did something he had not done before: he ran into the sea, swam and then dived while the skeletal nun floated past. He came to a cave and entered it and he saw the withered old woman sitting cross-legged, naked, her eyes closed. He sat before her and willed himself not to move.

The following morning, when the nurse came to his bed, he whispered, 'Water, water.'

And she smiled and said: 'Ah, Mr Sarjeant. You're back with us.'

He was indeed back in the world of the living. Within days he could sit up in bed without assistance and became cognisant of his surroundings, a large, high-ceilinged room with rows of beds in which men slept or lay with blank expressions on their faces.

His own bed faced tall arched windows and beyond them was a view of a green, sloping field. The view changed as the day progressed, from pale, misty green in the morning to bright green when the sun was at its zenith. He daily willed himself to view the field and the longer he gazed at it, the stronger he felt. But some nights the dream of the skeletal nun recurred, and he would wake up feeling exhausted and robbed of the desire and the willpower to recover. On those days, the painful knowledge of his failure, the scrappy memories of the dissolute lifestyle which had led to him walking through a strange London street late at night, of the pleasure that preceded the disaster, kept him on his back in an almost vegetative state, unable to see the consoling view through the windows.

The green field also exercised a powerful hold over the man who occupied the neighbouring bed on Marshall's right.

His name was Patrick Boyle. With a gaunt, fretful face, and wearing a white dressing-gown, he daily walked to the far end of the room and sat looking out of the window, remaining there for hours gazing at the field. His face was still young, despite the grey streaks in a head of thick dark hair. His mobility gave the impression that he was further along the road to recovery than all the other patients in that ward where rest appeared to be the only prescribed cure. But one night Boyle woke up the entire ward shouting, 'There is no God. We are all damned.' Somebody shouted back, 'You're the one who's damned,' and a babel of voices and the banging of bedpans against metal bed frames created a cacophony which was only silenced when a nurse switched on the light.

That same night Marshall was again woken, this time by a new noise, a muffled sound, and became aware of arms thrashing about and a figure leaning over the neighbouring bed. Somebody was trying to suffocate Boyle. Marshall shouted, struggled out of bed and hurled himself against the figure. Suddenly the ward was flooded with light and two nurses came rushing to his assistance. With the help of a male nurse they overpowered the would-be killer, who kept on shouting, 'He doesn't deserve to live.' He was strait-jacketed and led away, and a nurse tended Boyle, who was unharmed.

Later that morning, as Marshall sat up in bed gazing at the pale green field, Boyle left his own bed and spoke to Marshall for the first time.

'There was a field like that in our home in County Galway, too. We used to play in it as children.'

'It reminds me of the mountains back home, in Jamaica.'

'You saved my life,' Boyle said. 'I don't know whether it was worth saving. But thank you.'

Over the next few days a strong friendship developed between Marshall and Patrick Boyle in this makeshift psychiatric hospital converted from a mansion. Their conversations, slow and difficult at times, revealed that they had much in common. Both had lost something precious and vital to a war that they viewed with equal abhorrence.

In Boyle's case it was his faith. He had been a young Catholic priest in France at the time of the German conquest of that nation. Disobeying Vatican directives, which his immediate superiors followed to the letter, he had secretly assisted the French Resistance movement. His downfall came when he gave sanctuary to a trio of Resistance fighters who had been sabotaging German communications lines. One Sunday, during Mass, a squad of Gestapo descended on the church following a tip-off. They surrounded the building and held the congregation hostage. The priest insisted that the freedom fighters were not there, but the soldiers threatened to shoot a member of the congregation every hour until he yielded up the saboteurs. An hour later, the first member of the congregation was shot on the altar, beneath the cross, under the blessed Mary holding baby Jesus, the son of the God who had died for the soul of mankind. By evening and four more dead civilians, Patrick Boyle broke. He revealed the whereabouts of the Resistance fighters. The three men were found in a mausoleum, dragged out and executed in front of the worshippers and their bodies left sprawling on the church steps.

Although his parishioners did not reproach him for his decision, Boyle suffered ineffable pain. Eventually he walked away from the church wearing his soutane, clutching his Bible and crucifix, and wandered around for weeks. During the battle of Rouen, he walked about the battlefield for ten minutes praying over the bodies of fallen soldiers, Allied and German troops alike, with bullets flying about him, but miraculously he escaped death or injury. But the frayed thread by which he had clung to sanity finally snapped with that incident. The allied troops found him cursing God over the muddied and bloodied dead bodies of two young soldiers, mere boys, one British the other German; they had killed each other in combat. Patrick Boyle's war against the war ended there, on the Rouen battlefield, praying over the corpses through rain and darkness. He was seized and flown to England where he had been in and out of psychiatric hospitals.

Marshall could not reveal to Boyle the nature of his own loss, but spoke in general terms of having come to the Mother Country to help in the war and found destruction on a scale which left him disoriented, and prone to seeking escape in pleasure, which led to his being caught in a flying bomb attack on London. He had no heroic tale to tell. Nevertheless there was sympathy from Boyle and this relieved his feeling of guilt.

In mid-November Marshall suffered a serious relapse which brought their conversations to an end and returned Marshall to the nightmare of the skeletal nun. When he recovered Boyle had been discharged.

Christmas came and went like a furtive, timid visitor. Between Christmas and New year, light snow fell daily, then a heavy blanket of frost settled over the countryside. Each morning Marshall woke up to see the green hill whitened by frost which would thaw in the weak sunlight, and around noon shine like silver before the long dusk covered the land in ever-thickening layers of darkness.

On good days Marshall gazed out of the arched windows, as if the landscape beyond concealed some mystery which would only reveal itself with prolonged and dedicated scrutiny. If there was a mystery in that landscape, it lay in what made it beautiful. How could something so cold and at times bleak appear simultaneously beautiful to one who had known the warmth and exuberance of the tropics? For he could not deny that the copse of beech trees which crowned the hill to the south was beautiful: some days the sunlight defied the clouds and streamed down on that copse in a fan-shaped strip that created an almost numinous effect. Then at dusk those same trees took on a sinister, menacing appearance and at those hours he would retreat to his bed, defeated in his attempt to understand the mystery of the landcape's beauty, a little resigned to the futility of the task, a little more aware that it was as absurd as trying to understand what made a woman beautiful, her nose, her lips, her eyes. Nevertheless the next morning, if he had not been weakened by the dream of the skeletal nun, he would return to the window; for to look inward was to see only the confusion of his failure.

In early January Marshall received a letter from Patrick Boyle. It described a busy life of meetings, without saying what the meetings were about, gave his London address and invited Marshall to treat it as his home when he was discharged from hospital. It signed off: 'Your Comrade.'

Marshall thought the parting line strange, but was too heartened by Boyle's generous invitation to dwell on how he had become the ex-priest's comrade. Although still prone to occasional relapses, he was making a steady recovery. And as his strength grew, he began to confront his own future. He had failed in his mission and he could not return to Paradise with his mission unfulfilled, now unfulfillable. Temporary exile had become permanent. He could not face Pharaoh, Eleanor Sarjeant and the women of Banyan and live there with the knowledge that he had betrayed their trust. He would have to start anew, find somewhere in England to settle down, a hole into which he could disappear and try to forget his past.

Towards the end of the month a team of medical inspectors came to the hospital. The two men and a young woman went through the building with a fine-tooth comb, checking its sanitary conditions, talking, or rather attempting to talk to, patients. On the second and last day of their visit the sun made one of its rare wintry appearances, and Marshall borrowed a greatcoat from a nurse and went to sit outside on a bench. He was gazing at the green field, which had now lost its veneer of frost, when the inspectors walked past him. He had spoken to one of the men – who had told him about the splendid job the colonial troops were doing in the war, and that when it was won Britain would be forever indebted to them – but he had not met the other inspectors.

A few yards past Marshall, the young woman stopped, turned and walked back to him. She bent and looked him in the face and said: 'Excuse me, haven't we met somewhere before?'

It was not one of Marshall's better days. The dream of the skeletal nun had visited him the previous night and though it had not left him as exhausted as in the early days, he was weak. Nevertheless, he recognised the voice immediately and it triggered a flashing memory of his first kiss. Her name followed quickly – Constance Castle.

She sat beside him and said: 'What happened to you?'

Marshall recalled the explosion in the East End, omitting, of course, what he had been doing there.

Constance looked at him with grave solicitude and shook her head, saying: 'I'm sorry, so sorry.'

One of her colleagues called to her, but she waved the man away and said: 'When do you expect to be discharged?'

'Soon,' Marshall said. 'Soon or I'll go crazy.' He laughed lightly.

Constance grimaced and said: 'Then what?'

'Back to Liverpool, to the factory.'

Constance's colleague called again, for they had finished their inspection. She stood up and said: 'I must go. But you'll hear from me soon.' She touched his shoulder and shook her head sympathetically, which made Marshall feel ashamed. Then she was gone.

Some weeks later, a nurse brought Marshall a hand-delivered parcel. It contained a suit of clothes, and a brief letter from Constance asking Marshall to make contact with her when he was discharged. The clothes cheered him up somewhat but he was not certain that he would be in touch with Constance Castle. Though she had been there briefly, she was a part of the Paradise past that he had decided to forget.

3

Marshall was released from hospital in early March, with the dream of the skeletal nun still an occasional feature of his nights, leaving him exhausted the next day, but he was as well as he would ever be again.

Wearing the grey tweed suit Constance Castle had sent him, he travelled back to Liverpool, devoid of any definite plans except to collect his belongings and to start drawing a curtain of forgetfulness across the window of his failure, to delete the past that had brought him to England.

The moment he re-entered Toxteth a curious visceral thrill invaded him, as if he had reached home. He felt it most powerfully whenever passing strangers greeted him with a slight nod and whispered 'Bro'. 'Bro.' How that simple, truncated word resonated with warmth and acceptance, filled him with a powerful sense of having crossed an unmarked boundary between hostile and friendly territory.

But Marshall's plans received an immediate setback. The building which once housed the World's End Club had been reduced to a pile of rubble, and a vacant space, like a missing tooth, interrupted the elegant flow of the terraced street. Brown and white children played on the mounds of brick and plaster in the bright spring sunshine, seemingly oblivious to the dejected stranger who looked on from across the street. Then, mistaking him for an American GI, they swarmed around him with outstretched hands asking: 'Got any gum, chum?' He gave them the few sticks of chewing-gum in his possession, wondering what had happened.

It was the owner of another shebeen, an Ibo called Chucks, who brought him up to date on events in Toxteth. It seemed that

Holy Joe's past had caught up with him when a sinister-looking Kru sailor appeared in Toxteth one day and started asking for Joe, claiming that Joe owed him a vast sum of money. Joe must have known about the Kru's imminent arrival because some days before he had evicted his tenants, closed the club and vanished. Then one night, with the Kru sailor wandering around Toxteth threatening to kill various people whom he believed were hiding Joe, an almighty explosion destroyed the building. Whether it had been a flying bomb or Joe had sneaked out of hiding and wrought that destruction was now speculation. And speculation that was secondary to the fact of the ruin, which now marked where the World's End Club once stood, serving as an undeniable monument to Holy Joe's reputation as a clairvoyant protected by the spirit of his dead ancestors.

Chucks laughed knowingly as he shared with Marshall the whispered speculations that Holy Joe had gone underground in Manchester, Cardiff or London, cities where he had families. The Kru sailor had, meanwhile, gone to South Shields on the strength of some misleading advice.

'That fellow better have X-ray eyes to find Joe. That Joe is one Anancy,' Chucks concluded, chuckling with a mixture of conspiratorial knowingness and triumph.

Chucks delivered his other piece of news with less amusement: Bernie Parker had died in a flying bomb attack in London, and Augie had returned to Trinidad with his brother's body. This information stunned Marshall, not least because he surmised that the incident had probably happened on the same night as the explosion which had knocked him senseless for over six months.

Marshall rented an attic room in a house near the Ibo Club. He frequented the club, and similar places, where he played cards for small stakes in smoky back rooms and affected a devil-may-care countenance. Although he had lost his purpose he had retained his luck. Money came so easily to him that some nights the card tables held no appeal, and he hugged the bar and got drunk on whisky, then he would walk back to his attic room through the cold vespertine light, too drunk and too tired to dream.

In the privacy of his room, sipping from the whisky bottle that was his companion while waiting for the night to arrive, he discarded the carefully cultivated mask of insouciance and wrestled with his future. He was tempted to stay in Toxteth, to make a home in this strange neighbourhood, free himself from the burdensome chains imposed upon him by the Sarjeant family. It seemed a cruel irony that he who had wanted a quiet, peaceful life of watching sunsets over the sea and the rainfall on the mountains, to farm the sea, or failing that the land, inhale the intoxicating odour of the earth after a heavy rainfall, should now be in permanent exile. His mission to save the unborn children of Paradise from Sybil's curse seemed like an evil trick of fate. He was trapped in a Toxteth of the mind, a wasteland of nostalgia and an uncertain future. But come the evening, he washed, put on the tweed suit, and, depending on his mood, went in search of a card game or a bar to prop up.

It was Barbara who finally drove him out of Liverpool. She was one of several young women who hung out at the Ibo Club night after night, ostensibly in search of a good time, actually looking for love and escape across the invisible wall which encircled Toxteth, but prepared to accept the comforting arms of a stranger who might praise their beauty. And if he stole away with the morning light they would settle for some notes left on the dressing table, and continue clinging to the dream of being transported by love. It had been done before: women who had married American GIs and migrated with their husbands to the States had become legendary figures. But Babsy, as most people called her, would never be one of those women. She was always the one who made her way home alone, late at night or early morning, or ended up with someone who wanted to put her on the street or beat her black and blue with his black anger. The handsome, decent

GIs could not see her beauty, only the withered left arm with the limp, lifeless, dangling hand like a flower broken on its stem; only the stiff, awkward parodic dance which she often danced alone when the music moved her and nobody asked her to dance.

Marshall had seen her and she him, and they had exchanged pleasantries. Then one quiet weekday night some weeks after the war had ended, Marshall found himself sitting beside her at the bar, with music evocative of another, warmer island, and, moved by both the music and the request, he asked her to dance. They danced, once, twice, thrice and Marshall would later remember thinking at some time in the dance that her awkwardness was only evident when she danced alone because as he held her, as she pressed her not so young but youthfully eager body against him and clutched his back with her one good arm, he felt as though it was only in this brief union of bodies that she became whole, complete, normal. He was young, an inexperienced dancer, but it would be many, many years before he met another woman who blended so perfectly with his own rhythm, who anticipated every twist he made, and teased and emboldened him to follow her down unexplored paths of this language called dancing. Yet when he finished and felt her limp, lifeless left arm against his body, he was anxious to be free of her, to put some distance between himself and this disturbing, crippled beauty. But she would not let him go so easily.

The following day he could not find the will, nor see the point in going out, because his wallet was full. He had forgotten the dance with Babsy until a gentle, hesitant yet insistent knock roused him and when he opened the door to the first visitor to his attic room there she was: Babsy, breathing a little heavily from having climbed the stairs to the attic room, looking straight into his eyes with her own pale green eyes bright with desire.

He had been spoilt by the women who had slept with him for adventure and did not then know that love with a woman from his own people came with a price. He admitted her into that chilly attic room and laid with her on the stained, hard mattress of a bed rusty with memories of previous doomed couplings. How those weary bedsprings sang, sang out loud and clear; but their choral cautions, washed away in the profusion of sweat, fell on ears filled with the passionate music of release from loneliness. In union with his body, her own body acquired the suppleness of a dancer and they repeatedly declared love for each other.

She stayed with him for a whole week, leaving the attic room only to buy grocery and whisky. Towards the end of that week of hallucinatory love she became talkative, revealed in one unbroken monologue all the details of her life.

Her mother, Vivienne, had peddled love to sailors and she had been born from an error, an obdurate error which survived an attempted abortion. The birth of a curly-hair-thick-lipped-father-unknown-jetsam-from-a-ship-that-passed-in-the-night-brown-baby, with a floppy, dead arm had changed her mother. Vivienne had degenerated from regarding herself as a respectable member of the oldest profession into an accursed whore, a compulsive drinker, a pursuer of oblivion.

A sister, Bernadette, was born three years later, father also unknown. She was less dark but she sealed the coffin of her mother's irreversible banishment. Bernadette had a special kind of beauty, though. She radiated it in her smile and large blue eyes and crinkly straw-coloured hair. If she had wished, she could have passed for white, escaped the prison of colour. But Bernadette had been proud of her shade and that pride paid off because two years ago she married an African-American GI and now lived in Chicago with his family. She sent money to her mother once a month, which Vivienne wasted on alcohol.

While Vivienne was determinedly drinking herself to death, Barbara haunted the Ibo Club every night to escape from the sight of that interminably slow suicidal ritual. She, Barbara, had been mauled countless times by that miserable creature called betrayed love; had slept through many tear-stained nights with the icy cold spirit of unrequited love. Unlike the other women who hung about the Ibo Club she had given up hope of escape, until Marshall came along.

Her story moved him and he held her and whispered that she was beautiful, that he loved her. But when he woke up the following morning he began to recognise the quality of his error. He had confused pity with love. She had thrown her fragile, brittle heart at him; entrusted it to his trembling hands and he had caught it and was bound to let it drop to the hard ground of his own indifferent heart, breaking and scattering here and there like glass. Every day he thought of fleeing, but for some inexplicable reason, he stayed, postponing the inevitable. They danced every night at the Ibo Club, and each night their embrace became more desperate, as if they both knew that this romance, like spring or summer, was nothing more than a season. He dropped hints of departure, spoke of the need to find work. But she ignored these, praised his sensitivity, his goodness, which distinguished him from the men she had known, continued holding her head up high and proud as she walked through the streets with her man.

Then one July morning, when the sunlight streamed through the window and illuminated her face he was suddenly struck by her resemblance to Pharaoh. They shared the same proud face, and the longer he looked the more certain Marshall was that she bore the stamp of his former teacher. He recalled the delirious afternoons when Pharaoh talked about a woman he had loved in Liverpool after the First World War. Barbara, whose age he did not know because she refused to reveal it, could have been the offspring of that brief union. She could have been his cousin. He tried to get her to talk about her father, but she knew nothing about him. Yet he could not rid his mind of Pharaoh whenever he looked at her, and when he thought of Pharaoh he thought of his failed mission and his resolution to forget his past. He knew then that this season was coming to a close.

One August morning he stole aboard the Liverpool-to-London train, having drunk and danced late into the night with Barbara, chased the night with ominous fury and left her exhaustedly asleep in his bed. He was on the run from a crime of the heart and his conscience. Intermittently on the journey he imagined that he saw her standing at empty railway stations, above flower-strewn banks, amid cornfields, wearing her best dress, her limp arm at her side, weeping at his wretched cowardly flight.

Distraction from this inner turmoil came when the train stopped in Manchester and two men, both darker than the sun-baked farmers of Paradise, entered the compartment. The older one had a high, shiny forehead, hairline receding in the shape of a horseshoe, and a calm, rather self-important bearing. The younger man was deferential towards his companion.

Genuinely tired, after greeting them in the brotherly way all dark strangers greeted each other in England, Marshall closed his eyes in search of respite from Barbara's accusing ghost. Nevertheless he heard every word spoken by the two men, whom he surmised were Africans from different parts of that continent, for they spoke in English. He gathered that they had been in Manchester to arrange a meeting which would happen in the autumn, and the older man was pleased with the outcome of the visit. The younger man did not share this optimism, though: the rather doleful tone of his voice betrayed a pessimistic disposition, in spite of his easy laugh.

The older man chose his words carefully, as if distrusting the third person in the carriage. He alluded to a late-night conversation he had had and said with powerful conviction: 'Our cause has friends here. They understand, they will help.' The younger man iterated his scepticism by recalling the difficulty he had experienced getting served in the hotel bar. The older man calmly and not without sympathy retorted: 'If I were to recall every instance of petty colour prejudice I suffered in America and since arriving here, you'd think that my optimism was misplaced, wilful blindness born of insanity. But I do believe that times are changing. In a peculiar sort of way, though I would never dare say this in public, we have something to thank Mr Hitler for.'

Marshall opened his eyes, found the older African looking directly at him and closed them again quickly as if satisfied that he'd signalled his incredulity.

The younger African also wore an expression of disbelief and the older man allowed a long moment of silence to pass before he continued. 'Look at it this way,' he said softly, as if the compartment walls might have heard his blasphemy, and told this parable.

'A long time ago a certain chief led his people into a victorious war against a neighbouring people. The conquered people became slaves, minions, and the chief's people enjoyed decades of prosperity. They built vast cities, great monuments; their artists and thinkers flourished, their storytellers invented long and elaborate tales extolling their virtues and justifying the continued subjugation of the subject people. But one day the chief's own people were threatened with invasion by an aggressive neighbour from the north. The enslaved people and the chief's friends rallied to his support, for despite the unfairness of the chief's regime, they recognised in the aggressor a potentially far worse ruler. With the help of their allies, the chief's people repelled the envious aggressor. At the end of the war, the chief, now an old man, his head white with wisdom, counted the dead among his own people, his supporters and those of his enemies, surveyed the war ruins of his chiefdom and, in a moment of epiphany, realised that he could not rebuild his chiefdom without risking another destructive war. So he granted all his subject peoples freedom. And there was peace everywhere.'

Marshall opened his eyes again and kept them open as the older African went on calmly: 'You see, we stand at a crossroads in history. There can be no going back to the past, the empire is dead and we must give it a dignified burial by seeking the co-operation of those within the empire who understand the significance of the moment. Unfortunately, it will be a protracted and at times painful process. There will be more wars, but not, I pray to God, on the scale of the one we have just experienced ...'

Eerily, Marshall heard an echo of Pharaoh's voice in the older African's, and that compelled him to strike up a conversation with these men. He started by expressing his scepticism of the older African's analysis of the historical moment: 'If only the world were as simple as that in which your enlightened African chief lived,' Marshall said.

Unruffled, the older African smiled and said: 'I doubt that such a chief ever existed and if he did the council of elders would have dethroned him on the grounds of insanity and replaced him with somebody sensible.' He laughed sonorously.

Thus started a conversation between Marshall and the two Africans which lasted until they reached London. The older African dominated the conversation. His name was Martin Mayini and he had studied in the United States, travelled extensively through that vast nation and seen much that he admired there, despite its many shortcomings. He expatiated at great length on his dreams of African independence and unity, spoke with such confidence about its inevitability that Marshall was left in no doubt that it was not a matter of if, but when.

Listening to Mayini discourse on world affairs and the place of the African in them, Marshall felt as though he were being toyed with by the gods. They would give him no respite until he accepted his responsibility; they would force on him more encounters with men like Mayini, envelop him in the world of politics, regardless of his own apolitical wishes. How could he both make his own way through life and fulfil the duties imposed upon him by history? Was there space for both? While he had no answers to these questions, of one thing he was certain: Pharaoh's training had ensured that he would never be allowed to give expression to the real Marshall Sarjeant.

At Euston Station they swapped addresses, with Marshall giving them Patrick Boyle's address, where he would be staying. As they were parting Mayini invited Marshall to what he described as a Pan-Africanist meeting. Marshall was anxious to be on his way and said without conviction that he would try to attend. He shook the older man's hands, turned to walk away, but as he did so he heard a cry of pain. Mayini had stumbled and fallen; his assistant was some yards away, and Marshall rushed to help him up.

Dusting himself down and thanking Marshall profusely, Martin Mayini said: 'For some reason I feel this will not be the last time you come to my assistance.'

Out on Euston Road, Marshall hurried through the crowds, determined to put as much distance as possible between himself and the Africans. He sensed that he would meet Mayini again; the man emanated something of a destiny shared. But as he threaded his way along, he was aware too of being in this great city called London, and something about it appealed to his youthful energy. Here, he thought, a man can begin again.

4

This time round, London welcomed Marshall with kinder arms, embraced him, engaged him by expanding his world to such a degree that he had little time for debilitating self-reflection. Subsisting on a few hours of dreamless sleep, he ran through the city like a child discovering a new playground abounding in fantastic apparatuses. He devoured its sights, from Tower Bridge to Buckingham Palace to the East End slums; he admired its imperial architecture, marvelled at the destruction it had withstood as evidenced in its innumerable bombed-out buildings and pockets of wasteland; he stole glances at women whose beauty demanded attention; he watched military parades; he imbibed intoxicating ideas such as revolution, communism, pacifism, Pan-Africanism; he found friends among a disparate legion of men searching for a path across a city nursing the lacerations of war, itching to remove the constricting plasters over its wound, and overshadowed by universal fears that unless humanity mended its self-hatred and warmongering ways its future lay in the same path as the dinosaur. He felt the sharp sting of racial insults, the fleeting warmth of strangers, and one morning, as he walked along Euston Road, he heard the quickening pulse of the city as it prepared to rise from its war-weary slumber.

Patrick Boyle, in whose house he lived for six months, had found a new Church in the Communist Party and brought to this faith the manic energy of the apostate whose new conviction is held with fear of a permanent loss of the ability to believe in anything at all. Gaunt, ascetic-looking, he could recite the entire content of the *Communist Manifesto,* investing whole passages with a liturgical tone, and held the rare distinction among his comrades of having read two volumes of *Das Kapital.* Apart from his party duties, he was a part-time student at a working men's college and a shop steward with the railway workers' union.

His little terraced house near King's Cross, bequeathed to him by his grandfather, a former railway worker, was a shrine to the communist cause. Breakfast and dinner were occasions for intense discussions: how to take advantage of the post-war uncertainty to reshape the world along communist lines and avoid a third world war.

For a time Patrick Boyle's communist circles completely absorbed Marshall. He even considered joining the party, but held back because it seemed to require of its members blind dedication to ideas that he did not entirely share. The party, he was certain, would in the long run turn him into an invisible man. Furthermore it would have left him with little time or energy to pursue his numerous other interests, not all of which were compatible with being a card-carrying communist.

Some months after arriving in London, Marshall ran into Martin Mayini in Holborn and the genial African invited him to hear him at Speaker's Corner one Sunday morning. Marshall went along initially out of curiosity, but went back on subsequent occasions because after listening to the eloquent man declaim the evils of colonialism and exalt the inalienable right of Africans to manage their own affairs, an idea began to form in his mind that their cause could also be his, a route to some kind of redemption, of creating harmony between what he wanted and what others expected of him, a vague notion of doing good in order to make amends for his failure, of paying homage to Nana Sarjeant, and silencing Pharaoh's harsh disembodied voice which occasionally waylaid him with accusations of wasting his life, of failing to become a duppy conqueror. Introduced to the Pan-Africanist network by Mayini, Marshall became a regular face at meetings held in halls and kitchens, helped to produce and distribute a small magazine on colonial affairs, and dipped his hands into his pocket when a brother looked hungry because the dreams of independence were then like the dreams of a pioneering artist, to be achieved only by self-sacrifice and privation and bloody-minded perseverance. And faith.

Neither the austere communists nor the exiled Pan-Africanists knew that when Marshall left their company after a meeting, no matter how late, he headed for Soho, to smoky basement nightclubs of bohemians and artists and drifters, where spivs made deals in dark corners, where African-American GIs danced with their English sweethearts to syncopated music played by itinerant jazz musicians, where fruity laughter signalled merriment as well as danger. Then to illicit gambling salons in back rooms where players swopped gambling tips between games of poker and kalooki. The experienced gamblers welcomed his presence at their table as an apéritif for the larger games which developed with the night and sometimes sent him home broke, compelling him to hock his clothes or, on one desperate occasion, find work in a factory for a few months. But they noticed that his luck exceeded skills that improved with every game.

Laconic in speech, with a quiet intelligence, a solitary but not unfriendly air and a taste for well-cut suits, Marshall danced across London wearing an imperturbable mask that concealed the angst of failure, the loneliness of the exile and a longing for love. Barbara had taught him that love always comes at a price, so he exercised tremendous self-restraint and avoided making eye contact with women who gave him those little friendly smiles that are really arrows of cupidity that lead ineluctably to the tears of broken hearts. If the need for feminine company coincided with a successful run at the card table, he bought the sort of love that came without duty and expired without money, leaving a rancid odour of guilt. The sort of love that placated, momentarily, a deeper hunger.

Constance Castle, the woman who had given him his first kiss, often entered his mind at such moments, arousing not a desire for love but for intimacy. He had written to thank her for the suit and then, as part of his effort to put his past behind him, refrained from making contact again. But one day, in between a Communist Party public meeting and an appointment with Martin Mayini, he saw a woman who looked so much like Constance that he started to approach her and realised his error only when she hastened away, no doubt alarmed at the prospect of being accosted by a 'coloured' stranger. Some days later, to appease his perturbation, he wrote Constance a letter. The reply, immediate, gave him a quiet satisfaction.

They corresponded for several months and her letters conveyed the impression of a woman settled into domestic harmony, with twin daughters, a war-wounded husband to care for, a house full of servants to oversee, and a job that was part of her contribution to the war. They were cheerful and filled with the minutiae of her domestic life. Knowing an ordinary person, someone who was not fighting for something, someone anchored in a definite space, living out the unvarying routines that he had once imagined would be his life, was pleasant in the London of his exile.

It did not occur to him to seek a reunion with her and he would have contentedly continued corresponding until both got bored. But in the summer of '46, in the same letter in which she informed him that she had left her job with the Ministry of Health, Constance initiated a meeting.

They met on a fine July afternoon on the steps of the Albert Memorial, the monument to the Consort of the imperial age, hidden from the bombers, as though its destruction would have rent some irreparable hole in the collective psyche of the nation. Wearing a beige raincoat, blue flowery silk headscarf and sunglasses, Constance seemed dressed for a clandestine rendezvous. None the less her smile was true and she pronounced his name in a tone of secret intimacy.

They walked to Kensington Gardens and sat in a secluded spot under a horse chestnut tree dense with dark green leaves, and all around them, under nearby trees, other couples were engaged in talk. She did not remove her sunglasses for a while, but when she took them off Marshall saw that she had not been trying to remain incognito but to conceal how much the war had aged her: shallow but distinct saucers darkened under her eyes, and when she loosened her hair from the scarf, the sunlight betrayed silver strands in brown hair thinner than he recalled in the frozen memory of his exile. He now recognised in that broad, freckled face, with its green eyes, an archetypal beauty he had seen in many other English women, but Constance Castle brought to it the elegance and refinement of class.

She remembered Paradise in an orgy of nostalgia for the mountains, the flowers, the sea, as though it were her last memory of peace before being caught up in the war, a glittering diamond polished and repolished over the terrible war years. She asked about Soledad, Scoop, Denzil Stewart and other Paradisians with such affection in her voice that it sounded as if they had been her dearest childhood friends. He told her what he could and enquired after her brother. Alexander Castle was, she reported, in Australia as a visiting scholar, was due back in London in a year, and hopeful that he would be selected for a parliamentary seat should a by-election arise.

Marshall ended the longest pause in their conversation when he said: 'You gave me my first kiss.'

'Yes, it was very forward of me, but at the time it seemed the only way I could express my appreciation for what had been a beautiful, almost magical day ... What will you do in London?'

'Try to create a Paradise here, maybe move on after a few years.'

'You sound like one who has lost something.'

'I don't mean to, but maybe I am. As I move around this

city, yes, I feel I've lost something, that somewhere in my past I was severed and displaced and in the process lost something.' Though he wanted to, he could say no more because to say more would have meant sharing a secret that marked the boundary of his desire for intimacy.

'I'm so happy the war is over,' Constance said. 'Sometimes I feel it changed my life, stripped me of the power to choose.'

'Would you have made other choices?'

Her quiet answer exposed the cheerful letters as works of fiction. She had sacrificed her youth to the war, laid on that bloody altar all her carefreeness and personal ambitions. In its afermath she now saw how far it had deflected her from the life she had once envisaged for herself. She had married a handsome RAF officer, given birth to twin daughters, Jessica and Penelope, twice endured the news that her husband had been shot down behind enemy lines, nursed him back to health the first time, to see him returned to her on the second occasion in a wheelchair, crippled, uncertain whether he would ever walk again, prone to violent mood swings. Her subordinates at the Ministry of Health secretly used to call her Constant Constance because she was trustworthy, unwaveringly reliable, dedicated. She served on charity boards, and between these public duties managed a household which included her crippled husband, the twin girls, a nanny, and four full-time servants, and she was profoundly unhappy.

'Am I wrong to feel this way, Marshall? Am I being selfish?' she finished.

'I don't know, Constance. I'm still trying to work it all out for myself. I'll share with you any answer I find.'

She laughed, the laughter dispelled the gloom, and they spoke about happier times. Marshall shared with her the ideas he had discovered, and she recalled amusing incidents from the war. And so the afternoon slipped into an evening when the setting sun cast a red sky over the city, and in the stillness of the park the war seemed like a century away.

As Marshall walked her back to the Albert Memorial, Constance said: 'Thank you for a lovely afternoon, again.'

'I should thank you,' Marshall said. 'It's your city and I wouldn't have discovered the pleasure of sitting in a park without you.'

'One of the better legacies of our Victorian forebears. This and the railway.'

He watched her disappear down Exhibition Road, then headed home, feeling that in their nostalgia, the swapping of complaints, in her fragrant scent, he had experienced intimacy and it felt good to be alive on this fine summer evening. When he reached King's Cross he realised that his watch had stopped at the exact hour of their appointment.

They met again some months later in Regent's Park, with London resplendent in autumnal colours of gold and russet, even on the wastelands. With more time on her hands, Constance had been attending to neglected family matters and one in particular preoccupied her. Mrs Castle, who had been living in California, was back in London and, Constance feared, in poor health. An inveterate eccentric, she spent an inordinate amount of money on astrologers, tarot card readings, seances to speak to her late husband, Constance's father. Her lovers had got younger and she drank gin in frightening quantities. Constance rued her childhood of boarding-schools and separation from her mother, who now seemed to be more distant than ever, and their recent reunion had exposed how little they knew each other. And now it was too late because Mrs Castle lived in the permanently sad world of the alcoholic.

'She told me that madness runs in the family on her side,' Constance said worriedly.

She further stripped away the veneer of contentment that Marshall had mistakenly attributed to her by mentioning her mother's upbringing in an orphanage.

'Did you know that's why we were in Jamaica? Mother has it fixed in her head that an ancestor of hers came from

Paradise, somewhere in the West Indies. But she has no name for him or her. That's why we visited six islands with towns called Paradise back in '39. It's just a wild, fanciful notion.'

'It's not that wild,' Marshall said, recalling the many Sarjeants who had left Jamaica and disappeared for ever.

'I do wish she would cut down or stop drinking,' Constance said, and then, as if hearing her own tone of maternal solicitude and disapproval, she laughed and they spoke about lighter things.

Before they parted she said: 'Marshall, be my friend.'

'But I've been that since you gave me my first kiss,' he said, and they laughed, and stole a fleeting embrace, then went their separate ways. He was confident that he had a friend in Constance, felt stronger for that certain knowledge and was puzzled why his watch had stopped again on the hour of their meeting.

It was shortly after the second encounter with Constance that Marshall began to experience a run at the card tables that professional card players dream of. The table in the Tropicanos on Berwick Street, run by an urbane but lugubrious, rubbery-faced Afro-Cuban called Santos Santeria, favoured him, sent him strolling into a crisp cold bright morning with more money than he had ever had, sent him floating on a stratospheric high, and he felt as though the gods of the city had smiled on him. But four days later the impassive veterans sent him out into a chilly friendless morning, broke, with the mocking laughter of the capricious gods pursuing him along Euston Road. For the next few months he chased another big win but it remained elusive.

One night, prematurely retired by the merciless rapacity of the veteran card players, he was treated to a consoling drink by Santos Santeria. With avuncular concern, Santos told Marshall that he had once owned the Tropicanos and lost it in a poker game. He had had no need to continue playing – the club gave him a living – but he had not known when to stop and like Icarus he had flown too close to the sun. Only the magnanimity of the new owner, who employed him as the manager, had saved Santos from sleeping the final sleep in the cold, wet arms of the River Thames.

'I tell you this,' Santos said, 'because one day you will win very big, you have luck, and you must not make my mistake.'

As Christmas neared, Santos paid Marshall the honour of introducing him to Tony Gillam, a Maltese who ran a table above an off-licence on Edgware Road. Tony Gillam's table changed his life.

On that night a brilliant full moon hung in a taut wintry London sky, the River Thames snatched restlessly at the Embankment, lovers quarrelled, drinkers became violent, the dying gave up their rage against the fading light. On that night, you knew the morning would bring a palpable calm and some subtle rearrangement in the order of humanity's affairs.

Harry Bough was the biggest loser. Bough had inherited a London chain of pawnbroking shops, and spent much of the war years sinking into a life of dissipation. He had long been careering towards ruin when on this night of lunar madness, in the poker game that climaxed a run of extravagant bets, he gambled an entire building on a full house, jack high, against Marshall's possible poker of fours. In the calm of the morning, Tony Gillam said: 'Gentlemen, we'd better call it a night.' Bough was an honourable man: two days later he signed the deeds over to Marshall, simply said, *'C'est la vie,'* and strolled away down Edgware Road, towards Marble Arch, like a man utterly at peace with the prospect of death.

When Marshall Sarjeant surveyed the Praed Street building its size shocked him: a cavernous basement, and three floors of rooms. What was he to do with it? He strolled through Hyde Park, down to the Serpentine and as he stood there gazing at the icy surface, inspiration touched him like a warm breeze in winter: he would open a nightspot and call it the Island Club.

5

Between deciding on the Island Club and its opening in the first month of '48, Marshall worked with frenetic energy to create a space from his imagination. Over the Christmas period workmen installed a bar and stage in the basement and he spent the next few weeks painting the walls. He festooned the basement ceiling with plastic bananas and pineapples and tropical leaves, and a pair of papier-mâché coconut trees – all bought from an auction in an East End warehouse – framed the small elevation which served as a stage. Simultaneously, he found a Maltese barman, and two English waitresses.

Advertised by word of mouth and in the various small magazines circulating in London's minuscule African and West Indian population, the opening evening was attended by a cross section of Marshall's friends, from communists and African nationalists, to card players who were disappointed that he would not be running a table. A quartet of Caribbean jazz musicians, who had been in London since before the war, entertained the guests.

Constance revealed a new side to her character by arriving with a group of thespians wearing outlandish clothes. Patrick Boyle seemed out of place until he fell into conversation with a Trinidadian communist. Martin Mayini arrived late and gave a brief speech, which sounded more as if he were welcoming a new-born baby than a nightclub. Everyone congratulated Marshall on his good fortune. The dance area was not large but it would suffice, and the twenty tables were covered in red check cloths like the bandanas worn by women on the island of his exile's memory. He gave his closest friends guided tours of the building and outlined his plans to open a restaurant on the ground floor with a private dining-room above it. The top floor – a later addition to the original building, and less spacious, but with a southerly view through a wall of windows – was Marshall's private quarters.

The Island Club was not an immediate success. The little Soho nightspots, more centrally located, were also more accessible and better known. None the less it attracted a steady stream of customers who seemed to enjoy its lack of popularity. But when Marshall booked Harvey and Ellen Jackson, an African-American piano player and his wife, whose repertoire of bluesy songs had taken them through war-torn Europe, the Island Club experienced its most successful fortnight. American GIs brought their sweethearts there, avoiding the rather notorious spots in Soho which were inseparable from the street trade; bohemians and artists got to hear about it, and gathered at its tables to discuss art and existence and listen to the music of a people who had invented nothing but whose songs, harvested from fields of suffering, reached out to all sentient beings.

From the outset Martin Mayini and his friends were regular patrons of the Island Club. Mayini kept a tab, and always had the same table where he and other Africans would converse for hours about independence.

Occasionally Mayini loosened up there, danced, and one night, merry with drink – though not drunk for he was an abstemious drinker – he said to Marshall: 'When I become President of Kinja you will bring your nightclub to our capital city.'

The proprietor of the Island Club laughed, not because Mayini had said something preposterous, but because Marshall suddenly recognised that, in spite of his failure, he would reach Africa.

'It would be a great honour,' he said, forgetting that Mayini's tab, unpaid for weeks, had reached an unacceptable level.

'Then we will dance the dance of independence late into the African night,' Mayini said.

It was already apparent to Marshall that Mayini possessed some quality that inspired belief and loyalty. The Kinjaian held his convictions without fear or doubt, and was distinguished from his African nationalist brethren by a vision not only of an independent Africa, but also a united Africa – from Alexandria to Cape Town, from Dakar to Mombassa, from the Nile to the Zambezi – that reached out to the descendants of Africans taken into slavery. With Indian independence achieved, African independence did not seem so fantastic a goal, but Mayini's insistence that it would be meaningless without unity promoted him to the rank of a colossal visionary.

'You see, the old man, the European, is tired,' Mayini continued. 'For centuries now he has persuaded himself that we Africans are children, undeserving of freedom until we have learnt the rudiments of civilisation. The war has humbled the old man, he has seen that his civilisation is an inherently destructive one. We Africans now need to set an example of an alternative future, one built on fundamental respect for the oneness and indivisibility of humanity. There are some who say that the twentieth century will become a battleground between communist and capitalist ideas. I say that may well be true, but regardless of whether communism or capitalism triumphs, as long as the philosophy is practised which holds one race superior and another inferior, then there will be war.'

That night, having closed up and retired to his apartment above the Island Club, Marshall stood by the window and looked south, towards Marble Arch and Buckingham Palace and the River Thames. As he stood gazing at the sky, it began to drizzle, an unusual drizzle with individual drops striking the window. Then it started snowing. The flakes floated and spun and touched the glass and turned to a film of melting ice. Soon the grey roofs were covered in a white blanket, and a nearby bomb site was defined by white.

He felt strangely at peace with himself and thought about all Mayini had said, and remembered all the sorrowful scenes he had witnessed during the war. At that moment, watching the snow fall over London, it seemed to him that the gods of the city had given him a second chance, had renewed his purpose, transformed it from one focused on himself and the Sarjeant family, to one focused on an entire continent and ultimately all humanity. On that night he recognised in sharper terms than he had ever done before that he was a man of the new world returned to the old world, as part of an inescapable personal destiny, to help shape the future.

Late in the spring of '48, Marshall was one of eight men in attendance at a meeting above the Island Club, in what would later become the restaurant. Mayini had called together two other Kinjaians, a Nigerian, two Ghanaians, and two men from the Americas – including Marshall – to announce his intention to return to Kinja to agitate for independence.

'I have done all I can here. I am satisfied that our cause has friends, supporters and sympathisers. But I have been away from home for many years and feel that the time is ripe to return, to accelerate independence for Kinja and all Africa, and lay the foundation stones of African unity. It will be a long, hard road, brothers, but never let us lose sight of the ultimate goal. Let us not rest until all Africa is free; let us not go into the twenty-first century burdened by the Europeans' delusions of superiority; let us rise up and remind them that the pyramids, the oldest monuments to civilisation, are not located in Africa by accident, remind them it was on that continent that their ancestors first learnt to fashion tools. Let us build cities in the forests, roads across the savannah and plant flowers in the desert ...' Mayini ended his speech: 'Brothers, share with us your strength.'

Wade Mayana, a Kinjaian who was the oldest man present

and had the quiet authority of the scholar, the guardian of ancient rites, asked for a bowl and knife, and when Marshall arranged for these to be brought they were passed round the table and each man drew his own blood and as drops dripped into the bowl only the traffic noise could be heard.

Then Wade Mayana hummed a melody, stood and told a long tale of a people who had built monuments to their gods on the banks of a great river and when they offended their gods, how war and drought and famine sent them crossing a vast desert in search of the sea, and when they had settled, the unforgiving gods sent pirates and warmongers to inflict further suffering on them.

Dr Kenneth Braithwaite, the other West Indian present, spoke next, and recalled the slave trade, the middle passage, and the iniquities of the slave plantations that caused the African to despise himself, and how independence for Africa would end that self-contempt. 'Freedom for Africans,' Braithwaite said, 'will mark the beginning of a higher level of freedom for us in the diaspora.'

From being a sympathiser and supporter of the African nationalist cause Marshall became a player. The independence cause would need men in London, the heart of the empire, to keep the momentum going, and he would be one of them. He felt honoured to have been included in the ceremony above the Island Club, and in the days that followed he became more voluble, more willing to express his own opinions. Ownership of the Island Club had already given him the air of a man of property, now he had the air of a man who knew where he was going, a man of destiny. He was slower in his movement, his voice deeper, and he began to cultivate private habits such as ensuring that he daily listened to the news on the wireless and read a newspaper. Seen in the Island Club he was quick to smile as was necessary to make his customers feel relaxed, but behind that practised amiability was a man who gave careful and serious thought to the issues that preoccupied world leaders.

The farewell party for Martin Mayini was held in August and used all the facilities of the Island Club for one night, thus sealing its reputation as a place of relaxation for political activists. The small stage was draped with the future Kinja flag – three horizontal bands in red, gold and green – and the Kinjaian community, a small almost invisible minority scattered in English universities, turned out in force for the occasion. A handful of communists, two Labour Members of Parliament, their wives and the English wives and girlfriends of Kinjaians, were the only Europeans present. There was much pouring of libation, and long farewell speeches littered with proverbs, calling on the gods to bless Mayini's voyage, and heaping encomiums on him and his parents, all his illustrious ancestors, children and unborn children. A trio of Kinjaian singers, London University geology students wearing resplendently voluminous robes, sang a cappella ancient songs, evocative of seas and forests and savannah.

Marshall had seen and heard Mayini speak on numerous occasions, but that night the Kinjaian mesmerised his well-wishers with a valedictory speech of extraordinary brilliance. This dazzling performance was briefly interrupted by heckling from a balding Kinjaian who accused him, in English, of betraying his mother's people by aligning himself with the majority tribe, the Ekans, his father's people. The heckler was silenced by the unanimous protestation of Mayini's admirers, and for the rest of the evening alternated between sullen muteness and drunken outbursts that further isolated him. Like everyone else present, Marshall was overwhelmed by Mayini's charisma and eloquence. Such was the urgency of the independence moment that any distraction was ignored like a malodorous scent wafting through a genteel gathering. Marshall, who had yet to experience the reality of Africa, was still then subscribing to an idea of Africa in which all Kinjaians were one, and Mayini, bathed in an iridescent aura, was their undisputed leader.

At some point in the night, that hour in a celebration

when the flow of alcohol has removed the masks that men wear, Mayini embraced Marshall and whispered into his ear: 'Remember this moment.' And Marshall would remember, for in that brief embrace, he sensed the palpitations of fear in Mayini's heart and saw doom in those bright brown eyes, and recognised that Mayini's courage was the courage of all great men because it persisted despite their fear.

In the weeks following Mayini's departure, Marshall set about opening the Island Club's restaurant. Work on refurbishing the ground floor had been completed and he now needed a chef. One afternoon, as he brooded over the qualities he would look for in a chef, he received an unexpected visitor. Carrying a small suitcase and looking like an Edwardian gentleman, he introduced himself as Mr Delisser. A thin, tall man with a slight stoop, his pencil-thin moustache curling up at the edges, he spoke with a superior air, as if he were doing Marshall a favour by enquiring about the vacancy which Marshall had not yet even advertised. He claimed to have worked in Paris, Havana, Bahia and New Orleans as a chef in exclusive restaurants frequented only by élite epicureans. He spoke at great length in sonorous language about the culinary arts, of which he was a supreme maestro, but stressed that the secret of a good meal, a fine meal, did not lie just in how it tasted on the palate – the myopic ambition of a lazy chef – but how smoothly it flowed through the digestive tract, climaxed in effortless bowel movements that infused one with a feeling of wellbeing such as might be experienced after a hot bath.

'That is the secret, *mon ami,*' he said. 'And crucial to achieving that effect are the herbs and spices that the alchemist of antiquity fought and killed for. The proof of the pudding is not just in the eating. No, my friend, it is also in that much maligned act, inseparable from eating, and essential to our humours.'

Mr Delisser talked his way into a job and Marshall was not

disappointed: the man's meals were not only sublime in taste, they produced the most wonderful evacuation as part of his morning ablutions.

The demands of the nightclub and restaurant now devoured most of Marshall's time, though he never missed the monthly meeting with Wade Mayana, Kenneth Braithwaite and other nationalists. Ensuring that the bar was well stocked jostled for attention with the hiring of musicians – London then teemed with entertainers – and waitresses, who were all too often young women looking for lovers and therefore quick to abandon their jobs. And looming above these routine demands was Mr Delisser.

Mr Delisser insisted that his creole dishes would neither taste right, nor have the desired purgative after-effect without the freshest fruit, vegetables and meats. Tinned food, Mr Delisser maintained, was an abominable crime against the discerning palate and comparable in its coagulative effect on the colon, that most crucial digestive site, to eating wet cement. The arduous task of procuring the scarce fresh produce fell on Marshall, who was not above being rebuked in the most excoriating terms by the punctilious chef. To keep Mr Delisser happy, he sedulously cultivated contacts with spivs, who seemed to control everything. When they failed him it was not unusual for him to close the Island Club at two a.m., sleep for an hour, then set off to trawl round Smithfield, Covent Garden and Billingsgate Markets in an old van that he used for ferrying supplies. And at that early hour of the morning, he felt as though the city belonged to him.

6

The Island Club oscillated between dire dull nights and nights when a fantastic energy flowed, between sessions when a single couple danced on the small floor and sessions when the tables seemed like obstacles to the principal purpose of the moment: to dance. Such a night happened in late November when a barrel-chested man strolled, uninvited, on to the stage where a trio played, took out an alto saxophone from a black bag, hooked it around his neck and began to blow notes which did not belong to this world and transported first the drummer, then the guitarist and the pianist – demanding of them skills they did not know they possessed – and then everyone in the Island Club. Afterwards, after the strange sax player left, following two hours of vertiginous flight, some people said it was Bird and others that it was Dizzy and both were equally right.

It was shortly after that exceptional night that something extraordinary happened: the *Empire Windrush* docked at Tilbury with over three hundred migrants from the West Indies. Hundreds of thousands more would arrive over the next decade. Men in zoot suits and Panama hats, men with stylish walks. Lured here by appeals to help rebuild the Mother Country, by the death convulsions of empire, they came clutching their past in fragile suitcases and their hopes in passports which declared them British subjects.

They roamed across the city in search of room and board, and congregated in the poorest, most run-down neighbourhoods – like Brixton, Paddington, and Ladbroke Grove – between the wastelands of a dying imperial city. They got into scrapes with some native men whose aggression owed much to the atavistic instinct to protect their women, an aggression all the more ferocious because these subjects of empire, these patent outsiders, bore British names, claimed to be insiders, and some had obscure ancestral roots in the shires of England, the highlands of Scotland, the valleys of Wales. Signs of an ancient loving. They colonised pub corners where they reminisced about home and swapped anecdotes on their experience of being immigrants. And soon enough, as if it were a pioneer outpost created specially for them, they discovered the Island Club.

Marshall welcomed the newcomers but he was not at ease with them. They seemed like naive islanders who had been reared on a myth. Initially, he felt compelled to disabuse them of the notion that the streets of London were paved with gold. He told them about Liverpool where the small African population huddled together for safety, about the profound and pervasive antipathy towards people of colour. But these men laughed at him, pointed to his own good fortune in owning a night club and restaurant – within walking distance of Buckingham Palace, no less – and charged him with selfishness. He soon gave up trying to caution them because he recognised that each man would make his luck or not. He wished them good fortune, gave them whatever advice he could on finding work and accommodation, and secretly hoped that they would make friends among the natives as he had done with Patrick Boyle and Constance Castle.

When a customer's expression betrayed that he had suffered some wounding insult or was missing home, Marshall was none the less capable of listening sympathetically. And not all had tales of woe to tell: a Barbadian once described how, when he saw the pavement in Holland Park Avenue covered in the golden leaves of the plane trees, he knew there was gold to be found in this city, and a week later won a small fortune on the football pools. A Trinidadian married an Englishwoman within six months of arriving because her milk-white skin was matched by kisses that tasted as sweet as honey.

By the start of the new decade Saturday nights in the Island Club were electric. It was on such a night that a skinny man with a long face strutted into the Island Club with the flamboyant air of a circus master, beside him two beanpole-thin peroxide blondes whose exiguous raiments caused that night's drummer to miss a beat. It was Scoop Fearon.

Marshall recognised him, and when he went to Scoop's table there was a loud cry of disbelief as Scoop leapt up and hugged his friend as though he had never betrayed him, and Marshall hugged him in return as though he had never once wished the traitor dead. They could not talk then, but Scoop came back on the Monday and they repaired to the top-floor apartment and settled down over tumblers of rye whiskey, courtesy of an enterprising American GI who ran an illicit liquor trade.

Only the restaurant part of the club opened on Mondays, and Marshall trusted Mr Delisser to manage without him, so there was ample time to settle an old score with Scoop Fearon. He set about this with considerable cunning, plying Scoop with alcohol, and affecting the expression of naive credulity with which he had once, before his own baptism in the ways of the world, greeted Scoop's fantastic lies. He had met innumerable men like Scoop over the poker table, at bars, during the building works on the Island Club, and took pride in his ability to judge a man's character, to recognise the sincere from the insincere, the hustler from the businessman. Nevertheless, by the morning he found himself back in Paradise, unable to separate Scoop's truths from his lies, knowing that Scoop was lying but not sure what he was lying about. Only time would bring him to an understanding of Scoop Fearon's unique gift: he believed his own lies so completely that they amounted to alternative interpretations of reality.

Consequently Marshall was not sure what to make of Scoop's account of his life in the intervening years. According to Scoop he had laboured on a sugarcane plantation in Cuba until he got a chance to go to America. There he had landed up in New York and been forced to live off his wits, worked for a Harlem numbers runner called Daddy George, a garrulous, gargantuan man who boasted that his grandfather had come from the islands and on account of that he was soft on islanders. He recalled the scrapes he got into, the enemies he made, the friends who saved him, though these were not as reliable as the guns he had owned. After two years in Harlem he was sitting pretty, drove a Buick, ate in the best restaurants, wore the finest suits and had the keys to several apartments occupied by the most delicious and accommodating women that any man could wish for.

Then one day his employer, Daddy George, called him into his office and with him was a short, not pretty but not ugly either, woman who had the refined air of college education. She was Daddy George's daughter. Then Daddy George, who trusted Scoop completely, went into a long spiel of how he was an only child and how his wife, whose portrait dominated the office, had found higher ground prematurely, leaving him to bring up their only child, unable to look at another woman, and how he had always seen himself building an empire that would last for generations but how on account of his condition he had only been able to father one child and she was the most precious thing to him and now he wanted to see that child happy.

Scoop said he didn't see it coming, and should have done when Daddy George started flattering him about how they were alike in character, their gritty determination, their ambitiousness; that the blood of islands flowed in their veins. And he was flattered, thought he was just doing Daddy George a favour when the doting father gave him Roxelle's telephone number and suggested that he might want to take that beautiful girl out for an evening. He obliged dutifully.

One night he took her to a quiet speakeasy on Lennox Avenue, and spent four anxious hours worrying whether

Chantelle, one of his ladies, would be home later that night because he was hungry for some serious loving and had already decided that the demure, bespectacled Roxelle was not, was definitely not, his type. Even when they danced close, cheek to cheek, thigh to thigh, his Pete refused to stir, remained as limp as a dead snake. But when he took Roxelle home he erred in accepting her invitation to come up for a nightcap because two mornings later he crawled away from her apartment with every muscle in his body aching and needed three whole days of sleep to recover from the voracity of her loving.

After that his life acquired a dreamlike quality. Next thing he knew he was walking up the aisle of the Abyssinian Baptist church dressed in tails, a top hat and white gloves, then slipping a diamond ring on to Roxelle's finger while Daddy George looked on, six foot six and 300 pounds of supreme paternal pride and happiness, and five hundred guests.

Daddy George presented them up with a palatial apartment on Riverside Drive, a maid, a car and twenty-four-hour chauffeur. And when three months later Roxelle announced that she was pregnant Scoop was still dreaming, and when she gave birth to triplets, two boys and a girl, he was still dreaming, and thought that there couldn't be a greater monument to his manhood.

With Roxelle engrossed in the demands of triple motherhood, Scoop went in search of his neglected girlfriends, but didn't think anything of it when he discovered that they had all changed their locks. One had even moved to Chicago. He thought she was only upset with him because he had married and she had been particularly sweet on him and was always saying that she wanted to have his baby. Then he noticed that the bars in Harlem were always closed to him, as if the whole neighbourhood was conspiring to keep him on the straight and narrow path of fatherhood and marriage.

That suspicion was horribly confirmed on the day he saw one of his old girlfriends, Maveline, a southern gal with one of those whining accents and kisses that were sweeter than guava jelly. She was dance-walking down 125th Avenue and when Scoop called to her she hurried away as if he were the man from the IRS. When he caught up with her, he found that she had clearly been running from him, and that she was scared, and it was from Maveline that he learnt what had happened. Daddy Joe had put word about that she – and all of Scoop's ladies – was to keep away from Scoop Fearon, his son-in-law, and if she didn't her job would be the least important thing that she would lose.

It was only then that things began to make sense to Scoop: the bartenders who always enquired after his wife and children and who sent him home in a cab when he had had one drink too many; the friends who only took one drink with him then hurried away; the persistent feeling of being watched once he stepped outside the apartment. He was a prisoner in Harlem.

He tried to adjust to this not altogether unpleasant sentence, marriage, fatherhood and freedom from want. He spent his days playing with his triplets, sought pleasure in their triple cooing. When Roxelle's monstrous sexual appetite revived, fuelled by a diet of roast yam, pork and collard greens, he went into battle each night with the courage of St George but each morning emerged with his feeble lance broken on the impenetrable pachyderm of her insatiable appetite. But he abandoned any attempt to reconcile himself to this domestic incarceration after Roxelle's stomach began to swell again, filling him with fear that she would once more give birth to triplets. He slumped into despair, and involuntary dreams of flight, escape, freedom invaded his mind. When the midwife announced that Roxelle had earned a place in the record books with a second set of triplets, he wandered up into Manhattan and drank himself into oblivion.

Recovering from that binge, he started to plan his escape. A wife whose fecundity had made the *American Scientific Review,* a father-in-law who would stop at nothing to ensure his daughter's happiness – it was too much for him. One day he emptied a secret account he kept, bought himself a counterfeit passport, left a pile of clothes on the Brooklyn Bridge and that same morning boarded a flight to Paris, free to resume his roaming. Now and again he was stricken with guilt but on the whole he wasn't worried. Daddy George would look after the children and maybe one day, when he recovered his manhood, Scoop would return to Harlem.

Marshall listened to Scoop with sympathy and outrage and laughter. Nevertheless he remained determined to get Scoop to confess the theft of the treasure map. He did this in a circuitous way, told Scoop about how somebody had broken into Pharaoh's cabin, knocked the old man out and had stolen the map. Scoop seemed genuinely surprised, but Marshall was not fooled by his incredulity. He said that Pharaoh had seen his attacker as clear as day and described him and named him: Scoop Fearon. Scoop leapt up indignantly and said that Pharaoh must have been mistaken because by then he was in Port Columbus and besides, how could he have seen the thief in the dark? Marshall was then more direct. He said only three people knew about the map, Pharaoh, himself and Scoop.

At this point Scoop's defence crumbled and he admitted that he had indeed stolen the map, but swore that he had not meant to injure Pharaoh. When Pharaoh woke up, fearing that he would be seen, Scoop had struck him over the head with a pot, and run. In his plea for mitigation, he said he'd been so infatuated with Soledad that he would have killed to get her. Stealing the map it seemed to him then was the only way he could secure the sort of wealth that would enable him to win her love.

When Scoop mentioned Soledad, Marshall heard a sadness in his voice, as if he had truly left all his love with Soledad and no other woman could repair his broken heart. But when Marshall asked whether he still loved Soledad, Scoop dismissed the question with an exaggerated 'Naw', claiming that he had met and had women who made Soledad look like a hag and he had abandoned them.

But what had happened to the map? Marshall demanded.

Here Scoop's account of his adventures since leaving Paradise, though fantastic, echoed Pharaoh's account of his confrontation with the spirit of Alegba. The map led Scoop to a spot some thirty miles north, some yards from the most hideous banyan tree he had ever seen, a monumental plant draped in vines which hung off it like ropes, holes which resembled eyes, an immense knot like a nose and another hole which seemed like a mouth.

He began digging with the spade he had brought. The ground was hard, and he dug all day and then slept. When he woke up in the morning the spot where he had dug had been covered over. Undaunted, he attacked it with the spade again and kept on digging until sunset, cutting his way through the roots of the banyan tree. Then at last he struck something solid, wooden. But at this point, with the night fully descended, he saw, standing over the hole he had dug, a bald-headed man with gold earrings, his muscles thick and an expression of murderous grimness on his face. Thinking that the stranger had come to steal his find, Scoop tried to drive him off, but the man leapt in the hole and wrestled him to the ground, shouting what sounded like some dialect of Spanish or some strange language.

When they had been wrestling for some time Scoop realised that the hole they were in was deepening, its lips disappearing. At that point he decided that something was amiss, he threw the stranger to the ground, and scrambled out of the hole. As he stood over it, he saw the roots of the banyan tree pressing down on the casket and the stranger sinking further and further into the earth until he was looking into a bottomless hole, a dark void. By now he realised that he had fought a duppy, but not conquered it, and he was lucky to be alive. He ran for his life.

Marshall was laughing as Scoop finished. He had not heard

such an outrageous lie for years. Scoop did not, however, laugh. He ordered Marshall to stop laughing and insisted that he had told the truth. He, Scoop, had really fought a duppy and lost, and that moment of defeat had also marked the moment when he had stopped loving Soledad.

'And what did you do with the map?' Marshall insisted.

'I posted it back to Pharaoh. I knew it wasn't mine and what it led to would never be mine. Anyway, that's all in the past,' Scoop said, 'another continent, another island. Right now, I need work, Marshall, badly. And you're just the man to help me.'

It was already clear to Marshall that Scoop was in need of help, that he had fallen into some deep hole. And while he did not doubt Scoop's ability to claw his way back to the surface, he was profoundly uncertain as to whether he should extend a helping hand. Scoop's betrayal had hurt him too deeply for him to forgive lightly.

'We'll talk about it in the morning,' he told Scoop. And on that note they went to bed, with Scoop sleeping in the spare room.

The following morning Marshall woke up early and went to Hyde Park. It puzzled him that Pharaoh had never mentioned the return of the map, but unable to work out why, he dwelt instead on a more urgent concern: should he employ Scoop? Everything Scoop had said suggested that he was reckless, irresponsible and dishonest. Yet Marshall could not deny the affection he still felt for his incorrigible boyhood friend. As in the Paradise days, Scoop's presence served to remind him of what a solitary and ultimately lonely life his own temperament encouraged. Should he or should he not readmit Scoop? He asked himself this question a thousand times as he strolled round the park. Unable to arrive at an answer, he took a coin from his pocket, tossed it in the air, and watched it fall to the ground. Heads he would employ Scoop; tails he wouldn't. But as if reluctant to bear the onerous burden of deciding for him, the coin rolled and came to a stop against a small stone, with the head showing. That was good enough for Marshall. Years later he would regret that he had not tossed that coin again.

But that was several years later. For Scoop soon proved himself a hard-working and invaluable member of the the Island Club staff. In fact, if Mr Delisser was responsible for the popularity of the restaurant, then Scoop was the moving force behind the basement. His knowledge of the latest stateside music was encyclopaedic and he had a surer instinct than Marshall, whose taste did not extend beyond bluesy ballads.

After six months of general duties, Marshall appointed Scoop the house manager. It was Scoop who greeted customers with that broad smile and direct gaze, and moved about all night ensuring that people were comfortable, having a good time. When Scoop laughed everybody within earshot laughed with him. He simply possessed the gift of making people feel good. Scoop was in his element amongst these men. There was not a Caribbean island he had not visited, and to show his familiarity he would enquire after Gwyneth in Georgetown, Pauline in Port of Spain, Brenda in Bridgetown. 'You must tell me the brand of aftershave you use,' was his favourite line to men. And the ladies loved Scoop. He had an inexhaustible store of lines for massaging the female ego and could reel them off in Spanish, Portuguese, Dutch, French and even the obscure language of a little known South American tribe. When Scoop greeted customers at the door, he made them feel as if they were the most important people to cross the threshold of the Island Club in years.

His relations with the staff were not always helpful, though. Caught *in flagrante delicto* with a waitress in the storeroom by Mr Delisser, Scoop pleaded in mitigation, 'If a man can't appreciate the women of the country he's living in he's got no right to be there, he should move on.'

7

Marshall had unwittingly created a goldmine. The steady influx of immigrants from the Caribbean provided the basis for him to expand into property. He built a small and profitable portfolio of houses and shops around Paddington and Notting Hill. These mostly dilapidated, freehold properties were managed on his behalf by an estate agent who, not knowing the landlord's identity, must have thought it strange that the letters of instruction from his solicitors explicitly forbade any racial discrimination in their lettings policies. Their compliance ensured that a fortunate few among the newcomers escaped the bruising rejections which greeted so many elsewhere. Some of these tenants also discovered the Island Club as a place where they could relax on weekend nights, but none suspected that the fleshy, somewhat princely-looking restaurateur and nightclub owner also owned the roofs under which they slept.

In spite of his worldly success and his air of benevolent calm, Marshall was not at peace with himself. The private man, the man behind the mask, continued to be haunted by powerful feelings of loss and loneliness and failure. In the solitude of his top-floor apartment above the club, through overlong nights, vivid, macabre images of Nana Sarjeant, Pharaoh and the crippled children of Paradise drifted across the landscape of his dreams. On some nights Nana Sarjeant was a skeletal figure in a rocking chair on a bright red veranda and behind her stood Pharaoh, dressed in coral-black military regalia with sparkling gold buttons, while an unending procession of crippled children hobbled and crawled past them towards crimson mountains from which came, borne on the wind, peels of a chilling female laugh. On other nights, he dreamt that winged demons with filed teeth were nibbling at his heart while making clamorous conversation, as if his heart were an apéritif for a feast of his soul.

Quite by accident, he discovered a palliative in the form of his female employees. He acquired the habit of inviting, through Scoop Fearon, a barmaid or waitress to share his Sundays. When a particular young woman lost her ability to banish the dreams, to placate the demons, when the quality of her tenderness no longer gave him respite from their noisy voracity, when her body had yielded all its secrets, he swapped her for another one. Consequently, the turnover of female staff at the Island Club was phenomenally high. It did not matter that the proprietor had a reputation as an insatiable devourer of female flesh, a callous heart-breaker who was so corrupted by his power that he had lost the ability to feel or love. Scoop always seemed to know young women who were looking for work; and once Marshall had employed them, Jean Myers tried to encourage their early resignation from the job.

Marshall and Jean Myers had enjoyed several gloriously erotic Sundays together and in the throes of passion she had sworn undying loyalty to him. But he had soon tired of her and substituted her with another of his employees, abandoning Jean to pick up the pieces of her shattered heart. Another scorned woman would have left the job but Jean stayed on, with some toxic brew of masochism, desire for revenge and optimism fermenting deep inside her heart. She became the senior waitress, the stern major-domo whose infatuation with the seldom seen proprietor was obvious to the young subordinates to whom she lectured about the perils of accepting an invitation to Mr Serjeant's apartment.

Far from deterring her charges, Jean Myers's warnings had the opposite effect: she transformed Marshall into a mountain, the scaling of which became an irresistible challenge to young women determined to test the power of their beauty.

And when they felt themselves ready for the challenge, they sent surreptitious signals to Scoop Fearon, who dutifully guided them to the path which led to the mountain top and awaited the ineluctable fall which followed after Marshall had cooled on them, after his heart had frozen over and his indifference become a violent blizzard.

Constance Castle's visits to the Island Club probably did more to enhance the aura of mystique surrounding Marshall than Jean Myers's embittered strictures. During its early years her visits were infrequent and fleeting, and made en route to one or other of the appointments with which she filled her days. But over the years she developed the habit of dropping in during the afternoon to sit with Marshall in the basement as he auditioned a band. Constance would tap her feet to the music and laugh a curiously ebullient laugh, as if the near-empty club afforded her a rare chance to express some wild spirit which yearned for freedom, as if her presence in a place like the Island Club was a deliciously secret pleasure, a vice in an otherwise conventional life of privilege and wealth. Her impeccable manners and graceful poise distinguished her from the working-class English women and the small group of rather bohemian Whites who mingled with the club's mainly immigrant clientele. There was an air of mystery about Constance herself and the nature of her relationship to Marshall. The staff always received her as if she were a visiting dignitary. They never addressed her by name, always 'ma'am', and referred to her between themselves as 'the White Lady', Mr Delisser's coinage, or 'the English Lady'. The most common speculation, started by Jean Myers, held that she was the real owner of the Island Club and Marshall merely her employee. Far from undermining Marshall that rumour added to his charisma because it begged the question of what qualities he possessed to win the confidence and friendship of such an esteemed lady. Even Scoop Fearon, though he had once been to tea with her in Paradise, seemed somewhat restrained in her presence, as if he knew she was immune to his peculiar brand of flirtatious charm.

One afternoon, after Marshall had seen Constance into a cab, Scoop observed: 'Man, that lady looks like she needs some serious loving.' Now, Scoop was in the habit of releasing a lascivious chuckle and remarking of this or that woman that she was in need of serious loving. He was more often right than wrong. Just how right he was became apparent a week later on Constance's next visit.

Some hours before she arrived Marshall had learnt that the band he had hired for the approaching weekend had pulled out, leaving him with a disastrously blank weekend and the prospect of having to cope with disappointed customers. He was too distracted with exploring alternative arrangements to notice immediately Constance's pale, drawn face and general air of quiet anxiety. He was on the telephone when she arrived and took a seat opposite him at the corner table which often served as his office and where they had passed many hours in idle conversation over the years.

While trying to negotiate a reasonable fee with a Guyanese musician who claimed he could, as a favour, assemble a quartet for Saturday night, Marshall poured her a drink. She did not touch it; instead she lit a cigarette and the smoke which soon enwreathed her face accentuated the colour of her lipstick, making it seem uncommonly red. He winked at her and it was her failure to return this gesture of complicity which reminded him of Scoop Fearon's remark. It occurred to him then that admiration and gratitude had caused him to place Constance on a pedestal where she was beyond desire and possession. Had he allowed her wealth, her self-confidence, her belonging to a country in which he was a foreigner, to blind him to the simple and undeniable fact that she was a woman, not a goddess? Suddenly she turned her gaze to him and he was flushed with embarrassment. Agreeing to the exorbitant fee being asked by the musician, he hurriedly concluded the telephone conversation. Surmising that her somewhat melancholy appearance might have something to do with her children, who had recently been sent away to boarding-school and whom he knew she missed, he enquired after them.

She sipped from a glass of Scotch and said: 'The children are fine. But I'm not. I've left my husband, I've left Phillip.'

If Marshall had been less insensitive, less preoccupied with the Island Club and less self-absorbed he would have seen the signs which presaged Constance's revelation. Now he recognised them with the benefit of hindsight: how in the recent past her visits had become more frequent and lasted longer, as if she did not want to go home; her copious drinking, her chain-smoking. He admonished himself for his blindness and resolved to be a pillar of support for her in this crisis.

The full details of why Constance had left her husband emerged over the next few weeks in the capacious Notting Hill Gate apartment to which she had decamped from the family home. The apartment belonged to her mother, Frances Castle, and almost all its deep walls were covered in portrait and landscape paintings, hanging carpets and giant tapestries. Frances, Marshall learnt from Constance, had maintained the apartment for some years before the war as a love nest. It reeked of neglect and this musty odour was only attentuated by the scent of lilac, which mysteriously wafted from the bedroom at irregular intervals through the day.

Marshall called there on alternate afternoons, and ignored the mask of contentment which Constance wore, trusting his instincts that though she had not requested it, she needed his help. They would talk until early evening, then he would walk back to the Island Club through Bayswater, meditating on their meandering conversation which lacked the light tone and the laughter of better times.

According to Constance her marriage had long reached a terminus of mutual boredom and indifference. While the children were still at home she and Phillip could shower them with the affection which they were no longer able to give each other. Once the girls were despatched to the Somerset school that Constance had also attended, Phillip began to withdraw. He had never been comfortable with her wealth and his negligible contribution to their opulent lifestyle. With his ability to walk restored by a team of American doctors and his own formidable willpower, he had tapped into the old-boy network and secured a job in the City. His work had become his passion, just as flying had once been, and he seemed determined to replicate the daring aerial exploits which had won him the Victoria Cross, this time in financial deals which, if successful, would win him not medals but millions of pounds.

The weekly letters home from the girls were the only topic of animated conversation, and once it was exhausted Phillip would excuse himself and retire to the attic, where he had constructed a model battlefield.

Constance had sought advice from her twin brother, Alexander, but he was too busy politicking. He had been elected as a Member of Parliament in the 1951 election and, true to his youthful ambition, was making a name for himself as a foreign-policy specialist.

Her mother had been more forthcoming with advice. On Frances Castle's last visit to London, a fleeting one en route to Nice, the elderly romantic adventurer had merely told her daughter over tea in the Savoy, 'Men must have dragons to slay for their lovers,' and counselled her to keep herself busy and maintain an appearance of youthful beauty, which required dedication and self-sacrifice. And if she, Constance, felt neglected, she should consider taking a lover which, paradoxically, would keep her husband's interest alive.

After parting with her mother she realised that she had been misunderstood: she had not been seeking advice on how to save her marriage, but how to extricate herself from its suffocating familiarity, its vacant routines, its maddening ennui. Then she had acted, acted with sudden brutality before she lost the courage which came with that insight, before a sense of responsibility prevailed again. Phillip's response to the letter informing him that she needed time to herself had been coolly understanding. He would wait for her return.

One Sunday Marshall listened with disguised calm as she unearthed her memories of Paradise in a monologue which lasted for a whole hour. He could almost see her groping in the dark for the door that would lead to inner peace. He was relieved when she said: 'Do you realise, Marshall, that we, the British, practically ruled the world before the war, and now the empire is being slowly dismantled? We've lost India and, from what Alexander says, much of Africa and the Caribbean will follow soon.'

He welcomed this conversational departure because he felt she needed some respite from her obsessive self-examination, the perpetual turning over of her past, as if trying to identify the precise wrong turning which brought her to this impasse.

'All empires are transitory,' he said, 'whether they last ten years or a hundred.'

'Yes, I suppose you're right. It's strange, I didn't attach any importance to the empire until recently. It has always been there, and the realisation that it soon won't be has made me realise how much it shaped me, us, and how much we will have to unlearn.'

Then she began to talk about the three months she had travelled through the Far East with Alexander and Frances, and Marshall understood that she had not alighted on the topic of the empire to lament its passing. In some oblique way she was still talking about herself.

One of the Island Club's periodic crises interrupted Marshall's visits and a fortnight passed before he saw Constance again, though they spoke over the phone. On his next visit to the apartment he found many changes. The rooms had been stripped of their paintings, hanging carpets and tapestries and most of the furniture. Only a rosewood chaise longue, covered in red velvet, and two Victorian spoon chairs remained in front of the black marble fireplace. The vast living-room was now like an almost empty hall. The blank walls were complemented by thick white sheets which covered the enormous semicircular bay window and gave the light in the room the quality of dusk.

Constance had changed, too. She wore a long velvet dress which trailed on the floor and the evidence of her anxious months was visible in the svelte figure which the dress made more pronounced. Her hair had somehow darkened from light brown, and seemed to be darkening before his eyes. Her cheeks, once fleshy and full, were flat and her complexion as white as chalk. It was as though Constance were trying to reinvent herself by creating around her as blank a space as possible onto which she would draw some imagined new life. But she was still the old Constance, projecting an outward calm which belied her inner unrest.

During the first hour of that visit she complained repeatedly of the noise from the street. When Marshall observed that he did not know it was possible to find such a quiet place in London, she rose from the chaise longue, swayed unsteadily and said: 'I think I might be going mad.' He urged her to lie down again, and when she complied, he pulled his chair over to her and began to stroke her ashen forehead. 'No, you're just going through a difficult time, Constance. Everything will be all right.' With her eyes closed and in a whispering voice she recalled how Alexander had visited ten days before and they had quarrelled, though she could not say about what, and since then she had become so sensitive to even the slightest noise that she could only fall asleep with the help of a mixture of alcohol and Valium. Marshall implored her to stop talking and he continued stroking her forehead until she fell asleep. While she slept, he telephoned the Island Club and informed Scoop not to expect him there until further notice. Then he carried Constance to the lilac-scented bedroom, placed her on the bed and lay beside her. She did not wake up until the next morning. He stayed with her until late afternoon, and as he walked back to the club, Constance's remark on waking up, that she could not remember having slept so peacefully in years, played in his mind because it echoed his exact feelings on floating out of sleep on her bed. And now, as he walked, he felt that the mystery that was his life had somehow deepened overnight.

Constance added to that mystery some days later, after they had taken the short step towards making love and lay naked on the bed.

She said: 'Marshall, sometimes I feel that our lives, yours and mine, are in some strange and preordained way tied together.' Her voice sounded faint and distant, as if she were not lying beside him but speaking from some far-off place where only ghosts and memory dwelt.

'Where will it lead, this shared destiny of ours?' he said, and his own voice did not seem to belong to him, but to Pharaoh. Her reply, slow in coming, was even fainter and this time hoarse as if she were reluctant to answer: 'To death.' She rolled away from him, to the far side of the bed, creating a vast, cold chasm between them, and they plummeted into it when he, lost for words, reached for her pale, slender body. Reached for his destiny.

The physical passion between Marshall and Constance was quickly spent and superseded by protracted conversation in bed which sometimes lasted into the morning. Marshall did not lose his desire for her, but having reduced her intake of food to cream crackers and water, Constance was always weak and the simplest physical task left her breathless and faint. One night Marshall held her, and felt her ribs and the sharpness of her pelvis against his thighs and for a horror-filled moment imagined that he was holding the skeletal nun of his nightmares. After that he tried to get her to eat, brought her meals from the Island Club restaurant but she complained that it was all too rich in spices and vomited the few mouthfuls she had forced herself to swallow.

As she continued losing weight, she surrounded herself with stones bought on frantic shopping expeditions to Bond Street. Large pieces of ruby, turquoise, beryl, jasper, agate and amethyst were scattered around the apartment floor. Marshall would arrive to find her walking among them, picking this or that one up, as if trying to divine in them the future. In the same month that she started collecting cloth – silk and satin in rich vibrant colours, which she pinned to the walls and the doors – over several nights Marshall found her sleepwalking around the apartment, naked and feverishly hot. That phase of somnambulism climaxed what amounted to living with Constance because he felt he dare not leave her alone.

Then one evening, Constance turned up at the Island Club and informed Marshall that she was going away to southwest England so she could be near her daughters. He did not hear from Constance for over a month and when he did it was in the form of a long letter. She had spent a week with the children, and then taken the opportunity of being in that part of the country to visit a cottage which her great-aunt had bequeathed to her and Alexander. The building had been in danger of falling into extreme disrepair, but she had had the roof mended and was staying in the cottage. Its age and bucolic setting had charmed her, pacified the restless unhappiness that she had been feeling, leaving her more at peace with herself. The easy, conversational tone of the letter suggested to Marshall that Constance was enjoying a much-needed respite from London.

Constance returned to London in late spring, glowing with rude health. She no longer smoked, and spoke calmly. It seemed that Phillip had visited her in the cottage and begged her to come back home. For the sake of the children, she would be making another attempt at being a wife.

While Marshall was still breathing a sigh of relief, mixed with some regret, Martin Mayini was arrested in Kinja and imprisoned on sedition charges. Mayini's friends in London quickly formed a committee to raise funds for his defence and Marshall was co-opted on to the committee. Over the next three years the Free Martin Mayini Campaign would absorb all his time, pulling him closer to the reality of Africa.

8

The arrest of Martin Mayini, General Secretary of the National Freedom Party, did not come as a surprise to his supporters in London. Since returning to Kinja, he had been touring the country giving speeches which had disturbed the European settlers and won him the adoration of the people. Under tamarind trees, on makeshift rostra, with the sun hanging low in the sky, he demanded the return of land stolen by colonial settlers from his people and warned that the ancestral spirits, to whom the land truly belonged, were growing impatient and nothing short of national independence would placate their anger.

Some months after Mayini's visit to the Plateau region of Kinja, where there was a large settler community, several European families were slaughtered and an organisation called the Kinja Warriors claimed responsibility and promised further deaths. Mayini distanced himself from the terrorists, denouncing them as bushmen whose barbarity threatened to set back the independence cause by a decade.

While Mayini was denying that the National Freedom Party 'knew' the terrorists, Sir Anthony Watson, an old colonial hand experienced in quieting restive natives, was appointed Governor of Kinja. He imposed an emergency order and sent five hundred soldiers to scour the hills of the Plateau region.

After a month they announced that they had caught one of the terrorist leaders, Mazo Kwayan. The photograph of Kwayan carried on the front pages of all British broadsheets, showed a fearsome man with a mane of thick rope-like hair and bulging, glassy eyes, a figure redolent of the supernatural, of ritual sacrifices, of ancestral vengeance. In his confessions in Hosa, capital of the Plateau region, Kwayan claimed that the spirit of Martin Mayini had ordered him to carry out the slaughters, and had given detailed instructions on how to claim his victims and make propitiatory sacrifices to the ancestral spirits.

Sir Anthony Watson, urged on by the small settler community, had already targeted Mayini as an agitator, and Kwayan's confession became the final link in the chain they had been forging for Mayini. Mayini was humiliated before his family and charged with sedition and being an accomplice to murder. Two days after Mayini's arrest, another European family in the Plateau region lost their lives to killers who left no trace of how they entered the house, no footprints in the dust.

Marshall developed a morbid curiosity about events in Kinja. He read every newspaper article he could lay his hands on and started a cuttings file. In idle moments he found himself filling in the details of the lives of the dead European settlers and their killers. These reports gave him a disturbing thrill, a sense of something approaching a climax, a mixture of revulsion and fascination, a violent swirling mass of contradictory emotions which revealed to him how little he knew himself. He was a confluence of two rivers, calm on the surface but filled with treacherous, turbulent whirlpools.

Every day some minor incident brought this inner conflict into sharper focus. Walking down the street, he saw that he was expected to weave his way along, while white people walked in straight lines. He noticed that even Whites engaged in the humblest occupation related to him, a man whose bearing, stature, mien, radiated success, as a lesser being. One day a shopkeeper on Edgware Road placed Marshall's change on the counter instead of in his hand and something inside him snapped and he demanded the return of his money, threw his purchase on the counter and walked out.

Later that same day he took out the cuttings of the killings in Kinja, and the photograph of Mazo Kwayan, carried in most national newspapers, reminded him of Pharaoh. It was as though Pharaoh had removed himself to Africa and resurfaced as a guerrilla, a terrorist, a freedom fighter, a deadly emissary of ancestors who were now demanding of him, Marshall Sarjeant, to do his duty. He felt he was looking at a part of himself which he had so far refused to acknowledge because it frightened him, because he was a coward, because he did not know how to give it expression without destroying himself. Yes, that dreadlocked figure with the protuberant eyes dwelt within him.

He would not remember much about that night when that terrifying realisation seized him, as if the scar of some old wound had erupted pus and refused to heal unless he dressed it with the right medicine. But he would, for many years, remember leaving his apartment in a state of violent agitation and walking through the empty streets for some time until he realised he was lost and had to stop to find his bearings. A cobbled mews to the north, he knew, would bring him out onto the main road, which would eventually lead back onto Edgware Road. But walking down the narrow mews, he found himself facing a dishevelled bearded man, a tramp, whose breath reeked of methylated spirits. The fellow demanded money from him and while in the light of day Marshall had often dipped his hand into his pocket and tossed a coin to a beggar, he found this request menacing and offensive. He refused, the tramp stepped closer, and Marshall pushed him away, causing him to fall. Then something inside Marshall snapped and he found himself kicking the man on the ground, striking him in his stomach and head several times before regaining control of himself. He looked down on the writhing, pleading figure and, seized with horror at his own violence, hastened away.

When he had gone some distance guilt and remorse descended on him like a sudden shower. He returned to the spot where he had left the tramp and found it empty but for a pool of blood lit by the streetlamp. He emptied his pockets of all the money he had on him and threw it on the ground and a few coins fell in the blood. He arrived home rebuking himself, reminding himself that he had chosen to be a man of peace, that he would take no life, no matter the strength of his belief in a cause. And that night the dream of the skeletal nun ruined his sleep, leaving him tired and irascible the whole of the next day.

This inner turmoil was, of course, invisible to the people who saw him daily. At the Island Club he remained outwardly the calm proprietor with the boyish but rare smile and the dignified bearing. The most obvious changes were his indifference to the young women whom Scoop Fearon sent up to his apartment, and the responsibilities he delegated to Scoop and Mr Delisser. For Marshall was now pouring all his energy into the Free Martin Mayini Campaign. Apart from making generous financial donations, he helped to edit its newsletter – which grew in size and popularity with each issue as intellectuals and academics from Africa and the African diaspora, outraged by the blatant injustice of Mayini's incarceration, contributed free articles. He also served on its co-ordinating committee. Within weeks he was co-opted onto another committee following attacks by the natives here against Caribbean settlers in Nottingham, Liverpool, Cardiff, and the London neighbourhood where his properties were concentrated, Ladbroke Grove.

It was the Free Martin Mayini Campaign which consumed most of his time. It met twice weekly in various places, including the middle floor of the Island Club, but mostly in the luxurious Barons Court home of Dr Kenneth Braithwaite, a Barbadian-born general practitioner who had lived in London since between the wars. Braithwaite was a partner in a flourishing Harley Street clinic and ran another, less well-paid, surgery in a poor West London neighbourhood. With his curly white hair, pale skin and soft voice with a tinge of a West Country burr, he was often mistaken for a full-blooded Englishman. But in his home, over the fireplace in the room where the committee met, surrounded by an ornate gold frame, hung a giant oil painting of his mulatto mother. Through that portrait of a handsome, fiercely proud, strong-willed woman – painted when she was on the cusp of middle age – Braithwaite asserted his Africanness to those who doubted it. When the committee faced a difficult decision, or when the proceedings dragged on late into the evening and he was exhausted, he would look up at her steely gaze, as if seeking her counsel and strength. Braithwaite was chairman of the committee, and his political connections included two members of the House of Lords and several radical Labour politicians.

Another notable member was Victor Rampersand, a Trinidadian of African and Asian descent, who was most famous for his comment: 'With Indian independence I have liberated half of me, when the African continent is free, then the other half will be free.' Victor always sat beside Wade Mayana, one of two Kinjaians on the committee. Ageless and slow of speech, Wade Mayana came from a long line of griots and his people had chosen him as a teenager to live among Europeans. To this end he had studied in Harvard, the Sorbonne, Heidelberg and Oxford universities. Though his contributions to the committee meetings were always terse, his words carried great authority.

Less humorous and it seemed at times far less thoughtful was Dr Rudolph Lacoste, a Guadeloupean psychiatrist based at St Bartholomew's Hospital. Lacoste shared a similarity of position and temperament with Jeffrye Washington, a mysterious African-American who had served in the US Army in Europe and remained in exile in London, earning his living through freelance journalism. Both men consistently took the most bellicose stance. They articulated it with an eloquence fuelled by an ancient anger, a deep hurt which rang in their impassioned voices. Marshall found their contributions disturbing, not because they were irrelevant and forced him to disagree, but because he sometimes sensed that they were seeking the same visceral satisfaction that kicking the white tramp had given him, but on an infinitely grander scale.

The differences, ideological and philosophical, between members of the committee were not insuperable as long as the committee's work remained focused on the legal battle to free Martin Mayini. All its members shared, tacitly, more than a sense of history in the making: that by their actions and words they were fulfilling personal destinies; this was what they had been placed on earth to do.

Martin Mayini was found guilty of sedition and being a member of a proscribed organisation, and sentenced to life imprisonment in one of the most inhospitable corners of Kinja, an abominable place, an island in the desert. The committee members were devastated, but resolved to exhaust all the legal channels of appeal.

Shortly after the Privy Council rejected the petition for leave of appeal, the Kinjaian bushfighters not only escalated their attacks on white settlers, they began to kill prominent Kinjaians who supported the status quo. An entire village and its colonial appointed chief were slaughtered.

The reports of that massacre reached London on the day of a committee meeting whose members were still reeling from the severity of the sentence imposed on Mayini. The latest slaughter would have dominated the meeting anyway, but now there was an added ingredient in the form of a substantial donation from an anonymous source towards the committee's work. All the differences that had been simmering beneath the surface erupted.

Jeffrye Washington, seconded by Lacoste, proposed that the money be spent arming the Kinjaian bushfighters. He and Lacoste had never concealed their belief that violence was an inevitable and essential part of the liberation process. Speaking for his proposal, Washington argued that Britain's hold over its colonies was part of the same order which kept American 'Negroes' at the bottom of American society, and that subjugating grip, so rewarding to the powerful, could only be broken by armed force. He spoke exultantly of the violence that would erupt in American cities over the next ten years, and with chilling prophetic certainty of the urban armies that would rise out of the black ghettoes like Harlem and Watts and Chicago and wherever 'Negroes' lived.

Lacoste was less belligerent than Washington but supported him on medical grounds. For him, the oppressed needed to inflict violence on his oppressor, not simply to liberate himself from political and social oppression but also to free his mind. Violence was a necessary cathartic experience after years of colonial subjugation.

Wade Mayana's counterproposal urged the committee to donate the money towards supporting schools, hospitals and trade unions in Kinja. Victor Rampersand, a trade unionist, supported him.

Marshall pitched his tent with the Mayana camp, but midway through his speech, Jeffrye Washington interrupted him by banging on the table and shouting: 'The world is being rearranged, we must do our own rearranging. We must play a part in determining this new order. That is our historical mission. We must seize the time or time will seize us as it has been doing for five hundred years. We must arm those fighters. Give them the best weapons we can. Russian, American, Chinese – it don't matter. Give them guns ...'

Braithwaite banged the table and Marshall said with all the calm he could muster: 'If certain Kinjaians decide that violence is the only way to liberate their country, then that is their prerogative. Mayini's imprisonment will not stop Kinjaian independence; more likely it will accelerate it, and his freedom is the price he is paying. Let us look beyond this phase of the struggle.'

'I say no,' Lacoste spoke up. 'I say it's crucial that we look at this phase of the struggle. The colonised *need* to spill the blood of the coloniser. Let us arm the bushfighters.'

Joseph Kante, the other Kinjaian present, pitched in, speaking directly to Marshall: 'It is not mere violence we are proposing to support. It is armed resistance. The white man has been using violence against us for centuries. But he calls it the force of law. We do not recognise the legitimacy of that law and he will not deter us by branding our struggle violent and terroristic.'

Washington leapt up and shouted: 'Send them guns. Let the sound of gunshots be their language, a language the European understands –'

'And where will it end?' Marshall interjected. 'When will man stop killing man? Let our mode of liberation be an example of the sort of future we want to build. A peaceful future, a future of love –'

'Blood must flow for that. And not just the enemy's blood,' Washington said, glaring at Marshall.

Marshall stood up suddenly and glowered at Washington, and for an instant the two men seemed like two bulls sizing each other up, ready to fight.

At this point Braithwaite reasserted his control of the meeting and put Washington's proposal to the vote: should the Free Martin Mayini Campaign committee fund the bushfighters? A show of hands revealed deadlock. Dr Kenneth Braithwaite had the deciding vote. He looked around the room slowly, then he looked imploringly at the portrait of his mother and cast his vote in favour of Washington's proposal. Marshall immediately tendered his resignation and the meeting descended into a noisy row. Having again lost control, Braithwaite closed the meeting and asked everybody to leave.

While the others departed quickly, Marshall remained behind with Braithwaite and Wade Mayana. Braithwaite spent half an hour trying to persuade Marshall to reconsider his decision. Marshall conceded that he had been hasty, promised to give the matter a few days' thought.

As they stood on the doorstep, Braithwaite said: 'We need men like you and Wade Mayana, Marshall. We have entered a moment in history when a war which predates all our lives is reaching its climax. We need men who are not afraid to remind us of our common humanity.'

As he and Wade Mayana walked silently through the night, Marshall found comfort in the presence of the older man. Parting at the underground station, they spoke for the first time in the fifteen-minute walk.

Marshall said: 'I don't understand you. You opposed Washington's proposal but you don't think it's a resignation matter.'

'No. But that is my conscience. I cannot resign from history. And, I suspect, neither can you. For when the warlords have triumphed, we, the warriors of peace, must be there to spread reconciliation and harmony among the living.'

'Well, good night, my brother. May God give you peace and rest,' Mayana said as they parted.

Marshall walked for many hours that night and on the bank of the Thames, he resolved to remain on the committee, to speak up for a pacifist path for independence. He continued attending the meetings and arguing his case and when another large sum of money boosted the campaign's coffers he was instrumental in getting it directed towards the building of a hospital in the Middle Belt region of Kinja. And he and Jeffrye Washington buried their differences.

Nevertheless, it was Washington who caused Marshall's next crisis of conscience. For some time Alexander Castle had been writing a column in *The Times.* These largely anodyne scribblings were redeemed by their elegantly classical style and the writer's breadth of knowledge of foreign affairs. Castle, clearly, was no mere hack: he believed what he wrote. During the trial of Martin Mayini Alexander Castle's 'Foreign Eye' column had become more polemical and stridently imperialistic. Week after week, the columnist railed against the dying of the British Empire and Britain's declining status and influence in world affairs. He argued that the empire had brought the light of civilisation to dark corners of the globe, citing the end of savage practices such as widows' suicides in India, and slavery. It had brought technology, the railways, roads; it had brought about peace and co-operation between warring tribes, thus creating the basis for nations to emerge. Many of the peoples incorporated in the empire were not ready for independence, but if they forced the issue, Britain's historical mission obliged it to ensure that independence took place slowly and involved only those natives who were moderate in their views and prepared to continue co-operating with Britain.

One week he dedicated his entire column to an excoriating attack on Martin Mayini and his ilk, which elicted a strongly worded letter from the Free Martin Mayini Campaign. The next week he warned against Egypt's Nasser, whom he dubbed the 'Arab Hitler'. Foreshadowing the ecology movement, he warned of the vast tracts of land, the 'lungs of the earth', that would be destroyed by unbridled industrialisation as governments in the former colonies rushed to emulate the West. He warned against the spread of American civilisation, with its crude consumerism and cultural vacuity. He condemned the Soviet Union as the most sinister state on earth, and dismissed its totalitarianism and lack of democracy as retrogressive steps, anathema to the spirit of the twentieth century. He called for more exchange programmes between Britain and her colonies, and once went so far as to express mild approbation for the increased presence of dark-skinned people in Britain. Lest he be seen as a champion of immigration, in another article, he called for immigration controls in order to improve race relations. Contradictory and sanctimonious, his erudition impressively wide, his pieces made for compelling reading.

Castle's articles were often discussed before the committee meetings, or afterwards, as members drank and chatted informally. There was a general consensus that Alexander Castle, for all his undoubted intellectual brilliance, was not an astute politician. He had offended too many of the Conservative

Party's kingmakers by exposing their intellectual inferiority, and while he enjoyed some support from a small extreme right-wing clique, his views were of marginal importance. None the less Dr Kenneth Braithwaite found them deeply offensive, expressive of the worst sort of British arrogance which presumed that they, Britons, could be guardians of the world and keep Britain white. The doctor often entered a committee meeting waving a copy of *The Times* and spitting, 'Have you seen what that idiot has written this week?'

One week, when Alexander Castle wrote of Britain's West Indian possessions as Gardens of Eden, Arcadian islands peopled by natives whose simple way of life would be ruined by independence, thus depleting the sum total of happiness of mankind, Braithwaite entered the meeting in such a state of violent indignation that it took him almost an hour to find the composure to start the meeting. But halfway through, he lost control of himself again, picked up *The Times* and shouted: 'That arrogant, sanctimonious English bastard!'

Jeffrye Washington sighed impatiently and said: 'Look, I'm tired of hearing about this jerk. Let's take him out.'

Braithwaite looked at Washington puzzledly, but Rampersand seemed to understand Washington. 'You mean, bowl him a bouncer, aim for the head.'

'Or shoot him, or arrange an accident. Thing is to take him out of the game,' Washington said.

'Retired hurt,' Rampersand said. 'Good idea.'

'Dead would be better, easily done and irreversible. But I'm not bothered. Thing is to take him out.'

The rest of the committee now understood Washington's suggestion and a fever of gleeful mischievousness infected the room after they had dismissed a solution as extreme as assassination. Joseph proposed sneaking into Castle's bed a famous poisonous Kinjaian snake, the venom of which was used to zombify people. This suggestion triggered a roar of laughter, which heightened Alexander Castle as a target deserving of the worst sort of mischief. It was Washington, again, who suggested – not for minuting – that they start compiling a dossier on Castle. And in that mischievous spirit it was agreed.

The dossier grew over the weeks, but it contained nothing that could be used to harm Castle. It revealed that he was a solitary, and deeply private man whose family wealth went back only to his father. He was a lover of music, country walks, the theatre and belonged to an exclusive club. He worked hard and was ambitious. His political views apart, Castle seemed a model of moral rectitude.

Marshall agreed that it would give him great pleasure to see Alexander Castle silenced, but he contributed nothing to the document. Nor did he reveal his connection with the Castles.

One evening, as he, Victor Rampersand and Joseph Kante were sitting in the Island Club, drinking and talking, Washington strode in in a mood of great excitement. He had just found a chink, soon to be a massive hole, in Alexander Castle's armour. 'And I've got just the person for the job,' Washington said.

Minutes later Sweet P. McCorquodale sidled into an empty chair, wiped his forehead with a polka-dot handkerchief and purred: 'Darlings, ah am fatigued. The things a girl has to do to make ends meet.'

Now, great cities like London are full of people who do not exist, people who have several names, addresses, identities but are unknown to the authorities. Sweet P. McCorquodale was one of those privileged non-persons. He was an habitue of the Island Club. He preferred being a woman but found the cost of that identity prohibitively high – the cosmetics, the clothes, the wigs, the jewellery – and so, to give his purse a respite, he sometimes dressed as a man. But in whatever gender he presented himself to the world, he was never lost for admirers, male and female. Sweet P. was recruited to the Pan-Africanist cause in a campaign which its architects have never recorded, and which filled Marshall Sarjeant with feelings of unspeakable shame.

Jeffrye Washington directed 'Operation Bouncer' – as he, inspired by Rampersand, called it – and for almost two months, when asked how it was going, he would sit back, smile cruelly, and say: 'Just fine. Got me a sweet potato pie in the fire, and it's coming along just fine.'

That pie turned out to be a collection of photographs of Alexander Castle with a submissive Sweet P. dressed in stockings and suspenders. A week after Washington, with a triumphant flourish, showed committee members the photographs, Alexander Castle announced his resignation from Parliament ostensibly to spend time with his sickly wife. His name continued to appear in *The Times,* but only in other columnists' puzzled speculation as to why a young politician with a brilliant future ahead of him should suddenly resign. His own column never appeared again.

Then one morning, not long afterwards, Marshall Sarjeant opened the morning paper to read the headlines: 'Former MP in suicide attempt.'

9

With the legal process exhausted, the co-ordinating committee of the Free Martin Mayini Campaign somewhat lost its focus and the Alexander Castle affair woke up some of its members to that regrettable fact. Marshall now turned his attention to a much neglected area of his life: the Island Club. A good thing, too. For over the years of the Mayini campaign, the Island Club had been toppled from its paramountcy in the league of London Caribbean nightspots. There were now fewer free-spending African-American GIs in the capital, and venues similar to the Island Club but more locally based and therefore cheaper, had opened in other parts of London. While the Island Club retained the prestige of the sort of venue that a man keen to impress a new lover, show off a new suit or mark some special occasion, might saunter into, the sad and undeniable truth was that it had known better days. In fact, without the dedication and sacrifices of Scoop Fearon, Jean Myers, and Mr Delisser's culinary skills and boundless gastronomic imagination – which had won the restaurant a loyal group of diners who shared the maestro's belief that the quality of the aperient effect of a meal was as important as the meal itself and who, to the distress of uninitiated visitors, could often be overheard exchanging notes on the dishes responsible for recent exceptionally pleasant evacuative experiences – the whole operation would have been running at a loss.

In an effort to revive the venue's popularity, Marshall invited suggestions for special events they could stage. Mr Delisser floated the idea of a month-long festival of New World cuisine, dishes from different islands and countries within the Americas, and worked himself up into a lather at the prospect of introducing Londoners to a sublime Amazonian delicacy: steamed tarantula eggs wrapped in young sweet potato leaves. Marshall bought the idea.

Jean Myers suggested refurbishing and redecorating both the nightclub and the restaurant. She despised the white tablecloths which, anyway, were now frayed and stained beyond cleaning. She wanted to use various shades of blue to create a soothing atmosphere and attract certain kinds of people, those who knew that blue is the colour of misadventures in love. Marshall welcomed her suggestion, but made the mistake of agreeing to spend time with Jean choosing the new colour scheme. He found himself, yet again, having to extricate himself from her tenacious embrace.

Scoop initially seemed disinterested in the whole project and for days went about with a rather resentful expression and hinted darkly that he considered himself overworked and underpaid; and he was fed up with being Marshall's locum and shadow. Marshall got wind of Scoop's disaffection and offered him a week's paid holiday. Scoop accepted, and on his return, apparently rejuvenated, put forward a brilliant idea: a series of beauty contests, climaxing in the crowning of Miss Island Club. It was pure Scoop Fearon.

Sadly, transportation difficulties prevented Mr Delisser from securing the necessary ingredients for his arachnidan delicacy, but even so the month-long festival of New World cuisine was a resounding success. Two days after eating a meal which included sautéed bull-calves' testicles lightly coated with fresh black pepper, from Argentina, and a guava and mango salad sprinkled with the maestro's secret spices, one diner, a visitor drawn there by the novelty of the event, came back to seek out and thank the chef for not only giving him a gastronomic adventure of epiphanic intensity, but also curing him of years of constipation. Mr Delisser's new admirer, John Meadows, was, it transpired, a restaurateur and he attempted to lure the maestro away to start a Mayfair restaurant, which he, John Meadows, was convinced would be a *scandale de succès.* Unfortunately, John Meadows's regained laxity did not reach as far as his wallet. Mr Delisser took umbrage at the parsimonious salary being offered and drove him away with some spicy insults. Jean Myers's shades-of-blue scheme attracted many compliments and there was a noticeable increase in the number of lonely-looking men and women in both the restaurant and the nightclub. They included a melancholic woman who always wore blue dresses, danced alone, and was prone to fits of lachrymosity in response to sad songs, and an impecunious young poet who, in exchange for drinks, offered to compose epic poems for the brokenhearted but over the course of a month managed to produce only a single haiku, which so disappointed and offended his patron that Scoop Fearon had to rescue him from a poetic pounding.

Scoop's beauty contest followed the festival of New World cuisine. In keeping with the spirit of the New World ethos, the competition was open to all nationalities and races but, possibly due to the venue's Caribbean image, British entrants were scarce. This had been expected and Jean Myers – out of concern, of course, that the exercise could turn out to be a costly failure – had expressed some reservation as to whether there were enough female immigrants to sustain a contest.

There was no shortage of contestants. But they were not always of the right sex. The winner of the first round – decided by the audience, with Scoop as compere – was a leggy lady who had to be disqualified because she turned out, to the chagrin and consternation of her wolf-whistling supporters, to be none other than Sweet P. McCorquodale.

The remaining rounds were trouble-free, and the audience, which was alternately raucous and stunned into awed silence, grew weekly. Men who had left their wives or their girlfriends back on the islands came to ogle, cheer and admire women who reminded them of mist-enshrouded mountains, rhythmic tropical rainfalls, gazing at the sea at midday from under a coconut tree, sunset over undulating valleys, the reflection of the moon on a still lake, clear river water rushing over white rocks and cascading into limpid pools surrounded by giant ferns and fantastically coloured flowers with petals which sweetened the water to an intoxicating scent, sweaty and sticky after a day's labour and strolling home through the dusk laden with the aroma of fried plantain, and looking forward to a shower under a cold water stand, then lying with your lover in the humid night and watching the dancing light of the fireflies.

Marshall did not notice Zenobia Blomfontein until after she had been crowned Miss Island Club 1955. By then he was almost too late, for Scoop Fearon's amorous ambitions had settled on her; she was one woman he would not be sending up to Marshall's apartment. Scoop had engineered her victory in a field of finalists who, between them, covered the Greater Antilles, the Leeward Islands, and North and South America – and choosing a winner had been as difficult as choosing between a view of mountains and a view of the sea.

She was not the most beautiful but she was the boldest. When asked about her greatest ambition, she had caused uproar with her answer: 'To find a man who loves me enough to run away with me regardless of his ties and responsibilities.' Seeing himself as just such a man, Scoop had whipped the audience into a frenzy because the winner was decided by the loudest and longest applause. Between announcing her victory and crowning her, Scoop had invited her out to dinner and for the rest of the night hovered over her with an air of proprietorial solicitude.

It was Jean Myers who observed to Marshall – they were sitting at the same table watching the event – that Zenobia Blomfontein was trouble incarnate. Miss Island Club was introduced to Marshall later in the evening and he found her intelligent, with a wry sense of humour, and thought he could smell the Guyanese coast on her breath. But that night, as he was emptying his pockets, he came across a note which, unknown to him, had been slipped there. It read: 'I would like to discuss my future with you. Signed, Zenobia Blomfontein.'

Scoop was not seen in the Island Club for several days after the crowning of Miss Island Club 1955, and when he turned up, he had lost weight and had the distracted appearance of a man wrestling with love. Zenobia herself reappeared one night looking like no woman should look who was aware of the perturbation the feminine presence can cause, and nobody could deny that the lady had style. Scoop was all nervy and distracted, and clearly cross with her because he was overheard reproving her for disobeying his injunction not to come to the Island Club again. For her part she spat back: 'I've told you, Scoop, you don't own me.'

Marshall happened to have been at a committee meeting that evening and arrived at the club after midnight and took his seat at his special table to relax and enjoy the performance of that week's act: a duo composed of a piano player and a female singer with a wonderfully controlled soprano voice and a repertoire of blues songs.

Jean Myers was already at the table and Zenobia came to join them, swiftly followed by Scoop. Marshall danced with Jean while Scoop danced with Zenobia. Then Jean Myers did a most unusual thing: she asked Scoop to dance and with obvious reluctance to be separated from his beloved, he agreed, leaving Zenobia and Marshall together.

She turned to him and said accusatively: 'Why haven't you replied to my note?'

Astonished by her forwardness, Marshall made a feeble excuse and left her fuming alone at the table.

Months later, as he tried to save their friendship, he would relate to Scoop all Zenobia's predatory manoeuvres – such as the desperate notes she sent him, the urgent telephone calls, the accidental encounters in shops and on the streets.

Then on a Sunday morning he went to answer his door and found Zenobia Blomfontein standing on his doorstep, shorn of cosmetics and jewellery, a plain headscarf hiding her wild hair, dressed in white and altogether looking like a paragon of wifely virtue. She invited him to accompany her to Mass at a church she knew where the choir was glorious and uplifting.

For some time now, especially since the committee's decision to fund the Kinjaian bushfighters and the near-tragic Alexander Castle affair, Marshall had been feeling a hunger in his soul, a curious need for atonement and spiritual cleansing, as if he were personally responsible for the killings in Kinja and Alexander Castle's suicide attempt; as if his soul were protesting at his excesses and demanding that he stem the encroachment of the desert which would leave him without the ability to feel compassion and therefore to be truly human.

It was a measure of Zenobia Blomfontein's prescience that she recognised that his spiritual hunger was the key by which she could gain entry to his life. Still resisting, he made her wait downstairs while he dressed hurriedly, then they went to a Catholic church, where they prayed, sang and watched the confirmation ceremony of three children, and he was reminded that he had never been confirmed and remembered Binta Sarjeant.

Afterwards Zenobia invited him back to her home for Sunday lunch. He was feeling so stilled by the service, so peaceful within himself, that he received her invitation with trusting innocence. On the way she refused to answer his questions about her relationship with Scoop beyond saying that he was a 'dear friend', and made him promise never to discuss Scoop with her.

Her modest bedsit overflowed with miniature dolls and stuffed toy animals and potted plants, and the closed air was saturated with a cocktail of scents like a glade in the forest at the height of the rainy season. From the single armchair, with its fussy antimacassar, he watched her prepare lunch, and as he followed her slow deliberate movements around the stove he became aware that she was dancing for him, and, for all its space, his apartment seemed like some far-off place of exile, stark and bare and lonely.

The meal was simple and plain, and presented before him with engaging artistry. When they had eaten she invited him to rest on her single bed, with its kaleidoscopic patchwork quilt which she claimed to have stitched with her own hands, and dismissed his feeble protest by stretching her wonderful body out between him and the wall and lowering her voice to a whisper. Then he lay on the bed and was seized by the most violent concupiscence, as though she had laced the meal with some potent aphrodisiac.

The rest of the Sunday passed like a dream, and he strolled home early the next morning with the smell of mangrove swamps in his hair, the taste of guava in his mouth and visions of ships floating across the sky.

Over the next week, he avoided Scoop and when they met, he could not meet his friend's eyes, because every night he was drawn back to trespassing in that wondrous place that was Zenobia Blomfontein. None the less, like all his infatuations, her appeal was short-lived, and though he fought hard to keep his passion alive he was called back to the spartan solitude of his apartment above the Island Club.

For a while he was able to conceal the ugly fact of his spent love with extravagant gifts, but she was not fooled. She revealed that she knew he was tired of her when one evening he went there in response to a desperate telephone call from her, and sat unmoving as she narrated the tale of her aunt who had made her lover wait for ten years before agreeing to marry him, and another three years before sharing the pleasures of her body with him because she wanted to be absolutely certain that he would love her in perpetuity. She, Zenobia, a quintessential child of the twentieth century, born in one place and now living in another, regretted that she had not learnt those old ways.

He offered his apologies for inflicting himself on her, for

succumbing to her advances when he knew full well that some personal flaw undermined his ability to sustain love. He told her he did not mean to hurt her, and urged her to find somebody who could give her enduring love. He mistook her tears for resignation, failing to see in their abundance a preparation for battle.

A month later, she telephoned and insisted that they had to meet. They met on Paddington Green, walked among the moss-encrusted gravestones beneath plane trees that were shedding their bark. Then she told him: 'I'm carrying your baby.'

The prospect of fatherhood terrified Marshall beyond the normal terror of men receiving such news because he feared that any child of his would bear the mark of Sarjeant's curse. He explained but she refused to believe him and called him a coward and cried, and hours later he lay awake in her bed wondering how he had come to propose marriage to Zenobia Blomfontein.

They moved into one of his houses, married at St Christopher-in-Marylebone and the bride wore white and the bridegroom top hat and tails. Scoop Fearon found it within his wounded heart to forgive Marshall and Zenobia and serve as best man, and gave a speech at the wedding reception which rang with sadness as he wished the newlyweds happiness and expatiated on the chaos of love.

Despite his apparent magnanimity, Scoop was never his old self. His appearance at work became erratic, he was seldom seen without a glass of Scotch in his hands, and after the stag night, he never again entered Marshall's apartment and sat with him to drink and reminisce about their island home. His clothes became looser with each day, his face more lugubrious, and late into the night, drunk, he would corner an unsuspecting nightclubber and tell him about the children and the beautiful rich wife he had left in Harlem when he was young and foolish and cowardly.

One night he reduced Jean Myers, a woman whose skin

was of elephantine thickness, to tears with a long rambling account of the innumerable women he had lost through stupidity and restlessness. Jean Myers, having now abandoned hope of ever getting Marshall, took Scoop to her home and there, in a room impregnated with the scent of frankincense, palliated his stricken heart with the tender strokes of one who knew the cruel twists and turns of love.

Then they started to plot against Marshall.

10

Marshall was still adjusting to marriage and fatherhood a year after Zenobia had given birth to a normal, healthy boy, whom they named Martin-Johann (the Johann came from Zenobia's Dutch grandfather). Although he was inclined to work late at the Island Club and occasionally slept over in its top-floor apartment, Marshall looked forward to the quiet hours with his family, playing with his baby son in the comfortable and beautiful home created by Zenobia. Given a free hand and a generous budget, Zenobia had filled the house with lacquered mahogany furniture evocative of her own childhood home in British Guyana. Her habit of appearing to dance while performing the most mundane domestic chore still delighted Marshall and made him feel, if not happy, at least contented. But this period, the most settled he had known since leaving Paradise, was short-lived. It was disrupted by Constance Castle, who re-entered his life like a sudden storm.

He had seen Constance only once and fleetingly over recent years – around the time her mother died – and knew that she had left her husband again to live alone in a cottage in the Welsh mountains. They met in Hyde Park at the height of the summer of '57. She was bony and frail-looking, with broad streaks of white in shoulder-length hair, and her face had acquired a hieratic quality. She wore a long white cotton dress with a matching hat, which accentuated the paleness of her skin. As they walked around the park, Constance reminded Marshall of her late mother's belief that there was a West Indian connection in the family. On her deathbed Mrs Castle had made Alexander promise to trace the connection, and Alexander, since retiring from public life, had searched out family members, consulted parish records and established the family's Paradise connection. It was Thomas Sarjeant, who came from Paradise, Jamaica.

The little that was known about Thomas Sarjeant came from a nonagenarian grandaunt, whom Alexander had discovered living in Barton, a village near Bristol. The tawny-coloured former sailor from the West Indies had settled in Bristol in the late 1840s, married Vivian Carter and fathered six girls. A philanderer, drinker and gambler, Thomas Sarjeant quite possibly also had children out of wedlock. His gambling debts resulted in two of the girls being sold into domestic servitude. Another two migrated to Australia and one ran away to the United States. The youngest, Lilian Sarjeant, was Constance's maternal great-great-grandmother. Thomas Sarjeant died in Newgate Prison in 1861.

Marshall now knew the meaning of that first kiss on the day, almost twenty years ago, when they sheltered in the damp, musty interior of the cotton tree and watched the rain churning the earth outside. The liaison between Neal Sarjeant and Nana had created a family tree with branches which circled the globe. Escaping its reach, which would always remind him of his failure, seemed impossible.

'So you were right, our destinies are intertwined,' Marshall said.

'Our pasts certainly are,' Constance answered. 'I'm no longer sure about our destinies. I will be living in a convent for the next three years.'

Remembering the dream of the skeletal nun, Marshall was suddenly struck by the realisation that his life was a puzzle with its pieces scattered far and wide, and even if he could assemble them all together they would still make no sense. As he looked at her in dismay, she revealed that she was pursuing a solution to the persistent agitation which had caused her to leave her husband. A convent of Carmelite nuns on an island in the Pacific Ocean would, she hoped, give her inner peace. If she was still there after three years, she would take holy vows and live out the remainder of her life in silence and solitude. She could see no reason to continue secular life.

Phillip, her husband, had turned the children against her with malicious tales which questioned her sanity for wanting to live solitarily in a cottage without running water or electricity as far away from people as possible. She was confident that her daughters, to whom she had given more affection than she had received, would soon be able to stand on their own feet.

She was more concerned about Alexander. Recalling how, from a young age, Alexander used to practise his oratorical skills with her as his audience; how, several times, he cajoled her into playing the Queen to his loyal servant, a dignitary who had travelled to foreign lands and returned with some rare and exotic plant or animal, treasure for the felicitation of her royal highness, she expressed bewilderment that he could have lost so completely his appetite for politics, the consuming passion of his youth. Not that his life was empty. When he was not reading in his vast library, he pottered about in his hothouse which, designed to resemble a rainforest, was home to a pair of toucans, a boa constrictor and a shoal of fish. Since the outbreak of the Suez crisis he had been approached by several party movers to re-enter politics but refused.

Marshall coughed when Constance said she could not understand Alexander's stubborn refusal to discuss the reason for his sudden loss of interest in politics. She interpreted his unyielding silence on the matter as further proof of the unbridgeable gap that had developed between them in adulthood.

Hearing the hurt in her voice, Marshall now understood, more fully than he had ever done, the peculiar search that had overtaken Constance's life. She was looking for her other half, a part destroyed in the passage from adolescence to adulthood, a part that Alexander had once played. He had, Marshall now recognised, briefly replaced Alexander as her complementary half. Was her inability to lead a settled life a manifestation of Sarjeant's curse?

He told her about Neal Sarjeant and Nana without mentioning Sybil and the curse because he was not certain, after fifteen years in Britain and fathering a healthy child, that he believed in the myths of Paradise any more. Like Blyden's creation story, his belief in the curse seemed to belong to another age and time.

She expressed regret that her mother had not known, for the search for ancestral roots had been her obsession, while she, Constance, was concerned with finding inner peace.

Marshall then invited her to meet his wife and child. 'After all, you are family, you're my cousin,' he said.

The Sunday afternoon Constance spent with the Sarjeants was a disaster. Zenobia took an instant dislike to Marshall's willowy white female cousin, spoke to her with icy formality, and for the first time in her marriage, burnt the rice. Martin-Johann seemed equally ill at ease with Constance, bawling loudly whenever she tried to pick him up.

Conversation was so strained that Marshall felt relieved when Constance prepared to leave. He walked her to a waiting taxi and when they embraced in a farewell gesture he felt her bony shoulders and an image of the skeletal nun flashed in his mind. And as the taxi sped away, he was overcome by a powerful feeling that he had not seen the last of Constance Castle.

Constance's visit marked the beginning of the end of Marshall's domestic bliss. Zenobia, a woman of brutal candour, wasted no time in letting him know that she had found Constance unnerving, unsettling. She drew his attention to a number of strange occurrences which marked Constance's visit. An aspidistra she, Zenobia, had been cultivating since coming to England had almost overnight turned yellow, and defied all her efforts to resuscitate it; cats had gathered in the garden for days afterwards and two dead pigeons had fallen down the chimney, spreading soot over the furniture; all the clocks in the house had stopped, and the baby, since being held by Constance, had become difficult, crying through the night and resistant to all her maternal comforts.

Marshall dismissed what he saw as Zenobia's attempt to blame Constance for her domestic failing and regarded his wife's animosity towards his friend as nothing more than an expression of jealousy. He began to spend more time in the Island Club and a month after Constance's departure, missed his first Sunday with his family. This enraged Zenobia. She accused him of failing to love her and their child and charged him with callous neglect. Marshall refused to get drawn into a quarrel and, having given work as his excuse, promised not to allow it to happen again. But a few weeks later he missed another Sunday with his family, and Zenobia could not be appeased by promises.

Her complaints increased daily, and seldom a day passed when she did not attempt to pick a quarrel with Marshall. The more fractious she became, the less time Marshall spent in the family home. One day, transported by anger and still believing that Constance had disrupted their domestic harmony, she heaped on him all the imprecations she had learnt from mixing with the wrong company, and told him to go back to his 'white woman friend who was so skinny she looked like a skeleton'.

Marshall did not go home for a whole week, and only returned because Zenobia telephoned the Island Club to inform him that Martin-Johann was ill. Their concern for the child's health kept them together that Christmas, and for a while there was a semblance of domestic harmony, sustained by both their efforts to wear masks of marital bliss. Nevertheless, unable to meet Zenobia's exacting standards of filial and paternal devotion, Marshall soon resumed his lengthy absences.

He squeezed Zenobia and the child, who now cried through the night in defiance of a potent cocktail of soporific concoction, in between the Island Club and the Free Martin Mayini

Campaign, and several organisations concerned with West Indian immigration.

Then his complacency about his marriage and fatherhood was suddenly destroyed. One day he found in the mail a typed, unsigned note which read: 'Are you sure that child is yours?' He tried to ignore this malicious letter, but the seed of doubt had been planted and every day it grew, watered by the memory of how he had stolen Zenobia from Scoop, until it became a monstrous weed, invading the corners of his mind on which keeping up his multifarious activities depended. Scoop, who had recovered some of his former flamboyance as a result of the tender and secret ministrations of Jean Myers, became the subject of constant speculation. Had he, Scoop, who had already betrayed him once, given him a responsibility? Was Zenobia colluding with Scoop?

Within a week another note came and it read: 'While the king is in his chambers counting up his money, the queen is in her bed loving up her honey.' From then on he could not look at Scoop without seeing in his friend's eyes the glint of mocking, vengeful laughter. Marshall made sure he went home every night, not because he had suddenly found it within himself to love Zenobia, but because the notes had stirred in him the fear that he was a cuckold and everybody knew but him.

Zenobia's behaviour did little to allay his suspicions. She had quickly regained her youthful figure and started spending beyond the limit of the generous monthly allowance he gave her, and, having employed a nanny, spent many unaccountable hours away from home. Sometimes Marshall picked up the telephone at home and the caller hung up, fuelling his suspicion that Zenobia was having an affair.

One weekend Scoop telephoned to say he would not be able to make it to work due to illness. His usual duties – introducing the Saturday act, welcoming guests, supervising the waitresses – fell on Marshall's shoulders. As was his habit, he did not go home on closing up the Island Club, but slept in the upstairs apartment.

He woke up at midday on Sunday with a rare hunger for a few quiet hours with his son and his wife, whose beauty, despite his weakening affection for her, he still appreciated. On the way he bought her a bunch of carnations from a streetside stall. But the house he entered was empty. Clothes spilled out of Zenobia's wardrobe, and the drawers from Martin-Johann's dresser were piled on the bed with not a single item of clothing in them.

A note stuck in the mirror above the living-room fireplace read: 'Sorry, Marshall, but I need a man whose love is strong, a man who loves me enough to run away with me, regardless of his ties, responsibilities and duties. Yours Zenobia Blomfontein-Sarjeant.'

Marshall folded the note, put it in his pocket, then went for a walk around the local park. From there he caught a cab to Scoop's Kilburn flat. One of Scoop's neighbours said he had last seen Scoop leaving with a suitcase on Saturday evening. And Marshall knew then that Scoop had betrayed him again and absconded with Zenobia and Martin-Johann.

He spent the remainder of the day in Hyde Park, moving from one bench to the next, as if searching for some view that would pacify his troubled heart and restore his equanimity. He told himself that he had not loved Zenobia, but he would miss his son, that Constance's visit had nothing to do with the discord which appeared in his marriage after her visit, that Zenobia would come begging forgiveness when she learnt the truth about Scoop, that he did not care and the pain in his chest was the result of excessive smoking and not the pain of betrayed love.

Finally, as night fell, he walked to the nearest church and tried to enter but its doors were locked and only then did he notice that the church had fallen into disuse.

II

A month after Zenobia left, Martin Mayini was pardoned, released from prison and allowed to participate in the Kinjaian independence process. But Marshall Sarjeant, who had worked tirelessly for the Free Martin Mayini Campaign, was in no mood to celebrate. He was falling, falling as swiftly and as loudly as a ripe breadfruit crashing through leaves and bouncing off branches and splattering on the ground.

Over the years he had delegated more and more responsibility to Scoop in the everyday running of the Island Club. It was Scoop who ordered the provisions, kept the bar stocked, booked the acts, hired the waitresses and generated the *esprit de corps* among the staff. It was Scoop who greeted visitors, familiarised himself with their needs, cultivated their loyalty, engaged them in badinage, and floated through the night bringing happiness and harmony to the tables where he alighted. Marshall owned the Island Club but Scoop's spirit had animated it.

With Scoop gone Marshall discovered that he had lost the ability to mix easily with his customers. They bored him with their insistence on nostalgic conversation, alternating with embittered anecdotes about life in England, and they annoyed him with enquiries about Scoop – whom they were told had had to make an emergency trip to the Caribbean to be with his dying mother. Each night he looked forward to locking the doors and retiring to the solitude of his apartment. The dream of the skeletal nun now visited him every night and only a generous measure of whisky could give him a few hours of dreamless sleep.

The customers, of course, soon began to sense that they

were unwelcome at the Island Club, and so found other nightspots where the owners' eagerness for their company and their money created a convivial atmosphere. Sepulchral Saturday nights in the Island Club became commonplace. One night, The Aces, a popular four-piece American rhythm-and-blues band, were so disappointed with the sparse, unresponsive audience that they ended their performance early, packed up their instruments and reproved Marshall for failing to warn them that they would be performing in a graveyard. Word soon spread that the Island Club was finished because it only attracted the dead, the ignorant and the uncool.

The proprietor of the Island Club had already graduated to starting his day with a tumbler full of whisky when George Mahoney, the least copacetic visitor to step through its portal, made his first appearance. Preceded by two potbellied bodyguards, he strolled into the basement one afternoon and introduced himself as the man who could save Marshall from ruination. Dressed like an English civil servant in striped suit and bowler hat, thin and straight, with a permanent smirk and cold, calculating eyes, George Mahoney described himself as a rescuer of failing businesses. His proposition to Marshall was simple: to turn the Island Club over to his management. He would then take advantage of the club's proximity to the West End, with its theatres, concert halls, and hotels, especially its hotels. Businessmen and tourists a long way from home were always looking for adventures and the new Island Club would provide just that.

While Mahoney spoke in a soft voice of saccharine reasonableness his bodyguards were glowering at Marshall from behind hooded eyes, and their menacing expressions left him in no doubt that this was no mere business proposition. He dealt with them tactfully, offered them drinks and invited them to sample Mr Delisser's cuisine – both of which they refused. Then he promised to think about Mahoney's proposition, which seemed to disarm the thugs. As he watched them leave, Marshall knew they would be back. Mahoney had the look of a man who got his way.

Just in case Marshall did not get George Mahoney's message, the following Saturday night, one of those now rare occasions when the Island Club pulled more than a handful of customers, saw the first fight on the premises. It started when Larry Lovelace asked an Englishwoman to dance. Larry Lovelace hailed from Trinidad and was renowned for his highly developed predatory instincts and vigorous dancing which usually left his partner weak at the knees, disoriented and susceptible to his amorous advances. The woman was a stranger to the Island Club and she had been sitting by herself most of the night, and Larry was the first to approach her. While the couple were dancing, out of nowhere a burly white man appeared, pulled the woman away and reacted to Larry Lovelace's mild protestation at this ungentlemanly behaviour by throwing a wild punch at him. A scuffle broke out, tables were overturned, and a free-for-all ensued.

For the first time in its history, the Island Club was invaded by the police, called by Marshall, who came to put an end to the fight. When the dust had settled the *femme fatale* and belligerent white man responsible for starting the fracas were nowhere to be seen.

That incident was the forerunner of several altercations involving white couples who had not been seen in the Island Club before. And always George Mahoney would telephone some days afterwards and offer Marshall mock sympathy and reiterate his proposal, which had extended to part ownership.

Marshall instructed his doorman to be extra vigilant and deny entry to people who looked like troublemakers. None the less, one night, a month into this season of violence, a young Jamaican immigrant, who had been in England for less than a month, was stabbed at the Island Club. He died two days later in hospital. The Jamaican nurse who had watched over the hapless young man in his dying hours swore she could smell the aroma of freshly roasted coffee when, with his last breath, he begged her to promise him that his body would be taken back to the village in the foothills of the Blue Mountains where he was born.

Marshall paid for the young man's body to be shipped to Jamaica and closed the Island Club as a gesture of respect to the deceased. The restaurant remained open and it was there, one evening, that he confided to Mr Delisser that he suspected that George Mahoney's hands were dripping with the blood of guilt. Mr Delisser listened to Marshall's account of the visit and telephone calls from the sinister businessman, then suggested to Marshall that he invite Mahoney to dinner, ostensibly to discuss some sort of deal, and the rest would be taken care of.

Mahoney was delighted to hear from Marshall. The next day he came to the restaurant and engaged Marshall in a long discussion about his plans for the Island Club, all of which sounded attractive to Marshall, except that they came from a man whom he found morally reprehensible. While they talked Mr Delisser served up a simple dish of steamed Dover sole in its own stew and young potatoes garnished with parsley, as George Mahoney was a fastidious eater with a preference for plain food. The meeting was inconclusive and arrangements were made to continue negotiations. After Mahoney left, Mr Delisser said with a tone of quiet satisfaction: 'Don't worry, you won't see him again.'

Marshall would remember the drained, exhausted expression on the maestro's face, as if he had poured all his energy into that simple fare, as if he had been compelled to summon powers that could not be wielded without harming both protagonist and antagonist.

Mr Delisser did not lie. The rumours that reached Marshall's ears from various sources told of a sudden victim of some mysterious malady which began with itching of unbearable intensity. A bath full of calamine lotion gave George Mahoney temporary relief, but as the irritation grew worse that soon became ineffective. Mahoney sought help from all quarters but to no avail and eventually resorted to hiring a team of private nurses. They worked around the clock to soothe his inflamed skin. But neither the nurses nor the doctors he then consulted could help Mahoney when the itching reached his brain. In one of his now rare lucid moments he is said to have compared the sensation to having an army of ants in his skull. Marshall's prospective business partner was, supposedly, last seen being bundled into an ambulance, straitjacketed and screaming profanities between pleading for someone to douse the fire in his brains.

These apocryphal accounts of George Mahoney's last days among the sane were, however, little consolation for Marshall because around the same time Mr Delisser fell gravely ill. He collapsed in the restaurant's kitchen, and suffered what seemed like an epileptic fit accompanied by the utterance of feverish, incomprehensible monologues. While Jean Myers called an ambulance, Marshall clung to the tremulous, babbling figure. Then Mr Delisser was suddenly still. Speaking calmly, he tried to assure a terrified Marshall that he would be all right, and was only paying the price for ridding the Island Club of George Mahoney. Mr Delisser was hospitalised and Marshall stayed with him through a long night of febrile ranting, copious sweating and violent palpitations. Although Marshall's linguistic knowledge did not extend beyond English, he could have sworn that, in the course of ten hours, Mr Delisser's babblings, which often attained an incantatory pitch, were expressed in a plethora of languages, as if he were fluent in all the languages of the innumerable recipes he had dedicated his life to mastering.

The morning light brought the stillness which the medication could not give the chef, and when Marshall was satisfied that he was in deep sleep, he set off for home with the growing realisation that Mr Delisser was far, far more than a masterchef. On subsequent visits to the hospital Marshall was told that it would be a long time before Mr Delisser could work again. The doctors confessed that they couldn't diagnose his condition, compared it to a form of extreme mental exhaustion, and made a gloomy prognosis based on their estimation of Mr Delisser's age, about which they were uncertain because he had the desiccated skin of a centenarian and, on his better days, the heartbeat of an ox.

Marshall could not help them with Mr Delisser's age, nor his first name because he had only ever addressed him as Mr Delisser, like everybody who came into contact with him; neither could he make them understand the patient's refusal to touch the hospital food.

Despite Mr Delisser's reassurances Marshall did not believe he would ever recover until he saw him sitting up in bed, advising the head nurse on ways to improve the hospital diet. Marshall had already started looking for a new chef and his suspicion that Mr Delisser would prove to be irreplaceable was soon confirmed.

Anxious to reopen the restaurant and believing that he was not in a position to be too choosy, he employed the first chef who answered his advert for an expert in Caribbean cuisine. The new chef was a Mauritian who persuaded Marshall that he could cook West Indian dishes. But in his first week he caused a fire in the kitchen, blamed it on the antediluvian cooking appliances and resigned before Marshall could sack him.

The next chef seemed to bring with him a plague of rats whose excreta was everywhere, and after a time became so bold that one fought a diner for his meal and the incident, reported to the authorities, brought the local health inspectors swarming over the restaurant before they issued a health hazard warning and closed the restaurant down until sanitation was improved.

The nightclub fared only marginally better. Bands and acts were still reluctant to perform there and last-minute cancellations were not unusual. Sometimes the acts simply failed to turn up, and Marshall was forced to refund money to customers. A full bottle of whisky, and sixty cigarettes daily were now indispensable crutches to him.

Nevertheless the Island Club enjoyed a period of revival. The fights and the fatal stabbing had earned it notoriety and many of the new customers were themselves already notorious. Pimps, prostitutes and petty gangsters made the Island Club their Saturday night haunt, driving away the hard-working men and women who had sustained it in its earlier days. Yet Marshall took to these disreputable characters with surprising warmth.

Then some weeks before his alcohol and entertainment licence came up for renewal he received another visit from someone wanting a stake in the Island Club. This new interloper was Detective Inspector Milligan, a man who oozed corruption in his smile. He warned Marshall that the police might oppose the Island Club's licence renewal because the place had become a seedbed of vice.

Hardened by his experience with George Mahoney, Marshall asked what it would take to ensure that his licence was renewed. Detective Inspector Milligan smiled his corrupt smile, mentioned a figure which he euphemistically called a commission and the matter was settled. Every Monday from then on Milligan called at the Island Club to collect a brown envelope of notes. The licence came through but Marshall now found himself with an expensive employee whose regular pay demands ate up his profits. To add to his troubles, several tenants in his houses claimed that his rent was exorbitantly high for the standard of accommodation and he was named in a local newspaper report as one of Westminster's new slum landlords.

Around the time Mr Delisser was transferred to a sanatorium in Cornwall, Detective Milligan brought five girls to the Island Club and installed them as resident whores. Within a matter of months Marshall's business went from being the most respectable, the classiest Caribbean entertainment venue and restaurant in London to being the embodiment of all the loose morals which Caribbean immigrants were accused of bringing to Britain, and corrupting innocent English girls.

The police raided it one night and arrested several whores and drugs dealers, who had not been licensed by Detective Inspector Milligan, and threatened to charge Marshall with running a brothel. The next week his special employee's salary had to be doubled. Now, when he looked at himself in the mirror in the mornings Marshall thought he saw Mephistophelean horns sprouting through his hair.

His political work gave him no respite from these troubles. As the Kinjaian elections approached, the committee meetings became more and more fractious and protracted and seemingly futile.

Jeffrye Washington, who had been sent to America to raise funds for the Kinjaian cause, disappeared off the face of the earth with the proceeds of several fund-raising balls in New York, Chicago and Washington. Three months later rumours began to circulate that he was really a CIA employee, an *agent provocateur*, and the secret representative of a huge American arms manufacturing company. Other rumours claimed that Jeffrye Washington was really Ilyich Konstadt, the progeny of an African-American who had migrated to revolutionary Russia, and an agent of the KGB. Nobody knew what to believe. Only one thing was clear: Jeffrye Washington was not who he said he was. There was no record of him having existed beyond the committee meetings and the Pan-Africanist circles where he enjoyed a reputation as a fiery revolutionary.

The mystery of Jeffrye Washington dominated the committee meetings, caused bitter quarrels and spread distrust as everybody was now required to give an account of their credentials. When Marshall refused to say how he had got the money to start the Island Club he became a target of suspicions. Meetings took place without him, papers were circulated to other members but not him. He found going to the meetings a laborious chore but feared that his absence would be interpreted as a sign that he had something to hide. When he turned up at Kenneth Braithwaite's house and discovered that that evening's meeting had been cancelled and he was the only person who had not been told, his interest in the Free Martin Mayini Campaign suffered a fatal blow. He withdrew further into himself and began to dwell on his failure and the people and things he had lost.

One night he reached such an emotional nadir that as he passed Jean Myers's flat he decided to call on her. She seemed delighted to see him and her visible excitement cheered him somewhat. And when she surrendered her shrivelled, starved body to him, he felt relieved of some great pressure and that for the first time in many weeks he would be able to sleep through the night.

But halfway through the night he was woken up by Jean Myers, who said: 'Marshall, you'd better go home. You've been crying in your sleep.' Her voice sounded hard and unforgiving, as if after all these years of pursuing him she had discovered that he was not a man, but a weakling, unable to withstand the pressures of life, a baby who sought comfort at a woman's breast.

The following day, she revealed her role in Scoop's and Zenobia's disappearance and resigned from her job.

Christmas approached and Marshall found himself in the grip of an unbearable loneliness. He went in search of Pat Boyle, a neglected friend, but discovered that since the invasion of Hungary, Boyle had resigned from the Communist Party and was considered a non-person by his former comrades. Nobody answered the door of his house and it looked unoccupied, but Marshall hung around for a while until a neighbour told him that she had not seen Pat Boyle for months, and believed that he was studying somewhere in the north of England. Some days later, passing a toyshop, he bought a rocking-horse and struggled with it through a crowded Oxord Street, and because he could not get a cab decided to take the underground. He brought it to the house where he and Zenobia and Martin-Johann had lived, and only on his arrival did he remember that his wife and his son no longer lived there.

The Island Club suddenly went through another drought and Marshall spent Christmas Eve there with a few sorry-looking customers. All strangers, they had not heard the rumour that Marshall Sarjeant had been cursed and anybody around him would be cursed too. The atmosphere of the place suited his mood. Much of Christmas Day passed in an alcoholic daze, and in the evening when he went out the empty streets and tinsel-clad shop windows so saddened him that he took a bottle of rum and mixed it with Scotch and did not wake up for three days.

The act that had been booked for the New Year's Eve Party at least had the decency to call and let him know that due to illness they would not be performing at the Island Club. Two days later when, on one of his meditative strolls, he ran into a customer and was told that this same act had performed at a nightclub in Brixton and would be there for New Year's Eve he adjusted his mask, shrugged his shoulders and walked on, ending up on the Embankment and staring into the River Thames where he thought he heard the mourning of the river's ghosts and an invitation for him to join them in their watery repose. Only the thought of his unfulfilled mission kept him from throwing himself into the river of his despair.

That night he woke up to the smell of burning, dressed hurriedly and fought his way down the stairs through the thickening smoke. There was fire in the basement and he could do nothing about it. He waited for ages on the pavement before the fire engines arrived. By then most of the ground and first floors had been destroyed. When the firemen left, he went back upstairs and lay in bed wondering why he felt so relieved, as if some great weight had been lifted off his shoulders, as if he were free to start again.

But he did not start again: instead, he returned to past

habits. An encounter with an old gambling associate revived his passion for poker. Forgetting Santos's injunction, he began to play wherever he could find a game. When his cash ran out he sold several of his houses and gambled the proceeds away.

He was seldom abroad during the day now. His nights were passed in smoky basements where men coughed with such violence that it was a wonder their chests were not rent apart. Yet he felt at home in these subterranean dives, felt a serenity which the world above no longer gave him.

The spring found Marshall in dispute with the insurance company who claimed that they had clear evidence of arson, and held him responsible for starting the fire with the intention of collecting the insurance money because his business was failing.

News of his wife and son came via a friend who told him that they had been seen on the Orinoco river, had taken up residence at a house on a bend there and were farming the land. In the privacy of his apartment, above the burnt-out restaurant and nightclub, Marshall wept in his sleep.

Then one morning, not long back from a marathon poker game in which he had lost thousands of pounds, the doorbell stirred him from sleep in the arms of a young whore whose time and love he had purchased because alcohol alone was no longer enough to give him peaceful nights. He tried to ignore it but it persisted, and when he went to answer the door, he found Dr Kenneth Braithwaite standing outside. Even in his somnolent state he could see the surprise on the doctor's face and imagined that his horns were showing.

Braithwaite had brought good news. He had just returned from Kinja's independence celebrations where he had been a guest of Prime Minister Martin Mayini, who had expressed regret that Marshall Sarjeant, one of the most energetic supporters of the Pan-Africanist struggle, was not there to mark that great day.

Marshall asked Braithwaite what year it was. And when

Braithwaite answered, 'It's 1961,' Marshall realised that he had lost almost three years of his life in the fall.

A month later Marshall locked up the Island Club, handed the keys to his solicitors with instructions to dispose of the building, and start divorce proceedings against Zenobia. Leaving a 'Closed until further notice' sign on the door of the Island Club, he set off, accompanied by the thought that if the vultures of misfortune which had been picking at the carrion of his life, stripping him of friends and possessions, threatening to leave only the bare white bones of a life once so rich with promise, if those vultures chose to swoop on the building they were welcome to it. He was a man on the run, a man desperately in search of the inner calm destroyed by the recent years of betrayal, loss and defeat. His greatest defeat, of course, lay in setting off for Africa, the final destination of his odyssey, without Nana Sarjeant's ka.

PART III

I

Roused from a stupor of personal disasters, Marshall Sarjeant was astonished at the political changes sweeping across the African continent. The Union Jack and the French Tricolour were being folded up, in some places with relieved haste, and dispatched back to Britain and France, the two principal nations which had altruistically burdened themselves with the thankless task of civilising Africans. A few unreconstructed colonialists still clung to their swathes of Africa in Angola, Mozambique and Rhodesia, and in South Africa the spirit of Nazi Germany had been given flesh in a monstrously racist state, a mocking monument to the aspirations of Africans everywhere. But Africans could now boast universities, colleges, schools, tarmac roads, railway systems, airports; and these belonged not to tribes – that most rudimentary of social groupings – but to nations with national flags, anthems, armies, budgets, development plans, parliaments, prime ministers and cabinets.

Although the military brass bands that had once played 'God Save the Queen' now sounded somewhat discordant as they played the newly composed national anthems, accompanied by the faltering, inharmonious singing of prime ministers and cabinet ministers, schoolchildren and soldiers who could not remember the words which were supposed to express the spirit of the new nations carved from diverse peoples, it was hoped that time would bring about greater harmony. Freedom was still an unfinished song.

Africa, Marshall recognised, was not alone in shouting out this song of freedom. The falling apart of the thing that was the British Empire also meant independence for several West

Indian islands, including Jamaica. While many West Indians of African descent were happy with their island homes, a small minority saw in the crumbling of empire, a chance to reclaim and celebrate the Africanness that had survived centuries of exile. In the United States, the African descendants there were also nearing the climax of a long struggle, which was not about independence, but an end to inequalites and injustices. The civil rights movement was gathering momentum, along with a plethora of radical political organisations.

So it seemed that Africans everywhere, those on the continent and their descendants in the Americas, were finally being admitted to the free world as equals. This would be the decade of Black Power, Afro hairstyles and dashiki shirts, clenched-fist salutes, the humility of Martin Luther King and the implacable anger of Malcolm X. Though these disparate events, personalities and trends seemed unconnected, to men like Marshall Sarjeant they belonged to the same order of historical events as the countless plantation uprisings which marked slavery days, the Haitian revolution, the abolition of slavery in the West Indies and later the United States – key battles in the centuries-old war between Black and White, African and European.

It seemed to Marshall that no other African leader personified the spirit of this awakening African world more than Martin Mayini, the Prime Minister of newly independent Kinja. Mayini's autobiography, written during his imprisonment, had been published to universal acclaim while he was campaigning for the prime ministership of Kinja. Titled *Facing the Atlantic,* the book showed an extraordinarily comprehensive knowledge of Africa and the African diaspora. Mayini saw himself as part of a tradition which included Toussaint L'Ouverture, Nat Turner, the Jamaican Maroons, King Jaji and Emperor Menelik. When the Harlem-based national newspaper the *Amsterdam News* ran extracts from *Facing the Atlantic,* for weeks its letters page was dominated by correspondence from African-Americans who recognised in some of the customs and folklore recalled by Mayini the beliefs of their grandparents.

Three months after Kinja gained independence Mayini spoke at the United Nations headquarters in New York and thousands of African-Americans gathered outside, hoping to catch a glimpse of the slim, white-haired figure with the beatific smile and air of saintliness. His unscheduled stroll through Harlem, where he had lived briefly while a student at Columbia University, brought Manhattan to a virtual standstill. His impromptu invitation to all Americans of African descent to regard Kinja as the portal back into the home of their ancestors was greeted with raucous cheers which could be heard far across Brooklyn Bridge. Portraits of Martin Mayini dressed in white voluminous robe, leopardskin hat, and holding a flywhisk made from the tail of a lion outsold pictures of Jesus Christ. His words and images penetrated even the remotest corner of the Amazon jungle where, according to a report in the *National Geographic,* a group of Yorubas, who had a century before fled the slave plantations in Brazil and recreated their own culture, elevated the former political prisoner to their pantheon of deities and attributed to him the qualities of patience, resolution and faith.

The UN visit which transformed Mayini into a Black icon had repercussions in Eko, formerly Victoria, the Kinjaian capital. This steamy coastal city of lagoons, grandiloquent colonial buildings and urban slums was already being transformed by extensive land clearances to build highways, flyovers, skyscrapers, stadiums, and monuments that would reflect the nation's great aspirations. It would become the Mecca of Africanness, attracting pilgrims from the Americas who had been inspired to visit the continent and explore their roots. Identifiable by their colourful dashikis and Afro hairstyles, they slept rough on the streets, rented rooms in shacks, swelled the few hotels.

When a shrewd Kinjaian called Butu Mwaka appointed himself 'Keeper of the African Gates', and charged these pilgrims five dollars for participating in a ceremony of return, the main beach around Eko would be crowded on Sundays with people dressed in white. The ceremony included a long period of immersion in the Atlantic, during which time the participant, starved of oxygen, was supposed to be possessed by the spirit of a slave bound for the Americas, who had, centuries before, drowned him or herself rather than endure the middle passage. On emerging, the person would be given a new name, and instructed to wrap his or her United States passport in a bag of stones and throw it into the haunted ocean.

From the Caribbean basin came large contingents of Rastafarians. Most of these dreadlocked figures stopped in Kinja en route to Ethiopia; but others, on hearing familiar words in the languages of the coastal peoples of Kinja, made a not inconsiderable intellectual leap and concluded that the Zion of their destination had all along really been the languages, names, myths, gods and rituals that their ancestors had lost on the slave plantations, and that their deification and worship of Ethiopia's Emperor Haile Selassie was an error born of their disorienting captivity in Babylon, so they remained in Eko.

These disparate groups from the African diaspora with their dreams of racial redemption combined with the diverse and numerous peoples who also flooded into the capital from within Kinja and other parts of Africa, to make Eko an exciting, heady place, a veritable Black metropolis the likes of which had not been seen anywhere in the world since the Harlem of the 1920s, a bustling city full of energy and optimism, a symbol of the African spirit, vanquished and humiliated over four centuries, and now rising in the early afternoon of the twentieth century.

It was into this tumultuous African dawn that Marshall Sarjeant fled from a London that had sucked him into its bowels of depravity and dissolution. The islander, now a grossly overweight chainsmoker, saw in Africa a chance to start anew, to placate the often debilitating feelings of failure caused by the loss of Nana Sarjeant's ka, to heal the lacerations of his heart inflicted by Scoop Fearon and Zenobia Blomfontein, to find redemption, love and peace. But his arrival in Kinja was memorably unpromising. His flight, delayed in London and slowed by air turbulence, landed after midnight in an airport that seemed more like an airstrip carved from wilderness because only darkness lay beyond the perimeters of silhouetted coconut trees.

The few airport taxis were snapped up by more experienced travellers to Kinja and Marshall was left standing at the taxi rank, alone and bereft of any idea as to how he could continue his journey and find a bed for the night. He had begun to reconcile himself to the possibility that the morning might still find him waiting for a ride when a noisy, beat-up cab came to a shuddering halt at the rank. The driver was a muscular dwarfish Kinjaian with a broad brilliant smile which swallowed his face, and an air of manic energy.

Squashed in the tiny car, sweating copiously, Marshall spent an unsuccessful hour scouring Eko for a hotel room. Even the shabbiest establishments were full to capacity. After the twelfth attempt, even the diminutive Kinjaian taxi driver, who had been full of confidence, sighed in weary despair. Then he suddenly perked up, and suggested that he knew of a hotel five miles outside Eko, along the coastal road, that was bound to have a room. There was something trustworthy about the driver so Marshall surrendered himself to his care.

They struck the city limits quickly and entered a pure thick syrupy darkness, punctuated by the scent and sounds of the sea, and these once familiar emanations from the nights stilled the doubts Marshall had about this desperate search for a hotel room. Suddenly, it started to rain and the visibility created by the car's headlights was halved by the downpour as the windscreen wipers were slow and ineffective. Yet the driver did not slow down, rather he accelerated, sped through the darkness and the rain as if inspired by it. Now fear invaded Marshall and he thought of death on this darkened African road within hours of reaching his destination after a twenty-year journey, of Paradise to which he would never return, of the son he did not know and who would now never know him, of Constance who had given him his first kiss and was now searching for inner peace. But death did not strike him on that road and when they came to a halt outside the Brighton-Lisbon Hotel Marshall felt as though the driver had been sent specially to deliver him here.

That night saw the onset of a fever which quickly reached a crippling intensity and kept Marshall confined to his room. Behind wooden slatted windows, on a metal bed with a thin mattress, with the persistent whirr of mosquitoes and the sound of the ocean – so similar, he often thought, to the steady drone of urban traffic – he emerged from his febrile nights drenched in sweat and shivering violently, as if naked in the snow. Sleep came to him at erratic, unpredictable hours and was always accompanied by the dream of the skeletal nun on the red island. The perpetual chase continued around and across the mountainous island, just him and the bony figure clad in a white habit and, as in the past, the closer he approached, the more distant she seemed. How he wearied of this eternal chase which, in some indecipherable way seemed to resemble his waking life.

Just when his exhaustion seemed soul-deep a new figure joined the landscape. It came to him at first only in epiphanic flashes: a vision of a dark woman clad in only a piece of cloth around her waist, her bare breasts rising from her chest as proud and magnificent as the mountains, and she carried on her head a large purple fish. She held its neck with her right hand, while its fins rested on her slender shoulder, and seemed frozen in a walking pose. There was no movement from her; she was always still, like a statue, though the texture of her flesh and the water dripping off the fish all suggested that she was as human as Marshall. Then he started seeing her with greater frequency and clarity, as clearly as the skeletal nun. He saw her beside banyan trees festooned with vines; in the shadow of smooth, rain-polished, sun-bleached rocks, between palm trees bent by the wind, on the long, desolate golden sand of the beaches with the surf washing her immobile feet; he saw her in torrential rain, water rushing off her dark skin, and at those moments, though she remained still, the fins of the fish thrashed her shoulder, as if animated by the heavenly water. He wanted to stop and ask her name, and enquire how he could escape this perpetual chase, this never-ending dream, but his legs did not belong to him, they belonged to the pursuit of the skeletal nun.

Then on a night when an electric storm played in the sky above the ocean, Marshall wandered from his room, and across the sloping lawn of the hotel, down to the beach. As he stood there looking out to sea, he imagined that he could hear the deformed children of Paradise weeping at his failure. The mourning gradually subsided and was replaced by the celebratory music of triumphant horns and drums, which none the less resonated with the melancholy of things irrevocably lost. That night was his eighth in Kinja and he later slept a dreamless sleep and woke up feeling that he had finally arrived in Africa.

The next day, following advice given him by Kenneth Braithwaite, Marshall reported to the Bureau of Foreign Africans. This was attached to the Ministry of Internal Affairs and staffed by African-Americans who had been involved in the Free Martin Mayini Campaign. It was his ambition to gain audience with Prime Minister Mayini, but he learnt that Eko was teeming with other visitors with the same purpose. Marshall would have to take his place in the queue. He reported to the Bureau of Foreign Africans on alternate days and spent the rest of his time wandering around Eko, tramping through its dusty streets from the Arab quarters to the leafy government reservations where colonial civil servants once lived. He spent long hours beside the sea in silent contemplation of the enormity of his achievement in recrossing the Atlantic, allowed himself to be led by half-naked little boys to see rusting slave chains on old derelict quaysides and sometimes felt so moved that he sought solitude to weep alone because tears were the only response to those horrendous relics of men's greed-inspired cruelty.

He had been in Eko for two weeks when the good fortune of landing in the Brighton-Lisbon Hotel began to register on him. Located in a small horseshoe-shaped bay, from a distance it looked like an English manorial house. Its African staff were all immaculately and uncomfortably dressed in starched uniforms, but each day had nothing to do because, despite the dearth of hotels in Eko, visitors rarely stopped in this one.

The owner did not seem to mind. He was a Brazilian by the name of Alfredo Costamanta and he told Marshall that the hotel had been built originally by a Dutch merchant who kept his most highly prized slaves in the cellar. Costamanta spent most of his days alone in the games room, reading from sea-stained books, or playing snooker on a full-sized table with lion-shaped legs carved from ebony wood. A handsome thick-set man with luxuriant, curly black hair, and a waxed moustache, bovine eyes, a penchant for three-piece linen suits, and an air of fretful languor, Alfredo Costamanta was delighted by Marshall's presence because, though he had been in Africa for thirty years, he regarded himself as a child of the Americas, a progeny of the New World. Unfortunately, he had been thrust back on to this ancient continent by family obligations.

Costamanta had inherited the Brighton-Lisbon from his father, who in turn had inherited it from a paternal uncle. The whole family had uprooted themselves from Rio de Janeiro while Alfredo was still a child, but his Spanish-born mother had detested the building. She was haunted by the stench of blood which she imagined came from the cellars, now used to store provisions, and though Costamanta senior employed three hundred Africans to wash down every stone with lime water, the odour remained obdurately ineradicable. Fearing for his wife's sanity, Costamanta senior had sent her back to Brazil, where she died within a month of returning.

Alfredo had been a student in Europe when he suddenly found himself thrust into the hotel business after the war because his father took ill. The old man's dying lasted a whole decade and was marked by frequent bouts of fever in which he called out for the late Clementina Costamanta, the only woman he had ever loved, to return to him and share his paradise here in Kinja.

Alfredo did not conceal his love of the bright lights and theatres and fashion salons of Europe. But out of loyalty to his father, he had repressed his longing for Madrid, Paris and Lisbon, the cities of his youth where he had spent many idle hours playing snooker, drinking absinthe in pavement cafés and discussing the latest ideas in philosophy. He fancied himself as both a proficient snooker player and philosopher and loved nothing better than to while away the night drinking rum and pontificating on his favourite subject: the African condition. Nevertheless, his silences were long and his sighs expressed the weariness of a man of multiple exile.

Once a week, always in the afternoon, one of his concubines shared his bed, and he was convinced that the Brighton-Lisbon Hotel was an accursed place that had robbed him of the power to procreate, for despite the seraglio he had once kept, no woman had presented him with a child. How he longed to be out of Africa, to be back in Europe, back in the metropolis, but he had sworn to his dying father that he would remain in Kinja. He regretted that he had been true to his word because he now sensed an imminent season of chaos. Europeans with deeper roots than himself had fled, frightened away by independence and the prospect of African rule.

One morning he drove Marshall along the coast and showed him an unfinished ten-floor hotel, and recounted how the owners, on hearing of Mayini's release, brought all work to a halt. In one rainy season, the building was already being reclaimed by the bush, sea salt caked the bare concrete walls of its windowless rooms and a flock of gulls had colonised the tenth floor, as if it were just another piece of rock thrown up by nature's eruptions. Had he been in love with the Kinjaian coastline, as his father had been, he would have sought to buy the building, but his heart belonged elsewhere and he was looking for an opportunity to gain his independence from the tyranny of his legacy. 'My past is my chains,' he often said, 'my father the lock for which I must find the key.'

Marshall felt a strong affinity – born of a shared sense of being prisoners of their inheritance – with Alfredo Costamanta. They passed many hours together in the games room of the Brighton-Lisbon Hotel playing snooker, with the Atlantic Ocean visible through the windows, and talking about their pasts. Both were in need of reliquaries into which they could pour their stories, unburden themselves of the strange adventures their different but similar legacies had given them.

When, after two months of living in the Brighton-Lisbon Hotel, Marshall received a much delayed letter from his London solicitors instructing him that they had received a serious offer for the Island Club building, it occurred to Marshall that he could help Alfredo escape from Kinja. The Brazilian exile did not leap at the suggestion he exchange the Brighton-Lisbon Hotel for the Island Club (still in need of repair after the fire), the fog-bound capital city of a former empire for the edge of a continent, a city and a jungle. He would have to give the proposal careful thought.

His deliberation lasted for a week and during that time he wandered from the balcony, with its view of the ocean, down to the beach where he rested under the wind-sculpted sea-grape tree planted by his father, to the four corners of his demesne where he struggled with memories of happy times and reasons to remain in Kinja.

Then he challenged his guest to ninety-nine frames of snooker, with the exchange of properties, plus some cash from Marshall, as the prize. They played at a leisurely pace over six days. They played through nights when the distant sound of the Atlantic crashed against the coastal rocks, the crepitation and brilliant flashes of lightning from electric storms over the ocean synchronised with the hypnotic drumming which came from a nearby fishing village. They played through a day when the crackling of hailstones assaulting the roof vied with the clacking of the ivory balls, and another day when the damp coastal heat reduced their movements to a slow, ponderous pace as they waded through the humid air, which made nonsense of their best strokes.

Alfredo Costamanta would later maintain that he played to win out of respect for his opponent and even greater respect for his legacy, but some unseen force robbed him of victory on the very last frame. And so Marshall became the proprietor of the Brighton-Lisbon Hotel, confident that it was an honest swap. All the signs suggested that at the rate Eko was growing, the location of the building would soon place it in a suburb of the city.

Though Alfredo Costamanta promised to keep in touch, even come back as a guest one day, Marshall would not hear from him for many years until the former proprietor had married an American and migrated to Philadelphia, where on hot summer days he sometimes pined for the Kinjaian coast and rued throwing away his legacy in a game of snooker.

Not since being compelled to leave Paradise had Marshall felt so contented, so at peace with himself as in his first few weeks as the owner of the Brighton-Lisbon Hotel. His little corner of Africa had revived something in him, a zest for life, a passion for the simple pleasures of witnessing the slow unfolding of the morning, the light playing on the ocean surface, the brief dusk that preceded the long nights. He was a child of nature who had been exiled to its opposite extreme – the city.

Early each morning he swam in the calm water of the bay, rediscovered swimming strokes that were once as natural as walking, rolled in the ocean like a mighty whale once beached and now reunited with his element. Then he would take breakfast on the balcony of his room-cum-office and watch the fishermen row past the mouth of the bay in crude boats, and read the previous day's newspapers to catch up on the news, while sipping fresh coffee grown in the Kinjaian highlands.

2

Under the reluctant ownership of the lugubrious Brazilian the Brighton-Lisbon had been the well-guarded secret of a select group of European settler farmers from the Plateau region, their overnight stop when business matters brought them down to the capital, their seaside sanatorium when stricken with the enervating melancholia of the harmattan, their peaceful retreat when the haunting sound of the drums across the plateau nights frayed their nerves.

The new Brighton-Lisbon Hotel held no attraction for distressed highland settlers. Eko suffered from a housing shortage and Marshall, exploiting his government contacts, filled all the rooms with long-term guests, all civil servants, prepared to suffer the inconvenience of commuting to and from Eko daily. Their recompense came in the evenings and at weekends, and in many guises – the games room, the sea breeze and the Africa Bar, one of Marshall's innovations. Sited in the topmost corner of the gently sloping lawn, shaded by a riotously sprawling tamarind tree, the Africa Bar was a circular thatched building with comfortable rattan easy chairs and low bamboo tables. Bar food was provided by an adjoining barbecue and customers were invited to challenge the cook – Akante Ousman, a skinny northern Kinjaian of limited gastronomic skills – and eat as much as they could from a cornucopia of peppery-hot meat, fish and poultry. On Friday and Saturday nights, highlife music, as sweet and slowly intoxicating as palm wine, played by Prince Limpopo and his All Stars Band, drifted out to sea and lured into the bay such an abundance of fish, especially Atlantic sole, that the local fishermen took to casting their nets at those hours and repaid the owner with free supplies.

Most of the hotel boarders were married men with wives and children upcountry, and the last weekend of each month – when civil servants were paid – they deserted the Brighton-Lisbon for the family comforts awaiting them in the villages and towns nestled in the tropical forests beyond Eko and returned bearing yams and pineapples and mangoes for their landlord.

The only exception to this monthly exodus was Baku Mathaku. Baku arrived at the Brighton-Lisbon one day on a Raleigh bicycle, bought, he would later reveal, from a retired district commissioner, with a small suitcase strapped on the handlebar. He eschewed all motorised transport. He would stay for almost a decade and during that time he would never own more than enough clothes to fit into his small suitcase.

It took Marshall some time to understand why the other residents shunned this homunculus of a man with the bright eyes, permanent abstracted air about him and an uncommon fondness for bananas, which in his idle hours he could often be seen chomping under a tree in a secluded spot like the ancient philosophers were supposed to do. They referred to him as 'that madman'. After his first conversation with Baku, on a weekend when the Brighton-Lisbon was deserted, Marshall retired to his room feeling violently antagonistic towards him, and vowing to avoid the argumentative civil servant's company. Baku was not mad but he possessed a great talent for maddening people.

By the time the other guests returned, Marshall realised that Baku was perhaps the most intelligent man he had ever met. They would spend many hours together in the Africa Bar, strolling round the lawn and along the short beach, arguing – you did not discuss things with Baku; he always demanded an argument – about African and Kinjaian politics. A conversation for Baku was like a game of football without goalposts or a duration, something to be kicked around indefinitely. One of his most common conversational gambits was, 'Remember that point you made?' Then he would proceed to voice some new angle of disagreement while Marshall rummaged around in his memory for the remark which could have been made weeks, months or even years ago and which Baku had stored in his own incredible memory, which also contained knowledge of ten of Kinja's two hundred languages as well as Arabic and Swahili.

One day, early in their relationship, Marshall, wearied by Baku's disputatiousness, said to him: 'Baku, why do you argue so much?'

Baku replied instantly: 'If we agreed, there would be nothing to talk about; if we agreed knowledge would die; if we agreed there would be no universities, no newspapers, no books. There would be silence and stagnation.'

His uncle was the Kinjaian Ambassador to France and Baku himself could have held a highly prized foreign posting but for a few quirky, irremediable flaws. His lack of respect for authority and excoriating tongue played their part, but far more important was his hobby: Baku was an amateur entomologist, specifically an amateur hymenopterist, with an obsessive interest in the construction of anthills. Most weekend mornings, he set off on his bicycle in search of ochre-coloured mounds built with patient industry by ant colonies, and the greater the size of the anthill, the greater his excitement. What intrigued him, he told Marshall, was the intricacy of their architecture and their ability to withstand droughts and floods. He claimed that the pyramids of Egypt were inspired by anthills and that somewhere in Kinja was a thousand-year-old anthill which contained the secret of all anthills that would make cement obsolete. Marshall once accompanied Baku on a safari in search of termite mounds and though his friend and tenant showed him an impressive example and waxed lyrical at their strength and harmonious structure, he, Marshall, could not appreciate it. Indeed, when Baku disturbed the mound and ants ran out, Marshall's mind was flooded with the discomforting memory of seeing Teacher Lee's ant-ravaged face.

It was soon after that expedition that Marshall's stay in Kinja underwent a dramatic change. The revamped Brighton-Lisbon Hotel had remained for several blissful months the secret of its civil service residents, their friends and a few aficionados of highlife music. When it became common knowledge that the proprietor was on first-name terms with Prime Minister Martin Mayini, things were never the same. Their friendship was renewed when Marshall was invited to the unveiling of the Prime Minister's statue in Independence Square. On that day all government buildings in central Eko were festooned with the national flag and the standard of the ruling People's National Party, as the National Freedom Party was now renamed. Thousands of excited people lined the streets leading to Independence Square, which had been cordoned off. Only those with an official invitation were admitted through gates guarded by fearsome-looking soldiers in sunglasses and clasping rifles across their chests. To his surprise, Marshall discovered that he had a seat in the VIP section, right at the back of some twenty rows of seats behind the Prime Minister himself. The Prime Minister – flanked by the First Lady and cabinet ministers and military men – was buried in a plush, deep red, high-back chair that resembled a throne. Elsewhere in the makeshift stand of privileged spectators were haughty, rotund chiefs swaddled in gold-embossed cloth, their faces polished from birth with shea butter, surrounded by their wives, some almost pubescent in appearance, their necks and wrists draped in gold jewellery.

The event began with a marching military brass band playing the national anthem, followed by the Eko Regiment of the army and then hundreds of marching khaki-clad schoolchildren waving the nation's red, yellow and green flag. They were followed by a column of dancing women, horsemen, more dancers and praise singers representing every region of Kinja and every sector of society. Then the speeches came. The Oni of Maraka, the spiritual centre of the Western region, delivered the longest peroration with all the selfadoration of a man who loved his own plummy public school English accent. The speeches of the representatives from the North and East were considerably shorter, which was much appreciated because noon was approaching and an intolerable heat emanated from the sky.

Then the Prime Minister left his seat and ceremonially pulled the rope which instantly billowed aside a canvas sheet to reveal a thirty-foot stone statue of himself, enrobed but without his famous leopard-skin hat, with outstretched arms, upturned palms, and a smile of Messianic benevolence such as might be seen on one of those mass-produced images of Jesus Christ hung in the homes of poverty-stricken Christians for their daily succour. The seated spectators applauded, and the people denied admission to the square roared. After the unveilings VIP guests mingled with the Prime Minister and members of his cabinet in a vast marquee. Champagne and beer flowed like a heavy rainfall.

Marshall was standing with Wade Mayana – who was a special adviser to the Prime Minister – and a group of African-American colleagues from the Bureau of Foreign Africans, when he was summoned to the Prime Minister's side. As they stood face to face for the first time since Mayini's valedictory celebration in the Island Club, they smiled warmly at each other, and Mayini ignored Marshall's outstretched hand and instead reached out and embraced him, clasping him to his chest as if he were a long-lost brother, as if they had shared some perilous voyage in a storm-tossed vessel across the oceans of the past. When the Prime Minister released Marshall, they shook hands, and perhaps because silence now prevailed, as most people within seemed stupefied by the national leader's exuberant display of friendship towards this mere restaurateur-cum-hotelier, Mayini gave a brief speech on the important role played by diaspora Africans, men like Marshall Sarjeant, in Kinja's independence struggle.

The following morning Marshall found a photograph of himself beside Prime Minister Mayini in all the daily newspapers. Over the course of the next month he was interviewed on radio, television and by several newspapers about his involvement in the Free Martin Mayini Campaign. His distinguished handsomeness, his modest dignity, his enthusiasm for Africa and admiration of Martin Mayini, and his lilting Caribbean accent, softened by his years in England, were so appealing to radio listeners and television viewers that he became a regular guest on current affairs programmes. Furthermore, he received a postal avalanche of marriage proposals from around the country. They included an impassioned scrawl from the disaffected teenage wife of an impotent octogenarian chief in the Middle Belt region, detailing her knowledge of some of the more arcane practices in the African art of lovemaking, which had never been recorded in print and were known to only a select number of initiates.

The Brighton-Lisbon, of course, benefited from this deluge of publicity. Suddenly it became the popular entertainment spot in Eko. Foreign and local businessmen, politicians, and high-ranking civil servants flocked to the Africa Bar. They came for the cooling sea breeze, to escape the harsh heat that reigned from early to mid-afternoon, inducing lethargy and indolence in all those whom it touched. They came in brand-new cars which, like the nation, were as yet undamaged by the treacherous, pothole-ridden roads of progress. They struck business deals, formed alliances, plotted under the cool circular thatched hut shaded by the tamarind tree while the African sun raged and the Atlantic Ocean massaged the beach at the end of the lawn. Wealthy Kanjaians sometimes hired the Africa Bar and the lawn for ostentatious marriage receptions.

When one of the many scurrilous newspapers – which thrived under Kinja's liberal press laws and the people's insatiable reading appetite – claimed that the Prime Minister maintained, in the Brighton-Lisbon, a suite with a golden four-poster bed specially imported from Harrods of London for amorous trysts, the hotel began to acquire a reputation as a temple of love. This, of course, was a monstrous calumny. It was well known that Prime Minister Mayini's ascetic lifestyle, busy routine of foreign and national travel, and philosophical meditations on the contemporary African condition which he shared with the nation in lengthy newspaper articles and books, did not allow him the time, energy, or disposition for illicit liaisons. The real miscreant was the Home Secretary, Kende Tometta. Kende Tometta possessed a voracious carnal appetite – surpassed only by his greed for money and food – which he sated in several secret love nests around Eko, on the sturdiest iron beds, necessary to support his titanic frame. He was the only customer to win the Africa Bar's meat-eating competition.

When Marshall's Kinjaian acquaintances brought foreign visitors to the Brighton-Lisbon, he was introduced as Marshall Sarjeant, a friend of the Prime Minister's, as if he and the Father of the Nation regularly drank together while discussing affairs of state. This apparent intimate friendship acquired an almost mythical status after the Nkanda incident.

Sunday Nkanda, then the Minister of Commerce, and an occasional visitor to the Brighton-Lisbon, was renowned for his punctilious manners towards his superiors and insistence on total deference from his inferiors. One afternoon he and a party of friends drank and ate in regal quantities, then refused to pay because of an alleged slight from the waiter. Challenged by the barman and waiter, Nkanda, drunk on beer and bushmeat, abused them with such ferocity that they both fell to their knees and begged his ministerial pardon for daring to request payment for the food and drink that he and his party had consumed. Brought to the bar by the commotion, Marshall ordered the two men off the floor and, when briefed, repeated the request for payment.

Nkanda exploded with righteous indignation, as if he were the wronged party, and shouted: 'Look at this son of a sugarcane cutter, this son of a cottonpicker.' He then boasted that he would one day own the Brighton-Lisbon Hotel as it rightfully belonged to a Kinjaian and not a foreigner.

Marshall was deeply wounded but none the less kept his composure and told Sunday Nkanda that he was drunk and should go home and sleep it off. A member of the party settled the bill and apologised for the fracas. Nkanda himself returned the following day and apologised for his offensive remark about Marshall's ancestry and pleaded overwork and marital strife in mitigation for his lapse in manners. With that apology Marshall forgot the incident.

But three months later Sunday Nkanda lost his ministerial portfolio and was given a parastatal to run, as part of Mayini's routine cabinet reshuffle designed to stymie the corrupting influence of power. This demotion was widely interpreted as a sign that he had incurred the Prime Minister's wrath and incontrovertible proof of the sodality between Marshall and the Father of the Nation.

Marshall, however, had to pay a price for this new-found fame and success. He was once again drawn into politics by the man who was now his patron and protector, Martin Mayini.

From his London years, Mayini had distinguished himself as a fervent believer in the total liberation of Africa. He had never been a mere African nationalist, but a Pan-Africanist, and this was reflected in Kinja's foreign policy. It sought to strengthen links between African nations and was the moving force behind the creation of the Pan-African Congress based in Addis Ababa. Representatives of liberation movements in Southern Africa were accorded diplomatic status in Kinja, and in all his speeches on foreign affairs Mayini made it clear that he considered African independence incomplete until Africans in Namibia, Angola, Mozambique, Rhodesia and South Africa had gained majority rule. He was less vociferous on the fate of the descendants of Africans in the West, but his autobiography and occasional speeches could leave no one in doubt that he supported the radical movements for change in the United States, the Caribbean and Britain.

At Mayini's written request, hand-delivered by a messenger from the Prime Minister's office, Marshall was invited to sit on the African Diaspora Committee and the Southern Africa Liberation Committee. Both bodies, created by the Prime Minister and answerable only to him, were responsible for disbursing funds to organisations in the Americas, Europe and Africa. The civil rights movement in the United States of America was by far the greatest beneficiary of Mayini's largesse. Lesser sums went to the Black Panthers, a splinter group of the Nation of Islam, and several radical organisations in Britain. The Southern Africa Liberation Committee's principal task was to fund the training of guerrilla recruits from South Africa, Angola, Rhodesia and Mozambique in the mountain forests of northeast Kinja.

In both fora Marshall continued to voice, with the same passionate conviction which marked his London activities, his non-violent beliefs. Reconciled to the impossibility of resigning from history, recognising that its making or unmaking was his destiny in a century of war and bloody liberation struggles, it was his way of appeasing a personal conscience that would not allow him to sanction the taking of another human life, however just the cause. As in London, he advocated funding schools, hospitals and associations like trade unions. His pacifism was tolerated by other committee members, but around the time of the Sharpeville Massacre, he found himself so isolated that after a fractious committee meeting he wrote despairing long letters imploring the Prime Minister to release him from his public duties because his beliefs rendered him unsuitable to make decisions about Africa's future.

Mayini's brief reply read:

> Were you a priest, as a few of your fellow committee members seem to believe is your rightful vocation, your

voice would echo with the hollow phrases of religions compromised by avarice and lies and, therefore, carry less authority. You worship the god of humanity, most fervently and purely. That is your strength, the strength you must share with us. I need not remind you that our god is no different from your own but imposes on us different, and no less exacting duties, in pursuit of the same dream. Universal peace, love and happiness. One God. One Humanity. One Destiny.

Yours, Martin.

So Marshall continued to attend the meetings – sometimes abstaining or voting against the funds for buying weapons – and government functions, and his face remained a familiar sight at public events, near the Prime Minister's box, a warrior of peace in violent times.

3

In spite of his international fame and popularity, Mayini's domestic base was far from secure. His incarceration by the colonial regime had given him an iconic status as the Father of the Nation, but from the outset anti-Mayini forces were at work within Kinja. The most powerful of these were centred in Onaland. The Onas formed only an eighth of the Kinjaian population, but having experienced centuries of contact with European traders and missionaries they were amongst the most westernised of Kinjaians and believed it was their God-given right to govern the nation. They were the main force behind the leading opposition party, the Kinja National Party, and their MPs, though outnumbered in Parliament, derived confidence from the fact that Mayini's People's National Party had not secured a single seat in Onaland. The end of the Onas' co-operation with the Mayini government was signalled by riots in Onaland.

Sparked ostensibly by a fuel shortage, and eventually quelled by soldiers, the riots lasted an entire week. Mayini was attending an Organisation of African Unity conference, and Mali Nbentata, leader of the Kinja National Party, punished him for his absence in a moment of National crisis by playing the tribal card. In a series of newspaper articles, Nbentata accused Mayini of packing his cabinet with his fellow Ekans, overlooking the talented amongst other ethnic groups, especially the Onas, deliberately starving Onaland of fuel, and spending an excessive amount of time and the nation's wealth on foreign hobbyhorses. There was little substance to these charges. Mayini's paternal link with the Ekans – a tiny ethnic group from the eastern coast – had played no part in his choice of cabinet ministers; indeed he seemed to have striven to ensure that his cabinet reflected all the nation's major ethnic groups.

Returning from Addis Ababa early, Mayini immediately embarked on a tour of Onaland. As always, wherever he went in Kinja, Mayini was greeted by thousands of ordinary people, who regarded him as the personification of Kinja. But the tour began to go wrong when the Fon of Onaland, Mzene II, snubbed Mayini by refusing to meet him, sending a clear signal to all Onas that the great-great-grandson of Mzene I, who had defeated the British in the famous battle of 1776, the incumbent of the golden throne – carried across the Sahara by the ancestors of all Onas – did not welcome Mayini in Onaland. The remaining legs of the tour were abandoned after a rally in the Onaland capital, Canabar, where Mayini was heckled and booed by supporters of the Kinja National Party.

Marshall, who happened to be a guest on a current affairs programme which had been discussing the assassination of Malcolm X, suddenly found himself drawn into Kinjaian politics when the presenter asked him to comment on the riots in Onaland.

He said: 'They're an unfortunate development, but I don't believe there is a conspiracy against Onaland. I know the Prime Minister places the highest premium on national unity and the equitable distribution of resources. But, you know, the nation has a long way to go towards building the infrastructure that would make the ideal of national unity a reality. Accusations of tribalism will not help matters. They're inflammatory and will hold back progress.'

It was a fairly innocuous answer, echoing sentiments that had been expressed by most reasonable Kinjaians. But having, for the first time, commented on Kinjaian internal affairs, Marshall began to feel frustrated by his status as a foreigner. A longing to wield power to help shape this young nation grew inside him, and he dreamt of schemes for unification, from youth exchange programmes between the regions and ethnic groups, to abolishing the army. To console himself he took to writing, late into the night, long letters to the Prime Minister proffering advice on matters of state and commenting on events elsewhere in Africa. All these letters went unanswered but Marshall was inspired to continue when he began to hear Mayini use phrases that he, Marshall, had coined in his nocturnal missives in his monthly radio addresses to the nation: 'Progress in unity and unity in progress'; 'The long walk to the glory of nationhood'; 'Let Kinja be the black star of Africa'.

During the three-month period leading to independent Kinja's first national elections, when Mayini promised the poor piped water, the return of land stolen by the white settlers so the people could feed themselves and offer propitiatory gifts to their gods, when he promised them hospitals where they could dress their wounds and give birth in comfort, schools where their children could acquire the education that would bring prestige to their families; when he promised those educated Kinjaians who had studied in the great universities of the world, who had gazed upon grand buildings such as Buckingham Palace and Versailles and the White House, and who sat in the shadows of great monuments like Nelson's Column, the Arc de Triomphe, who had marvelled at jet planes, and trains of those countries – when he promised them to catch up with the West, he did so in words and phrases borrowed from Marshall Sarjeant's letters.

But the pleasure Marshall achieved from hearing Mayini utter his words was undermined by the chaos and violence surrounding the next elections. Throughout campaigning, ethnic rivalry reared its ugly head and took a serious turn when the Fon of Onaland, abandoning the political silence which the constitution required of him, not only threw his weight behind the Kinja National Party, but called on all his fellow traditional rulers to support the election of a leader who spent less time abroad. A rarely sighted figure, who seldom left Onaland and never appeared in public without a veil of cowrie shells, the Fon of Onaland gave a controversial interview to the *Kinja Guardian,* a leading national newspaper, in which he accused the government of discriminating against Onas, and charged Mayini with trying to liberate the entire world while neglecting Kinjaian affairs. 'You do not build a house by starting with the roof,' the Fon was quoted as having said. These were not new charges, but coming from one of the most powerful traditional rulers, they set the tone of the election.

All Mayini's campaign speeches dwelt on the inseparable link between the future of independent Kinja and the rest of Africa, and warned against the dangers of tribalism. Concluding one famous speech, delivered in Independence Square to loyal party supporters, Mayini picked up the gauntlet thrown down by the Fon of Onaland and warned all traditional rulers to stay out of politics or face the consequences. While Mayini fought his campaign on strengthening national unity, the Fon withdrew to his palace in Canabar, the Onaland capital, amid rumours of ill-health.

The announcement of the election result – a resounding victory for Mayini, with his party gaining sixty per cent of the seats in Parliament, the remainder divided between the three other parties – was for Marshall the proudest moment of his years in Kinja. The Brighton-Lisbon Hotel was the scene of a three-day celebration for Party stalwarts. But when the celebrations had ceased, controversy swiftly followed.

The ethnic demagoguery that had marred the elections remained very much alive. Mayini's People's National Party had again failed to win a single seat in Onaland. The Kinja National Party claimed that the ballots in other parts of the country had been rigged but evidence that they had themselves indulged in the very wrongs of which they had accused the victorious party undermined the charge. Mayini ignored his opposition critics and interpreted his victory as a mandate for reforming the parliamentary political system inherited from the former colonial rulers, which, he said, was incapable of containing the ethnic passions and threatened the unity of the country.

Six months after those elections, the government declared Kinja a republic with twelve states, Martin Mayini its first President, and revealed plans to move the country towards one-party rule.

Alarmed at this prospect, but emboldened by his friendship with Mayini, Marshall one night sat down and wrote a long discursive letter, voicing reservations about the one-party state – from its stifling of debate to its tendency to encourage corruption. He requested an audience with the President to present his case but his timing was poor. For Mayini had begun to surround himself with 'yes men' and sycophants. Not only did he not receive a reply to his letter, in the next presidential address to the nation, Marshall noticed that all the phrases the President had once freely plagiarised from his letters were now absent. Never again would he hear the President utter his words.

Although he wrote again to reaffirm his loyalty to the President, soon the invitations to functions at Government Castle ceased and he was relieved of his positions on the African Diaspora Committee and the Southern Africa Liberation Committee, with a thank you note expressing profound thanks for his services to the African cause.

Retired from public duties, Marshall could do no more than watch President Mayini stagger from one political blunder to the next. When the Internal Affairs Secretary announced the date for one-party rule, Marshall watched in silent despair as the newspapers began to attack the Mayini government. Mayini himself was unassailable, but his ministers were not. The newspapers seized upon every discrepancy between the government's stated socialist leanings and the behaviour of its ministers. The Internal Affairs Minister, Kende Tometta, was exposed for building himself a forty-room palace in his village to house part of his extended family and for sending his son to Gordonstoun school in Scotland. The

Minister of Education and Culture, Peter Mandake, was accused of running a flourishing business smuggling Kinjaian artefacts to America. Some of the allegations were true, and others downright malicious. Between these daily allegations of corruption the ethnic issue began to erupt.

The ruling party's office in Onaland was destroyed in a mysterious fire. But this incident was overshadowed by the first attempt made on the President's life. A bomb, exploding as Mayini was making his way to his car, killed his personal security guard and destroyed the façade of the presidential house. A special unit within the security service pursued the conspirators with ruthless tenacity. Caught and interrogated, they confessed that their paymaster was Mwene Alatan, a senior opposition politician, and an Ona.

Mwene Alatan was not seen in Kinja again. Smuggled out of the country, he turned up in London and gave media interviews in which he condemned the Mayini government for its corruption, tribalism, and lack of legitimacy in Onaland. The trial of the conspirators, three semi-literate peasants, was a farce which ended in guilty verdicts and death sentences.

Marshall stayed up all night composing a letter which urged the President to show them clemency, which would be interpreted as a sign of his magnanimity, but received only a frosty silence in reply. He was fortunate because when the Fon of Onaland appealed for clemency, President Mayini publicly derided the old man and dismissed him as a voice of the past, the worst aspect of Kinjaian tradition.

A week after the conspirators were executed, rioting broke out in Onaland and several northern cities. Suddenly soldiers began to appear on the streets of Eko, and wherever Marshall went, he noticed the men in green uniforms.

A brief period of calm was followed by more rioting, this time in Eko as well. Mayini now dissolved the senate and declared a state of emergency, which lasted a week. From that moment Kinja was effectively a one-party state moving with alarming rapidity towards dictatorship.

Mayini's monthly presidential address to the nation on the radio became a weekly sermon in which he tried to justify his increasing centralisation of power. He argued that Kinja's army, civil service and political system were like new, unwieldy tools in inexperienced hands. It would take Kinjaians decades to handle them effectively in the interests of all the people. With between one and two hundred ethnic groups, each served by a layer of traditional rulers who had enjoyed enormous privileges under British colonial rule, and who now found their influence and privileges diminishing, Kinja was fragile and volatile. These monthly speeches were veiled, then overt, attacks on Kinja's traditional rulers, and Mayini's assault seemed to be directed in particular at the Fon of Onaland.

It was a grave mistake, for some of the major newspapers were owned by Onas, and they interpreted the President's attacks as being against all Onas. They came out in favour of the Fon, and for the first time began criticising the President himself. Mayini's iconic status was now being eroded in a bitter exchange of views. Unfettered by censorship, the newspapers criticised Mayini's government with fierce abandon and surprising unanimity.

This sudden twist in Kinjaian politics surprised and perplexed Marshall. It was Baku Mathaku who opened his eyes to the earlier portents of this escalating crisis.

One night, as they sat alone in the Africa Bar, Baku said: 'Remember years ago, the unveiling of the Mayini statue? Did you notice that the Fon of Onaland was absent, but sent a band of dancing warriors?' Marshall remembered the dancing warriors but did not grasp the point Baku was making and said so.

Baku said: 'It's very simple. The Fon is hostile to Mayini and all he stands for. Has been since before independence. He was signalling that he is prepared to go to war with the central government.'

'Why?'

'There are many, many reasons. But fundamentally, I believe, because there's oil in Onaland, enough to finance a fifty-year development plan that could take Kinja into the modern world.' He explained that he had worked in the Ministry of Natural Resources and seen a report which detailed the size of the oil field.

'Then it should be exploited for the whole nation's benefit.'

'That's what Mayini wants. Mayini is Kinja. Eko is Kinja. Beyond Eko and men like Mayini are bushmen, the bush, darkness, where man's primeval loyalty reigns supreme. If we're not careful, the bush will swallow us.'

Distraction from this mounting strife was provided for a time by news of the Butu Mwaka scam. Mwaka, now famous for charging visiting African-Americans a ten-dollar fee for undergoing the ritual of return, was implicated in a passport racket. The *New York Times* exposed Mwaka as a fraudster who reclaimed the passports thrown into the sea by those undergoing the ritual, and sold those from the United States to Kinjaians wanting to migrate to the land of the free.

The implications of these reports preoccupied Marshall long after the newspapers had returned their attention to the unfolding political drama. He came to recognise the naivety of the foreign Africans who gathered in Eko. They were here looking for an Africa that they could never find because they had irrevocably lost it. Exiled in the West for centuries, bereft of tribe or nation, they had claimed their race. But to the Kinjaians race and nation were abstract notions, mere ideas beside the everyday experience of being members of a tribe.

The fierce exchange between the President and the Ona newspapers resumed against a background of coup fever in other newly independent African countries. Reports from Nigeria, Ghana and the Congo showed that the only unique feature of Mayini's problems was the refusal of the Fon of Onaland to stay out of politics. Having recovered his health, the Fon was daily quoted in newspapers or photographed performing some traditional ceremony. Mayini suddenly ended this spate of publicity for his arch enemy by introducing harsh press laws which strangled the papers and starved the Fon of attention.

Then one morning, Eko was shocked into silence with the announcement that the President had invoked a colonial law still on the statute books and exiled the Fon. According to various sources, government troops invaded the royal palace, and the revered ruler and his family were given twenty-four hours' notice to vacate it, and then placed on a plane bound for London.

Marshall Sarjeant watched helplessly and with growing disenchantment as Kinja, following the exile of the bellicose Fon of Onaland, spiralled downwards into chaos. Violent clashes between anti-and pro-Mayini gangs, between conservatives and progressives, began erupting all over the nation, like lesions on a diseased body.

President Mayini started threatening all his critics, branded them subversives and traitors, poisonous elements that would be extirpated from the ailing infant body politic and discarded into the dustbin of history, their rightful place. Special security squads scoured the country arresting these malefactors, and intelligence agents infiltrated meetings of trade unions, tribal associations, and even the most innocuous social gatherings. As the prisons swelled with incredulous criminals, who included many apostates from the ruling party, a powerful myth-making machinery attempted to consolidate President Martin Mayini's image as the benevolent Father of the Nation, a man whom the gods had blessed with divine wisdom and protection, a man dedicated to the unity and progress of all his peoples in the face of Western imperialist agents, and ruthless, unscrupulous, self-serving tribalists; the fractious relics of tribe, and tribal kings.

A year after the Fon of Onaland had been exiled, and two months after Martin Mayini had declared himself President

For Life a bomb destroyed the President's statue in Independence Square. The new one, erected within twenty-four hours, came from a huge warehouse, somewhere in Eko, full of such facsimile statues.

In the Brighton-Lisbon Hotel, Marshall Sarjeant remembered the fate of the statue of Queen Victoria in Paradise, and recognised the disturbing reverberation thousands of miles on the other side of the Atlantic. He knew without doubt that Mayini's days in office were numbered.

4

Seeing no space for him in this new phase of Kinjaian politics Marshall Sarjeant confined himself to the Brighton-Lisbon. He agreed that some of Mayini's opponents had overstepped the boundaries of propriety but he could not condone the consequent strangulation of freedom; he did not welcome this harmattan of silence which had swept over the nation from some Sahara of the African soul. He could not become a devotee of the cult of Mayini and lay flowers at the base of the President's statue. But as he also suffered from a pusillanimous fear of expulsion from the country, another upheaval, another exile, another displacement, he kept quiet.

Besides, he was comfortable here. The Kinjaian love of music was irrepressible, and the Brighton-Lisbon's now legendary reputation for jazz, soul and highlife ensured that it remained a popular venue. But the clientele had changed, become younger. The business of politics and the politics of business no longer dominated the conversations in the Africa Bar, not least because everybody believed that the President's ubiquitous special intelligence agents were constantly on the lookout for subversives. The new clientele were in any case more interested in amorous encounters than in the uncertain future of Kinja. They came to the Brighton-Lisbon to dance and to court.

Marshall was now seldom seen in the Africa Bar. He remained mostly in the main building and left the daily running of that extension to Akante Ousman, who had proved himself an honest and loyal employee, and on the rare occasions when he mixed with these carefree youngsters, Marshall moved amongst them with an avuncular smile and the imperturbable cool of a man racing through his middle years witnessing the demise of his dreams.

When he was alone inside his rooms, he surrendered himself to his melancholia, imbibed its bittersweet juice, until he was drunk on memories of Paradise, Soledad, Constance, Scoop, Zenobia, and Martin-Johann, the son he had known for a few short years.

Some nights, he and Baku Mathaku stayed up late playing chess and talking. It comforted Marshall that even Baku, a staunch Mayini supporter, had begun to have misgivings about the Father of the Nation's dictum that good citizens should be prepared to sacrifice short-term freedom for the long-term good of the nation. On other nights he composed imaginary letters to the President, asking him what had happened to their dreams, letters that would never be written because he was now beginning to recognise that dreams, like freedom, always come with a price, and that regardless, like freedom, they must be pursued, though they constantly threaten to become our worst nightmares. Dawn often found him awake and at that hour, dressed in a white ankle-length kaftan, he would wander down to the beach and there, before his constitutional swim, pace the silent shore of his latest exile. Only at that hour would he know peace because it seemed then that the world, like the day, was new and not yet sullied by failure and regret and loss.

Then he lost even this fleeting respite from the ineluctable fury of the day. Around the time his divorce from Zenobia was completed he began to dream again of the skeletal nun on the vermilion island with mountains like cathedrals. In this new appearance of the dream, the female fish-bearer walked beside him, regardless of his speed, and when she was not beside him he saw her outlined in the trees, clouds and mountains. When Baku Mathaku observed, over the chessboard, that Marshall looked as though someone had touched him, cursed him with a juju, he straightened his back, composed his weary, fretful face, donned his mask, and declared he was fine, then chased his friend away – not just because Baku Mathaku suggested that perhaps he needed some loving and knew a place in Lipi Market with an excellent reputation, but because his opponent was about to checkmate him in three moves and he did not have the strength to face the ignominy of defeat that night.

Nevertheless, he took Baku's advice and began to pay weekly visits to Lipi Market, to its famous amorous quarter of tents, hovels and grand houses built on the profits of selling love and staffed by an astonishing variety of young women, some of whom had come from as far away as Ethiopia, Libya and Mozambique.

First he laid with a Kanuri girl with intricately patterned blue scars on her cheeks and forehead; then a Fulani, who smelt of milk and the savannah during the rainy season; then a complaisant Hausa with skin the colour of a moonless night, a Tiv with an ample yam-fattened derrière, an Ibo whose kisses tasted like egusi stew, and a Yoruba with beads around her waist and Shango in her eyes.

For a whole month he was loyal to Ceri, a Mandingo from Senegal, because the quality of her tenderness, her soothing touches, lasted longer than those of the other women. But even Ceri's spell soon wore off, and his torment resumed, exposing the depth of his hunger for an intimate and constant companion, for enduring love.

Then one afternoon, for some inexplicable reason, Marshall wandered down an unfamiliar alleyway in the market and found himself walking behind a half-naked woman carrying a large Atlantic sole on her head. Slender, with a gently rounded stomach and pointed protuberant breasts, her movements were slow and graceful and she walked a straight line as if the narrow, crowded passage was empty. He attempted to catch up with her but an unbridgeable gap remained between them as he collided into other pedestrians and incurred their anger for his haste and carelessness. Delayed by these collisions, some of which sent him sprawling on the ground, he became frustrated and started shouting: 'Stop that woman!' But everyone ignored him, as if the figure he was pursuing were visible only to his eyes.

He was dripping with sweat, and aching from his falls, when he came to a bewildered stop on the edge of the market, with the subject of his pursuit nowhere in sight. He looked around and saw that he was standing outside a Portuguese-style house, with ornate verandas on both floors, and a roughly painted sign bearing the legend: 'Water for Sale'. He entered through a door to the side of the house and stood in a courtyard lined with jasmine, guava and pomegranate shrubs, and rising above them and the walls were papaya trees bowed by clusters of huge oval fruits, and in the centre a young woman stood beside a well.

Marshall bought a cup of water and the liquid was so sweet that, though the single cup slaked his thirst, he could not resist a second cup. When he had finished this second cup of water and sighed with loud satisfaction, he found the young woman looking at him with eyes that sang, danced and laughed simultaneously, set in a face of disturbing beauty, her hair plaited in intricate, geometric corn rows. Her gaze unsettled him in a peculiar way and he laughed and apologised for laughing and then declared that he had never tasted such delicious water.

'Maybe because you were very thirsty, sir,' she said, and smiled a smile as radiant as the sun breaking through a gloomy, overcast sky, as glorious as a rainbow.

When her gaze shifted to his clothes, he self-consciously glanced down and realised that the thin cotton shirt he wore clung to his chest and body with perspiration. That night, alone in his rooms, ejected from his first dreamless sleep in weeks, Marshall felt the tremulous stirrings of love.

He went back to the waterhouse daily but an entire week passed before he saw the same watermaid again, whose name he learnt was Kaya. She shared her duties at the well with a bevy of equally stunning beauties, though none touched

Marshall so deeply. Whether she worked at the well on a certain day was entirely up to Madame De Souza, the owner of the waterhouse, the well, the papaya trees, and Kaya herself. This Madame De Souza, Marshall discovered from Baku, was a legendary, almost mythical figure in Eko; so much so that Marshall's friends were surprised to hear that she actually existed. They had until then considered her the invention of picaresque bar-room raconteurs and streetside myth-makers. She was a member of Eko's small community of Afro-Brazilians and as a young courtesan of spellbinding beauty during the colonial years, she had been at the centre of numerous scandals involving senior colonial civil servants. She had caused the transfer of at least eight colonial officers, and drove another officer mad with love and then to suicide when she refused to marry him and rubbed salt into his bleeding heart by denying him her expensive affections altogether.

But her amorous cunning had not been matched by political astuteness. She had fallen in love with Joseph Mtaka, a journalist with political ambitions. Mtaka had persuaded her to pitch her tent with a faction in the defeated opposition party. With independence she had drifted into obscurity. Her most enduring legacies were her name – it had entered the street argot to signify a whore who ensnared wealthy men and blackmailed them: whenever a rich man's wife left him after learning that he was in the habit of visiting whores, it was said that his marriage had been 'desouzed' – and the substantial donation she was rumoured to have made to the building of Eko's Catholic cathedral, Our Lady of Africa.

From her base in the Brazilian quarters near Lipi Market, Madame De Souza now sold water, and loaned money to the poor at usurious rates, and if they could not service their debts she settled for payment in kind, which provided her with a lucrative sideline. The watermaids were not merely her employees, they were her property, to be used and disposed of as she saw fit, the hapless victims of parents who had got into debt with Madame De Souza and then, unable to settle their debts, had surrendered their daughters to her. The girls were not ill treated. In fact, the improvidence of their parents sometimes saved them from a life of hardship. For Madame De Souza trained some to be courtesans to rich and powerful men and sold a select few into marriages for fantastic fees which reflected the time she had invested in training the girls and her belief that love is rarer and more precious than diamonds.

Kaya was born in Eko and her mother came from the Western region but her father, Modupe Ogbomosho, was a Dahomey Yoruba who had migrated to Kinja during the colonial years. Modupe Ogbomosho was a man of astonishing pretensions, even greater profligacy, and ruinous incompetence in business. He had borrowed large sums of money from Madame De Souza and when the debts became unmanageable, packed up his family and fled to his wife's village in the Western region. Madame De Souza had pursued him with two henchmen, and on finding him demanded full payment or some compensation of her choice. Kaya was the compensation. She was bondaged to Madame De Souza for twelve years, the estimated time it would take to discharge her father's debt, and had served five years of her time.

Unknown to Marshall, Madame De Souza kept a vigilant eye on Kaya from the top floor of the house, and one day, as he stood talking to her beside the well, she presented herself to him. Corpulent, with a golden complexion and voluptuous blood-red lips, she was swaddled in fine yellow lace, carried a white flowery parasol, and an ostentatiously large golden crucifix hung from her neck. She smelt of myrrh, and the gold bangles on her wrists and ankles jangled with her every move. Cone-shaped diamond earrings hung from her ears, and her bulbous cheeks glowed from the shea butter which one of the maids administered thrice daily. Though she had gone to fat in her middle years, she retained an extraordinary beauty and the probing gaze of a woman quick to recognise a man's weaknesses.

She spoke harshly to Kaya, sent her inside, and said to Marshall: 'Some thirsts cannot be quenched by water alone. But there are no thirsts that cannot be quenched at the waterhouse, Mr Sarjeant.' She smiled and handed an incredulous Marshall her parasol, waddled past him with her fine lace wrapper trailing the dusty yard. Then she picked up a long pole, expertly dislodged a ripe papaya from the tree and caught it with equal skill.

'How did you know my name?' Marshall said.

'Names carry our strengths and weaknesses, so a lioness should know the name of the hunter stalking her pride.' She came back and placed the papaya on the well wall. It was a beautiful fruit; a yellow streak bled through the green and Marshall regarded it intently and thought it would be ripe to eat in about two days. 'This papaya has been ready for picking for some time. But the girls lack the skill to pick it. Some can be stubborn, but once picked the stubborn ones are the most delicious. I will sell it to you, Mr Sarjeant. Can you afford the price?'

'A papaya, they are two-a-kan in the market.'

'Not this papaya, Mr Sarjeant,' Madame De Souza said archly. 'This papaya is very special. I noticed it when it was very small, and swore that one day it would be mine to sell. Only God knows the cunning I used to gain it. Only God can forgive me my sins. So I could not take less than five thousand kwanzas for this papaya.' She fingered her gold crucifix.

Marshall was about to laugh at the preposterous price, enough money to build a sizeable house, that the businesswoman had placed on this most common fruit when he suddenly realised that it was not the fruit she was pricing, but Kaya. He glared at her with disgust, indignation and anger.

'You are nothing but a slave owner,' he spat at her.

'But you and me, we are the descendants of both slaves and owners, Mr Sarjeant, and what fine specimens of humanity we are. You are a friend of the President and I am one of the richest women in Kinja,' she said, and released a loud, dry cackle.

Marshall stumbled backwards, composed himself, then walked out of the waterhouse. Madame De Souza's cackling laughter pursued him into the street, the night, and even his morning swim.

But when he had regained some semblance of equanimity, the stirrings of love occasioned by Kaya, and the terrible fact of her enslavement remained a persistently visceral itch. He confided in Baku Mathaku, attempted to share his sense of outrage, but his Kinjaian friend responded with the sanguinity of one who knew his people's ways.

He said: 'There are many Madame De Souzas in Kinja. And as long as there are foolish parents they will prosper. Besides, in my village, when a chief sees a girl he wants to make a wife, he must pay her family or her guardian a dowry. And when the drought ends the clever farmer does not stand about asking who sent the rain.'

Marshall vowed to stay away from the waterhouse but within hours of making that vow, he wrote a one-line letter to Kaya. It stated simply: 'Do you want freedom?'

Three days later he received a reply which read: 'Yes, yes, yes. But not to become a prisoner of a man's love because my love awaits my release.' The honesty of her response shocked him.

The next day, having started the morning repeating his vow to keep away from the waterhouse, Marshall impulsively made his way there intending to buy Kaya her freedom. The roll of notes in his possession was almost the price of liberty, and the monetary value of his defeat in love. Madame De Souza was not surprised to see him, indeed she had been expecting him for some days, and commended his self-restraint before doubling her original price. In her shuttered room, impregnated with the scent of jasmine and myrrh, she revealed that he was the fourth man to have expressed an interest in Kaya, but she had refused to go with the others, and she, Madame De Souza, was not in the business of forcing her watermaids into unsuitable marriages because she had enough enemies in Kinja already.

They haggled over the price for some time and when they had reached an agreement Madame De Souza said: 'I can see why she chose you. Kindness sparkles in your eyes, Mr Sarjeant. But you are just a short-sighted man. You have confused the beauty of youth with beauty itself. A man like you, a vulnerable foreigner, needs a love that can protect him from his enemies.'

She smiled and Marshall, though struck by her sudden charm and bold advance, parried her thrust: 'And who would protect me from that love, madame?'

Madame De Souza exploded into a rich, fruity laughter which filled the whole room and seemed to last a whole minute. Then, with tears streaming down her golden cheeks, she said: 'Touché. All the same, I will be your friend. And one day you will need my friendship. In return for that day you must pray for me.'

Marshall agreed to this unusual request, and as they shook hands it occurred to him that Madame De Souza's loneliness was as deep and vast as his own and the inevitable consequence of her wickedly acquired wealth.

Kaya accompanied Marshall back to the Brighton-Lisbon and there then followed the most difficult forty-eight hours in his life. He began to equivocate about granting her freedom. From the balcony of his room, he watched her wander along the beach and imagined a future of marital bliss with the young woman who had touched his heart. When she returned to his rooms, he told her all about himself and proposed to her. She revealed that she longed to be with her parents and her siblings, yearned to see again the village in the rainforest where she had lived for three years before Madame De Souza claimed her in lieu of payment for her father's debts, to be reunited with Kende, the love she believed awaited her liberty, the youngman who had sworn to work until his hands bled and his back bowed for her release. She did not beg for her freedom but when she had finished revealing her desires, Marshall could not bring himself to detain her. How could he, an exile and a man who had known the ineffable pain of lost love, deny her the freedom to return to her source where the love of family awaited her? Only the most ignoble cruelty and selfishness would allow him to prevent her being reunited with her family.

So on the second day, he gave Kaya her fare to her village in the Western region, and when she left his sorrow was an implacable ache. Regardless of their exotic provenance, the tenderness of their ministrations, none of the girls in Lipi Market could now soothe his troubled heart. He ceased going there. He rarely left his rooms in the Brighton-Lisbon, ate sparingly and with reluctance, and became a somewhat spectral figure, as if his obsession with Kaya were causing him to fade away. Such was his despair, that even the tragic news of the death of the Fon of Onaland in a London council housing estate flat, the subsequent riots in Onaland and skirmishes between government troops and rebels in the Onaland forest, failed to penetrate the hermetical walls of his sorrow.

It was Baku Mathaku who saved him from the consequences of his generosity. Without seeking Marshall's permission Baku travelled to Kaya's village, Elaka, intending to attempt to persuade her to return and rescue his friend and landlord from the inferno of unrequited love. He quickly discovered that conditions favoured a successful mission. The village and the life which Kaya's memory had preserved during her time with Madame De Souza had become for her something of a nightmare. The Ogbomosho family were in disarray. Her father, Modupe, had forsaken Kaya's mother, Epeka, and taken a much younger woman as a second wife, as well as becoming indebted to the village chief, and an addict to ogogoro, the local gin. Every day Modupe, a great lover of city life, visited the house to admonish his daughter for passing up the opportunity to marry a wealthy man and live in Eko just to return to this backwater village where the primeval sounds of the surrounding jungle could drive a man crazy. Meanwhile, Epeka had joined a revivalist Christian sect, changed her name to Faith and wore only white as a symbol of virtue. Kaya's two brothers had left home and were believed to be in Lagos or Abidjan or Dakar. Furthermore, her beloved Kende had left Elaka some months after her departure and had not been heard of again, except in various rumours which claimed that he had died in a fire in Eko.

Baku set about trying to persuade Kaya to abandon hope of seeing Kende again and return with him to Eko, where she would bring happiness to a kind but foolish man who failed to understand that an act of selfishness inspired by love was a pardonable sin. Modupe Ogbomosho appealed to her sense of filial loyalty and tried to make her see how the entire family would benefit from her marriage to the wealthy foreigner. Even Kaya's mother, Epeka, joined in the campaign. If Kaya had not herself often thought of Marshall, his kind eyes and sad, lonesome air, if regret had not slept beside her on the mat that was her bed and accompanied her on the daily two-mile walk to the river for water, no amount of smooth words from Baku or appeals from her parents would have convinced her to make the Brighton-Lisbon Hotel her home.

There were two marriage ceremonies. Baku Mathaku was the best man at the wedding held in Eko's Catholic cathedral, which was famous for its stained-glass window image of an African-looking Virgin Mary and Jesus Christ. President Mayini could not make the wedding but he sent the couple a four-poster bed made from iroko, and a card to Marshall with the message: 'Now you have really arrived in Africa.'

Modupe Ogbomosho travelled to Eko to give the bride away, and Marshall loaned him a small fortune to pay off the village chief on the condition that he stayed away from Eko until he had learnt the virtues of frugality and acquired some business sense. Nevertheless by the end of the week-long traditional marriage ceremony, Modupe – swearing on pain of death by the sword of Ogun, his personal deity, that he would never again borrow money – persuaded Marshall to grant him another sizeable loan. Modupe would eventually strike it rich, enabing him to take a third wife, five years younger than Kaya, and offer to pay Marshall back. By then Marshall had known so much happiness with Kaya – in spite of the difficult times – that he waived the repayment because it seemed like an insult to Kaya's priceless love.

Three months into the marriage of Marshall Sarjeant and Kaya Ogbomosho, a Colonel Makanja, a nephew of the deceased Fon of Onaland, declared the Eastern region a sovereign nation by the name of Sankafa, with its own flag, and Provisional Ruling Military Council. For days an air of uncertainty hung over Eko. On the evening President Martin Mayini was due to give his monthly radio speech to the nation, the radio played non-stop Kinjaian music. The following morning, the steely voice of a General Raafu Bamako announced on Kinjaian radio that he was the new Head of State, and ex-President Martin Mayini and his cabinet – who were out of the country – were wanted for embezzlement.

The soldiers, however, underestimated Mayini's popularity and thousands of demonstrators, drawn entirely from the poor, took to the streets of Eko demanding Mayini's return. The soldiers responded with draconian measures which made Mayini's own repressive acts seem liberal. All demonstrations were banned, and a group of protestors who defied this military decree became the sacrificial victims to power when soldiers opened fire on them and slaughtered over a hundred people. The few remaining independent papers were closed down, and those who resisted had their printing presses destroyed, the government-owned paper was turned into a broadsheet for proclaiming the countless military decrees which the Ruling Military Council daily issued, and a dusk-to-dawn curfew was imposed throughout Kinja. General Bamako's Military Council then declared war against the secessionist forces in the East, invoking Mayini's famous dictum, borrowed from one of Marshall's letters – 'One nation, one destiny.'

The gods of war were abroad in Kinja and rivers of blood would surge through the nation before their terrible games ended.

5

The civil war would last a thousand days, claim over a million lives and become such a permanent scar on Kinja's collective psyche that it made the colonial years seem like a blissful interlude in four centuries of tribal wars and slave raids. Waged entirely in the Eastern region, some eight hundred miles from Eko, its most visible effect on the capital was the daily waves of refugees which streamed into the city like lava from an angry volcano, like blood from a deep wound, like ants rushing from a disturbed termite mound. The Eastern roads teemed with women with babies strapped on their backs and bundles balanced on their heads as they trudged with weary stoicism; premature war veterans, men in the prime of their lives, hobbled on twisted crutches or leant on children forced to become adults overnight; elderly couples, bent by the unrelenting vicissitudes of life, their faces marked by the imperturbable patience of the aged, straggled in the rear.

The healthy and strong carried beds, tables, chairs, stoves, refrigerators and other household belongings on their backs and in rough homemade carts. They created makeshift homes in every available open space, on roadsides, in Independence Square, first in the shadow of Mayini's vandalised statue and after the statue had mysteriously vanished no – doubt to become the walls of somebody's new home – they made sleeping berths in the hollow plinth; they built brittle shantytowns on the Eko lagoons and every so often these aquatic ghettos erupted in flames and claimed even more lives, accentuating the Ona people's sense of persecution and reaffirming the growing belief that the death and exile of their Fon was an inescapable pestilential curse.

Late into the night, over kerosene fires at the roadside, they recounted stories of the horrors they had witnessed: whole villages razed to the ground by government troops; girls and women raped by drunken, undisciplined soldiers; bloody, turbulent rivers of bloated human corpses and slaughtered cattle; thousands of starving rebel prisoners in makeshift camps, their faces ravaged by diseases, their bodies emaciated; drugged children and teenage soldiers in the rebel armies clutching rusty rifles and the Bible as they launched suicidal attacks against the tanks of the government soldiers, and screaming, 'Long live the Fon, long live Sankafa.'

They told of ships anchored in Port Cana, and the tanks and armoured vehicles and crates of weapons that rolled from their holds, of planes that arrived at night and disgorged grim-faced mercenaries from Europe and America. They told of the vultures that pecked on the half-severed limbs of stricken creatures, of the malevolent mistral that fanned the flames of wrath and transformed a blaze into an inferno of human suffering. They told of the harmattan, which seldom penetrated into the East, which blanketed the region with the onset of the war, and speculated that it had been sent to obscure the evil that men were perpetrating against each other.

Meanwhile, ex-President Martin Mayini, granted asylum in Guinea, grew Egyptian roses in his seaside villa in between penning another volume of his autobiography, condemning the Ruling Military Council and the secessionist government as imperialist agents, and attempting to rally support from progressive forces in the West. He would die eighteen months into the war, and his critics would say of him that power corrupted him, and the loss of power drove him mad; his supporters, that he made history, but history unmade him.

Life at the Brighton-Lisbon Hotel, far from the crimson sky over the East, acquired a slow, constricted, predictable rhythm. Frequent dusk-to-dawn curfews, combined with an erratic electricity supply, restricted customers to the afternoons only. Live bands ceased playing. Marshall's status as a foreigner, friend of the ex-President and renowned pacifist, excluded him from this internecine conflict. He was by now anyway thoroughly disenchanted with politics, but retained enough faith in mankind to make writing an account of the Mayini years appear a worthwhile project. Provisionally titled *Letters to the President,* he worked on it from early to mid-morning, but despite his many hours of labour would not get beyond making notes because he was too close to the events he sought to describe, still a part of the African chaos.

Late mornings he attended to the now diminished affairs of the Brighton-Lisbon, followed by lunch with Kaya, then a long siesta. Afterwards he helped Kaya in the vegetable garden which she insisted on cultivating rather than pay the astronomical prices demanded in the markets.

If Baku Mathaku was home, he and Marshall played chess and discussed the war and the enigmatic generals who now ruled Kinja with the aloofness of foreign conquerors. They agreed to reserve judgement on the soldiers until after the war. Most nights, Marshall and Kaya sat together and listened to the news programmes, dramas and documentaries on the foreign radio stations, or read extracts from books to each other. For a spell she tried teaching him Hausa, the most widely spoken of Kinja's indigenous languages, but he lacked concentration and lost interest quickly.

He sometimes worried that this unexciting, sedentary lifestyle would bore his young wife, and sought reassurances that she was happy and not merely a prisoner of his love. On such occasions she would recall the day he stumbled into the waterhouse and inspired her with hopes of freedom and love, which her young and foolish heart misinterpreted as an opportunity to be reunited with Kende, the village lover from whom she had been separated, and the weeks of torment as she wandered through the ruins of an irretrievable past. Yes, she was happy. Yes, she loved him. But first she had had to learn to relinquish her adolescent memories, to recognise that we can never really go back. Her answer would assuage his doubts.

And there were nights they sat together on the balcony, listening to the music of the ocean, only the white of Kaya's eyes visible as her ebony face merged with the darkness. On such nights Marshall felt a sublime tranquillity, a happiness that seemed numinous in origin, and he would reach over and hold her hand and whisper, 'Thank you.' There were mornings when the sun fell on her dark face buried in the white pillow and he looked on her and felt like thanking God for this undeserved blessing, this island of beauty in the ugly chaos of Africa.

A year into their marriage, Marshall became aware of a subtle change in Kaya's mood. Her laughter lost its lightness, her voice became strained, when he stole glances at her he noticed a faint sadness on her face, an almost imperceptible dolour. He began to fear that love, that most mysterious and capricious of emotions, had deserted their marriage. He pestered her with daily questions, but the answers remained the same: nothing was troubling her. But one night she revealed that every month, since their marriage, she had looked for signs of life, the ultimate expression of their love, and every month they had failed to appear. Marshall reminded her of the curse which plagued his life and robbed him of any enthusiasm for further adventures in parenthood. But she retorted: 'I am not a woman unless I give birth and if the child has no arms, no legs, if he has an elephant's trunk for a nose, if he talks like a donkey, I will still love him.' Her voice resonated with an elemental longing, a desire so pure and true and powerful that it reverberated through the night and challenged the restless murmur of the ocean.

After that night he could not look at his young wife without seeing her hunger, her sorrow, her silent resentment of his indifference to her plight. He attempted to distract her by redoubling his efforts to learn Hausa, but now it was she who lost patience with the lessons and cut them short. On his journeys into Eko, he scoured the Lebanese quarters for delightful gifts: the finest Irish linen and Dutch wax cloth; ivory and gold earrings, amethyst pendants, malachite brooches; shoes from Paris and London, dresses from Rome. He invited the dwindling group of lodgers to dinner in the hope that their admiration would please her. But her nonchalant receipt of the gifts, her lacklustre smiles in response to the dinner guests' flattery and her eventual expression of boredom convinced him that he could not provide a substitute for Kaya's desire for motherhood. Only a child would restore their marital harmony.

Marshall, the uxorious husband, now paid for his wife to consult Kinja's best medical experts. He and Kaya subjected themselves to exhaustive tests which showed that there were no reasons why the couple, though he was getting on in years, should not eventually conceive. After all, this was a land where octogenarian chiefs regularly fathered children and looked forward to many more years of procreation. They were given fertility pills but after six unsuccessful, disappointing months, the doctor suggested that perhaps they visit a London clinic and benefit from the superior medical knowledge and resources.

The prospect of revisiting London did not excite Marshall. He had known too much pain there, too many racial slights and humiliations. None the less he buried his reluctance in the face of Kaya's growing despair, now visible in the expression of inconsolable sorrow on her face, now audible in the elegiac ancient songs that she sang to herself, and began to make plans to fly to London with her. But a week before their departure, he received an urgent message from Madame De Souza requesting that he call on her.

The purpose of Madame De Souza's urgent request was to discourage Marshall from leaving Kinja for even a day.

In her luxurious dimly lit parlour, swaddled in fine lace, her earlobes distended by gold orb earrings, her voice taut and solemn, she warned him: 'Your enemies are lurking in the undergrowth. If you leave Kinja you will lose everything you own and you will never be able to return.'

This was Marshall's first inkling that he had enemies in Kinja and their identities perplexed him. The Ruling Military Council had shown nothing but indifference to his presence and allowed him to pursue his business without any interference. He pressed Madame De Souza for more information, to name names, but she could do no more than remind him of the European settlers in the Plateau region who had lost their farms to Kinja and the inestimable value of the Brighton-Lisbon Hotel in a peaceful, prosperous Eko, the politicians and civil servants, disgraced during the Mayini years and rehabilitated under the military, the soldiers themselves who, once they had defeated the secessionist forces, would arrogate to themselves and their friends the best land and businesses in all Kinja. She promised to find out more from her extensive network of paid informants and former watermaids, some of whom were now courtesans and enjoyed the patronage of high-ranking military men.

It did not take Marshall long to decide to postpone the London trip indefinitely. Kaya flew out with her sister as a companion. During Kaya's absence, Marshall made several visits to Madame De Souza's waterhouse. With war raging in the East and refugees flooding into Eko, Madame De Souza was back in her element. She hoarded staple goods which forced up prices; she dabbled in the intrigue brought in by the secrecy which came with military rule. The quiescence forced upon her during the Mayini years, after she had backed the wrong candidate in the wrong faction in the losing party, had been one of recuperation. Political influence was now back on her personal agenda. Although hundreds of miles away, she knew more about the civil war than reporters on the spot and even some of the commanding officers in Eko, and boasted that after the war she would be the most powerful woman in Kinja. Already she had accumulated one general and two colonels who were beholden to her for favours rendered, secrets betrayed, complicity in black-market deals.

When she spoke of her military friends, she cackled with the same contempt and sense of superiority which Marshall had heard in their first encounter. Yet she was always warm and welcoming to him. On one occasion he arrived at the waterhouse to find her in the company of a young major, who was obviously enamoured with her mature, exotic beauty, and regarded Marshall with proprietorial hostility. She introduced Marshall as her cousin, and hinted that it was time for the major to leave. He extracted from her a promise to see him again soon and reluctantly departed.

As she closed the door after the soldier Madame De Souza laughed gleefully and said: 'Poor boy, he's hopelessly in love with me. He mistakes me for his mother.'

'When did we become cousins, Magdalena?' Marshall said. (They were now on first-name terms.)

'Your innocence is beyond correction, Marshall. Of course we are family. We belong to the tribe of foreign Africans. Here in Africa, everybody must belong to a tribe. You're respected because of your tribe, despised because of that same tribe. Never mind the uniforms, or the suits. It was something Mayini did not understand, or if he understood it, he thought he could eliminate it. Maybe in a hundred years. Maybe.'

Madame De Souza did not however always exude boundless optimism, power hunger, or equable resignation to her African condition. On Marshall's subsequent visit she allowed her mask to slip. On entering her parlour, he had noticed a trace of intimacy in Magdalena's voice, a hint of cupidity in her smile, a seductiveness in the arrangement of her wrapper, which exposed her mountainous cleavage, and received the overwhelming impression that Magdalena was dissatisfied with their merely platonic friendship.

It was the most awkward visit Marshall had ever made to the waterhouse because Magdalena, sipping cognac, bared her heart to him: the lovers she had lost, the contempt and infamy her vocation earned her in so-called decent circles, especially those of her Brazilian compatriots, the unbearable loneliness of her life in the waterhouse, a state exacerbated by the watermaids with their youthful beauty and bright prospects, the wicked cunning she used to separate the girls from their families, the fortune she would share with the man who would illuminate the dusk of her old age with the light of love. She suddenly became lachrymose and Marshall was moved to comfort her. He held her shaking body and urged her to sip more cognac. She complied but whispered between fitful sobs, 'I need a man to hold me through the night.'

She dozed off in Marshall's arms and he laid her to rest on the divan and called one of the watermaids to put Madame to bed, then drove back to the Brighton-Lisbon through a dusk laden with the harmattan dust, past the hovels of the refugees with their naked fires and ramshackle kiosk selling single cigarettes and sticks of gum and dry, stony kola nuts. He was missing Kaya, and Magdalena De Souza's confession had deepened his melancholy, and it seemed to him then that the African sorrow was the palimpsest of all mankind's sorrow.

He saw Magdalena the next day and her mask of tough shrewdness had been restored, and neither mentioned the previous day's melodrama. She spoke with ebullience of the inspirational service she had attended that morning in the Our Lady of Africa Cathedral and the army captain who had expressed an interest in marrying one of her watermaids. As they parted, she advised Marshall to transfer the Brighton-Lisbon into Kaya's name.

It was Madame Magdalena De Souza who revived Marshall's church attendance. While Kaya was away, a daily visit to the Our Lady of Africa Cathedral became an important part of his routine. In one of its apses was a black Madonna, carved from onyx and supposedly of Ethiopian origin, and he discoverd that half an hour's meditation under her gaze filled him with a tranquillity comparable to his morning swim. The cathedral ran a large refugee programme, and he made generous donations to it on each visit.

6

Around the same time that the Ruling Military Council announced the capture of the Sankafa capital, Canabar, and predicted an imminent end to the conflict – wrongly, the war dragged on – Kaya returned to Kinja. The foreign doctors had confirmed the original diagnosis, advised her to be less anxious, laden her with new, more powerful fertility pills and asked her to return with her husband if the problem persisted. She exuded a calm cheerfulness which owed much to the break from the suffocating climate of the war and the suitcase of fashionable dresses and shoes purchased in London's dazzling emporiums with the generous allowance given her by her uxorious husband.

But the beneficial effects of the trip and the uniquely feminine joy of new clothes did not last long. Before travelling Kaya had been anxious about motherhood, now her faith in Western medicine as the exclusive solution to her problem weakened. Convinced that she was the problem, she turned inwards, and resorted, with fervid dedication, to the medicines her mother and grandmother would have used if faced with a similar predicament. She began to frequent the herbalists, juju men and babalawos who occupied a large corner of Lipi Market and claimed to possess cures for every affliction known to mankind. She tried all manner of teas, infusions and foul-smelling brews made from barks, powders, grasses, and the sundried organs of creatures renowned for their prodigious issue. She took to wearing fertility charms, made from multicoloured beads, around her neck and waist. Their bedroom became a shrine to her maternal aspirations as she filled vacant furniture surfaces with pairs of statuettes with protuberant stomachs, and fertility dolls, and festooned the walls with grotesque wooden masks, all bought in the belief that they possessed magical properties. For meals she served mounds of yam, okra and fresh talapia fish and stews made from bitter leaves because of their fabled properties for promoting female fecundity. Following the advice of one medicine man, she insisted that they make love at certain propitious hours and days in the month and in contorted positions, which strained Marshall's neglected and ageing muscles.

Though determined to make his wife happy, Marshall gradually withdrew his co-operation and urged Kaya to exercise greater patience. He picked at the new dishes, lightly mocked the new effigies, and voiced his preference for the conservative but less physically exacting missionary position.

Kaya was not insensitive to her husband's weariness. For an entire month she prepared familiar meals, but served them up with a petulance which attenuated their flavour. At the most favourable time of month, they made love with punctilious affection but without passion. Nevertheless, Marshall welcomed this return to the mundane and the ordinary.

The lull ended when Kaya heard about Chief Lakijo from an acquaintance who had suffered the misery of barrenness for a decade. Chief Lakijo had cured her, just as he had cured the wives of several rich men in Eko. On matters of pregnancy, the medicine man only saw wives in the company of their husbands, so Kaya begged Marshall to accompany her to Chief Lakijo's home and promised that if they failed to achieve a result, she would accept with finality that motherhood was not part of her destiny. For the sake of peace, out of exasperated love, he agreed.

Chief Lakijo was no ordinary babalawo, no mere peddler of nostrums and false hopes. He occupied a vast, sprawling compound with his four wives and fifteen of his twenty-seven children. He daily saw scores of patients, and many had travelled great distances to avail themselves of his healing prowess, a divine gift enhanced by two nomadic decades seeking the wisdom of herbalists, griots and marabouts, studying the Bible, the Koran, and arcane texts, and residence in Eko, which the ancients believed straddled the most powerful ley line on the African continent.

He received them in a gloomy room, squatted in its centre on an Arab carpet, an ornate calabash of water on one side, a fly whisk on the other. With his shrivelled body, incongruously large head, kola-juice-stained teeth, there was about him an air of erudite mysticism. He bade his visitors sit on separate wooden stools with carvings of elephants for legs.

They had agreed beforehand that Kaya would explain their problem, and as she did so with hesitancy, Marshall was discomfited by Chief Lakijo's stillness, and the slowly dawning realisation that the babalawo was blind.

When Kaya finished speaking, Chief Lakijo sent her out of the room, then asked Marshall to strip to the waist and sit before him on the carpet and close his eyes. Marshall obeyed and felt dry hands roam lightly across his face, then down to his neck and across his chest, leaving a curious warmth wherever they touched. Next, he clasped Marshall's neck and began humming from deep down in his throat.

Suddenly he stopped and announced: 'The problem is with you, not your wife. But I do not know if I can cure you. The blood of Europeans flows strong in your veins. You must tell me all you know about your ancestors. You must tell me everything you know. But first you must go home, and cleanse your home.'

The cleansing involved a ritual bonfire of all Marshall's possessions acquired before he arrived in Kinja, with Chief Lakijo in attendance. Then the mystic sprinkled a white powder on the bedroom floor as he chanted incomprehensible incantations. Marshall was required to fast for forty-eight hours and return to the babalawo's compound.

On this second visit, he was taken into a windowless room

lit by candles. Chief Lakijo awaited him and instructed him to undress completely and lie on his back on the bare bamboo cot which centred the room. In that supine position, he told Chief Lakijo about Paradise, Nana Sarjeant, Neal Sarjeant and Sybil's curse, his loss of Nana Sarjeant's ka, his failed mission, and the dream of the skeletal nun. The old man listened impassively but with intense concentration.

When Marshall had finished, Chief Lakijo said again with great solemnity: I don't know if I can cure you, but I will try, and you too must try. You must have faith. You will feel pain but you must float on the pain.'

Chief Lakijo handed him a calabash bowl and from it he drank a pungent liquid and almost retched. As he lay there in the silent bare room, drowsiness crept over him and he hovered somewhere between being and unbeing. He felt the old man applying a balm to his body and face which caked quickly, as if he had bathed in mud and then sat in the sun. He seemed to be alone for a long time, then a figure entered the room and he too was naked but for an elongated mask with two narrow eye slits and a circular serrated hole for a mouth. Clasping a knife with both hands raised above its head, the figure took high steps. It circled the bamboo cot while humming, chanting in a medley of tongues, and at times there was a rhythm in the voice which evoked in Marshall's mind memories of his blind days seated at Nana Sarjeant's feet. Suddenly, he felt two sharp pains in the corner of his eyes, and another two on his chest followed swiftly, and he felt the trickling flow of warm blood down his stomach and the side of his chest. The pain stung him and he convulsed and gripped the bamboo cot. He heard the masked figure say, in a loud angry voice: 'Be gone, Sybil; be gone, Sybil; be gone, Sybil, ancient spirit of evil. Leave this body now. In the name of Olodumare, in the name of Nyame, in the name of God, in the name of Allah, in the name of the Supreme Being, I command you ...'

He did not hear the remainder of this exhortation because

the pain in his chest shook him and propelled him into darkness.

When he woke Chief Lakijo was rubbing a grey powder into the four incisions.

With a feeble voice Marshall asked what it was and was answered soothingly and simply: 'Ashes from the ariba and baobab trees, one to heal the wounds of the past, the other to make you strong again to create the future.' He bathed Marshall, wiping the encrusted balm, and as he did so he said: 'Henceforth you will take the name Segun Dada and carry it in your soul only until the day you are forced to speak it.'

'When will that be?' Marshall asked.

'You will know, you will know,' Chief Lakijo answered simply.

That night, back in the Brighton-Lisbon, Marshall was gripped by a burning fever which drenched him with sweat. For days he could barely move a muscle and drifted in and out of a sleep haunted by the dream of the skeletal nun. The landscape across which the chase now occurred had darkened to a magenta red and the mountains were composed of writhing human figures, peaks of flaying arms, legs and heads, and every so often somebody fell from those great heights and their screams were ignored as the mountains pullulated with masses of stacked bodies which all seemed intent on reaching summits that were lost in dark swirling clouds, as if somewhere in those clouds they would find the gods who had created this chaos of human ambition and suffering. A stormy sea assaulted the shore with angry giant waves, and from somewhere in the sky came a cruel female laughter which chilled his soul as he pursued the skeletal nun around the red island.

Half conscious, he heard Kaya lamenting that her selfishness, her refusal to accept her destiny, was killing her husband and then he felt his neck and head being lifted onto her lap, and she stroked his hair and her tears fell on his cheeks and caused a rainfall in his dream. Late into the night, he felt her warm body close to his, holding him firmly, tenderly, desperately; holding him with a love supreme because it was the only love that could pull him back from the dream of death.

After a week the fever began to subside, but Marshall remained frail, with aching muscles, unable to stir from his bed. For days his sole sustenance was a bitter, foul-smelling drink which Kaya served him twice a day. Slowly his strength returned and on the first day he could stand alone he saw his reflection in the mirror, and was shocked not by scars near his eyes or the further two sets of raised scars on his chest, or the weight he had lost, but by his head of completely white hair, hair as white as freshly fallen snow.

Marshall's recovery was swift, and true to her word, Kaya seemed happier. It was as though, by subjecting himself to Chief Lakijo's blade, he had proved the strength of his love for her, and should that love not result in children, then it was the will of God. For though the months dragged on, like the war, without any signs of pregnancy, she seemed to remain buoyant.

Then one morning, his meditations on his stalled book, *Letters to the President,* were interrupted by a new sound: a crying baby. Marshall left his study and found Kaya cradling a baby girl of no more than six months old. She explained that an Ona refugee – a ragged distraught teenager – had given her the child in Lipi Market and begged her to give it a decent life because she, the mother, had exhausted all her resources and feared that she would harm the baby unless separated from it.

'Why didn't you take her to one of the refugee camps?' Marshall said.

'The conditions there are terrible, she would've died in a few weeks,' Kaya said. 'Her name is Alayli, which, in Ona, means a gift of God.'

She looked at Marshall imploringly, then at the child in her arms, and smiled and cooed in a way which suggested that in the brief time that had elapsed since acquiring the baby Kaya's frustrated maternal ambition had been satisfied and the bond formed between them would only be broken by a heartlessness of which he was incapable.

Marshall could not offer any further resistance. But he did not know that he was opening the floodgates of surrogate parenthood.

The next week Kaya came home from a trip to Lipi Market with a pair of twin boys. On their first night in the Brighton-Lisbon their screams, probably triggered by memories of horrors that no child should have seen, woke up the entire building. Other children, less scarred by the war, followed. Within the month all the rooms vacated by the civil servants were filled with children, the abandoned offspring of refugees from the war-ravaged East, rescued by Kaya. They played on the lawn, in the calm water of the bay, they stripped the tamarind tree of ripe and green fruit alike and bawled when their stomachs churned and burned, and on one occasion Marshall discovered two pre-pubescent children copulating wildly in the storeroom.

Disturbed by Marshall's account of the children's behaviour, Kaya, who had so far concentrated on ensuring that they were fed and clothed properly, imposed a militaristic regime on them and required the older ones to care for the younger ones, to make sure that they did their toiletries and laundry. Teenagers were required to instruct their juniors in elementary school lessons while Kaya herself gave the teenagers lessons. At night, as she lay exhaustedly beside Marshall, he would listen to her deep breathing and hear the rhythms of happiness.

The presence of these children had an ambiguous effect on Marshall. He loved their innocent, riotous laughter and the smell of their freshly washed bodies, but he now found himself thinking about his son, Martin-Johann, and wondering, with renewed regret, what had happened to the boy and his mother.

She had not challenged the divorce proceedings handled by his London solicitors and he still had no idea where she was. Though Zenobia had wronged him, he could not help feeling that he was responsible for driving her away with neglect and feeble love, and both his ex-wife and son belonged to the order of people lost in a careless life. But he discovered that by helping Kaya with the children – structuring their days – he could mollify the pain that accompanied his memories of his sole – and he was now convinced, last – adventure in fatherhood. Without acknowledging it, he was making the children the new source of his redemption.

He turned one of the empty rooms in the Brighton-Lisbon Hotel into a classroom for the under-elevens and used the basement storerooms for the older children. He spent his days with these older ones, told them stories and taught them history lessons and physical exercises and swimming. So it was that the end of the Kinjaian civil war found Marshall with a new ambition – the building of a school.

The older children called him 'Mr Sarjeant' or 'Sah', and the younger children, without any direction from him or Kaya, 'Dada'.

7

The Kinjaian civil war ended with inevitable victory for the Federal Forces and the imprisonment of Colonel Makanja. Although a bellicose minority within Onaland pointed to the Fon's missing golden throne – the symbol of power in Onaland since time immemorial, and which, apocryphal tales claimed, Ona loyalists had smuggled out of the royal palace and secreted in the northeast mountains – as proof of an unvanquished warrior spirit, proof of a people who would rise again, the vast majority of Onas welcomed peace and committed themselves to a future of 'One Kinja, one destiny'. The will for national reconciliation, powerful and ubiquitous, prevailed. And with peace came abundance.

The Ruling Military Council, headed by General Raafu Bamako, now had access to vast oil revenues, and he and his uniformed cohorts seemed determined to spend the money with the exuberant profligacy of a jackpot winner. Kinja experienced a wild, intoxicating period of growth and excess, as the soldiers revived Martin Mayini's project of transforming Kinja into the shining star of Africa. There was a proliferation of highways and airports, schools and universities, factories and offices, houses and stadiums. There was talk of a new capital city, one located in the mathematically exact centre of the country, so no ethnic group could make special claims on it. Everywhere, Kinjaians downed hoes and cutlasses and stampeded into the existing cities, to the bright lights far from isolated villages and towns surrounded by forests and savannahs, mountains and deserts.

Eko was the Mecca of this flight from the land, the epicentre of this seismic growth spurt. Elevated expressways and skyscrapers were constructed with astonishing speed. The few car assembly plants in Eko worked at full capacity – roads became so congested and deadly that over the next decade they would claim almost as many lives as the civil war – but still could not meet demand. So more vehicles were imported. And as Eko port's berthing facilities were too small to accommodate all the maritime traffic it attracted, from certain vantage points in the city, the horizon could be seen lined with ships laden with every conceivable electronic gadget, from America, Europe and Japan.

Nor did Eko sleep. It was a twenty-four-hour party, an endless urban carnival, that crackled, crepitated with incredible, inexhaustible energy. Many tragedies would be acted out in the shadow of these skyscrapers and expressways, many lives sacrificed to the merciless gods of this already great city in the throes of a parturition that would make it greater still.

Nevertheless, the new regime's enthusiastic embrace of the capitalist ethos was not complemented by any enthusiasm for democracy. General Raafu Bamako promised to organise a national constitutional conference to find a political formula that would contain the explosive passions of Kinja's fissiparous peoples, a vehicle that would not veer off the road and crash as driver and passengers squabbled. But as the months went by without such a conference, it gradually became clear that General Bamako saw himself as the personification of unity, the chosen driver.

Throughout the war the Ruling Military Council's edicts and proclamations had referred to him as Head of State, General Raafu Bamako. By the end of the first year of peace all government announcements referred to him as President Raafu Bamako. Few people noticed the change. Even fewer had the power or desire to object. Colour portraits of his solid, square, handsome face, with its grim, unsmiling expression below his military hat, his proud chest garlanded with medals, his broad shoulders weighed down by gold-coloured epaulettes, were hung in all public buildings, banks, the offices of any sensibly run business, and on the windows of the minibuses that plied the intercity roads.

Occasionally the General appeared on Kinjaian television in civilian clothes, the dashing, voluminous robes worn by Kinjaians at special ceremonies. The General then revealed his real plans. Independence Square was cleared of refugees, sealed off for three months, then reopened with a ceremony to celebrate, on the same spot where Martin Mayini's giant statue once stood, the unveiling of an even taller, mightier statue of General Bamako, with the legend 'Saviour of the nation' beneath. It was launched on a sea of champagne.

Like most people connected with the Mayini years, Marshall did not receive an invitation to that ceremony, or any other government function. But these years of obscurity were his most enjoyable in Kinja. They came closest to the future he had imagined, before Pharaoh burdened him with a mission destined to fail. Now the joyful laughter of children borne on the sea breeze filled his days, days when he rediscovered the pleasure of storytelling, learnt that he lacked pedagogic talent, abandoned the futile mental torture involved in writing the book on the Mayini years, and floated above life's daily vicissitudes on the oceanic love of his beautiful wife.

The Brighton-Lisbon was still in name a hotel, but as its grounds were now concealed behind tall, wildly overgrown roadside hedges of purple, white and red bougainvillaea, and a storm had blown down its road sign, which no one had bothered to replace, only a select few – its residents apart – knew of the hotel's existence and drove out to its Africa Bar for quiet, unhurried drinks beside the sea. The road sign was finally re-erected when the children and the school were relocated almost two miles away, in the year of Magdalena De Souza's death.

Magdalena De Souza did not live long enough to enjoy the latest fruits of her formidable cunning. In the first year of peace, she took to her bed one day claiming that somebody had poisoned her, and despite a plethora of decoctions known for their antidotal effects on a variety of toxins, never left it alive. The problem was she did not know which of her many enemies had administered the poison and without that knowledge, as the various babalawos to whom she resorted told her, the antidotes were useless.

Marshall sat with her for an hour on the night before her death, and throughout that hour, at her request, held her hand and listened to her pray for redemption. He and Kaya were two of a handful of mourners from outside Eko's small community of Afro-Brazilian returnees at her funeral service in the Our Lady of Africa Cathedral. Fulfilling a promise he had made to Magdalena, he placed twelve white anthurium lilies on her iroko coffin. The detailed instructions she had left for the funeral service included an eclectic mixture of taped music, from a Brazilian soprano's recording of Monteverdi, to Miriam Makeba's African elegies, and to Nina Simone singing African-American spirituals.

A month after her death Marshall learnt that Magdalena De Souza had bequeathed him a plot of coastal land – on which she had hoped to build a magnificent retirement home – and a substantial sum of money, both of which, her will stipulated, were solely for the school. A proper school building and dormitory were constructed.

For a long time the schoolboard – Marshall, Kaya and Baku Mathaku – argued over a name for the school. Baku wanted to call it the Martin Mayini School, which would have been a suicidal act under the Bamako regime, which seemed determined to expunge Martin Mayini's name from the history books. The name was arrived at by each member of the board placing three names in a hat and, at morning assembly, they asked a five-year-old boy to pick one out. The chosen name was that of the recently assassinated African-American civil rights leader: Martin Luther King, Jnr. Baku did not cavil: he accepted this arbitrary result as the will of the gods.

Kaya became headmistress, with a teaching complement of ten and numerous other staff committed to the education and welfare of the rescued street children. Marshall helped with the administration – a task which did not require his absence from the Brighton-Lisbon – and Baku Mathaku gave science lessons on a voluntary basis. The school's proudest moment would come five years later when three pupils – Latuk Nkene, Joseph Manaka and Victoria Banko – all of whom had been rescued from the streets, won places at the University of Eko. The small graduation ceremony would be a particularly proud moment for Marshall because he was fond of Latuk Nkene, had taken a special interest in the boy's welfare and had encouraged his academic pursuits. On that day Latuk Nkene would wait until Marshall was alone and then say to him, with ineffable gratitude in his voice: 'Thank you for sharing with me your strength.' Only a sense of manly decorum enabled Marshall to stem his tears.

The Martin Luther King Jnr School had been in operation for three fruitful years when Marshall received, from a messenger, two framed portraits of President Bamako. He disapproved of the General's refusal to initiate a programme of return to civil rule, and knew of the growing rumours that the regime was arresting its opponents without trial. But he recognised the expediency of hanging the President's portraits in both the school and the Brighton-Lisbon's reception area. He was still an alien in Kinja and did not want to give his enemies – who remained unidentified – an excuse to turn down his application for citizenship when he had fulfilled the fifteen-year qualifying period. So he hung up the portraits in the school and hotel and took solace from the knowledge that the flowers in his garden were thriving, despite the poor soil.

When Baku Mathaku first saw the President's portrait in the school, he cycled back to the Brighton-Lisbon Hotel, through the cruel afternoon heat, and subjected Marshall to a lengthy diatribe against the reprehensible General who had reneged on his promise to restore democracy after the war, seemed determined to erase all traces of Martin Mayini from the history books, and led a government so riddled with corruption that the stench of putrefying meat, which everyone knows is inseparable from deferred dreams, emanated from government house night and day. Besides, as a paying guest and a working man, who had to see Bamako's ugly, dishonest face in his office every day, Baku protested that he deserved a respite from it at home.

Marshall was innured to Baku's increasingly frequent anti-Bamako outbursts, and placated his friend by appealing to his pragmatic side: the school would one day need financial assistance from the government.

None the less, Marshall soon began to notice a certain secretiveness about Baku, a vaguely conspiratorial air, a furtiveness in his movements. He cycled home late at night and kept to his room. Their chess games and the termite mound expeditions, always indicated by Baku's shovel and bags, ceased. He continued to take lessons in the school without pay, but he no longer volunteered extra hours of teaching, as he often did in the past. He was always polite but all attempts to engage him in conversation were brushed aside because – so he claimed – he was busy with work, or family matters.

It was around this time that mysterious leaflets began appearing all over Eko. They littered the ground in Lipi Market and Independence Square; they were found on church benches, on the desks of civil servants, in schools and universities. Their message was a vitriolic denunciation of the Bamako regime as tyrannical, inept and irredeemably corrupt. No sooner were these gathered and burnt than another leaflet, equally well distributed, appeared. It claimed that the Ruling Military Council merely rubber-stamped decisions made by General Bamako in consultation with his pet goat, called Oitibo, which accounted for his capricious behaviour in office. The lampoonists then started targeting other members of the Ruling Military Council. The official car of Colonel Innocent Kaana, the Minister of Power and Industry, was plastered with leaflets, as he took a siesta with his mistress, accusing him of stealing millions of kwanzas intended to upgrade the electricity supply in Eko and importing faulty equipment. As the lampoons spread unchecked, the heads of the police and intelligence services – men famous in Eko for the frequency with which they changed their Mercedes Benzes, the preferred car of the powerful – were publicly upbraided and then exiled to towns on the edge of the Sahara and given camels for transport.

The authors of the lampoons eventually declared themselves the Kinjaian Liberation Front, a movement committed to restoring democracy in Kinja and stopping the soldiers squandering the nation's wealth. At the outset the Kinjaian Liberation Front were mere nuisances, embarrassments to the government and President Bamako – especially President Bamako, as he was the target of most of the lampoons – and they were utterly without support in a populace wearied by war and too busy making money to worry about democracy – indeed, regarded politics as a distraction. But the Kinjaian Liberation Front soon progressed from attempting to ridicule the government, to exposing the scale of corruption, to issuing a ten-stage programme for civil rule.

In response, the regime declared the Kinjaian Liberation Front a subversive organisation and offered fantastic monetary rewards for information about its leaders. The Kinja Intelligence Surveillance Service was created to identify, hunt down and eliminate the subversives. But far from thwarting the activities of the Kinjaian Liberation Front, the security service fuelled its popularity. Known by the acronym Kiss, theirs was a fatal kiss. These young, semiliterate thugs, conspicuous wherever they went by their dark glasses and penchant for loose-fitting, broad-shouldered linen suits, descended on the homes of suspected and actual dissenters in the early morning, and husbands, brothers, fathers were Kissed. Most of their victims disappeared without trace, but some turned up as corpses in the bush or the lagoons. Others were tried in camera and their executions became well-publicised macabre Sunday morning spectacles on Lipi beach.

Six years after the war, the mere mention of Kiss would cause a hushed silence to descend on the most private gathering. Guests would whisperingly exchange stories about friends and relatives who had been Kissed, express shock at rumours that Kiss agents hired their deadly services to ruthless businessmen to eradicate their rivals and then fabricate evidence of politically subversive activities on the victim's part.

Marshall did his best to ignore these auguries of renewed unrest. He worked hard at the school and the Brighton-Lisbon Hotel, and avoided all political discussions. This wilful disinterestedness came to an end when he witnessed four Kiss members in operation.

One afternoon, as he strolled through Lipi Market, a man tore past him with the fear of death on his face. Seconds later, as another two men raced by, the sound of a gunshot rent the air, a man cried out in agony and several women screamed. The hunted man had run headlong into the other half of the Kiss team – they always worked in fours – and they had shot him dead. They walked away, brushing and adjusting their clothes and laughing, like mischievous schoolboys on an exeat.

The following day, recovered from the shock of witnessing such a casual killing, Marshall wrote an angry anonymous letter to General Bamako, signed it 'An alarmed citizen', and posted it in a central Eko district.

A week later, as if in reply to the letter, a Kiss team called at the Brighton-Lisbon Hotel. It was nearing midday and Marshall was working in the hotel office, behind the reception area. A power cut had disabled the air-conditioning and forced him to open the windows for the cooling effects of the sea breeze, which fluttered through the curtains. He saw the thugs arrive in a white Peugeot car and, fearing the worst, he assumed his most inscrutable mask. Two of the team remained in the car, two entered the lobby of the Brighton-Lisbon and demanded, from the receptionist, to see Baku Mathaku. Marshall called them into the glass-encased office adjoining the reception desk. They reeked of eau-de-Cologne, and their height and sartorial elegance gave them the appearance of male models, but their sinister, arrogant air exposed their purpose. The two scars on the cheeks of the silent one betrayed him as an Elak. The other was nondescript and he did the talking while chewing gum, parodying the hard-boiled American cop portrayed in Hollywood movies. Marshall had not seen Baku since the previous day, which was not unusual, given the frosty state of their friendship. When told that Baku was out, Chewing Gum demanded to see his room. Marshall asked if they were from the police department, and if so, did they have search warrants?

Chewing Gum pulled out a gleaming revolver and said coldly: 'This is my search warrant.'

The Elak laughed with malevolent glee and Marshall glared at him and said: 'Young man, there are twenty rooms in the Brighton-Lisbon. Go ahead and search for Baku Mathaku, but you won't get any help from me until you learn some manners.'

At that very moment, from the corner of his eye, Marshall saw Baku Mathaku coming down the stairs, saw him recognise the Kiss men, halt, and begin to turn at the same time as the Kiss agents, alerted by Marshall's distracted gaze, also spun round.

With incredible presence of mind, Marshall suddenly shouted: 'Ah, Mr Nzaka, Mr Nzaka, these men are looking for Mr Mathaku. Can you help them?' All those hours of playing chess and debating, of two minds anticipating each other, would never be better deployed.

Baku stopped and replied with a quizzical, abstracted air:

'Mr Mathaku? He has gone to his village today for his mother's funeral. He left very early this morning.'

'Are you sure, Mr Nzaka?' Marshall called out. 'These men are very keen to see him, Mr Nzaka.'

'I will let Mr Mathaku know as soon as I see him. Now, excuse me, I have forgotten my wallet.' And so saying, Baku patted his pockets, and turned back up the stairs. Marshall gave the men a smug smile, shrugged his shoulders.

'One day Mr Nzaka will forget his own name. A very forgetful man.'

The Kiss agents clearly had no idea what Baku Mathaku looked like. They frowned and returned their attention to Marshall.

Suddenly, the Elak reached for the framed photograph of Kaya Marshall kept on his desk, picked it up, scrutinised it intensely and said: 'Is this your wife, Mr Sarjeant? She is very beautiful.'

'Thank you,' Marshall said graciously.

The gun was put away, and after warning Marshall that they would be back, the thugs made to leave. At the door the Elak turned slowly, eyes hidden behind shades, and said in a chilling drawl: 'Tell Kaya that Kende has found her.'

8

Marshall tried to keep his knowledge of Kende's existence to himself, while deciding what to do. But some days later, Kaya returned home in a fit of tears and convulsive tremors. It was several hours before she regained enough calm to confirm what Marshall suspected.

Kaya had found out for herself that her teenage lover, the boy to whom she had pledged everlasting love, the boy whom she believed had died in an Eko shanty-town fire, was alive and worked for the notorious Kiss. Kende had gone to the Martin Luther King Jnr School, interrupted a class Kaya was taking, ordered the children out, and confronted her with all the bilious fury of a betrayed lover. He'd recounted how he had tried to make contact with her at the waterhouse and was discovered and beaten to within inches of his life by two thugs, presumably hired by Madame De Souza; how he had almost died in a shanty-town fire. He had ripped off his shirt to show her his horribly scarred back and arms. He had recalled in the minutest details his subsequent struggle to recover, then to gain a foothold in Eko, the humiliation and degradation he had suffered since leaving Elaka on his mission to rescue her from bondage, unaware that she had escaped and married a brown, white-haired foreigner, a man stained with white blood, a damn sugarcane cutter, a damn cottonpicker, and was living in luxury; how he had suffered without knowing that the love of his life was no better than one of those shameless whores who plied their trade at every international hotel in Eko. He ranted and railed in English, pidgin and Elak, and showered her with the bitterest imaginable imprecations. He poisoned her heart with anguished guilt and reduced her to tears that flowed, intermittently, for days, and left her face so bloated she was ashamed to be seen outside their quarters.

While Kaya wept Marshall acted with urgent swiftness to protect his wife. It so happened that Modupe Ogbomosho, Kaya's father, had become wealthy under the Bamako regime. A man of irrepressible optimism and a blindingly charismatic smile, he had struck it rich when, by some devious means – though he would always claim it was entirely due to his devout worship of Ogun, the god of iron – his fledgling construction business secured a government contract to build a government ministry. In short, he was well connected.

Modupe Ogbomosho's immediate intervention resulted in Kende being transferred to Lanu, Kinja's northernmost city, nine hundred miles away. But such was Kende's rage that he did not leave Eko without first letting Kaya know in person that one day he would return, and meanwhile, she and her husband had better watch their backs.

Kaya would never entirely recover from her encounters with the brutish Kende, a young man hardened and twisted by his travails in Eko. Once he had established to his satisfaction that Kaya no longer loved Kende, Marshall did all he could to help her fight the guilt and terror Kende had instilled in her heart. But Kaya met Marshall's efforts to calm her with an urgent demand: she wanted them to leave Kinja, to flee to another part of Africa, even Europe or the United States.

Marshall opposed flight and continued resisting this cowardly option in the face of Kaya's daily entreaties. One night he told her: 'We cannot run. His fury will respect no national borders or oceans. No rocks can hide us. We will stay here in Kinja.'

Marshall invested these words with such a tone of immutable finality that Kaya did not argue. None the less her fear was beyond control. Marshall watched as his slim, svelte young wife became a voracious eater, a pathological devourer of four, sometimes six, meals a day, and she put on four stones in an equal number of months. The slightest unusual noise would cause her to start, set her heart racing and moisten her forehead with sweat. He resolved to love her with greater ardour in the hope that the strength of his love would restore the peace she had known since becoming a surrogate mother to the street children.

Marshall's efforts to aid Kaya's recovery were conducted under the scrutiny of security agents who watched the Brighton-Lisbon Hotel every day. As part of an intensified campaign to catch the most wanted political subversive in Kinja, the supposed mastermind behind the Kinjaian Liberation Front – Baku Mathaku – they drank in the Africa Bar and twice turned up at unexpected hours and searched the building, including the rooms where the proprietor and his wife lived. Neither Marshall nor Modupe Ogbomosho could bring a halt to their persistent attention, and Kaya's nervousness increased.

The Kiss agents were wasting their time. On the same day that he had almost walked into their arms, Baku left the Brighton-Lisbon Hotel for good. He had embraced Marshall, thanked him for his mental alacrity, expressed regret and understanding that Marshall could not be a part of the struggle and then ridden off on his bicycle. Over the subsequent months, as Kiss agents scoured the country for Baku, he was reportedly seen in every major city in Kinja, on every point of the compass. His ability to breach the securest buildings to plaster their walls with lampoons was legendary. These daring exploits earned him the sobriquet The Ant, because, like that minute creature, a burning sting announced that he passed by. When Juku, a popular singer of the day, joined the protests against President Bamako's overdue departure from office by releasing a song titled 'The President's Got an Ant in his Pants', the unfortunate musician disappeared without trace, though as a lampoon reportedly found on President Bamako's twenty-four-hour-guarded statue pointed out, the problem wasn't the ant in the President's pants but the goat who advised the President.

The Bamako regime met these petty acts of subversion with even greater repression, which in turn inspired fully organised opposition across the nation, from trade unions to students. Workers struck for higher pay as the price of staple goods hoarded by traders friendly with the regime soared. Campus demonstrations became commonplace as students protested against the arbitrary arrests and detention of radical lecturers, identified by semi-literate Kiss agents, who only had to hear mention of the names Karl Marx or Vladimir Ilyich Lenin to brand a lecturer a radical, condemn him as a subversive and arrange his disappearance.

Led by Latuk Nkene, a former pupil of the Martin Luther King Jnr School, the students at the University of Eko one day brought central Eko to a halt as they marched in thousands, occupied Independence Square and threw paint over President Bamako's statue. The frightened soldiers guarding the statue fled, but later they returned with a squadron of reinforcements, which encircled the square and trapped the young protestors. That day Kinja witnessed a most terrible hour.

Intoxicated by the power of their collective voice, the students ignored appeals to disperse and go home. Some danced to music played on portable cassette stereos and smoked marijuana, while others scaled President Bamako's statue, tied ropes to it and hauled it down. At the same moment as the statue toppled, the soldiers opened fire. The shooting continued for ten minutes as young men and women ran here and there for safety, their pain-filled screams filled the air, and bodies fell on top of bodies. By the time the commanding officer gave orders to cease, the air was heavy with the smell of sulphur and death.

When the acrid clouds cleared, amid the shattered pieces of General Bamako's statue, lay hundreds of dead, dying and wounded students. In the aftermath of that slaughter, rumours circulated that the commanding officer was an Ona, a vengeful, misguided secret Fon loyalist. On the first anniversary of that national tragedy, at the exact hour of the shooting, the thirty-foot spray of the fountain – which replaced Bamako's statue – would turn blood red and some people would claim that they heard the screams of the dying students.

They came for Marshall on the morning after the carnage in Independence Square. In deference to his age – for his white hair made him appear older than he was – the Kiss agents gave him enough time to dress. As he did so, he instructed Kaya to contact Wade Mayana, with whom he had served on the Free Martin Mayini Campaign committee in London, and who now lived in retirement in the savannah region of Kinja. Only Wade Mayana, a revered scholar and consummate political survivor who had advised the Bamako regime on many matters, could save Marshall from the fate he feared awaited him.

Marshall was driven to Maroko Castle, a former slave fort now a notorious prison for political prisoners. Placed in a brightly lit cell, he barely slept for three days and ate only bowls of gruel served to him once a day through a door hatch. Throughout this time, he kept his mind focused on Kaya, hoping she had removed herself to the safety of her father's home, hoping she had made contact with Wade Mayana.

Weak and disoriented from sleep-deprivation, Marshall was taken by a guard to a semi-dark room where three men, their faces hidden in the shadows, sat behind a table. Behind them was a screen which suddenly lit up and photographic slides of the swollen, battered face of Latuk Nkene were projected on to it. Marshall grimaced in horror and struggled to remain standing.

One of the men at the table spoke. His calm voice had a grating, metallic quality.

'I see from your reaction that you know him. He called out your name under interrogation, Mr Sarjeant. Why?'

Marshall explained that the youngman had been a pupil at the Martin Luther King Jnr School. 'I knew nothing about his student activities,' he said.

'You knew nothing? But he was your pupil, Mr Sarjeant.'

'I am not a teacher. He was an ex-pupil of the school I co-own with my wife,' Marshall corrected him.

'We know that your school and hotel are nothing but fronts for spreading communist subversion in Kinja, and we do not take kindly to foreign communist subversives.'

'That is a lie,' Marshall said forcefully.

The man who had spoken opened a file which lay before him on the table. 'We know everything about you, Mr Sarjeant. We know that you associated with communists in London and that the communists are funding the KLF. Now tell us about your links with the so-called Kinja Liberation Front. Tell us where to find Baku Mathaku.'

Marshall wrestled with a powerful feeling of absurdity, and disparate thoughts connected with the act of returning to one's ancestral roots to answer: 'I don't know who the KLF are, and Baku Mathaku was my tenant at the Brighton-Lisbon Hotel. I don't know where he is.'

The same voice repeated the same questions over and over for hours, as if it were a recording. Marshall gave the same answers and was brought back to his cell, where he remained until he was taken to the semi-dark room again and subjected to the same questioning. Weaker than in the previous interrogation session, he collapsed after an hour and was brought back to semi-consciousness by a pail of cold water thrown on his face. Although he could not stand up, his interrogators assailed him with the same questions. When he heard himself involuntarily begging them to allow him a few hours' sleep, he felt ashamed and degraded.

He began to shout: 'Is this the African liberation I fought for? Is this the ancestral homeland I've returned to? No, we did not fight to replace white brutality with African brutality. We did not. We fought for a new world. A new world. You hear me? Damn you. You are the traitors. You are the subversives.'

Seized by a fit of dementia, he felt oddly filled with strength and did not care what they did to him. He railed against his captors until one of the men slapped him hard across his face. I will defy them, he thought. I haven't travelled this far, lived this long to betray my beliefs. But his body would not support his resolve and he sank into darkness, with his face stinging painfully.

Marshall woke up on a mattress in a narrow cell where three other prisoners slept. And he knew then that Kaya had made contact with Wade Mayana and the retired scholar had intervened on his behalf. But even the venerable Mayana could not secure his immediate release. That would require far more time.

Over the next few days, as he spoke to his cellmates, Marshall realised how fortunate he had been to escape their fates. The most voluble was Laki Butene, a former bank manager, and a man who, despite his ragged foul-smelling clothes, seemed as though he would have been a pillar of respectability wherever he lived. Butene's deceased son had, unknown to him, been a member of the Kinja Liberation Front. The security agents, Butene believed, had killed him under interrogation and, working on the principle that the family of an enemy of the state were also subversives, had arrested and tortured the father.

'You're lucky, my friend,' Butene told Marshall. 'They are moderate in the first two interrogation sessions. It is in the third that they start getting nasty. By the sixth, you would've been dead.'

The former bank manager's obvious conservatism had saved his life, but having witnessed the death of two previous cellmates, he was resigned to dying in prison. In the exercise yard, where the prisoners were allowed to walk for an hour each day, Marshall saw men with broken limbs, gouged eyes, and swollen lips, and heard stories of torture, with electric wires attached to the most sensitive parts of the body, that made him shiver. The prisoners' pleas of innocence, their solicitude for their families, moved him to a new depth of understanding of man's cruelty.

Initially, Marshall attempted to give these victims of the Bamako tyranny succour and hope inspired by his knowledge that General Bamako's days were numbered because his statue had fallen, but the squalid condition, the poor diet, and the maimed, broken figures in the overcrowded prison assaulted his spirits daily. Some days passed in listless silence as he struggled to find the strength to persevere.

On one such day, a man who had been in Maroko for two years and knew neither his crime nor the duration of his sentence, and whose face was covered in weeping sores, approached Marshall in the exercise yard and said to him: 'The gods must have sent you to share with us your strength.' Weak and fighting lassitude, Marshall laughed with irony as these words evoked a memory of his encounter with Martin Mayini on a London-bound train many years before. And he felt stronger for the laughter.

After three months in Maroko Castle he received a visit from Kaya, a rare privilege won for him by Wade Mayana. She had lost weight, and though her hands were shaky he could see that she was battling to maintain her composure. In the few hours they were allowed together, she told about the strikes that had crippled the country, the staff her father had put in place to run the Brighton-Lisbon Hotel, the thriving school, the widespread rumours of an imminent coup, and her recurrent nightmare about Kende, whom she had not seen since his banishment.

'I have tried everything to rid my mind of him, but he refuses to leave me alone. I don't know what to do,' she said, raising her trembling hands to her face, a face that belonged to a woman ten years older than she.

Angry, frustrated and dispirited, Marshall was even more aware that Kaya's recovery would require dedicated help over a long period, a lifetime even. He had to survive this ordeal, if only for her sake. They embraced and remained silent for the last fifteen minutes of her visit, and were then separated by a surly young prison warden.

Along with a bundle of clothes she had given him a letter from England. But many hours passed before he found the strength to look at it – it had been read by the security service, no doubt. Reading in the quiet of the cell, tears came to Marshall's eyes and joy erupted in his heart. It was a letter from his son, Martin-Johann. He was living in London with his mother and had located Marshall through a chance encounter with a former resident of the Brighton-Lisbon, who had been sent to London to study.

Marshall read the letter over and over again in that Maroko cell, that cell of exile, where death and life walked hand in hand. From that moment, whenever he could find a quiet spot, he began to compose a letter to his son. On the days when his spirits were low, he summoned his memory of Kaya, and imagined her, Martin-Johann and himself seated on the lawn of the Brighton Lisbon Hotel, and so he focused his mind on writing to the son he had not seen in almost twenty years.

9

The palace coup which ousted General Raafu Bamako five months after the slaughter of the students at Independence Square was greeted with euphoric celebrations in the streets. The people burnt effigies of the deposed military dictator on bonfires made from his framed portraits, and danced under the moonlight to the polyrhythmic sounds of the reawakened drums of freedom. Thousands of wrongly imprisoned citizens were freed and reunited with their jubilant families in homecoming parties where prodigious quantities of roasted goat meat, beer and palm wine were consumed.

The new Head of State, General Moidibo Haruna, an unassuming northerner and Muslim, held the conviction that the temperament and training of a soldier rendered him an unsuitable national leader because he would always, always tip the delicate scales of concensus and coercion, on which governance is predicated, in favour of coercion. Intent on cleaning up the military's tarnished image, General Haruna acted with inspired and admirable haste to form a transitional government comprising civilians and soldiers, fix a date for the return of civilian rule and remove the more notorious features of the Bamako regime.

The universally hated Kiss was abolished and its agents returned to the ranks of the unemployed, to the shanty towns from which they had been plucked, to serve penance amongst their former victims. For many months the stoning of men known to have been Kiss agents was a common sight in Eko. Many assumed new identities and migrated to different parts of the country but the ineradicable odour of their past cruelties pursued and exposed them to the implacable wrath of the bereaved families.

Against this background, Marshall and Kaya attempted to repair their lives. On his release from prison Marshall learnt that Kaya, on the morning of his arrest, alerted Modupe Ogbomosho and then drove six hundred miles through rainforests, along roads infamous for casting animated shadows that lured drivers to their deaths, across the great River Kijj, and deep into the savannah to the remote village where Wade Mayana lived, to plead for the sage's assistance in securing her husband's release. The following day she drove back to Eko, rested for a while, then began a relentless assault on the President's office.

She sought the complicity of women known from her days in the waterhouse. Trained to an incomparable degree in the art of loving by Magdalena De Souza, many were now the wives or mistresses of military officers, and they rallied behind her by pestering their husbands or paramours at hours when all these embattled soldiers desired were tender caresses to fortifiy them against the palpable hatred of the populace.

Far more important were Kaya's daily visits to Government Castle where she deployed a mixture of cunning, obvious distress and haughtiness to overcome the official indifference to her plight until she reached the inner offices of the Castle. Long after she knew Wade Mayana had made a personal representation to the General, she continued those daily visits. Though the General's office always tried to reassure her that the matter was being dealt with, she wanted personally to let the General know that should her husband die, her grief would haunt him beyond the grave.

The General, of course, never saw the possessed wife, but it used to be said that, though the slaughter of the students had made little impact on his iron heart, Kaya's daily visits soon produced in him a noticeable irascibility, and several times he enquired, with affected insouciance, as to whether the mad woman – meaning Kaya Sarjeant – was in the building.

Nevertheless, Kaya's campaign, and the months of Marshall's incarceration, had drained and aged her, further diminishing a vitality already weakened by Kende's terror. Marshall saw it in her early morning countenance, the bottles of black hair dye in the bathroom cabinet, the frequent involuntary sighs of a profound weariness which shadowed even this love supreme, this love forged in the crucible of suffering and mutual sacrifice. Kaya now seldom worked more than half a day in the school, and when she lost her patience with a classroom of obstreperous pupils and found herself torn between weeping and inflicting a frenzied beating, she decided that it was time to reconsider her future as a teacher.

This she did on a holiday with Marshall at Modupe Ogbomosho's recently acquired villa on Lake Kitaka. The reprieve from work and the city confirmed her belief that some vital spark had gone from her heart, some animating spirit was fading, some flame was dying. For the vista over the lake, with its flocks of graceful flame-red flamingos, snow-white egrets, hippopotamuses lazily bathing in the mud, served to expose a growing lassitude, relieved only by hours of supine stillness, and an intense disquiet if Marshall – as he was inclined to do in ruminant spells which had become frequent since he started writing to his son – wandered too far from the villa or could not be heard in the adjoining room. So, much of their time beside the lake was spent in the sumptuous blue bedroom, with Marshall reading to her from the eclectic collection of novels, short stories and poetry anthologies which Modupe Ogbomosho had purchased on one of his London trips.

By the end of a month on the tranquil lake, both were ready to return to Eko. Kaya expressed anxiety for her favourite pupils, her surrogate children, and the school. For Marshall also, Lake Kitaka's daily, timeless tranquillity had lost its charm. Kaya's poor health worried him and stirred dark intimations of death and renewed loneliness deepened by bereavement. There was, too, the letter he was expecting from his son, Martin-Johann. Perhaps it was waiting for him in Eko. And Eko itself. How he loved that city, loved it with the sort of stern passion generally reserved for islands.

He longed to be back there, for night-time drives along the expressways, for the sight of the moonlight on the lagoons, for the sweet aroma of roasted plantain borne on sea breezes also laden with lilting music. But could he love it without Kaya?

Nearing the River Kijj, Marshall noticed that Kaya looked weak, and though they could reach Eko before nightfall, he said: 'We can stop again for a few days by the River Kijj, if you like.'

Kaya pressed his hand and said: 'Yes, let's rest beside the River Kijj.' Her voice was faint.

They booked into a small boarding-house by the river and after a light lunch and a siesta, walked through the dusk along the bank of the mighty and beautiful river where north and south Kinja met, strolled through a market of fish, yam, basket and calabash traders drawn from all corners of this great country.

Under a nim tree Marshall said: 'Maybe we should leave Kinja.'

Kaya did not reply for a long time, but kept her gaze on a canoe approaching the bank. Then she said: 'No, Marshall. I do not want to die a long way from home. It is the saddest death.'

He knew they would never speak about this matter again.

Marshall would recall first seeing the ragged, half-dressed stranger near the entrance of the Brighton-Lisbon Hotel on the afternoon he and Kaya arrived back home. Men crazed by the lethal concoction of marijuana, ogogoro and the sun, or their spirits crushed by the cruel city, were a common sight in Eko, so the tramp did not really impinge on his consciousness until some weeks after getting back home, about the same time that Kaya took to her bed complaining of dizzy spells, intestinal pains and an inability to keep her food down. It was then that the skinny, bare-chested man with the matted hair and bloodshot eyes started registering on Marshall's distracted mind, and he remembered that he had seen the pitiful figure several times, wandering along the roadside, his skin baked black by the sun, the soles of his feet hardened and stained by the ochre-coloured earth.

Now curious, Marshall asked several members of staff about the tramp. Most claimed not to have noticed him. The sole exception was Mirima, the receptionist at the Brighton-Lisbon. She told Marshall she had first seen the tramp while Marshall was, as she euphemistically put it, going through his troubles, and believed the man slept on a piece of wasteland a mile from the hotel.

For some days Marshall forgot about the tramp because Kaya's condition suddenly worsened and his mounting anxiety about her health left him with little time to think about anything else. He became so concerned that he sent a message to Kaya's mother to come to Eko. Epeka Ogbomosho turned up with speed, and after fussing over her ailing daughter for two days concluded that somebody had touched her. She immediately set about administering a dazzling variety of decoctions, and nailed into the bedroom walls numerous charms intended to dispel the evil spirits that she believed had invaded Kaya. When her charms seemed ineffective, she sought the services of Alhaji Lakijo but the babalawo was on his annual pilgrimage to Mount Kinja in the northeast.

Marshall, meanwhile, went to the Our Lady of Africa Cathedral every evening and prayed with quiet fervour at the base of the Black Madonna for her divine intervention to save his wife. Should she recover, he vowed he would take her out of Kinja, out of Africa. Most evenings, lost in his entreaties, he had to be reminded by the bespectacled Senegalese curate that it was time to lock the cathedral doors, and on those occasions the curate walked with him in solemn silence to the steps outside.

The combination of prayers, charms, and medicines seemed to work because Kaya's health rallied for a few days, and one afternoon she asked to receive a visit from her favourite pupils. This was swiftly arranged, but as Marshall watched her stroke the children's heads, and heard her shower each one with a mixture of severe admonition and praise, he felt, against his most heartfelt wishes, that she was bidding farewell to them.

A week later the fever returned with a vengeful swiftness and she could barely sit up in bed, and retched up everything that passed her lips. One night, as Marshall sat at the desk he had placed in the bedroom to be always close to Kaya, writing a letter to his son, he heard her moaning softly in her sleep. He went to sit beside her and held her hand and was shocked by its raging heat.

He daubed her brow with a wet cloth and as he did so, she stirred awake, looked fixedly at him and, smiling weakly, said: 'Thank you for these years of happiness, my love.'

They were her last words. The following day, at the hour when the sun reddened the western sky, he found Kaya, his wife, his companion, his love in the cold, cold arms of death.

Marshall sat with Kaya's corpse through the long night and by dawn his sorrow had grown as bright and luminous as the sunrise in the east. Epeka Ogbomosho, who had been weeping throughout the night outside the bedroom, relieved him of his mournful vigil. From that moment the grief of Kaya's death would cease to be his alone, but that of the entire Ogbomosho family.

An hour later, with Eko preparing for the working day, as Marshall wandered back from the beach where he had gone to be alone with his sorrow, Mirima, the hotel receptionist, unaware that Kaya had died the previous evening, informed him that the tramp was dead. She had seen his body on the roadside, near the hotel gate, as she made her way to work, and she surmised that a car or truck had knocked him down and that the driver had probably stopped only to move his body to the verge.

Marshall abstractedly instructed her to telephone the Eko morgue or, like those which littered Eko's expressways, the body would be there for days, even weeks.

Then, for some inexplicable reason, Marshall wandered to the gate and along the road until he came to the bloodied, mangled corpse. And the dead face that greeted him, though caked in dirt and blood was, he now recognised with a tremor which shook his soul, that of the young man whose last words to him were: 'Tell Kaya that Kende has found her.'

Over the next couple of days, while the Ogbomosho family prepared to bury Kaya, a terrible madness of guilt and sorrow crept upon Marshall. He could not participate in their pagan rituals; he could not, as they did, worship God and gods. He turned to the God of his childhood, the Christian God, and sought solace and forgiveness in the Cathedral of Our Lady of Africa for the deaths for which he believed he was responsible.

He entered the confessional and poured out his guilt to the silent, unseen priest. He was convinced that his selfishness, aided by his wealth, had killed both Kaya and Kende because if he had not married her they would still have life and with life a chance to be reunited in love. Before the statue of the Black Madonna, under the crucifix, he prayed until his knees were raw and stiff. He asked God what penance he should suffer, whether he should strike off his right arm, abandon all worldly comforts and go into the wilderness and live like a hermit.

There were days in this madness of the soul when he doubted the existence of the very God to whom he had prayed the previous day because he saw no reason to believe in a God who had exiled him from Paradise, and stolen from him everyone he had loved, and sanctioned all the suffering of mankind he had witnessed in his lifetime. And at such times, in the grip of this spiritual insanity, taking his life seemed the only recourse, the only way to end his suffering, for the temple into which, as he travelled, he had sought peaceful meditation had become a temple of sorrow.

It was the Ogbomoshos who rescued him from his madness. They were the closest he had to a family and though he had never admitted them to the secrets of his soul, they knew him well enough to recognise the depth of his crisis. Modupe Ogbomosho persuaded him to rest in Elaka. And in that village in the heart of the rainforest, over many nights and months, Epeka and Modupe – who had not spoken to each other in years – began to make him feel whole again.

Epeka reminded him that the Kende who reappeared in Kaya's life was not the same Kende she had left in Elaka, but another person, a stranger born from his travails in Eko. She recounted to Marshall conversations she had had with Kaya in which her daughter exalted Marshall's name, praised his strength to feel, to empathise, to be human, to love, despite the risk and his vulnerability. She recounted how she, Epeka, in her youth, had loved a young man and sworn undying love to him, but when Modupe came along she realised she had made a mistake, and when, in adulthood, she saw her former lover again it merely confirmed that she had made the right choice, despite all the suffering Modupe had caused her, of which only a fraction was known to the world. Kaya knew more happiness with you than she would have known with any other man, she repeated again and again.

And during the day, when Epeka was not with him, Marshall was always surrounded by children, by their laughter, and their insistence that he join them in their games, and their songs, as if they possessed an ancient wisdom and knew that he, a foreign African, was in need of a healing which only Africa could give him because it had wounded him as it did all its children.

At night, Marshall and Modupe Ogbomosho, bearing a gun, went out into the forest, and stalked prey they would never catch. The further into the forest and the night Modupe Ogbomosho took Marshall, the more loquacious he became. He would start their journeys by singing hunting songs. Later he would recite Yoruba epic poetry. Their hunting expedition always ended under the same ariba tree, with Modupe pleading exhaustion caused by being spoilt by city life. Under that ariba tree he would recount the myths of his people, explain the attributes of the four hundred and one Orishas of the Yoruba Pantheon, and argue that the gods are always playing evil tricks on us mere mortals, which is why a man must choose to worship in the temple in which he is most comfortable. That way he has a greater chance of reaching the Supreme Being, whose omnipotence can abrogate the malevolent mischief of lesser gods. Whether we call him God, Allah or Olodumare, there is only one omnipotent, omniscient Supreme Being because there is only one Humanity, and each man can know that Supreme Being because he, it, she dwells deep in the soul of every person and we must constantly seek to reach God, to nourish our souls, because in His presence we will find the power to forgive ourselves, without which we cannot forgive others.

When Marshall had been in Elaka for three months, Baku Mathaku came to visit. Following directions from a Fulani herdsman, Baku had gone deep into the savannah to find the fabled anthill, which was as high as a mountain and more fantastic than an emir's palace. He had not found it, and on returning to Eko he learnt of Marshall's tragedy and was in Elaka to comfort his friend. He had brought his chess set, and they played in the shade of the village mango tree for days before Baku set off again in search of the fabled anthill of the savannah, which he believed would finally yield him the secret of their durability.

Some nights later, with Modupe Ogbomosho now back in Eko, Marshall dreamt the dream of the skeletal nun, and woke up drenched in sweat and feeling feverish. Paradoxically, that was the moment he knew he was on the road to recovery, though he would never be exactly the same again because he had lost Kaya for ever.

The months in Elaka, immured in the love and protection of the Ogbomosho family, would not entirely cure Marshall's guilt about his role in Kaya and Kende's deaths. But, like his failure, he would learn to live with the guilt and it became one of the pains concealed behind his enigmatic mask, a sometimes troubling memory which waylaid him when he was too tired to suppress or deny the emotions that accompanied his memories of that episode in his life, another silent accusing companion as he paced the shores of his exile.

10

Eighteen months after the coup which ousted the Bamako regime, Jibril Sokotan, the leader of the revamped People's National Party, was inaugurated as President, becoming Kinja's first elected leader in over a decade.

Baku Mathaku was appointed Minister of Housing in the new government, but within four months the diminutive reformed rebel resigned altogether from politics. He told Marshall that the daily effort required to resist the insidiously corrupting effect of political office placed an intolerable strain on his nerves, nerves better suited to the excitement of rebellion than the ennui of conformity. Besides, he preferred to concentrate his energies on researching into the mysterious durability of anthills.

Immediately after the elections, ex-General Raafu Bamako, now a coffee farmer in the Plateau region, published his autobiography. This slim volume justified his repressive policies by alluding to the ancient philosophical school which believes that the lives of men are 'nasty, brutish and short' and as a result need firm disciplining, scathingly attacked the ingratitude of Kinjaians, and warned in apocalyptic tones that the country would need his services again. The consensual opinion on the ex-General's literary effort was summed up by one newspaper reviewer who described it as 'nasty, brutish and, mercifully, short'. The proud ex-General was acquitted of conspiracy to murder the reviewer by attempting to run the hapless hack off the road in his souped-up American military Jeep, a trophy from his years in office.

After the trial he would retreat to his coffee farm, and await the urgent letter pleading for his return to office. No one ever wrote to the General. Good times returned to Kinja, and an atmosphere of freedom was now added to Eko's explosive growth.

Marshall was still grieving for his late wife and so followed Kinjaian politics from the secluded Brighton-Lisbon Hotel. He divided his time between the business, the Martin Luther King Jnr School, daily visits to the Our Lady of Africa Cathedral, monthly visits to Kaya's grave in Elaka, and corresponding with his son.

Persuading the boy to visit Kinja had become his paramount ambition, and somewhere in the back of his mind was the vague hope that he, Martin-Johann, would like the country and his father enough to settle here. But that ambition received a major setback when his application for Kinjaian citizenship, to which he was entitled, was rejected without reason. Magdalena De Souza's warning that he had enemies was confirmed. Determined to find out who they were he sought Baku Mathaku's assistance and when that failed to yield any result, he went to visit Wade Mayana.

Wade Mayana lived in retirement in the northwest savannah region of Kinja, beyond the River Kijj, in an isolated compound with his four wives. He was happy to receive Marshall and although he seemed remarkably healthy for a nonagenarian, he early on disclosed that he knew the exact hour and day of his own death. Marshall had been lucky to find him because he, Wade Mayana, following the custom of his people, would soon embark on that final journey, which would take him into a remote corner of the savannah to join the ancestors.

In the isolated compound, which stood like an oasis in the savannah, in a library replete with ancient tomes, on walks to the baobab tree which the retired scholar used to measure the distance and duration of his daily exercise, in the compound of the sagacious Wade Mayana, Marshall learnt why his application for citizenship had been turned down.

Mayana told him that there existed in Kinja a secret society of Ona loyalists, with members in the highest ranks of military and civil service, sworn to fight for the restoration of the monarchy and exact vengeance on those who had brought about its abolition and precipitated the civil war. The Ona loyalists would never again take to the battlefield, but they were still at war and would remain so until the monarchy was restored. They kept an unwritten list of formal and informal advisors to Martin Mayini, whom they were convinced had encouraged the then President's actions. Some names belonged there, others were there out of error, but all would suffer from some act of retribution.

'The name Marshall Sarjeant is on that list, I am certain. Their people will block your attempts to gain citizenship. My name is there, too. But they will not touch me. They know my day is closing.' The sagacious Wade Mayana stressed that he was relaying a rumour, but a rumour which had acquired, through repetition, enough force of truth to reach his aged ears.

'It was,' Wade Mayana said gravely, 'Mayini's biggest mistake, to disrespect the institutions of the past, to destroy them rather than concentrate on creating conditions which would, in the long run, perhaps, render them mere anachronisms for most people. He angered the gods with his impetuous haste.'

Wade Mayana revealed that he had been part of a delegation of elders to dissuade Mayini from abolishing the monarchy and exiling the Fon. 'The young fool would not listen,' Wade Mayana said bitterly, and then, with incredulity and irony in his voice, 'You know, it's strange, there were times when he seemed envious of the affection enjoyed by the Fon from his people. But there were times, too, in his presence, when I felt that he was in the grip of a terrible ancestral fury. You know the Onas were great slave traders?'

'No.'

'It is a little-known fact. One of those shameful secrets that their griots prefer to forget. A huge number of Mayini's people, the Ekans, were seized and sold to the Europeans by the Ona traders.' And Mayana shook his head and said, closing the conversation: 'Ultimately, of course, we can only speculate about that. What we do know is that if we judge a leader not just by his achievements in office, but also by the skill with which he handles his succession, then Martin failed.'

That night Marshall retired to bed and in the arid nocturnal silence of the savannah he heard the echoes of imminent upheaval. Wade Mayana had promised to make enquiries, speak to his contacts in the Ministry of Internal Affairs, attempt to reach the President's ears. But he was far removed from public affairs now, and could not promise a favourable outcome.

The next day, as they strolled to the baobab tree together, with Wade Mayana using a staff to aid bowed, aged legs concealed under a thin white kaftan, the sage said: 'I do not believe the soldiers will stay in the barracks. They have tasted the sweetness of power.'

'You have no faith in the new constitution, the new government?'

'Yes. Some. Sokotan is honest and clever. If he's lucky he will get two years in office. Maybe longer. But, the soldiers, the soldiers ... Part of our tragedy is that we have no foreign lands to send them to conquer, to revel in the glory of war against imaginary enemies and its bloodied spoils.'

'But we have the past to conquer, too,' Marshall said.

'Yes, that is true, very true. And much of this second half of the twentieth century has been about starting to conquer the past, undoing centuries of greed and lies and violence, centuries of barbarism.'

'We seem to have made little progress in conquering that past.'

'Now, young man,' Wade said chuckling, as they neared the baobab tree, 'it is I who should be the pessimist. Yet I am very optimistic. At the beginning of the century we who are the most ancient of people on earth, inhabitants of the continent which gave the earth mankind, we who once sowed seeds in the Sahara and built pyramids now reclaimed by the sand of Kush, we who have been here for far, far more than two thousand years, were everywhere under colonial rule, those in the diaspora not long freed from slavery, full of contempt for themselves and all things African, their souls divided. A little over one score years from a new century that is no longer so. Huge swathes of Africa have gained independence, the Africans in the diaspora are prouder of their ancestral roots, their wounded souls are healing. Though much of the South remains to be liberated, we have crossed the desert of despair, survived the savannah of misery, now we must survive the jungle of independence and freedom. We cannot afford to be complacent. As you have witnessed for yourself, this last journey is the most difficult. Many ghosts from that past remain to be put to rest and until then there will be much chaos, bloodshed and confusion. But with faith, love, forgiveness, an unshakeable belief in the indissoluble oneness and yet infinite diversity of humanity, the millennium light faintly visible on the horizon, driving away this twentiethcentury night when the heart of darkness revealed itself to be not on our maligned land, but elsewhere, in Auschwitz and the minds of those who bombed Hiroshima and continue the evil search for weapons of ever more destructive capacity. That light bleeding through the dark night must be the light of peace, the light of love.'

He paused, then said: 'Now our personal ghosts, those are another matter. They are always cause for pessimism. Perhaps it is that you have not yet conquered the ghost of your own personal past?'

Marshall did not reply but looked into the old man's eyes, those narrow savannah dweller's eyes set in a lined blue-black face swaddled in a white turban, then he looked away, across the flat, dry land to an inselberg in the distance and thought, with profound discomfort, of Nana Sarjeant's lost ka and his failed mission, the deformed children of Paradise, the letter he hoped would be awaiting him in Eko from the estranged son with whom he was now trying, through correspondences, to build a bridge strong enough to support a reunion.

He steered the conversation back to the state of Kinja, and as they set off for the compound, Wade Mayana soared in his reproof of Martin Mayini, which Marshall now recognised was also an exercise in self-reproach because the imprimatur of elders like Wade Mayana had been the foundation of his leadership. Mayini was one of Wade Mayana's personal ghosts.

'The young fool,' Wade Mayini said again. 'A few years in power and he would not listen to us any more. We warned him. He caused a terrible imbalance between the traditional and the modern. He tried to appropriate the traditional authority enjoyed by the Fon, when he should have focused his energies on shoring up the authority of the new state, the new nation. His failure to diplomatically negotiate with the past allowed that paranoid buffoon General Bamako to seize power.' Reaching the compound, Wade Mayana, slightly out of breath, said: 'Mayini authored his own downfall, but he did not do so in circumstances of his own choosing, which is why, with time, we must reclaim and celebrate him as the founding father of the nation and a Pan-Africanist visionary. We must throw light on the shadow that fell between the ideals and the reality. We must forgive him his errors, for they were our errors also.'

They parted the next day with Wade Mayana reiterating his promise to pursue the matter of Marshall's citizenship application. 'Do not worry,' Wade said. 'Your blood will not water the tree of their ambition.'

Marshall hugged Wade Mayana and as he drove away on the dusty dirt track, he glanced back at the dust-shrouded figure and wondered whether the Pan-Africanist cause would survive the passing of men like Mayana.

True to Wade Mayana's prediction, the second incarnation of democracy in Kinja was destined to be as brief and bright as the life of a butterfly. The flamboyant new president, Jibril Sokotan, had begun by dazzling Kinjaians with his vision of the future, which included a futuristic new capital to rival Brasilia, in Keita, two hundred miles north of the River Kijj, and an international Pan-African Arts Festival. These were not original ideas – the Pan-African Arts Festival had been mooted in the Mayini years, and the new capital in the Bamako years – but Jibril Sokotan packaged and sold them to the nation with the hypnotic flair of a super salesman. He set about realising these projects with the same mad rush that claimed thousands of lives on Kinja's roads. While an international consortium of architects began meeting to plan Keita, the Sokotan government raced ahead with the Pan-African Arts Festival.

When Marshall got back to Eko from visiting Wade Mayana, he threw himself into taking advantage of the impending festival. Organised in nine months, it brought artists from all parts of Africa and the African diaspora, and over a million foreign visitors to the country. Eko was its centre and for a month the city overflowed with arts exhibitions, music concerts, dramatic plays, poetry and prose recitals, films and fashion shows. The hasty organisation showed everywhere. It was not uncommon to see theatre troupes performing on wasteland beneath the expressways or hear poets reciting on street corners because the indomitable spirit of the artist refused to be squashed by the festival's poor management. Here was the spirit of Africa given imperfect expression but vibrant and resilient all the same.

Like everything else in the Sokotan period, the festival was overshadowed by the country's alarming level of corruption. Visitors discovered that it was impossible to get anything done through official channels without bribes. From the lowliest airport official to the most senior minister, everybody expected a reward for rendering services which they were paid to perform. Halfway through the festival, the Housing

Minister was caught trying to smuggle out four suitcases full of kwanza notes at the Eko international airport. He sought mitigation by exposing the depth of corruption in the Ministry of Natural Resources where a billion kwanzas had gone missing while senior officials in that Ministry bought up palatial buildings in London. '*Mea culpa,* he cried, 'but I'm only a small fry.'

The Ona loyalists took advantage of the festival to call for the restoration of the monarchy in the East with a series of newspaper articles which suggested that until the monarchy was restored, Kinja was doomed to a perpetual cycle of growth and decay, anarchy and order. President Sokotan, a Muslim with great respect for tradition, however, surprisingly ignored the intermittent outcry made by the Easterners for the return of their royal house.

The Brighton-Lisbon Hotel enjoyed a brief period of revived prosperity during the Pan-African Arts Festival. The sloping lawn was the scene of several concerts by the Harlem Jazz Ensemble. The ensemble had come to Eko expecting to play at the prestigious National Theatre but discovered on arriving that they had neither been scheduled on the already crowded programme, nor reserved accommodation. Marshall gave them beds and a venue, and though their performances attracted small audiences, the fishermen returned to the bay to net the fishes lured by the music.

There were also daily poetry recitals by an itinerant Jamaican dub poet, Vincent Bacchus. With his astonishingly graceful African-American wife and their three-year-old child, he was on a quest to visit every single African country. Marshall would long remember the young, toothsome poet because he once described him as priestly-looking and, when it became apparent that the poet was broke and could only stay in the Brighton-Lisbon on Marshall's generosity, took to addressing him as 'Father'.

The musicians and the poet gave Marshall happiness.

Nevertheless, the month-long festival was for the Brighton-Lisbon Hotel and its residents a mere interlude in its ineluctable decline. The bougainvillaea hedges, as if inspired by the festival, suddenly grew wilder and higher, and the signpost disappeared yet again. Disaster struck the Africa Bar when Akante Ousman resigned from his position as chef, and opened his own establishment, the Savannah Grill, in central Eko. Marshall then decided to convert the bar into a chalet and imagined it would be popular with honeymooning couples. But the workmen he employed only got as far as erecting the wooden walls and two windows before abandoning the job for more lucrative work elsewhere. For months it remained a shrine to a failed ambition.

Only three civil servants remained in the hotel and few visitors came there, as Eko's tourist industry, stifled by the country's reputation for widespread corruption, was almost nil, and anyway there was now an abundance of affordable hotels closer to the heart of the city.

Marshall persevered, for despite the lonely life, he kept himself busy. He wrote regular letters to his son, and on his visits to Kaya's grave, if Modupe Ogbomosho was around, a rare event, they would spend a night in the forest stalking prey they would never catch and discoursing on the gods under the ariba tree.

Back in Eko, there were days when Marshall's hunger for love and physical intimacy was like a fever, and on such occasions he drove to Lipi Market, to the bed of a beautiful Tiv courtesan trained by Magdalena De Souza, and a night in her fleshy embrace, like a homeopathic dose of love, temporarily sated his yearning for feminine tenderness.

On other days, when his loneliness raged like an angry lion, when failure weighed heavily on his heart, and the rain of guilt poured over his soul, and even his daily dawn bath in the Atlantic Ocean gave him no peace, he drove into central Eko, to the Our Lady of Africa Cathedral, to meditate and strengthen his soul in its atmosphere of sacred tranquillity.

But his remained an eclectic faith. He worshipped in many temples. He had now taken to wearing a gold cross around his neck, not because he was any more certain about his exclusive commitment to that faith, that Church – he also kept on his bedside cabinet a small statue of the Yoruba god Ogun, from which hung a St Christopher pendant – but because the sign of the cross was for him the most comforting symbol of faith in the possibility of redemption.

II

Six months after the Pan-African Arts Festival, with the Sokotan government sinking in a quagmire of corruption and its critics calling for the return of the military, Marshall Sarjeant achieved one of his most cherished ambitions: the son whom he had not seen in almost twenty years agreed to cross the bridge of letters. Despite repeated requests, Martin-Johann had never sent a photograph of himself, so the young man Marshall met at an Eko international airport swarming with soldiers was a total stranger, but a recognisable one.

Tall and wiry, and soft-spoken, with intelligent, alert eyes and a strong facial resemblance to his father, he bore the stigma of Sarjeant's curse in a withered, almost lifeless left arm which gave him a rather awkward gait.

He had not mentioned this deformity in his letters and it would be many days before Marshall extracted from him its curious history. He had been perfectly normal up until the age of eight. Then his left arm went numb and, though it grew in length, it lacked muscle. This handicap gave him a proud defiant air and any offer of help with any physical task was greeted with an almost aggressive refusal. Marshall early on detected that his son was shy and self-effacing but over the months Martin-Johann spent in Eko, he would learn that the boy was capable of garrulity when it came to talking about others. The son brought the father up to date with friends lost along the way.

No one knew the whereabouts of Scoop Fearon. The mendacious wag had fathered a string of children in Guyana, run up massive debts, and then disappeared into the Guyana jungle with a teenage Amerindian girl. The last thing Martin-Johann remembered hearing about him from Zenobia was that he had joined an expedition looking for the legendary golden city of El Dorado. Martin-Johann spoke with a compulsive fondness for Scoop which Marshall recognised and shared because, in the intervening years, he had forgiven his boyhood friend as an incorrigible liar, the sufferer of an incurable pathological condition. He could not help but smile at Martin-Johann's recollections of Scoop's foibles.

Mention of Zenobia, however, occasioned the rueful feelings of an error in love. Shortly after Scoop's flight, which happened when Martin was eight, Zenobia returned to London with her son. For many years Zenobia fancied herself a businesswoman and owned a string of businesses which included a hair salon and a basement nightclub in Brixton. She had an army of admirers, numerous lovers and several earnest marriage proposals, but she was dedicated to her son and running her businesses, and, perhaps fearful of trusting her heart to another man, took perverse pleasure in playing elusive games and setting them impossible tasks designed to prove the strength of their love for her. When a suitor failed, she would enumerate all his faults to her son while warning him against becoming a weak-hearted lover.

There was, or had been, between mother and son, Marshall sensed, a powerful bond, but a bond which had been subjected to some severe trials. Zenobia had wanted Martin-Johann to become a doctor, a lawyer or a teacher, and up until his mid-teens, the boy was obedient, despite showing a talent for art which his teachers encouraged. Then around seventeen years old, the rupture occurred. The boy began to grow his hair in dreadlocks. He barely scraped through his university entrance exams because by the time he sat them he was wrestling with whether he should become a Rastafarian. Looking back on those troubled years, when he was so estranged from his mother that they lived apart and he seldom visited her, Martin-Johann saw them as a period of absolute confusion, a season of questions without answers.

That bizarre faith gave him a home, a sense of community, of connection, of belonging, which seemed more strengthening than his mother's familiar love.

The boy's recollections of episodes from those difficult years stirred in Marshall memories of his own time in London. No, it would not have been easy for a fatherless youngman growing up in the shadow of a declining empire, a nation trying to come to terms with its loss of imperial glory, its citizens having to live on equal terms with people around whom they had woven so many monstrous lies and subjected to such denials. So what better than a faith, however bizarre, that shunned all things White and European and elevated to the status of a religon the occluded fragments of the African past? The son, suffering from the discomfiture of double displacement, had followed in his father's footsteps, without the benefits of his father's secret sources of strength, prey to any set of ideas that helped keep him afloat while he crossed that stormy sea where the confusion of adolescence is exacerbated by the confusion of race.

One day Martin-Johann said to Marshall: 'I was angry all the time, and full of hate, and I did not want to have those feelings, but I could not help myself.'

'Who were you angry with?' Marshall asked.

The boy thought for a while, then said: 'My mother, all Whites. Myself for my crippled arm.'

'And me, your father?'

Martin-Johann did not answer, but excused himself, and Marshall did not see him again for several hours. When they next met, over dinner in Marshall's quarters, Martin-Johann sat at the table in silence, refusing to meet Marshall's eyes.

Marshall said: 'You did not answer my question this morning. Were you angry with me?'

'Yes, I was angry with you,' Martin-Johann exploded. 'More than anybody else I was angry with you. I was angry with you for not being there to answer my questions. I was angry with you for not being there when my mother was secretly crying in bed because a relationship had ended. I was angry with you for this crippled arm, this dead limb hanging off my shoulder.'

It was the first of many cathartic confrontations between father and son. Marshall listened with unruffled calm as the young man poured out his anger, and when he had given vent to years of pent-up rage and stormed away from the dinner table, Marshall remained seated and reflected on the inevitable fragility of a bridge built from letters.

When Marshall felt the young man had eviscerated all his anger, he admitted him into the history of the Sarjeant family, his failed mission, and asked Martin-Johann for forgiveness. But Martin-Johann was not yet ready to forgive him – perhaps would never be ready, or perhaps was incapable of forgiveness at that young age.

None the less relations between them improved over the next few days. Marshall steered their conversations away from the past and to the future. Martin-Johann disclosed that he had been painting for over a year, and for the past nine months he had been sharing his modest bedsit with a young woman by the prosaic name of Ellen Smith. He showed Marshall a rather blurred photograph of a pretty young woman, who was clearly of mixed race, with a broad face and saucer-like eyes, and an air of otherworldliness.

'We're very close,' he told Marshall. 'She encouraged me to visit you, and though we are thousands of miles apart, we each know what the other is feeling and thinking.'

Marshall surmised that Martin had found love and from that love flowed the strength which enabled him to accept the invitation to visit Africa. He was happy for the boy, because he felt he could like him as a person and love him as a son. Martin-Johann reminded him of himself, his gentleness, his natural dislike of violence, and that he was committed to becoming an artist made Marshall feel as though fate had intervened and given the son the chance to become what he, the father, had been denied.

One day he said to Martin-Johann: 'Did you know that I, too, once had ambitions to be an artist? I was very young then, and in those days I was on my way to becoming a Catholic and part of the tradition which drew on religion to create art that consoled and exalted.'

Martin-Johann smiled and said curtly: 'That's an old-fashioned view of art. Modern art is created from the inner mind, not religion. I believe that the most powerful contemporary artists draw on the world of the unconscious, the world of dreams, from an inner vision.'

Marshall laughed, delighted by his son's directness and certainty, and they talked about art for hours, and when they finished Marshall felt he was reaching Martin-Johann

But there was still friction between them. Days of peaceful conversation could suddenly end with Martin-Johann withdrawing into himself or speaking to Marshall in a resentful voice. In this latter mood, the warmth of reunion between father and son evaporated. Accusations of neglect and abandonment were given voice. Why had Marshall never made an effort to find him and Zenobia? It was a question the young man asked several times, and implied in the asking that Marshall never loved him or his mother. In this accusation, Marshall could hear Zenobia's voice, Zenobia's hurt that he, Marshall, had failed to love her. When he tried again and again to explain how he had disappeared into Africa, about his failed mission, the boy seemed incapable of understanding and dismissed him as sounding like his mother, Zenobia, who claimed that her dead mother sometimes visited her when she needed comforting.

Marshall's reply was brief: 'It's a level of reality which few of us can see, and even fewer understand.' The vaguely knowing silence from Martin-Johann made Marshall think that he knew exactly what Marshall was alluding to but, perhaps due to his English reserve, was not yet ready to share his vision with this stranger, his father.

They did not spend all their time talking in the Brighton-Lisbon Hotel. Some days father and son drove into Eko, along its expressways, through its back streets, feeling the frenetic energy of the city. When Martin-Johann commented on the many soldiers on the streets, Marshall shrugged and said, 'This is Africa,' though he interpreted the sight of the soldiers as signs of the coup Wade Mayana had predicted.

They strolled through Lipi Market, with Marshall taking great pleasure in naming the goods for sale, and the son recalling similar scenes in his Guyana years. As they got to know each other better, Marshall advised his son to settle down with Ellen because so much youthful energy can be wasted chasing useless dreams and duplicitous spectres.

Some days, too tired for the heat and fury of Eko, Marshall encouraged the boy to go into the city alone and expose himself to whatever adventures it gave him.

One evening Martin-Johann returned in a mood of excitement and described how he had met a Ghanaian in Lipi who had mistaken him for his brother, Kwesi, and they had sat on Lipi beach and eaten egusi fish stew and drank warm beer and felt the powerful breeze blowing off the Atlantic and listened to the Ghanaian talk of his exile here in Kinja and the family he had left behind in Kumasi, and the Ghanaian had sung a lament for his long-dead twin sister and cried to the stranger, Martin-Johann, and as they parted the Ghanaian said: 'Thank you for listening to my sorrow.'

When he finished relating the encounter to Marshall Martin-Johann announced that he had arrived at an important decision as a result of that chance meeting with the Ghanaian stranger and being here, in Africa. He would take a new name – Kwesi. Marshall smiled with approval and said it was an apt name because he, Martin-Johann, was born on that day, but counselled that he should not abandon the names given him at birth because they represented five hundred years of history that could not be and should not be erased from his identity. Those names, too, were part of his strength.

The boy agreed and that same night they enacted a private ritual where Marshall poured libation on the beach and baptised the boy in the Atlantic Ocean, and Martin-Johann Kwesi Sarjeant was born. From that ritual Marshall felt that the bridge between their hearts, between father and son, had been immeasurably strengthened.

A month into Martin-Johann's visit, the third and worst coup in Kinja's history occurred. One morning Eko residents woke to hear the radio broadcaster announcing that President Jibril Sokotan had been deposed and until further notice the country was under a dusk-to-dawn curfew. The new leader of the Provisional Ruling Military Council, a General Aliyu Shendam, had, the announcement declared, intervened to rescue Kinja from the plague of corruption and chaos.

But far from ridding Kinja of chaos, the soldiers appeared to plunge the country into a fortnight of anarchy and lawlessness. The Eko international airport was closed and tanks blocked all roads on the city limits. In this atmosphere all sorts of wild rumours circulated, one of which claimed that President Jibril Sokotan, the Vice-President, Kane Makal, and three senior ministers had been woken from their beds past midnight in a co-ordinated military operation, driven to Lipi beach, and there executed while their wives and children watched. Another claimed that the Minister of Finance, Meleke Meleke, Kinja's most prominent Catholic, had with his family sought refuge in the Our Lady of Africa Cathedral but the soldiers had violated the sanctity of the church, battered the doors down, taken the Minister away and subjected him to the same terminal punishment as his erstwhile colleagues. Simultaneously, there came news of insurgents in the northeast mountains making raids into the capital of the East, and in the largest Northern city Muslim fundamentalists had rioted and attacked churches and property belonging to Christians and Southerners. Within Eko bands of criminals, disguised as soldiers, roamed the city at night, engaging troops in gunfire battles and raiding the homes of the rich.

This was no mere rumour. One night, four armed men battered down the door of the Brighton-Lisbon Hotel. Brought to the reception area by the noise, Marshall confronted them with all his stillness. While three of the men trained their weapons on him, the leader raided the office and seized a petty-cash box. Dissatisfied with his spoils he demanded more and threatened to shoot Marshall and kill all the residents. Marshall remained still, impassive.

Then one of the looters looked at Marshall, and perhaps seeing the scars to the sides of his eyes, shouted, 'Na Dada, let's go. Na Dada. Let's go, or we go suffer-o.' The other two lowered their weapons, and the leader ordered them to leave. Chief Lakijo's scarification had saved Marshall's life.

Other Eko residents were less fortunate, for this storm of anarchy claimed many lives before another broadcast announced that General Aliyu Shendam had been replaced as head of the Provisional Ruling Military Council by General Haruna Bello, a popular figure from the civil war, and the man rumoured to have engineered General Bamako's removal. The generals had changed places and the effect was immediate: an uneasy calm descended over the country.

Some days before the coup Martin-Johann had entered one of his periods of brooding withdrawal. He had for some time been painting sea scenes and, after buying several cans of paint, he had retreated to the half-finished chalet that had once been the Africa Bar and Marshall seldom saw him for almost a month, which spanned the storm, and when he did, it was only to satisfy Martin-Johann's request for money to buy more paint. But he felt his presence and was comforted by his son's propinquity even as he was disturbed by the boy's trance-like dedication to his work.

A week after some semblance of normality had returned to Eko, and the international airport was reopened, Martin-Johann declared with sudden urgency that he had to leave Eko because he felt Ellen calling him home. Marshall did not try to dissuade him but instead spent several days calling in favours owed from various friends to secure a seat for his son on the earliest flight. An exodus was taking place, and getting a seat was no easy matter. But he succeeded all the same. Marshall saw the boy, laden with some of the canvases he had painted – the rest, he told Marshall, were still in the unfinished chalet – off at a busy airport thronged with travellers anxious to escape the new climate of anarchy in Eko.

It was in the airport, after watching Martin-Johann's flight take off, that Marshall picked up that day's newspaper and read, with dismay, the news that among the civilians co-opted onto the Ruling Military Council to serve as advisors was Sunday Nkanda, the Kinjaian who had promised that the Brighton-Lisbon Hotel would one day be his. Furthermore, the newspaper article disclosed he was an Ona. The implications shook Marshall. He was still pursuing citizenship, a campaign into which he had now drawn Modupe Ogbomosho, Kaya's father, but with Nkanda back in favour he stood no chance of achieving it.

That same evening, while pondering his future, he wandered into the former Africa Bar to look at the paintings Martin-Johann had left him. But there were no paintings on canvas. Instead, he felt he had stepped into the dream of the skeletal nun. Almost every inch of the walls of the circular interior was covered in rough but unmistakably recognisable images from the dream that had been haunting him since he lost Nana Sarjeant's ka. From mountains obscured by clouds, to mountains that seemed animated with human figures piled on top of each other; from sea and landscape in various shades of red, from the old lady squatting in a sea cavern, to the woman bearing a fish on her head; from the skeletal nun to her pursuer. Only the last square of the wall remained blank.

A month after Martin-Johann left for London Marshall had still not received a letter from him and he was in a pensive mood every day. He now struggled to maintain the routines which once gave meaning to his life, but none held any comfort. The drive to Elaka to place flowers on Kaya's grave seemed too far, the schoolboard meetings seemed to be full of tedious details and the longer they dragged on the more querulous he became. His weekly visit to the Our Lady of Africa Cathedral lost its ability to give him peace, as did all the other distractions he had cultivated since Kaya's death. He tired easily, lacked concentration and suffered from insomnia, which was not even relieved by the few hours of sleep he would have enjoyed in the past that had given him the dream of the skeletal nun. Every morning he woke up believing he was living his last day in Kinja. Some nights, with a torch in hand, he wandered out to the former Africa Bar, squatted in its centre and studied the mural of his recurring dream painted by Martin-Johann, and longed for somebody to explain to him this bizarre life that was his own. He was only partly amongst ordinary men in those months, as he drifted between a past and a present that seemed as uncertain as the future. There were days and nights when he remembered some incident from his past and it made him feel that his life had been marked by cowardice, stunted imagination, and a penchant for comfort which had caused him to avoid facing the truth about himself, and now that he wanted to know the truth it refused to reveal itself.

So when the two men from the Kinjaian internal security agency called on him early one morning, ordered him to accompany them to Eko international airport, handed him his passport, and told him that he was being expelled from Kinja as an undesirable alien, a threat to national security, he felt strangely distant, estranged from himself, as if what was happening to him, like much in his life, was happening to somebody else because he had long lost any sense of belonging to himself. Seated on the plane bound for New York, he fell asleep for the first time in weeks.

PART IV

I

The Paradise to which Marshall Sarjeant was forced to return was not the enchanting place fossilised in his exile's memory. A few miles outside Port Columbus – now a prosperous tourist city, with skyscraper hotels, casinos, international banks and a marina crowded with luxury yachts – the road subsided at regular intervals and the final stretch leading into Paradise abandoned its violent pretence to being a road and declared itself a mean, dangerous dirt track running parallel to a sea of contrasting tranquillity.

Paradise town centre had the charmless appearance of a place forgotten by time and cynically neglected by progress. A desultory collection of sun-bleached wooden buildings surrounded a rough concrete fountain that seldom spouted water. The fountain had replaced the ill-fated statue of Queen Victoria, which disappeared on independence night, and its basin – used variously as a litter bin, a bed for town drunks, when not filled with rainwater, and an ideal breeding ground for mosquitoes – bore, in large red letters, the graffiti: 'Victoria Falls'.

The hurricane of '61 had destroyed that year's entire banana crop, and four years later a grey fungus had invaded the citrus orchards, broken the weakened will of even the most stubborn farmers and convinced them that farming, like Paradise, belonged to the previous century. Brighter prospects awaited them elsewhere. Some of the oldest, wealthiest families in Paradise had moved to Port Columbus or migrated to North America, with Florida, New York and Toronto being the favoured destinations.

Some had died on the land they loved. Mrs Duncannon-Henriques had passed away in the year of independence and every day for a month after her death a flock of John Crow vultures circled the house. Soledad had remained loyal to Paradise and farmed bird-of-paradise flowers, which found a ready market in Port Columbus and beyond, until her death. The house on Bonny View Hill was still an impressive edifice. It was now owned by an absentee landlord – he had been seen in Paradise only once – who rented it out to parties of tourists. St Christopher's Church remained prosperous. Along with its renowned college – a privileged, separate community on the edge of the town – it was a balm to the large number of congenital cripples and people with disfigured faces who lived in the hills around Paradise. The reasonably fit found work in the college, and it was not unknown for able-bodied, bright, serious-minded locals to gain admission there. If they survived their schoolmates' taunts, which claimed that they came from families tainted by centuries of untreated syphilis, incest and miscegenation, they fled as far from Paradise as possible.

The Sarjeants, accustomed to the sudden reappearance of long-vanished family members, though none had ever stayed away as long as Marshall, nor returned in such poverty, welcomed Marshall back to Paradise. Both he and his mission were unknown to the two generations of Sarjeants born since his departure, two generations who betrayed the signs of Sarjeant's curse in their stunted limbs and disfigured faces. They regarded Marshall, with his mass of white hair and eye scars, with the same avid curiosity with which they viewed the tourists who sometimes wandered off the beaten track and into the hills behind Paradise. The elders who remembered him placed him in a long line of heroic Sarjeant adventurers, and none mentioned that night, when seized by ancestral spirits, they chose him to leave Paradise on a doomed mercy mission.

Binta Sarjeant was one of few people who knew about his mission. Having lost three pregnancies, and seen countless crippled Sarjeants, Binta had come to believe in the curse. She had returned to Paradise and submitted herself to the instructions of the women of Banyan. Now almost blind, she had inherited the half-forgotten African wisdom that she had once scorned, without abandoning her Christian faith.

She reproached Marshall as if he were a boy again, rather than a man in the sixth decade of life, because he had allowed himself to become a prisoner of failure and prolong his exile. She explained that his mission had been a desperate attempt to end Sarjeant's curse and the return of Nana Sarjeant's ka had held no guarantee of success. The elders of Banyan had known the risk and he had been chosen because they considered him the most promising Sarjeant of his generation. She told him that Pharaoh had somehow followed his progress until he arrived in Africa and seemed less interested in whether he had succeeded in his mission than he was in Marshall's involvement in the Pan-African cause. She was in no doubt that Pharaoh did not believe in his mission. 'I told you that man wasn't trustworthy,' she said. The mission had been a convenient means of sending him away from Paradise to continue the war that he, Pharaoh, believed all peoples with African blood had a duty to wage in the twentieth century.

Pharaoh had died a decade into independence and on his deathbed he urged all Sarjeants to lend their strength to the struggle to rid the world of the remaining vestiges of racial oppression so that all mankind could enter the next century free of that evil burden.

'And the family, what about the Sarjeants?' Marshall said.

'I don't know, Marshall. Maybe only God can save this family,' Binta Sarjeant said with the weariness of age, the accumulated memories of a midwife who had delivered countless cripples, the weakened faith of a herbalist whose potents, attenuated by the amnesia of time, had lost their curative properties. She was the last remaining link between the Sarjeants in Paradise and the mythical Africa that once gave them the strength to endure the diabolical curse with stoicism and defiance and hope. And Marshall would spend many hours at Binta Sarjeant's bedside, as he once did with Nana Sarjeant.

Rita, Binta Sarjeant's only child and her likely successor, handled the practicalities of resettling Marshall back into Paradise. Small, active, inexhaustibly energetic, Rita had the indomitable will of previous Sarjeant matriachs, and carried evidence of the curse in the prominent black mole on her forehead, which gave her the appearance of possessing a third eye.

The most civic-minded of the Sarjeants, she belonged to a plethora of committees for improving Paradise, and when she was not sorting out family difficulties, she wrote streams of angry letters to the island's newspaper berating Jack Buchanan, the Member of Parliament in whose constituency Paradise fell, for focusing all his energy on Port Columbus to the detriment of Paradise. Buchanan owned hotels and casinoes in Port Columbus and it was not in his interest to see the road between Port Columbus and Paradise repaired. Her letters were either ignored or received the most patronising replies, but she remained an indefatigable campaigner and was forever seeking to rouse Paradisians from their apathetic slumber.

On Marshall's behalf, Rita supervised the refurbishing of the wooden cabin on the Rio Grande where Pharaoh had died. After a week in Banyan Marshall withdrew to the cabin, intending to nurse the wounds incurred in Africa, seek the solace of solitude, and plan his future, which centred on his son in London. He was determined that the bridge he had started to build between them in Eko would be continued in Paradise.

For the first month Rita was a regular visitor and from their long conversations Marshall realised that she too was a protégée of Pharaoh. She told him how, after his departure, Pharaoh had won the devout loyalty of seven young Paradisians. They sat at his feet for years, listening to his impassioned speeches and taking instructions from him on books to read and ways of thinking and ways of being and ways of seeing. When the young men reached their early twenties, Pharaoh persuaded them to leave Paradise. Three had gone to the United States, two to the island capital, Kingston, one to England and another had left Paradise with Soweto, South Africa, as his destination.

Pharaoh took to his bed a year into independence and Rita became his nurse. She recalled his feverish ramblings about the race war and its many fronts, how his health waxed and waned in harmony with the events of the 1960s, how he cried on hearing that Malcolm X had been assassinated, how she had had to sedate him when, on hearing of the assassination of Martin Luther King, he somehow dragged himself to the town square and, with a placard bearing a photograph of Martin Luther King, spent hours shouting: 'How much longer will we allow them to kill our prophets?'

She consoled Marshall with the disclosure that Pharaoh was proud of him, because he, Marshall, was not only Pharaoh's first disciple, but because Marshall possessed, by some accident of birth, the gift of compassion which made him a man of peace and therefore the sort of warrior who could help in the winning of the war. Wars, Pharaoh often said, are not won by men who love fighting but by men who so love peace and hate the suffering of their fellow men that they will fight only for that end. But Pharaoh had not been blind to Marshall's faults, his self-doubt, his pleasure-seeking ways.

Marshall asked Rita if she had been influenced by Pharaoh and she replied: 'Yes, but times have changed. Where Pharaoh saw the race, I see the family and we're a family made up of many races; where he saw Africa, I see this little town, Paradise; where Pharaoh saw the wrongs of the past, I see the possibilities of the future.'

Rita's visits prevented Marshall from succumbing to the fever of despair that had claimed him in the past. Her bustling energy and irrepressible optimism helped to keep his spirits afloat. But other Sarjeants played a part, too. By day, children, some whole and healthy, some with horribly disfigured faces, others on crutches, came to the wooden cabin and assailed him with questions about Europe and Africa. Seated amid the Sarjeant children and their friends, he told fantastic stories of the ancestral continent to which all could return but few reclaim. And as he entertained the children he found himself scanning their faces, looking for the boy who was himself, the boy to whom he could, perhaps, bequeath his vision of the future, which was not just about going back to an ancestral source, but also accepting the richness of the island's historical legacy, a richness that placed its inheritors in a privileged position. Children of the new world, unencumbered by ancient allegiances and enmities, they were free to create that peaceful and loving tomorrow for which all the blood of yesterday had been spilt. But when he thought of all he had endured, all he had lost, he possessed neither the necessary strength of conviction nor physical energy to steal a life.

At night the adults, many his former childhood friends, descended on him with bottles of white rum and the same eagerness as the children to hear about his exploits in the outside world.

Surrounded by his family, Marshall soon began to think of the many things to be done to restart his life again. He made casual enquiries about the map which Pharaoh claimed could lead to a fortune, but nobody knew anything about it and he quickly pushed it to the back of his mind and turned his thoughts to more prosaic ways of regaining his wealth. He had never known great wealth, but neither had he known this depth of poverty which forced him to borrow the clothes on his back from family members who had themselves received these garments as presents from Sarjeants healthy enough to migrate to the United States.

En route to the island he had written to Modupe Ogbomosho, alerting him to his illegal expulsion, and could now do nothing but wait. Once a week he walked to the Paradise post office with hope in his heart that there would be a letter from

Martin-Johann or Modupe Ogbomosho. In fact, the first letter he received, posted in the United States, came from Baku Mathaku. It described the unrest sweeping Kinja and the difficulties he, Baku, was experiencing organising protest at Marshall's illegal expulsion and the betrayal of the Pan-Africanist ideals espoused by the founding father of the nation, and swore to work tirelessly on Marshall's behalf.

The next set of correspondence he received contained mixed blessings. Modupe Ogbomosho had claimed the Brighton-Lisbon as family property, much to the chagrin of several Kinjaians who had long desired it, and sent Marshall a sizeable cheque, with promises of more to follow.

But the letter he received the following day cancelled the relief given him by the money. It came from Martin-Johann and informed Marshall, in a distraught tone, that Martin-Johann's girlfriend, Ellen, was pregnant and the pregnancy was surrounded by complications which threatened both her and the baby's lives.

Marshall went straight to Banyan and talked with Binta Sarjeant, who told him, with resignation, that was how Sarjeant's curse had struck many women. 'If she survives and loses the baby, she will have to keep on trying for a child,' Binta said. He returned to the wooden cabin with his spirit at its nadir.

The following morning, Marshall started making preparations to leave Jamaica again. He had never done anything for Martin-Johann and the least he could do now was to be there to give him emotional support.

But on the eve of his departure for Kingston, Rita came to see him and informed him that a woman by the name of Penny Wharton was in Paradise, staying in the house on Bonny View Hill, and had made enquiries about him and the Sarjeant family from shopkeepers in the town.

Later that day an intrigued Marshall set off for Bonny View. It was a cool late afternoon and as he strolled up to the house he ruminated on whether its present owners would be interested in selling, and what an excellent hotel it would make with some judicious modifications. From beside the gate he saw St Christopher's Church with its terracotta tiles and crooked spire, and to the north, smoke rose from Black Rock Beach, where the fishermen still gathered at this hour to amuse themselves and anyone who cared to listen with stories. Beyond Cuffee's Point the sun reddened the cloudy sky and transformed the sea into a bowl of liquid gold.

As he stood there surveying land and sea, Marshall allowed his imagination to range across the possibilities of a Paradise touched by progress, and dedicating the remainder of his life to that future seemed right and true and redemptive. If he could persuade Martin-Johann and Ellen to live here, close to family members who had lived with Sarjeant's curse for over a century, everything would be all right.

The woman who answered the door was in her late thirties with the ashen face of one recently arrived in the tropics from colder climes. Her broad face, with its saucer-shaped eyes and freckles, had a disquieting familiarity. She introduced herself as Penny Wharton. When he said his name, she sighed with relief, called the maid and instructed her to prepare Mrs Hartley to receive a visitor.

Then Penny Wharton led Marshall into the living room, invited him to sit down, and said: 'This may sound strange, Mr Sarjeant, but for the past three months my mother has been pestering me to bring her here. She kept on saying she had to see you, Marshall Sarjeant.'

'What's your mother's name?' Marshall said.

'Constance Hartley, though you may have known her as Castle, Constance Castle.'

At that moment the door swung open and the maid pushed in a wheelchair-bound, frail-looking old woman dressed in white lace. Thin, with a gaunt face and wispy grey hair, she was none the less recognisable as Constance Castle.

She did not seem to recognise Marshall, but then a light

flickered in her eyes as she studied him and she whispered with great effort: 'Marshall?'

'Constance,' he replied.

Marshall went to Constance, the very distant relative who had given him his first kiss and who, many years ago, told him that their destinies were linked together. As he held her hands and scrutinised the bony, pallid, wrinkled face with its hieratic profile and hyaline eyes, he felt he had finally caught up with the skeletal nun of the recurrent dream that once haunted his nights.

Penny Wharton spoke for her incapacitated mother. A near-fatal stroke had left Constance paralysed from her waist down and capable of speech that was at best aphasic and at worst unintelligible grunts. Driven by some preternatural force, she was determined to make amends for past wrongs, and to that end enlisted her daughter's support.

Since her period of intimacy with Marshall, Constance had lived a troubled, peripatetic life. For almost six years she'd been a novice in various convents in Europe and the north of England, engaged in a daily routine of prayers, silence, and withdrawal in pursuit of a peace of mind which none the less eluded her. She spent some years wandering across the world and had lived in an ashram in India and on a kibbutz in Israel. During this period she studied various mystic arts – from tarot cards, to the cabbala, to rune stones and a host of arcane practices – in the belief that they would yield an understanding of the peculiar source of her spiritual and emotional turmoil, and eventually lead to peace. Her restlessness came to an end when Alexander Castle, her reclusive and eccentric twin, fell terminally ill. Despite their childhood closeness Alexander had accepted her merciful presence with great reluctance and for six months she nursed her now curmudgeonly and cantankerous brother, became his companion and only source of comfort.

After burying Alexander, Constance developed a curiosity about the family past and resumed the research which Alexander had abandoned after discovering that one of their nineteeth-century forebears came from Paradise, Jamaica. Tracing her mother's relatives, she learnt that mental and physical ailments ran in the family. But at this point Constance's investigations were brought to a sudden halt by the stroke. Nothing was done until her daughter Penny Wharton, childless and a divorcee, who shared her mother's predilection for mysticism, went to live with Constance. The trip to Paradise was Constance's idea and became an obsession when she heard – through Marshall's ex-wife, Zenobia, whom Penny had traced – that Marshall had been expelled from Kinja.

Marshall gave Constance and her daughter an account of the curse that had hung over the Sarjeants since Sybil Sarjeant's discovery of her husband's infidelity with Nana Sarjeant.

When he finished, Constance was greatly agitated. For some minutes she struggled to speak and then, with surprising clarity, said: 'You must find the source of the curse, Marshall. The source must be here in Paradise, somewhere, somewhere.' Then she fell quiet, as if that moment of lucid expression had exhausted her. And somewhere off Black Rock Beach, the plaintive cry of the manatees sounded and rushed up Bonny View Hill, borne on the breeze.

Marshall did not need to be urged. Late into the night he left Constance and Penny, and walked down Bonny View Hill with one purpose in mind: to find the map that Pharaoh used to talk about and which Scoop had once stolen. He stopped at Banyan and quizzed both Binta and Rita about Pharaoh's last days, the things he had left to the family. But neither could tell him anything about the map. Though Binta Sarjeant, after much thought, much excavation of her memory, recalled the family legend of Sybil Sarjeant and the mute African, and the existence of a map which was supposed to lead to a fortune in gold. Whether that map existed, and if it did, its whereabouts, was unknown to her.

Back in the cabin and wearied by the day's revelations, but

too agitated to sleep, Marshall remained awake thinking of the thin, wheelchair-bound figure of Constance in the house he always associated with Soledad, of the flight he was due to catch in Kingston, of Martin-Johann nursing his ailing girlfriend.

It was a long night, a night when the need for redemption seized him, and his reflections reopened memories of all his many unwitting wrongs and miserable failings. He had failed on his mission, killed his wife, and inflicted Sarjeant's curse on two lives. And through them future generations would bear the accursed stigmatas. Far from being the redeemer of the Sarjeants, he had become the means of spreading the curse, the passive vessel of a cruel, inescapable destiny.

Suddenly the few rays of moonlight penetrated the slits in the wooden wall and the creeping fatalism retreated. It was as though Pharaoh's ghost, stirred by Marshall's defeatism, had entered the cabin and filled him with energy.

He started ripping up the floorboards of the cabin in search of the map. If Scoop had returned it, then Pharaoh would not have disposed of it. He would have hidden it to prevent another theft. By the time the sun had risen above the mountain all the floorboards were loose. And on the underside of a joist, he found the object of his frantic search. Covered in plastic, it was wrapped around the spear Pharaoh had brought back from Liberia. It was perfectly legible.

2

The map led Marshall past the ancient cotton tree on the western edge of Paradise, a derelict sugar mill, across the rickety wooden bridge which spanned Sacks river, a tributary of the Rio Grande, and on to an old cart track known only to the most knowledgeable in Paradise. It had been reclaimed by the bush and its outline was barely visible. He followed it down into Harkers Vale and up to and along Monmouth Ridge, then through the tiny village of Lincoln and up to Richmond Hill. On the second step up the Blue Mountains, Marshall came to what the map described as Arawak rock. Dusk began to descend and with its advent the air cooled and he shivered and recalled winters in England. He unfurled his sleeping bag, placed it under the rock and there he slept.

In the morning, nourished by bread, he counted twenty-one steps in the direction indicated on the map and started digging a hard, stony ground which was initially unyielding. He persisted, and as he dug, he hummed work songs remembered from his past, and these seemed to lighten his labour. Despite his strenuous efforts and copious sweating, by late midday the hole was no more than a foot deep, and the spade, blunted on the dry, stubborn, stony ground, was becoming less effective. With the sun at its zenith, Marshall ate and rested, and resumed digging some hours later. He worked faster in the cool afternoon, with his muscles adjusted to these unexpected exertions and as night fell he stood up to his knees in the hole.

The following morning, he began again in the dawn light, and continued digging through a drizzle which increased with the passing hours into a torrential rainfall, the sort of rain that when viewed from the lower level in Paradise, looked like mist rolling across the mountain.

The rain forced him to stop, and he was only able to resume the next morning after draining the waterlogged hole, first with his cup, and then, much faster, with his hands. The rain resumed that afternoon, came down at a steady pace and soaked him and blended with his perspiration. But he had reached such a rhythm in his digging that he laboured on.

With dusk nearing, the shovel struck something wooden and at precisely that moment his strength gave way and he decided to complete one last task for the day. Taking the spear Pharaoh had brought back from Africa, he tied it to a long sturdy piece of rope, stood over the darkening hole, summoned all his remaining energy, and hurled the spear down into the void. It entered the wood with a dull sound and for a moment the world seemed still and quiet and cold. He tied the other end of the rope round Arawak rock and, suffused with a feeling a triumph, prepared to eat and rest. The rain resumed and he sought shelter under Arawak rock. He was hungry and thirsty and could not make a fire since all the twigs he had gathered were wet. He settled for a tin of beans and bread, and then, unable to sleep, he squatted under the rock and watched the hole through the rain.

He had begun to doze, when, suddenly, the rope began to unwind towards the hole until it snapped straight and taut. Marshall followed the rope to the hole and, looking down, he saw that it was now as deep as the length of rope, far deeper than he had dug, as if the earth had tried to reclaim the box which the spear had pierced. A raw smell, evocative of the sea, rushed upwards followed by a powerful rush of air which flung him backwards. He scrambled under Arawak rock as the mouth of the hole began to glow brightly.

Unable to move, he saw, rising up from the hole, an awesome sight: a figure, naked but for a loin cloth, and so dark it shimmered blue, darker than any human he had ever seen. Curled up in a tight muscular ball, it hovered above the hole, then it started to uncurl slowly. First his head, bald and shiny, with two golden earrings and with his eyes still closed. Then he unfolded powerful arms to reveal a chest as bare and luminous as his head. Alegba had risen. Now erect, he opened eyes as red and bright as the setting sun over the sea and glared at Marshall. Shocked and terrified, Marshall none the less sat with the imperturbable stillness that came over him when faced with danger. Alegba remained encased in the glowing light, hovering above the hole, with the rain falling around him.

Then he stepped out of the light, on to the ground and moved with measured slowness towards Marshall. He did not approach directly, but took short diagonal steps, with arms outstretched to his side. He came closer. A few feet from Marshall he bent forward and looked into Marshall's eyes and Marshall remained still, and met his gaze. Alegba stepped back and advanced again. Marshall felt a sudden heat as his shirt was ripped off and he faced Alegba bare-chested. Again Alegba recoiled, and Marshall realised that the scars he had been given by Chief Lakijo were having this repulsive effect. Alegba advanced yet again, and reaching out he ran a finger down the side of Marshall's eyes, touching the faint scars there and then those on his chest. Marshall saw that the spectre also bore scars, three on either cheek, and the same on his upper arms. He seemed to be fascinated by Marshall's own scars, studying them with a puzzled expression.

Suddenly Alegba leapt back, as if frightened, and began to shake and change shape, becoming first a wrinkled, bowed old woman whom Marshall recognised as Nana Sarjeant. He changed back to the African for an instant, before assuming the shape of a dark-haired woman dressed in a white cotton smock with fancy-frill necking, and in this incarnation the figure released a wild, manic laughter as flames leapt up around her and she hissed, and screeched, 'Curse you, Sarjeant.' Now she raced towards Marshall, preceded by a scorching heat which caused him to erupt in sweat. He smelt burnt flesh, looked down and saw that the skin on his arms and chest was peeling off in the heat.

Suddenly the female figure vanished and Alegba faced Marshall. For a moment it seemed as if he were fighting with himself, to be either Alegba or the figure Marshall had surmised was Sybil Sarjeant. Alegba fell to his knees and clasped his ears as if in excruciating pain and violently tossed his head from side to side in the heart of the flames left by Sybil. The figure that rose again was the dark-haired woman and she raced towards Marshall with outstretched arms, her hands talon-shaped, and a demonic fury in her eyes, and again he felt the heat and smelt burning flesh, and the most excruciating pain triggered vivid flashes of lying in a white room encased in bandages, then on a wooden cot in an African hut.

Sybil slowed and her gaze fell on the crucifix Marshall had taken to wearing since Kaya's death. She laughed and reached out and ripped it off Marshall's neck, but at the same instant she was repulsed and the figure in the flames alternated between that of Sybil and Alegba. For some minutes Alegba seemed to have vanquished his *alter ego,* but it now advanced towards Marshall with a fearsome menacing grin, muscles tensed. He stopped before Marshall and said with a cold voice: 'What is your name?' And for the first time since Chief Lakijo had given his name Marshall used it and said: 'Marshall Segun Dada Sarjeant.'

Alegba leapt backwards to the mouth of the hole, then fell to his knees again. While he swayed from side to side clasping his ears, Sybil Sarjeant rose out of his back, this time holding a horsewhip with which she lashed him. But as she did so, another female figure rose from the African. It was Kaya. She wrestled with Sybil Sarjeant on Alegba's back, and balls of flames flew here and there. Then the figure was only the bent African again and it stood and began turning, and when it stopped and faced Marshall it was yet another person: this time an old white man dressed in tattered breeches and a smock, and holding a rusting shotgun. The old man placed the weapon to his head and pulled the trigger and an earsplitting explosion rent the air. When the cloud had cleared blood gushed from a huge hole in the old man's head. This was re-enacted several times before another figure emerged, this time that of a woman who looked like a young version of Nana Sarjeant, and she took the weapon from the man, bade him rest his head on her lap and they were joined by three young brown-skinned boys who looked on in bemusement, one sucking his thumb.

Calm prevailed for a few seconds and as those figures disappeared, the African re-emerged, kneeling and clasping his ears. Suddenly, he was Sybil Sarjeant again and she cackled triumphantly and floated towards Marshall with flames streaming behind her. He was resigned to defeat and death, and vivid images of his past life flashed before him. But before Sybil Sarjeant reached him a new figure blocked her way. Its back was towards Marshall and all he could make out were its white habit and raised bony, fleshless hands. It stopped Sybil and stepped into the flames and repulsed her and both were consumed by a raging flame that was alternately clear and obscure. When it cleared all that was visible was the African writhing on the floor as if in great pain. The heat was now unbearably intense and Marshall was seized by an impulse to flee but found himself transfixed. The images in the flames alternated between the pain-racked African and Sybil Sarjeant and the skeletal nun. Half-conscious, Marshall saw the skeletal nun's face acquire flesh, and alternately it resembled Nana Sarjeant, Kaya, then Constance Castle and finally a face he did not recognise immediately because he had last seen that face many, many years before. It was Teacher Lee.

He fought to remain conscious and succeeded until the figures in the flames faded and were replaced by an almost new apparition. Helix-shaped, black, and crowned by Alegba's head and face, the eyes of which glowered at Marshall, it spun at accelerating speed and simultaneously released a blinding white light. A sharp pain stabbed Marshall's eyes and he covered them with his hands. As he tightened the grip over his eyes, he felt himself falling at a vertiginous speed into the light.

Marshall regained consciousness on a still, dry, windless morning. Stepping from under the rock, he saw that the spear was buried in a large oak cask at the mouth of the hole he had dug. Removing the spear, he prised open the box, and saw not the gold coins of legend, but a leather-bound book. He opened the book and began to read. The book told the story of the man who had ended Sarjeant's curse, ridding future generations of Sarjeants of all afflictions by sacrificing his life and joining the spirit of Alegba, the mischievous African god, and his lover, Sybil, to ensure that they remained buried for ever.

When he had finished reading the book, Marshall placed it back in the cask. He lowered the box back in the hole, from which came the smell of the sea, and gathered everything he had brought with him and threw them in the open earth. He hesitated for an instant and glanced around at the land he had loved as a boy and continued loving through his years of exile. In that instant, a vision of all the deformed, disfigured Sarjeant children filled his eyes. He could no longer afford to hesitate. He leapt forward and plunged down to meet his destiny.

Many years later, as the sun set over Cuffee's Point, the fishermen on Black Rock Beach often engaged their listeners with the story of Marshall Sarjeant. They would tell how his preparation for doing battle with the ghost of his ancestors involved a forty-year exile in England and Africa – because, after all, no man can advance beyond his preparation – and how his victory was secured with the help of the spirits of all the women he had loved, because men who have lived without loving are doomed to be lost in the opaque mist of history. They would point to the mountain that overlooked

Paradise like a cathedral, to a certain configuration of light and shade, discernible only in the brief dusk, which formed three enrobed female figures. Then they would point to the sea and urge their listeners to look long and hard at the patterns cast over the sea's surface by the setting sun and try to discern there an image of the man they called the duppy conqueror.